REVIEWS

Darkly Delicious

"I feel absolutely head over heels in love with this book! It truly was dark & delicious. Mayhem, death, Demons, Pagan's, Druids and a kickass heroine!"
- Taking It One Book at a Time (Blog)

"I get excited for strong female characters and Dark Hope delivers…"
- For the Love of Bookends (Blog)

Sookie Stackhouse of Hell

"If you like the Sookie books, you'll love this. The main character was likable, well developed and, of course, had a special part to play that was much larger than her role as the personal assistant to Satan."
- Mandy Payne (Top Amazon Reviewer)

"This was honestly one of the best books I've ever read …
LOVED IT!! <3"
- Taylorv915 (Amazon Review)

"…WOW! HD Smith has seriously hit the mark with this book … a truly phenomenal read…"
- Chelsea (Goodreads Review)

"Dark Hope was amazing to the last word. I didn't want it to end. Claire totally kicks ass. I love the ending."
- Bestselling Author Ceci Giltenan

DARK HOPE

DARK HOPE

The Devil's Assistant

H. D. Smith

Wild Fey LLC

http://www.wildfeyllc.com

Copyright © 2014 HD Smith

Cover design by Robin Ludwig Design Inc.
http://www.gobookcoverdesign.com/

ISBN-10: 1942030002
ISBN-13: 978-1-942030-00-3

DEDICATION

For the living and the dead.
(I trust you know which list applies to you.)

CHAPTER 1

I'd like to say it could be worse. I'm sure lots of people hated their job, or their boss, or the people they worked with. I just couldn't relate to them. They had options. They could quit their job, move out of town, or drop off the grid. The only option I had was a guaranteed one-way ticket to Hell when I died, and that didn't include dental.

I picked up the latest issue of *The Daily Grind*, our inner office paper, before stepping into the waiting elevator. I groaned when I saw the caption: 'Maintenance to Strike!' I was sure I'd have to handle it. The Boss doesn't deal with the little things. His lowly administrative assistant got those jobs.

I made my way to the back of the full elevator. Jenny, one of the other executive admins, leaned over and whispered something to a dark-haired girl beside her. The girl snickered then glanced at me before mouthing "no way." I rolled my eyes and ignored them. I refused to let the plebes bother me today.

Only five percent of the human population on Earth knows the truth about the otherworldly among us. At Tucker Bosh—the New York City company I work for that doesn't really sell insurance— the stats are only slightly higher. I grouped my fellow employees into three categories: the plebes, the damned, and the demons.

The demons call The Boss their king—HRH Demon King on official documents—and the plebes are normal humans without a clue. Lucky me, I'm one of the damned—a human who knows the truth.

It wasn't always easy to tell the plebes from the damned, so I didn't have work friends. One wrong word from me about The Boss or my job and I'd get a co-worker killed.

The elevator bell dinged, pulling my attention away from the paper. I was surprised to see a gray-haired man blocking the door. His head was down, one hand rubbing the back of his neck. He wore a dark blue tailored suit that should have fitted him perfectly, but it was wrinkled and creased as if he'd been wearing it for days.

His head shot up when I cleared my throat. His creased forehead relaxed, and he smiled and caught the door as it started to close. With a nod and another friendly smile, he spun and opened the glass door to The Boss's office suite.

"Thanks," I said.

"That's no trouble at all, miss," the man said in a pleasant Texas drawl.

"Do you have an appointment?" I checked my watch. It was seven thirty. The Boss didn't make appointments at seven thirty a.m.

"Not exactly," he said.

The office phone rang as I opened my mouth to speak. "Excuse me."

I hurried to my desk, reaching over the top ledge to grab my phone. I stopped mid-reach. My gaze fixed on the vase of white roses taking up half my desk. *Surprise number two?*

Surprise number one had been two front row tickets to the hottest sold-out play in town. Jack had left them with a note for me in my gym bag this morning.

I completely ignored the phone—which was no longer ringing—and the man standing behind me. My thoughts were on Jack—my beautiful blue-eyed, dark-haired boyfriend I'd left in our warm bed two hours ago.

Scooting around my desk, I plucked the card from the flowers. It read, 'I love you, -J'.

The man cleared his throat. I'd see Jack at lunch, but now I had to work.

I lifted my head to speak to the man and noticed the red file folder in my in-box. Red meaning from HR. It explained why the visitor was here so early, in such a disheveled manner. He'd been summoned. He was being condemned. His one-way ticket to Hell was being processed.

The HR Department, which was staffed with only demons, referred to the process as "retirement". Their little inside joke I guess.

In the past five years, I'd handled hundreds of these. HR had a knack for knowing which unhappy soul would show up at the office to see The Boss. Those were the ones I got to handle personally. It averaged around one a week. For some reason today, this retirement felt wrong to me.

The man sauntered up to the desk. He leaned in, smiling.

When he opened his mouth, I spoke first. "I'll be right with you." My words were rushed. I had to pull myself together before I did something really stupid like letting him see The Boss. That wouldn't work out well for anyone.

The man pressed his lips together, nodded, and pushed back from the desk. Disappointment shone in his eyes. I actually felt sorry for him, which was ridiculous. This wasn't my first day on the job. He was no different from the other damned souls I'd processed.

I glanced at the flowers then shook my head. Was I feeling something for this man because Jack made me see a glimmer of hope and a future I hadn't dreamed of in years?

I opened the folder and scanned the first page.

The man had a name—David Janus. Fifty years of service. He was married with three kids and seven grandkids. He was the son of a preacher, which wasn't as surprising or as rare as one might think, and he worked in sales.

It was this man's life in a paragraph of text. I imagined my own paragraph: Claire Cooper. Five years of service. No relations.

"I was hoping—"

"Sir, please," I interrupted. "Give me a moment."

I kept my gaze on the file. I didn't want to meet his eyes. Would it have been business as usual if he had a mistress or two? Would that have made him less of a human in my eyes? I took a deep breath. This wasn't personal. It was just another retirement. Ignoring it wouldn't make it go away. HR would know—The Boss would know—David Janus would be retired.

I extracted the three pages he needed to sign. I lined them up on the ledge of my reception desk and plucked a blood pen from the pen cup.

Blood pens resembled any other pen, except they drew a small amount of blood from the finger as the holder clicked the plunger open.

I was about to ask him to sign the pages when I saw Junior outside the glass doors of the office. He held his right hand to his ear gesturing for me to call and mouthed, "Later." He winked, then disappeared.

From the corner of my eye, I saw Janus shift his weight. "Miss."

Disregarding him, I gaped blankly at the empty corridor. Why would Junior, The Boss's oldest hellspawn, want me to contact him? I remembered the phone call I'd ignored and pressed the log button on my desk phone. My heart sank. The number was Junior's extension.

What the hell was going on? First I have the best morning ever, then I get emotional over a retirement, and now The Boss's oldest hellspawn wanted to chat.

"Miss," Janus barked.

I stared at the man whose life was over. "I have three documents for you to sign, Mr. Janus. Please use my pen." I held out the pen, but he didn't take it.

"I was hoping to see The Boss. I think there's been a mistake." He wiped his forehead with his handkerchief.

"No one sees The Boss."

"So, this is it," he said, slapping his hand on the desk and making me jump. "After fifty friggin' years. All I get is a snot-nosed redhead sayin' 'sign here.'"

For a minute I didn't know what to say. I couldn't change his fate. Once the deal was struck there was no choice. No matter who struck the deal. My mother made the deal with the Devil, not me, yet I'd inherited the debt, making me just as screwed as Janus.

I couldn't stop any of this from happening. Seeing The Boss wouldn't help him. If Janus continued down this path he'd lose more than his life.

"I can assure you, sir, I'm fully qualified to handle your retirement. I don't have fifty years of experience, as you do, but I am completely capable of reading you the fine print necessary to complete the process. If you choose not to cooperate, then you will *not* get the severance package, which includes an indisputable natural death and the seventy-two hour grace period that will allow you to say goodbye to your loved ones."

I read this so often I had the passage memorized, which was the only reason I was able to get through the spiel today.

"Any refusal on your part to sign the documents will mean immediate forfeiture of all remaining benefits, which includes the aforementioned severance package. As I'm sure you know, they always suspect a family member when foul play is involved, and your life insurance doesn't pay out for suicide. Do you have any questions?"

The pain in his eyes and the strain in his voice were heart breaking. His shoulders drooped as he said, "This is the worst day of my life, and you couldn't give a rat's ass if you tried."

I swallowed. There were no words for him. I couldn't help him. "I'm sorry," I said.

He snatched the pen from my hand and clicked it open, drawing a small amount of blood into the chamber, and signed the documents. As if on autopilot, I verified the signatures, collected his company-issued credit card, and handed him a red box with a white bow on top. He opened the box, snorted, and chucked it back at me.

No one ever took the gift. Probably because it was a cheap gold watch or maybe it was the unsigned thank-you card curled inside the band.

Janus stomped away from my desk and punched the elevator button with his fist. I shouldn't care, and not because I'd become jaded over the last five years. I shouldn't care because he made his deal—just like the rest.

I shoved the three documents and his credit card into the red folder. I couldn't save him anymore than I could save me.

I gazed at the flowers again and remembered I would see Jack for lunch. He was the reason I got up in the morning. I loved him. He was the thing that kept me sane. I needed him, and I really wished I were still curled up in bed with him instead of staring at a red message light from the oldest hellspawn in existence.

I took a deep breath, picked up the phone, and pressed voicemail. In the five years I'd worked here, Junior never came to The Boss's office. Not willingly.

I concentrated on his voice from the message. "Summer sun and falling rain have only you to call my name. If ever joy and comets come, the end of ocean's eyes are one. Blue and deep the windows see, as far and wide as yonder be. The willow breaks and I must need the one who means so much to me...I'm sorry about before. I can't wait to see you. I'm coming up."

I'm not sure how many minutes passed, but at some point, the phone timed out, clicked off voice mail, and started an annoying busy signal. I was still holding the phone—trying to determine exactly what had happened.

I hung up the phone and stared. *What the hell was that?* I picked up my coffee, wishing it were a double espresso.

"A love poem?" I said. I pressed the call log again. His name was still there.

The intercom buzzed, and I nearly dropped my coffee. The mark on my right forearm tingled and burned. Symbols appeared. I had no idea what they meant and was too scared to ask. The four characters resembled Chinese script, but they were actually from a long-dead ancient language.

I clenched my fist as he made the blood of his mark boil.

The intercom buzzed again. I glanced at my watch—it was early for The Boss to be in the office. I quickly checked my desk. Everything was in order—just the way he liked it. Retirement complete, no messages, no meetings until later. Maintenance was planning to strike, but he'd ignore that. *Okay, breathe. Now find out what he wants.*

I pressed the intercom, ignoring the pain on my arm. *Be polite. Be courteous.* "Yes, sir."

"Come here."

He didn't look up as I entered the office. Usually his desk was the picture of organization, but today he was moving papers around as if he'd misplaced something.

A slight chill made goose bumps on my arm as I closed the door. It always struck me as peculiar that he liked his office cold given his realm was Hell.

His voice was dispassionate and clipped as he said, "I need you to fetch something."

I straightened. He wanted me to leave the office?

In a casual tone hiding a deeper meaning, he asked, "Who sent the flowers?"

My mouth went dry. I couldn't speak. His stark black eyes were on me now—waiting. The Boss had one rule that could never be broken. No ordinary human or plebe from the office could know who he was. If I told anyone, they died. Period.

"Jack," I said quietly.

After a moment of studying me, The Boss dropped his gaze to his desk. He was dressed completely in black. His shirt was open at the collar—no tie. His black hair was cut short with a few streaks of silver running through it. He had a strong jaw and angular nose. He was attractive—as always—but frightening.

I stood there, waiting for his command, but it never came. After several more minutes I asked, "What do you want picked up?" which came out more agitated than it should have. *Crap.* He had me on edge with the flower question, but that was no excuse.

He was staring at me again. His intense eyes flared as he sent a jolt of heat through my mark. *Be polite, be courteous, and be quiet.* I bowed my head. He dialed the mark down a few notches.

"You will go downtown and see a man named Wylan James."

My head popped up, and my eyes widened.

He ignored me and continued, "He has something for me. Tell him I sent you, and he'll give you what I need."

The words came out of my mouth before I could stop them. "I'm not allowed downtown by myself."

My survival instincts were forgetting several key bits of information. First, his mood—grizzly bear. And second, he didn't give a rat's ass about me. Why should he care if the druid mob that ran the Underworld—or downtown, as he liked to call it—had threatened to kill me if they caught me down there alone again?

He kicked up the heat on his mark. I clamped my mouth shut so I wouldn't scream, or say anything else to piss him off.

"Return to me by noon."

~ # ~

Trying to ignore the nagging unease in my gut, I headed to the motor pool. The Boss knew I wasn't supposed to go to the Underworld alone, so why was he sending me?

The Underworld was the place between the three realms and Earth. I remember thinking it sounded so exotic. It turned out to look a lot like New York City. The only real difference between the Underworld and Manhattan was the cops. The druids ran the police. They were the law keepers of the Underworld, but they weren't police. They were the mob, and they were as corrupt as any member of organized crime on Earth.

The druids were the reason I didn't go downtown alone. The first time I'd been sent, a ruthless druid named Johnny Flash trapped me in a circle of salt surrounded by rabid dogs for three days. They made me promise to get Maintenance dental by the winter solstice.

The Boss said no to dental.

I was barely sixteen, but I learned three very important lessons that day. The Boss cared nothing for me, no one gets dental, and druids were not to be trusted—ever.

I willed the bad memories away. I'd get in and out before anyone knew I was there. I had no choice. No one refused The Boss.

The motor pool was dead. Shiny black town cars were parked neatly in almost every available spot of the big underground garage. The normally bustling atmosphere was quiet. It always was the Monday after a big Underworld event. The guys had all worked the weekend, driving the executives to and from Fight Night, so they had today off.

I spotted the manager, a burly demon with wiry black hair.

"I got your car ready, Miss Cooper," he said with a smile. The glint of red in his eyes sparkled as he motioned to the smaller man behind him. "Your usual guy is out—stomach flu—and with the fight being this past weekend—"

"I understand. You're short-staffed," I said, stopping his explanation. My polite smile faded when I sensed the new guy's veil.

"This is Frankie," the manager said. "He'll be your driver today."

Frankie appeared to be in his early thirties, and the harsh line of his nose and jaw gave him a stern demon-ish look. I was being stereotypical, since he was a demon, but he triggered my veil detector. The anxious feeling in my stomach, the response my body had to being near a veil, wasn't helping to settle my nerves. He shouldn't have been veiled. It wasn't necessary. Not down here where humans weren't allowed.

There wasn't much physical difference between the beings of the three realms and humans. The pagans, druids, and demons veiled when around humans to hide what *was* different. Frankie's veil wasn't just out of place. It was wrong. His veil made him appear more *like* a demon.

I checked my watch. Frankie was busy typing on his phone, but if we didn't leave soon I'd never make it back in time.

"I need to see a man named Wylan James," I said. "It's important business for The Boss."

Frankie's eyes were blank, but his hardened expression was smug. "Hold your horses, toots. I gotta make the log entry before I can leave."

"I have to be back by noon," I said.

"Frankie," the motor pool manager hollered. "Get goin'—that's a VIP you're driving."

"All right, already." Frankie shoved the key into the ignition.

Finally. I waved a thank-you to the manager.

I looked up when Frankie muttered a curse. He was stabbing at the GPS, trying to clear the screen. I only caught a glimpse before the screen went blank, but I was sure the last destination had been somewhere in Paradise—which was impossible. No one who worked for The Boss could go there.

The three realms weren't exactly vacation destinations. I'd never been to Hell—thank God, but it was technically possible to go. My soul would be trapped in Hell when I died. Demons were souls who had already died, but had enough power or privilege to get out of Hell. While it wasn't impossible for Frankie to go to Paradise— the druid realm—what reason would the Druid King have for allowing him passage?

I checked my watch again, but before I could tell Frankie I'd wait for the next driver, the car lurched forward, and we were off.

I considered asking him to return to the garage, but I really didn't have time to wait. It was a quick pick-up—in and out—no big deal.

Ignoring my unease, I picked up my newspaper and settled back into my seat.

The entertainment section was taken over by the Fight Night debacle. The fight—Underworld's biggest event—became an uncontrolled brawl after several small fights broke out in the arena. The entire event had to be shut down. For the first time in a hundred years, Fight Night was cancelled.

I shivered when the tingle of the threshold passed through me. We'd crossed into Underworld. Buffered by the car, it wasn't much different from a change in the cabin pressure on an airplane.

My eyes widened as a white van screeched to a stop in front of us. Frankie slammed on the brakes, throwing me forward into the back of the front seat.

Four tough-looking goons piled out of the white van that was now blocking the road ahead. I gripped my phone to call for help. Panicked, I glanced at Frankie to see if he was okay.

I froze when I spotted the gun he pointed at my chest.

I gasped. "What are you doing?"

He grinned and then pulled the trigger.

I expected agony to rip through my chest. When I only felt a sharp pain, I lowered my gaze to see the damage, but there was no hole in my chest. Instead, there was a blue-feathered dart.

My eyelids drooped. Frankie had his phone to his ear. I couldn't hear what he was saying. He smirked at me, continuing his conversation. I was going to pass out.

I fought to keep my eyes open. Frankie ran a hand through his hair, drawing the illusion away. His dark hair changed to a mousey brown, and his eyes glinted a muddy caramel. I understood now why he'd been veiled.

"Angel..." I accused, just before I blacked out.

CHAPTER 2

My mouth was dry. That was the first thing I noticed when I came to. The second was the horrible smell of pickled olives—a druid delicacy in the Underworld, and a dead giveaway the mob was behind this.

Slowly, I opened my eyes. Light shot through my head, making me wince. I glanced around. The room I was being held in was a large pantry lined with shelves of food and crates of fresh vegetables and fruit. My hands and feet were tied behind me. I was cold, lying on the dirty concrete floor. At least there weren't any rabid dogs this time.

My chest hurt where the dart hit me. I attempted to readjust, but nothing was comfortable. The ropes around my wrists and ankles were too tight, but I didn't think I could get them off. When faint murmurs drifted in from outside, I stopped moving.

I closed my eyes and concentrated on the door across the room. At first, I didn't hear anything. Then, as if a set of speakers had been flipped on, clomping feet and chair creaks came through loud and clear.

"Hey, Frankie, how did you like working for The Boss?" a man with a heavy European accent asked.

Another deeper voice—not Frankie—chuckled. Two unknown men were outside the door.

A normal person wouldn't have been able to hear them so clearly—or understand them, since they were speaking in Druid, but I wasn't exactly normal, and I had gadgets.

The veil detector wasn't the only company issued perk I woke up with five years ago. I had no idea what made the veil detector work—spells probably—but the translator was technology. Totally manmade tech the plebes would kill for.

It translated everything but Ancient into English, and it magnified any sound within earshot to an audible level. I'd cursed it often until I learned to control it. Now I could pick up the slightest sound and draw it near enough to listen.

A loud scrape of wood on concrete and the deep voice bellowed, "What the—" bringing my attention back to the men outside the room. A loud grunt and what sounded like a wooden chair clattered as something big hit the floor.

"What's your problem?" the man with the European accent asked.

Scuffling, a few thumps, and a jarring thud.

"Fuck you, Frankie," the man with the deep voice growled. "Can't take being called an ange—"

A grunt of pain and another shove against the door before the European said, "Chill out. Let him go, Frankie, you ugly fuck."

Druids were so damn touchy. They hated to be called angels. It was their own fault. They called their realm Paradise for God's sake. What did they expect?

Sadly, that was the only similarity to angels they had. Druids weren't unattractive exactly, but they weren't beautiful. They weren't even cute; they were plain—average, ordinary, nothing special. I was stupid to have called him an angel, but he shot me with a tranquilizer dart. He deserved it.

"Enough," the European cried.

"I'll show her," Frankie snarled.

Shuffling feet neared the door. The click of a bolt sounded. I gasped, then relaxed, pretending to be asleep.

The door creaked open, but was yanked closed before anyone came inside. "Don't be stupid," the European barked. "She ain't worth it. Let it go."

In a breathy wheeze, the man with the deep voice added, "The Godfather's not going to allow it. He was pissed when she was hurt last time. He only wanted Johnny to scare her, not try to kill her."

Oh, shit. "The Druid King," I whispered. Why would he care what Johnny did to me?

"You hear too much," Frankie snarled. "Johnny knows what he's doing, and once he gives the word, she's mine."

I brought my attention back to the room. I couldn't stick around—I needed to get out of here.

Maneuvering to my back, I winced as I slammed my shoulder into a large crate. The jolt caused a small box, perched on the top of the stack, to fall forward. I rolled to miss the tumble of vegetables, but bumped up against a pair of shoes. I looked up. Frankie. The rigid edge to his face was gone. Now he was just pissed. I yelped when he kicked me in the gut.

A druid with dark brown hair wrenched Frankie away. "Enough," he said.

I recognized him as the man with the heavy European accent.

The second man—I assumed the one with the deep voice—strode around the two. He yanked me to my feet.

Frankie jerked his arm from the European. "Bring her," he commanded to the man holding me, before stomping away.

I was dragged into the restaurant's main dining room, a bad Little Italy knock off with checkered red tablecloths and bottles of Chianti on every table. The place was empty, except for Johnny and his latest squeeze—a plump brunette wearing red lipstick and light blue eye shadow—a walking cliché.

The woman eyed me as the men brought me around. Johnny's expression was nondescript. Aside from the vicious scar running along his right cheek, he appeared the same as he had five years ago, brown hair, brown eyes, brown suit. Not even the scar added anything interesting to his style. He was a druid—boring, plain—deadly.

"Who's this, Johnny?" the brunette asked. Her voice was high-pitched and nasally. She had big boobs and bigger hair. Her dress was short and fit all her curves like a glove. She was the complete package. I didn't see a wedding ring. She must be his mistress.

"Nobody." He dismissed her with the wave of a hand. "Now go."

"But I haven't finished—"

"Get out of here," he thundered.

Her high heels clicked a fast staccato as she left.

"Hey, Johnny, what's new?" Thankfully, my voice remained calm, but I wasn't. This guy scared me.

"You got a lot of nerve, coming back down here. I got a

reputation to protect, and you ain't done squat for me."

I glanced at Frankie. "You should really hope The Boss doesn't find out about this." I was bluffing. The Boss couldn't care less.

A low guttural snarl came from Frankie.

Johnny chuckled. "You know *Conrad* can't touch my people."

"You should show more respect, and you're not supposed to harass his humans, yet here I am."

Johnny's face was smug. "Everyone knows you're special, Claire. You aren't part of that deal."

Special. It was a cruel joke. I should have been protected like the others, but I wasn't. Not that I knew why, and I wasn't going to ask The Boss. It wasn't as if we had weekly one-on-ones. Johnny could do anything he wanted. There would be no ramifications— no retribution. The Boss would probably be more pissed that Johnny called him Conrad, the Devil's human CEO-of-a-Fortune-500-Company name.

"What about the Godfather? He might have something to say about it."

Everyone went quiet, which wasn't the reaction I expected.

Johnny's smug smile disappeared as he lost some of his swagger. Absently, he touched the scar on his cheek. "I run things here, not Harry," he said.

Was the Druid King named Harry?

Johnny tilted his head toward the guy on my left, the man with the deep voice. Before I had a chance to react, he sucker-punched me in the gut. The wind was knocked out of me, and it hurt to take my next breath.

Johnny's dark mood changed, and he nodded toward the European. I flinched, expecting him to hit me, but he didn't. He untied me, then stood me on my feet.

Wheezing, I straightened, rubbing my wrists to return circulation.

"You see?" Johnny said. "I can be cruel or nice—just like Harry—but if you try to run from me... Well, let's just say you shouldn't run." He had a wicked grin, and his cocky expression was back.

"What do you want from me?"

He kicked out the seat across from him. I hesitated for a moment, then took the seat.

"Moe," Johnny barked. A guy I hadn't seen, sitting off to the side behind Johnny, stood. "Get the boys out of here. I have private business to discuss."

"Sure, boss."

Moe ushered out Frankie, who still looked ready to throttle me, and the other two. Johnny and I were now alone.

He went back to eating, skewering an olive with his knife. "You caused me a lot of trouble with the union reps. I told them we'd come to an arrangement."

I would have laughed if I hadn't been so shocked. "Are you kidding me? That was five years ago."

He tossed another olive into his mouth.

"What exactly did you expect me to do?" I asked. "I told The Boss what you said, but he's not going to budge. Nobody gets dental."

"The Cleaners get dental."

I gaped at him for a minute, not sure if he was crazy or if I was. "Yeah, well the Cleaners don't count." This was a lame argument, but I didn't have control over any of this. "Why don't you ask him yourself? I can get you on the calendar early next week. You and *Conrad* can chat about it over lunch."

He glared at me. Okay, so it was a stupid suggestion, but what did he expect? He was the crazy who wanted Maintenance to get dental, and apparently, he was willing to hurt me to make that happen. As if that would work. I didn't get dental; no one got dental, but he was acting as if it was the holy grail of company perks. Why did he even care?

"I don't understand why you think I can make this happen. It's ridiculous you're even asking. He's already said no." And he hates me.

"Should I call my boys back? Have them rough you up? I don't believe I went far enough the last time." Johnny skewered another olive.

Worse things have happened to me since, but you never forget your first time. I didn't want to spend another three days in a locked room protected by a circle of salt. He sent me to The Boss with a message: Maintenance gets dental or next time he'd send me back dead. This was next time.

I forced back the tears that threatened to fall. What would Jack think if I didn't come home for a few days—or ever? I couldn't solve Johnny's problem, and he knew it.

He studied me, then chuckled. He was enjoying my fear.

I squared my shoulders and glared back at him. "I can't get you what you want. We both know that. If you aren't going to kill me, have Frankie bring the car around. The Boss wants me back by noon, and I still have an errand to run."

Johnny's brows rose, then he threw back his head and laughed. "You're something else, kid. You know that?"

"Why did you really bring me here?"

He stopped laughing and dropped his silverware onto his plate with a clatter. Pulling the napkin off his lap, he wiped his mouth then spoke. "The Families aren't happy about the fight." He tossed the napkin onto the table. "You cost us a lot of money."

"I have no idea what you're talking about."

"You were supposed to stay out of downtown," he said. "I made that clear the last time, didn't I?"

"This is the first time I've been down here in months." Although, in light of Junior's behavior, I was wondering if I had an evil twin who liked pissing off mobsters and hellspawn.

"It was all hooked up, until you showed up."

Hooked up was probably code for fixed. I remembered an article from the paper. It had mentioned something about the bookies taking bets against Wagner winning. Since the fight was canceled, Wagner didn't win. The bookies must have lost a great deal of money. That was probably what Johnny meant, but that had nothing to do with me.

"I wasn't at the fight."

He was about to say something when a fidgeting Moe returned. He rubbed the back of his neck, and a bead of sweat threatened to roll down his cheek. He hesitated when Johnny motioned him over. Moe leaned down and whispered something in Johnny's ear.

He frowned. "How did he find out?"

I focused on Moe's whispered voice.

"I-I called him," he admitted. "I thought you would want—"

Johnny's eyes narrowed. A choking gurgle came from Moe. His eyes bulged as Johnny's will wrapped around him. Moe had obviously made a mistake. Whoever he called wasn't someone Johnny wanted notified. Was it the Godfather? Johnny seemed dismissive before. Maybe he didn't want *Harry* involved.

Johnny tugged Moe forward, bringing his ear close to whisper. His words were so low I couldn't make them out.

Moe peered at me. Johnny growled when Moe shook his head. His face was turning red. With little effort, Johnny threw him against the wall. Moe crumpled on the ground, sucking in air as he tried to catch his breath.

"Frankie," Johnny shouted.

Frankie bustled back into the room. He glanced at Moe, who was staggering to his feet. "Yeah, boss?"

"Bring the car around. It's time for our guest to leave."

Frankie's brows lowered, and his lips pressed into a thin line. "Sure, boss," he said, staring daggers at me, then at Moe.

"Now," Johnny ordered and Frankie left without another word. Turning to me, Johnny said, "You come back again and I'll kill you myself."

The dark gleam in his eyes left no doubt he was serious.

"Oh, and another thing—" He eyeballed something above my head "—don't be late."

I turned just in time to see Moe's right hook.

~ # ~

I woke up in the back of the town car. I winced as I touched my eye. It would be black and blue by tomorrow. It had been a while since someone actually knocked me unconscious. My head hurt worse now. I hated druids.

Frankie sat in the front seat reading what was left of my paper. I checked my watch— half past noon. *Ugh. The Boss is going to kill me.* Probably what Johnny wanted. I leaned my head against the seat. Why did I have to tell him when I was supposed to be back?

I touched my bruised eye again. "Did you have to knock me out? Couldn't you just hold me until I was late?"

"Nope," Frankie said. "We had orders."

"What orders?"

He didn't answer.

"Was it the Godfather?" Not that it made sense, but whom else could it have been?

Frankie's eyes met mine in the rear-view mirror. His intense stare and clenched jaw were frightening.

I leaned back against the seat, not wanting to be near him.

"Yes," he finally said.

"Why does he care?"

"No clue. Maybe he wants you as a pet." He smiled, showing teeth.

I snorted, trying to lighten the mood. That was a bullshit answer. Harry, the Godfather and Druid King, wouldn't want me for a pet. He would have to bargain with the Devil for me—why would he bother?

I shuddered at the thought of being owned by the Druid King. The druid mob in the Underworld were his enforcers, and he was more feared than they were. I'd even heard he was more feared than the Devil—not that I'd tell The Boss.

I peered out the window. We were parked in front of a deli called Sunshine Sandwiches. I glanced around; nothing was familiar. "Where are we?"

"You said Wylan James."

"Yeah and?"

"He owns the place," Frankie said, as if it were obvious.

"Wait here," I said, getting out of the car.

The place, your average mom and pop deli, was wall-to-wall with customers. Surprisingly there seemed to be an equal number of druids, pagans, and demons. An elderly man with white hair stood hunched behind a glass wall making sandwiches. I did my best to slide past the other patrons to get closer until someone said, "Take a number."

I scanned for the number dispenser and took the next slip—number ninety-eight. The readout above the deli counter read forty-two. I didn't have time to wait.

"Wylan James," I called over the crowd. The place went silent. "I need to speak with you in private."

The elderly man didn't look up from the sandwich he was making. "Take a number."

A guy beside me chuckled, but he shut up when I said, "*The Boss* sent me."

The noise level dropped to almost nothing. The door behind me opened as a few customers hurried out.

James cocked his head. "Prove it."

A tingling sensation ran across my mark. I held up my right arm and lowered the sleeve of my suit jacket. The mark flashed bright red for a second then disappeared. A woman near me gasped. The door opened and closed again. More customers leaving.

James motioned for me to walk around to the back. There were a few grumbles from the crowd, but I ignored them.

"You were supposed to be here earlier, before the lunch rush."

He motioned me toward a door at the end of the corridor. "I don't appreciate the show. I've got a business to run."

"I got delayed." I touched my bruised eye, but dropped my hand when he noticed. "And you wanted proof."

I caught the red shine of his eyes as he turned toward the door. His rigid jaw and angry scowl screamed demon. Not all demons had a red glint, but red was always a demon. Just as brown was a druid and blue was a pagan. I'd never seen any eyes with a green shine, but hazel, violet, and gold were a few of the common alternates.

James stopped at the door. He knocked once then opened it.

The room was dark. I coughed from the smoke that wafted out of the room. The smoke smelled of incense and mint. In the dim light, I could barely make out the fine lines that trailed from the smoldering tips of the incense sticks. I inched closer to the door, but hesitated to follow James inside. My vision adjusted a bit, and I saw a small man perched on a stool in the corner.

"You're late," James reminded me. "Don't dawdle."

He was right. I was late. But he knew The Boss sent me. I had to believe he wasn't going to do anything stupid. Despite my nervousness, I entered the room.

The air changed and my ears popped as I crossed the threshold. The man in the corner appeared to be a small, frail Asian man, but the veil I could sense hid his real form.

He was bent over a calligraphy box drawing symbols in the sand. The symbols were similar to the ones on my mark.

The Asian raised his head when James closed the door behind us. The Asian studied me for a moment, then tapped the box. The sand settled into a flat plane. He was a seer.

I started to say something, but James held his index finger to his mouth.

The seer chanted and drew new symbols in the sand. After a few seconds, he spoke. In Ancient. I had no idea what he was saying.

James translated, "Your existence will bring about tyranny like no one has experienced in thousands of years."

My eyebrows lifted in shock. Was the Asian talking about me? James's expression didn't change, as if the words meant nothing to him. Were they supposed to mean something to me?

The seer tapped the box and started again.

James continued to translate. "You will cause a great divide between the realms. You will cause sons to fight their father and win."

Another pause while the seer reset the box. *I really hope he's not talking about me.*

"You will cause chaos. You will unleash the great destroyer. One will betray, and one will die."

Chaos? I'm supposed to create chaos—*this is ridiculous.*

The seer tapped the box a final time. The sand cleared and he once again drew his symbols in silence. James pointed toward the door.

Outside the room I said, "Do you really expect me to believe any of that crap?"

"Believe what you wish, but the truth of the reading will be known to you before the moon rises again tonight."

I arched an eyebrow then checked my watch. It was past one. "Whatever. Just give me the package."

"There is no package."

I stared at him. The Boss wouldn't send me for a package if there wasn't a package. "There has to be a package. The Boss sent me down here to pick it up. I can't go back without it."

"I have given you all I can. You must now go."

Go? Empty-handed, back to The Boss—late. Was this guy trying to get me killed?

A cry of incoherent Ancient came from the room we'd been in. James about-faced just as the door flew open. The seer fell into his arms, screaming in Ancient.

I shuffled out of arms reach, not sure what was happening.

"It can't be," James said, eyes narrowed on me. "You're the one? The harbinger?" His face was pinched together in disbelief. "*You* will save us?"

"Save you from what?" I asked, although clearly James didn't believe it either. Was this a new prophecy or something connected to the reading? "Harbinger of what?" Why was the seer saying this now?

"The Ancients," James said. "You must set right what was lost. You must—"

I shook my head and backed toward the door. "Oh my god. You're crazy."

James eased the seer to the ground. "Come, return to the room.

Another reading. Please."

"No, stay away from me." I continued to reverse. "I'll tell The Boss."

James's eyes widened. He shook his head. "No. Please. Come—"

"No," I shrieked and bolted for the exit.

CHAPTER 3

I arrived back at two—two hours late and empty handed. The Boss was pacing when I entered his office. A clearly irritated scowl on his face, he checked his watch. I stood still, trying not to appear as scared as I felt. I winced for the millionth time as I touched my eye. He glared at me, and I dropped my hand. The bastard didn't care I was hurt.

"What did James give you?" he snarled.

"H-he didn't give me anything. He said there was no package." My voice betrayed my fear.

I sucked in a startled breath as The Boss stopped pacing and stomped over to stand in front of me. I held my ground. Not because I wanted to. I wanted to run back to my office and hide behind my desk, but I wasn't allowed to run from him. If I took so much as a step away, I'd regret it. He ignited the mark. Not enough to really hurt, just enough to remind me it was there.

"What else?"

"He translated a reading of me by a seer."

The Boss inched closer—towering over me. The heat from his body surrounded me. I could hear the low guttural snarl as he breathed. He smelled of burnt wood and cinnamon. He ratcheted up the heat of my mark. "Claire, am I a patient man?" he asked.

I shook my head.

"Then speak."

The power in his voice pushed against me as if it alone could knock me down. This was the way he always treated me, but today it was different.

No, *I* was different. He was angry with me because I was late. I was late because the mob didn't treat me the same as everyone else. He protected the others, but I got nothing from him—nothing except intimidation. Something came over me. I was pissed, and maybe a bit crazy. "Do you even care that Johnny threatened my life *again*? I can't go back there."

He sent a searing hot jolt through my arm, which immediately quelled my rebellion.

"I'm sorry. I know there's nothing you can do." *Or will do, is more like it.* I had to stop pushing his buttons. I was being stupid. He'd send me down there every day to prove a point if I wasn't careful.

He dialed back the mark. "Speak."

I told him what the seer said, leaving out the part about being their savior, although to me it was all a load of crap.

His stony expression gave nothing away. I wanted to leave, but I had to wait until he dismissed me. My right hand started to shake from the pain of the mark. I squeezed my fingers into a fist. His hand moved, and I flinched. I closed my eyes. I was afraid if I didn't the fear would take over and I might try to move. To run.

After several beats of my heart, a cool breeze brushed across my skin. He'd stepped back. I took a deep calming breath as he extinguished his mark. I un-fisted my hand and opened my eyes. I caught a glimpse of an expression I'd never seen on him before. If he weren't the Devil, I would have described it as worried. It disappeared instantly.

With the nod of his head, I was dismissed.

I opened his door to leave and heard the bell for the elevator. *Crap.* I'd listened to my messages on the way back to the office, but had forgotten an important one until the bell reminded me. "Your ex-wife called. She said she would be coming down."

"Tell her I'm busy."

I pivoted on my heel but didn't return to his office. "Unfortunately, she's already here."

He closed his eyes and pinched the bridge of his nose. I took that opportunity to leave before he could take his frustration out on me.

"What were you doing in there?" a shrill voice asked as the

fourth Mrs. Pain-in-my-ass sashayed through the glass door.

She was a silver-haired barracuda with skin so tightly stretched across her face she resembled a mannequin. She had a sleek, sophisticated style about her. The look of a woman who'd always had money. She held her head high—haughty as if she were superior to everyone else. His other ex-wives were about the same, but this one was the worst.

I smiled sweetly, ignoring her attitude. "You can go right in."

She squinted her eyes into slits, then smiled as if she wasn't a cold-hearted bitch even the Devil couldn't stand. "You really shouldn't let him get so rough with you, dear. Not until you get him to put a ring on it, at least."

My mouth fell open in disgusted shock. She winked and lightly touched the skin under her eye, giving me an exaggerated sad face as if she understood my pain.

I wanted to scream. She was insinuating that The Boss had given me the black eye as part of some kinky office escapade. The thought made me ill. *Breathe.* I steadied myself. She wasn't going to goad me into sinking to her level.

She smiled, baring her teeth, as she glided past me.

My shoulders slumped when the door shut behind me. I should have been relieved to be back. I'd survived. The day was almost over. But something was off. The office was different.

I glanced around, but nothing was out of place. My reception desk and the small waiting area was austere—severely modern. Every surface was glass, stainless steel, or rich mahogany. It was sleek and minimal, cold and impersonal—just like The Boss. The magazines were all stacked neatly as they had been before but oddly, it was colder than it had been this morning. It wasn't the temperature of the room. Something that had been here and made the space more inviting was now gone. I shook my head. The day had been weird; it was probably my imagination.

I brushed off the sudden dread and dropped into my chair. I tossed my bag in the bottom drawer and picked up my desk mirror. My eye was already starting to bruise. It would be worse tomorrow. Maybe The Boss would let me go to medical. They could make it go away. Otherwise, I'd have to explain it to Jack. Mugged, maybe? But I'd already used that excuse once this year.

I blew out an exhausted breath and leaned back in my chair.

I bolted upright. "The roses." I caught the faint smell of the buds that still lingered in the room.

I scanned the office, but they weren't there. Who would steal my flowers? Had The Boss had them removed? He'd asked me about them this morning. I spotted the note in the trash. When I reached in to retrieve it, I saw a crumpled paper crane.

Dammit! I wasn't here when Jack stopped by for lunch. I'd completely forgotten.

I pulled the crane from the trash. Today was missing from my origami desk calendar—a Christmas gift from Jack. He always made me a crane when he stopped by the office.

I picked up my phone—there were no messages or missed calls from him.

I texted him: "I'm sorry I missed you. I was stuck in a meeting w/o my phone. See you tonight! XOXO."

Whoever stole the flowers must have tossed Jack's crane into the trash.

Oh god, I hoped it wasn't The Boss. Was it punishment for being late? I hated this place.

I smoothed out the crane and balanced it on the monitor. I wanted to go home and be with Jack. The phone on my desk rang, reminding me how impossible that was right now. "This is Claire."

"Claire, um, Mr. Taylor wanted me to tell you to tell The Boss we're being audited by the IRS," Jenny, the plebe from this morning said.

Unbelievable. "Taylor is the VP of Finance. It's his job to tell him."

"So, you'll do it, right?"

"Are you kidding?" This wasn't the first time we'd been audited by the IRS, or the first time the VP of Finance wanted me to tell The Boss the *good* news.

Ugh. My second line was flashing. "Fine. I'll do it this—"

"Great!" She hung up before I could finish.

Unbelievable.

I picked up the second line. It was Carlos from Maintenance. "What?" I snapped.

"Do we have dental yet?"

As if it wasn't enough, the Underworld Mafia wanted Maintenance to have dental; every few months for the last five years I actually had to deal with Maintenance too. "If I've told you once, I've told you a hundred times—nobody gets dental."

"You listen to me, *chica*—"

I stopped listening. Carlos continued to complain, but I didn't need to tune in. It was always the same. He would threaten to stop working. He would remind me the Cleaners worked for him too, on and on and on. Just once, I wished I could tell him *The Truth*. The Cleaners knew The Truth. They knew they weren't working for some multi-national corporation that sells insurance. They knew they were working for the Devil—*the* Devil. If Maintenance knew the truth, my life might actually seem normal.

I powered on my monitor. A meeting reminder flashed at the bottom of the screen. I frowned, not remembering any meetings this afternoon. I clicked on the reminder. It was a meeting with Junior, and it was thirty minutes overdue.

The events of this morning were coming back. He'd stopped by and left a weird love poem on my voicemail. Now he was adding meetings to my calendar. What game was he playing? I cringed at the thought of having to deal with him today. I was about to ask Carlos to call me back when Number Four stormed out of The Boss's office.

"I'm not going to wait all day," Number Four said. "You tell Conrad I'll be back tomorrow. If he's not here when I return, I'm calling my lawyer."

Huh? "He was just in there." Where the hell did he go?

"You're not a very good liar, Claire. He couldn't have just disappeared."

If only she knew how wrong she was. She hitched her purse high on her shoulder, spun on her heel, and marched off before I could respond. Why he needed wives to perpetuate this farce on Earth was beyond me.

I was still holding the phone to my ear and heard Carlos continue, "Why, you gonna pick the trash up yourself? The Cleaners—"

I hung up. He would have to wait. I dialed Junior's extension. The call went straight to voicemail. *Crap.* I had to find out what he wanted. The heir apparent was just as *nice* as his father, so it wouldn't do to ignore him.

I peered at The Boss's office door. He'd blown off his ex, which meant he'd be MIA for the next two hours at least; he might not return at all. If he wasn't back by four he'd be out for the rest of the day. I could leave early. I smiled. The Boss would never know.

Then I remembered Junior. I had to handle this now. He was up to something. Maybe he was trying to piss off his father. It wouldn't be the first time, but it was the first time he involved me.

I took money from my purse. I'd stop by Junior's office, hope to God I could convince him to leave me alone, then run down to the coffee shop on the corner for a latte. I might even drink it before I came back to the office. At the very least I wasn't going to rush.

~ # ~

The Boss had more hellspawn than a dog had fleas. That was the colorful way Midge, the kindly old demon from HR, explained it during my orientation five years ago. Luckily, I had only met a few of them, and thank God, they weren't all like Junior.

He was arrogant and conceited like the rest, which was bad enough, but he was also immortal. Not all the hellspawn were. Human mothers almost never produced one. A non-human mother's offspring would be long lived—three or four hundred years, but true immortality was rare. At least, that was how Midge explained it. There weren't many immortal hellspawn left. Junior was the oldest by more than a thousand years, which ratcheted his sense of entitlement up to an almost unbearable level.

According to Midge, Junior had survived over two thousand years climbing his way to the top on the backs of his dead siblings. This was one of the reasons his visit this morning concerned me. I rarely saw him. He was usually too busy avoiding his father to cross my path. He wasn't the favorite, which appeared to piss him off. Midge called him the black sheep of the family, which was why—considering the family—I was freaked out by the sudden interest.

I knocked on his office door, but no one answered. Hoping it was locked, I twisted the knob. It wasn't. I could leave, but that wouldn't solve my problem. I'd have to deal with him at some point. Resolved to handle this now, I took a deep breath and pushed.

With a gasp, I stumbled to a halt. Junior sat at his desk with his head back against the chair. He was dressed in his best navy blue suit with black hair falling away from his face. He could have been sleeping, but wasn't. The tiny hole in his forehead and the blood and brains on the wall behind him were a dead giveaway.

From Midge's stories I'd known immortal wasn't invincible, but

I'd assumed it would take a beheading—at least that was how it worked in the movies. I examined the small bullet hole in the center of his forehead. How the hell did something that little kill an immortal?

I tried not to panic—Quaid would know what to do. He was the Head Cleaner and The Boss's right-hand man. I took out my phone. This was exactly the kind of thing he handled. "Quaid, there's a problem on three."

"Call Maintenance."

"It's on three," I repeated. Quaid would know Junior was the only one with an office on three. "I need you."

Quaid chuckled. "What has Junior done this time?"

"I can't really put it into words." Not in words I wanted to say over the phone.

He sighed. He hated dealing with hellspawn bullshit as much as I did, but technically this was his job. "Fine, I'll be right down."

Quaid didn't seem surprised when he walked in. He was impeccably dressed, as always. Today he wore his usual black-on-black suit tailored to fit his impressive six-foot-seven-inch frame perfectly. His short dark hair was cut close to his head. Even dead, he'd be intimidating.

I didn't take his lack of emotion to mean anything. It wasn't as if the Cleaners were known for their sensitive side. They were all demons, and one did one's best not to cross them.

"Does the old man know about this?" he asked.

"Not yet."

"Did you kill him?"

Speechless, I gawked at him. His merciless gaze was just as unreadable as The Boss's. "No! Why would you think I had?"

Quaid remained silent, his eyes boring into me.

"It's not even like I'd know how to kill him," I hurried on. "That bullet had to be spelled, right? I mean you can't just kill—"

His lip curled as if he might smile, or sneer.

I stopped talking before I dug myself in deeper.

"The rumors aren't true then?" he asked.

My breath caught in my throat. "W-what rumors?"

Harsh maroon eyes pierced the space between us. He was serious. He actually wanted to know if I killed Junior.

"What rumors?" I asked again.

"You and Junior."

"What about me and Junior?" Oh my god, what had he heard? *Must be bad.*

"According to the grapevine, you two are an item."

"An item," I scoffed. Who the hell would start a rumor like that? Oh no, the love poem and the calendar appointment. Now there was a rumor. Quaid studied me as if I could have done it. Would The Boss think I killed Junior? My heart rate increased. This wasn't funny. "Who—who said that?"

"Jenny in Finance said she saw the two of you at the Grand Hotel downtown on Fight Night. She said you were being *intimate.*"

Downtown on Fight Night? Intimate! "I think I'm going to be sick." I remembered how Jenny and her friend ogled and whispered this morning on the elevator. The dark-haired girl had mouthed, "no way." Was she talking about Junior? Did everyone think I'd been with him at the fight? "Is she the only one?"

"No. All the admins claim you were there, but Jenny's the only one sure you two hooked up."

Why was everyone so certain they were seeing me in places I'd never been? The mob basically accused me of screwing up all the bets. Hell, they probably blamed me for the canceled fight too. I was beginning to think I really did have an evil twin who was running around pissing off mobsters. Only now, she was also being intimate with hellspawn. And Junior was dead.

"Do you have an alibi?" Quaid asked.

Did I have an alibi? I quickly thought back over my day so far. I was in the office early, where I saw Junior—and he left me a *love* poem. I was downtown most of the morning, then with The Boss in his office. Would The Boss know exactly when I came back? I had the taxi receipt. Would he believe that or question why I hadn't used a company car?

Without considering that I might be contaminating evidence, I put two fingers against Junior's neck. There was no pulse, but his body was still warm. Did that mean I could have killed him? The Boss was out of the office. He wouldn't know when I'd come to see Junior after he left. *Oh god, I had no alibi.*

I jumped when Quaid clutched my shoulders. He was almost a foot taller than me and twice as wide. I wanted to look away, but his stare fixed my gaze.

Everything about this situation was wrong. The Boss was already angry with me. He'd never kept an assistant as long as he'd kept me. Would this be the way it ended? Early retirement? My head was spinning.

I snapped to attention when Quaid chuckled. "Are you scared, Claire?"

All the heat left my body. I was sure the bastard knew I was scared.

He pressed his right thumb to my neck.

My body stiffened. I could feel my pulse thumping.

"Did you kill him?"

I swallowed. His thumb pressed harder. Was this some sort of lie detector technique? "No."

He raised an eyebrow. Did he think I was lying?

I panicked. "Give me until tomorrow to find out why Jenny started the rumor. It's bullshit, and you know it."

Quaid rubbed his thumb along my neck. He tightened his grip, snorting at my pathetic attempt to pull away.

"Please. The Boss isn't even here." My voice was weak.

His brows dropped into a flat line. He didn't believe me.

I steadied my nerves and cleared my throat. "You can check if you want, but he hightailed it out of here when Number Four showed up." I swallowed. "You know how he is with them, and he hates her the most."

Snorting Quaid closed his eyes briefly and shook his head. He definitely knew The Boss's habits with the ex-wives.

"I know you don't care," I said. "But I didn't do this. Just give me until the morning. Give me a chance to prove the rumors are lies. I swear I'll tell him first thing."

He glanced at Junior. Quaid would never lie to The Boss, but since The Boss wasn't here, Quaid could let it wait until tomorrow—*if* he wanted to.

He squeezed my shoulders. "Don't make me regret this, Claire. You won't enjoy the consequences."

My mouth went slack.

He chuckled again. "I'll seal the floor until tomorrow. No one in or out." He scanned the room. "Don't remove anything from the room. I'll know."

Quaid left me alone with Junior. I tried not to stare at his body. It freaked me out. I wasn't squeamish about the blood, but I couldn't get the picture of him and me at the Grand out of my head. My heart belonged to Jack. The idea of being intimate with

Junior roiled my stomach.

If I could prove the rumors were lies, The Boss wouldn't seriously consider me a candidate. I wasn't sure how Junior's love poem fit into this. Was he under a spell? Had Jenny seen him with someone else—someone who looked like me? Jenny would be my next stop, but first I wanted to check Junior's office for clues. Quaid said not to remove anything. He didn't say I couldn't snoop around.

Junior's desk was a mess. I lifted a few of the papers but found nothing. I moved the mouse, and his computer hummed to life. There was a video application running. At first I thought he'd been watching something. The webcam activated, and a video of me filled the window. My bruised eye stared back at me from the live feed. Had Junior been using it before he died? I clicked the Play button.

Junior's image replaced mine on the screen. He wore the same suit and tie—the video was definitely from today. "Claire, baby."

Claire, baby?

"I'm sorry about the fight. I knew you didn't want to go. We should have done something else."

He thought it was *me* downtown too?

"I know you're still pissed because you've been avoiding me, but please let me make it up to you. Please." He smiled. "Did you like the roses?"

My vision blurred, and I felt light-headed. The roses were from Junior! Had Jack seen the card from the flowers? Was that why the crane was in the trash? The roses couldn't have been there or he wouldn't have made the crane, but the card was definitely there. I took out my phone—still no text from Jack.

Junior was smiling back at me from the screen. I'd never seen him like this. He seemed so human—so in love. What had gotten into him—or better yet, who had gotten to him?

He reached forward to stop the recording then glanced up. He smiled at someone in front of him. "Claire—"

A bullet hit him between the eyes. He fell back into his current position, and the video froze on Junior's lifeless body.

I leaned over and threw up into his trashcan.

CHAPTER 4

He'd said my name—right before someone shot him. I fell to my knees.

My eyes shot to the screen as Junior's voice said again, "Claire, baby..."

The video had started to replay. I lunged for the mouse and quickly closed the application. The file save box flashed on the screen. "No, I don't want to save," I muttered.

I clicked the no button. The video of Junior disappeared from the screen.

My heart was pounding. I opened his mini fridge and snagged a bottled water. I took a drink and swished out my mouth, spitting the liquid into the trashcan.

Junior hadn't created that video because of a rumor. He spoke as if *we* had been together, which I knew was impossible.

I opened his mail program and scanned through his past appointments. The appointment with me for today was color-coded pink. There were other pink meetings, but the one for Fight Night was green. Its location was Grand Hotel-Penthouse—the origin of the rumors—at least the one I knew about. I ignored it and opened one of the first pink meetings from two weeks ago. The subject was just FC. The location was Home. The message body was empty. The other pink messages weren't that much different. No real detail, just a time and a place.

I opened the one for today. The subject was colon and right

parentheses—the electronic smiley face. The location said 'My Office'. I caught sight of the body. For a moment I thought it was swaying before I realized the movement wasn't his body. I clutched the desk to steady myself. I hadn't opened the meeting request upstairs or I would have seen it then.

The body of the email message said Fun Claire in the Office.

FC was Fun Claire. It was me—someone Junior thought was me. I checked all the pink messages. How the hell was he fooled? Was someone really walking around pretending to be me?

I gazed at Junior's body and had my answer. The double wanted him dead—or me framed for the murder—or both, but why?

I took out my phone and called Jack. It went straight to voicemail. "Jack, I love you. I'm sorry about before. I can explain—tonight, we'll talk. Please don't be mad."

I wiped away a tear. Home with Jack, that's where I wanted to be. Not standing in Junior's office worrying about a dead hellspawn and a rumor that was going to ruin my life. I wanted Jack to wrap his strong arms around me and tell me everything was going to be okay. The morning had started out so perfect. Now I wasn't sure I'd be alive tomorrow.

I wasn't Fun Claire. Now I needed a way to prove it. Getting Jenny to recant the rumor wouldn't help. Now I was sure she'd seen someone who resembled me enough to fool Junior. She wasn't lying. It didn't matter that I hadn't been downtown. My only alibi for Saturday was Jack, but I would die before I involved him in this mess.

I patted down Junior's jacket, trying not to press my hands against his cooling body. I found his phone in his inside pocket. My heart skipped a beat when I located FC in the contact list. The digits were mine. I reviewed the call log. Thankfully my number wasn't there showing that we hadn't talked. Maybe a point in my favor.

I put his phone back and scrolled through my contacts.

I called Omar. He was a seer—a friend, sort of—someone I trusted, and the only one who might be able to help.

~ # ~

I received four company perks when I woke up five years ago. The watch—which I couldn't remove—was the most annoying and useless item. My ability to sense veils was a necessity of the job. The translator, also a necessity, was by far the coolest trick in the arsenal. Second only to the translator was the cell phone.

It worked everywhere. There were no dead zones, black holes, or dropped calls, and the contact list contained *everyone*. If you had a phone, listed or not, landline or mobile—even if you were just standing near a payphone—my phone had your number.

Seers were a tricky bunch. They could literally see you coming, which was why I always used Omar. He was the one seer I could count on to answer my call. I found his name in my favorites. He didn't have a static phone number. I never actually knew where I'd reach him. Two years ago I was quite shocked to find him at the Lucky Lady Gentleman's Club in Vancouver. He'd assured me it was all business. Today's number wasn't familiar, but it was local.

"Come on, pick up," I said.

"Hey, beautiful, what's up?" Omar answered.

He was a hopeless flirt, but he never tried anything. It was one of the reasons I trusted him. He was as far from my type as possible, but that didn't seem to stop anyone else from harassing me.

I didn't have time for small talk. "I need your help."

"Well, hello to you too." He sounded annoyed.

"I'm sorry. It's just…"

"What is it this time? One of the wives causing trouble? Or is one of the hellspawn…? Well, it's one of the spawn. Who is it—Junior? What has he gone and done this—oh, shit."

"Exactly." I wasn't sure if all seers were like Omar, but talking to him was sometimes hard to follow. However, it didn't take him long to pick up on the exact problem. Now maybe he understood my urgency. "Quaid's got the place locked down. You'll need to use the portal on three."

"What makes you think I know about the portal?" a voice said behind me.

I spun to face him, shoving my phone back into my pocket.

Omar could have easily been mistaken for a high school chemistry teacher. He was short, fat, and balding. He wore a pair of horn-rimmed glasses shoved up high on his nose, a short-sleeved white, button-down polyester shirt, and a clip-on tie. He appeared to be in his late thirties, but almost anyone with lots of power wasn't what they seemed.

Omar was powerful. I'd seen him do some pretty cool things over the years, and I couldn't sense his veil. The only other person

I couldn't sense was The Boss. I didn't think Omar was as powerful as the Demon King—the Devil was in a league all his own, but Omar definitely had some serious juice. Since I'd never seen him without a veil, I had no idea what realm he was from. I'd always assumed he was a demon, but his homely human veil screamed druid.

I considered him a friend, which was saying a lot—especially if he really was a druid.

He was at least two hundred years old, but that was the extent of what I knew about his history. He wasn't any more secretive than the average otherworldly person, but considering our relationship, I was surprised he hadn't opened up a bit over time. I wasn't offended. It just put the crazy world I was living in into perspective. Still he was the closest thing I had to a friend.

"I need your help."

"Who clocked you—?" Omar ogled my black eye. "Oh, a run-in with Johnny. It's a good thing you have the looks of a pagan, my dear, or that shiner would be very unbecoming."

"No time for jokes today, Omar."

"Trust me, I never joke about your beauty, Claire."

I rolled my eyes. He was always so adamant about my looks.

"You're supposed to stay out of downtown," he continued. "It's a rough place."

"Yeah, I know, but I have bigger problems right now."

Omar concentrated on my face.

"Please don't read me," I begged. This wasn't the first time he'd wasted time reading my future or past or whatever it was he could see. "Please focus on the room."

He smiled. "I just needed a quick peek." Now concentrating on the room, he moved away before I could beg again. "Someone did a number on him," Omar casually observed while studying Junior. "Do you have any leads?"

"Yeah, me," I said sarcastically. "So can we maybe find someone else so The Boss doesn't kill me?"

Omar fixed his gaze on me again. This time worry lines stretched across his forehead. He rubbed his head. He paced around the office, closing his eyes, then opening them again. His hand returned to his forehead.

"Are you okay?"

"I'm fine," he said.

He wasn't fine.

He rubbed his forehead again.

"What's wrong?"

"How long have you been here?" he asked.

"About ten minutes. Why?"

He continued to pace. "No, you were here before that."

What? "No, I wasn't."

He glanced at me, then closed his eyes again.

"It wasn't me. There's someone else—with blue eyes—" I remembered Junior's love poem. Now it made sense why he'd gotten the eye color wrong. "Anyway. It's not me. I swear."

"You weren't alone."

"She wasn't alone," I corrected.

He shook his head.

What did that mean? Did he doubt me? I would know if I'd killed Junior. "Junior was fooled too," I said.

How could anyone create a veil that good? A magic user could veil themselves to resemble another, but a veil was sort of two-dimensional. It was impossible to make an exact copy. A human would be tricked, but not another magic user. Not if they knew the real person. Junior and I weren't best buddies, but he knew me well enough not to be conned by a normal veil.

Omar rubbed his head again. I didn't like his behavior. He'd never acted like this before. His eyes shot open, and he glared at me. "You belonged to another."

"What do you mean?" I belonged to The Boss and Jack, unfortunately in that order. There was no way Omar meant Jack.

A wild thought crossed my mind. Omar wasn't seeing me, I knew that, but he said it as if it were possible. Did that mean there was a way out of my deal with the Devil? "Are you saying there's a way out of my deal?"

He rubbed his head again. Closing his eyes, he went quiet.

No, no, no, he couldn't do this. He had to tell me. "Omar," I pleaded. He didn't respond.

He opened his eyes. This time, they were vacant, hollow, and lost. He opened his mouth to say something, but nothing came out.

I started toward him.

He held up his hand to stop me.

"What's wrong? What can I do?"

"Nothing," he whispered. A second later, he headed toward the door. "Out," he said, before he dropped to the ground like a lead weight. He was unconscious or God forbid, dead.

"Oh crap." I rushed to his side. "Omar." I shook his shoulder, but he didn't wake. I checked his pulse. It was faint, and his breathing labored. Out. Did he mean I needed to be out of the room or him?

He'd taken a few strides in that direction, so that must mean him, but he had to weigh close to three hundred pounds. Pulling him out wasn't an option. I tried it anyway. My grip slipped from his arm, and I landed on the ground with a thump.

I studied the situation. He was partially lying on his side across from the door. Could I roll him? I crouched behind him and pushed. He flopped over onto his back. I moved to the other side and hooked my fingers into two belt loops. Using my body weight as a counter balance, I wedged my feet against his hip and tugged with all my strength. I got him back on his side, one roll closer to the door. I repeated my actions until we reached the elevator.

By the time we arrived at the lobby, he was conscious enough to stand. It took him a minute to compose himself. He clutched my arms and locked our gazes. He opened his mouth, then closed it.

"Omar, what is it?"

He backed away from me, holding up his hand so I wouldn't approach.

"Omar, you have to help me. Tell me who was with me—the one who looked like me?"

"I don't know. I can't remember what I saw up there. It's blank."

"Blank? You remember nothing?" I was stunned. He was a seer. He rubbed his head again.

Oh, no, not again. Okay, new tactic. "What about my deal? You made it sound like it could be broken."

Omar seemed hesitant to answer, but the thought of a normal life—with Jack—was worth any risk. If there were a way out—a way to be free of this hell—I'd do everything in my power to make it happen.

"Dammit, Omar. Can I get out of my deal or not?"

"I can't remember—"

"I don't care what you saw. What you saw up there was a lie. Is it possible? Is there a way out?"

Omar averted his gaze.

I clasped his arm and yanked him back around. "Please tell me. If there's a way—?" I could barely even consider the possibility. "I deserve to know."

"I don't know what—"

"I don't care about that. You know what I need to know. Please just tell me. You're a friend. Tell me what I have to do. Please, I'm begging you."

He shook his head. "The answer isn't that simple."

"No shit. Nothing is ever that simple," I shouted, then remembered where I was and lowered my voice to continue, "I'll do anything to be free."

Omar gazed deep into my eyes. What was he looking for? As if in pain, his eyes squeezed shut. What was hurting him? A few seconds later, his lids came up. He shuffled away, holding up his hand, forcing me to keep my distance. "I can't see his decision, and there are forces that you—" He stopped, pushing his palm against the side of his head. A moment later he continued, "If you're truly willing to do anything, Claire, then you must risk it all—and that may not be enough."

"I'm willing. I'll do anything."

"You must discover Junior's killer. To do that, you must visit the quads."

The quads! *Oh, hell.* This was bad—very bad.

Omar's complexion paled, but I needed more information. He wanted me to go see the four most dangerous immortal hellspawn alive. The five-hundred-year-old quadruplets were the love children of the Devil and a pagan, and rumored to have more power than a hundred normal demons combined.

I opened my mouth to protest.

Omar shook his head, then disappeared.

"No," I yelled, but he was gone.

CHAPTER 5

A chill ran through me as if someone had brushed passed me. I spun around, trying to find the whispered voice I'd heard. Or was I just being paranoid? A man by the elevator glanced in my direction then said something to the woman he was standing with. Had he seen Omar disappear?

I took out my phone, quickly checking Omar's contact. There was no number listed by his name. When I put it away, I spotted one of the security guards from reception heading my way.

I backed toward the elevator. My heart pounded, and my breath came out in short gasps.

"Is everything all right, Miss Cooper?" the guard asked.

I nodded, moving quickly to the panel. Impatiently I tapped the up arrow three or four times, as if that would make it come faster. I had to get out of here.

Hurrying to my desk, I kept my head lowered. I opened a drawer and snatched up my bag. As I turned to leave, I paused when my eyes landed on the red file folder. Impulsively, I swiped Janus's corporate credit card.

I froze when the elevator dinged. A moment later the door opened, but no one stepped off. I released a breath I didn't realize I was holding. I had to get out of here. Now.

Normally I walked home, but I didn't want to be predictable today. Too many things had gone wrong. I took the subway.

There was no relief when I entered my apartment. Jack wasn't here and still no text.

Every part of my being was telling me to avoid the quads. They were dangerous, cruel, vindictive, and immortal. Because their mother was a pagan, they were very easy on the eyes, but Cinnamon, Sage, Sorrel, and Mace were as deadly as they were beautiful.

I hadn't lied to Omar. I was willing to risk it all for my freedom, but the quads were...more. More dangerous, more cunning, more uncontrolled madness. What had he seen? Could I really save my soul?

I attempted to call Jack again. No answer. I wanted to explain some version of the truth before I left. I didn't want to die thinking he hated me. Rushing to change out of my suit, I remembered seeing Jack's gym bag on the closet floor this morning. It was gone now. Sighing, I realized he was probably at the gym blowing off steam. His phone would be in his locker. I'd stop by the gym before I left town.

I changed into something less 'office' and more 'run for your life'—jeans and a t-shirt. I had no clean socks. I opened Jack's sock drawer hoping to find a pair that might fit. My hand brushed against something hard, and something under the socks in the back flashed red. I plucked it out, stumbling to the bed.

A ring box.

I sat there staring at the box. Was this what he wanted to talk to me about? With trembling fingers, I flipped up the lid.

Empty. I forced back tears and took out my phone again and texted, "Where are you? Please call."

Had he taken the ring with him? If only The Boss hadn't sent me downtown, I would've met Jack for lunch. We would've talked. I would know if this meant something. Why wasn't he responding? I wiped away a tear. Was he mad? My hand tightened around the box. Did he think I was seeing someone else? *God, I hope not.* I put the box back.

I slipped on my shoes and slung my bag across my body.

I was writing "I Love You" on the whiteboard in the kitchen, when I heard voices coming toward the apartment.

Jack? My hope disappeared when I recognized Quaid's deep voice. I closed my eyes and concentrated. Two people approached the door.

"Let me do the talking," he said.

"If that doesn't work?" the other man asked.

"Do what you have to."

I bolted for the back bedroom.

I opened the window and peered outside. The fire escape was old, but it was the only other way out of the apartment. I didn't see anyone in the alley. But they could be just around the corner. I sucked in a breath as a knock sounded at the front door. Before jumping outside, I looked up and down the alley one more time.

Trying to ignore the rickety stairs, I hurried down the steps to the bottom of the first floor landing. The ladder broke off its rails last month, and the super hadn't fixed it yet.

I hesitated for a moment—I didn't want to break my leg. I glanced up at voices coming from the apartment. *Crap.* I left the window open. There was nothing I could do now. I jumped over the railing.

I landed funny when I fell and hit the ground. I winced as I stood and hobbled over to the darkened doorway of the building next door. There were three or four steps to a basement door—the only immediate place to hide. Once I was hidden, I stretched out my foot a few times. It wasn't too badly hurt. I'd probably have a bruise and soreness, but no real damage.

Within seconds, Quaid's head popped out of the open window above. He scanned the alley. I slunk into the darkened doorway and breathed a sigh of relief when he went inside.

I had to get out of town.

I texted Jack, "I'm sorry. I have to leave town unexpectedly. I'll be back. PLEASE don't hate me...I can explain...please. I love you."

I wouldn't risk getting Jack tangled in my mess. It hurt to think he might hate me, or that he might think I cheated on him. But I believed our relationship was stronger than today's misunderstanding. I would make this right—after I figured out who killed Junior and who was walking around pretending to be me.

Omar said to visit the quads, but he didn't say in which order I should. They were almost never together, which was probably a good thing. Each of the four was powerful in their own right, but they were rumored to be unstoppable together. Horrible stories were told about the destruction they caused as children. I believed the stories. Midge said, "There'd be Hell on Earth if they could

41

actually stand each other."

I decided to see Cinnamon first.

She was the oldest, by seconds, and the only girl. She was hardly my BFF, but of the four, she was the one I distrusted the least. This was mostly because she couldn't be bothered to waste her time on me, not because she liked me; she just had better things to do than screw with me.

To avoid running into Quaid or the other man as they left my building, I headed down the alley in the opposite direction. I opened the address book on my phone. Motor pool wasn't an option. Quaid would have them on the lookout. I would have to use an otherworldly taxi.

By the time I made it to the street at the other end of the alley, I'd been turned down by every listed otherworldly taxi service. It was essentially impossible to get picked up on Earth—who knew? My only other option was a walk-through portal I'd never used. I wasn't sure I'd be allowed to, or if I even could, but I had to try.

I opened Google maps to find one. The closest was five blocks away, but it was back toward my apartment. Quaid would probably have someone watching my home. If so, he might be keeping an eye on the closest portal too. The next nearby location was twenty blocks in the other direction.

I stopped on the sidewalk, searching for the best subway route on my phone. I froze when the sound of car brakes squeaked behind me. Closing my eyes briefly, I prayed this wasn't the end of the road. I should be moving or ducking into an alley. Not standing in plain sight. I peered over my shoulder, ready to bolt.

"Need a ride?" the guy asked.

Oh, thank God, it's just a taxi.

I was about to say no thanks, until I read the ad on the top of his cab: Sunshine Sandwiches—The hottest place downtown!—the Underworld sandwich shop I'd been to earlier today. This was an otherworldly taxi.

I eyed the driver. He wasn't veiled, which was unusual on Earth and the reason I hadn't immediately noticed he wasn't human. If he'd been veiled I would have sensed it and realized he was from one of the otherworldly taxi services. In the right light, or lack thereof, even an unveiled supernatural appeared mostly human. It was the little things that made one think twice. The metallic shine to their eyes was their most noticeable trait. It showed their true eye color, only brighter. The Boss, for example, had eyes so dark they were almost black, but the glint when the light was just right was red.

The driver wasn't a bad-looking demon. His longer than average dark hair gave him a softer appearance, which was probably why he didn't bother with the veil. His eyes were dark like The Boss's.

"Need a ride?" he asked again.

"Yeah, how did you know?"

"I dropped off a guy a few streets over. When I checked in, dispatch said someone called who needed a pick-up. I guess it's your lucky day."

I raised both eyebrows. This guy couldn't have been more wrong. "Right—lucky."

I reached for the door handle then stopped. Should I trust this guy? I glanced inside the cab. Except for a few papers strewn about the passenger seat and a Starbucks to-go coffee in the cup holder, the taxi was clean. His story was plausible. I considered the walkthrough I wasn't sure I could use—and was twenty blocks away. I got in the taxi.

"Where to?"

Traveling through the Underworld was fast. It would take no time at all to get almost anywhere on Earth. Hellspawn were required to register their current address. I just hoped she'd be home.

"I need to see Cinnamon, The Boss's daughter. She'll be in the registry."

I couldn't imagine her being involved in a plot to kill Junior. She was too self-absorbed for that, but Omar had been very clear. I had to see them all to figure out who killed Junior, and Cinnamon was the least likely to want me dead for saying hi.

The cabby typed something into the GPS.

"My code is 4-3-9-2," I said before he asked. It was a risk, but I didn't think Quaid would be monitoring my registry access.

"It's going to cost you," the cabby said.

I handed him David Janus's corporate credit card. "I'm in a hurry. Twenty percent tip if you can get me there in ten minutes." The cabby wouldn't check the name on the card. They never do.

CHAPTER 6

"China? What is Cinnamon doing in China?" I said, glancing at a traditional pagoda across the street before leaning forward to see the cabby's GPS screen. China.

"Excuse me?" the cabby said over his shoulder.

"Nothing," I said. "This is right. I'll only be a minute."

"I can't wait. You'll have to call when you're ready to be picked up."

"I had difficulty getting you guys to come pick me up the first time," I reminded him.

"Sorry, it's a new policy, but here's my card. Call and ask for me. I'll come back for you. I promise."

I sighed, but there was nothing this guy could do about the policy. I had to hope he'd still be available. I had doubts anyone else would come out this far.

"Okay," I said, taking his card. "I'll call when I'm ready to be picked up."

"One more thing," he said, handing me a clipboard and pen. "Please sign."

I reviewed the receipt.

"Nothing to worry about, just signing your soul away."

"Funny," I said, clicking the pen open. "Ouch!"

"Sorry, it's the only pen I've got."

"Don't worry about it." This wasn't the first time I'd used a blood pen by mistake. And I was already bound by one deal; I

44

couldn't be bound by another.

As you can imagine, blood pens were everywhere in the office, but this was the first time I'd ever been surprised by one. I signed the receipt and passed it back to the driver.

"Sorry again," he said.

I glanced at his business card. "I'll call you when I'm ready, Mike."

"No rush."

It was dark—China's time zone was twelve hours ahead of New York—but the streetlights illuminated the area well enough.

The pagoda was on the other side of the street. I was standing in front of a brick wall that ran the length of a football field in both directions. At least that was what I was supposed to see. Mike had stopped in front of a cluster of bricks that were all a slightly different shade than the rest. The bricks formed a diamond pattern—one I'd seen Cinnamon use before—that hid the door from public view. I walked to the pattern and placed my hand on the center brick. The wall disappeared showing me the real entrance.

I glided through the illusion then looked back toward the taxi. It was already gone. A drunken couple was stumbling down the sidewalk—heading home from a night out—but they couldn't see me. I was now hidden behind the brick veil.

Two life-sized lion's head knockers guarded the entrance to Cinnamon's Chinese fortress. They were mounted on a pair of heavy iron doors at least thirty feet tall. Odd didn't really cover what I was seeing. Uptown Manhattan was more Cinnamon's style.

My phone chirped. *Please be Jack.* I pulled it out to check the message. Not Jack. A sigh slipped from my lips. It was Jenny in Finance. "Quaid was just here looking for you. Is there something I should know?"

I shoved my phone back into my bag. That plebe needed to mind her own damn business. In an hour, the rumor mill would probably have me connected to Quaid, leaving Junior broken-hearted. At least that meant she didn't know Junior was dead.

I stretched out an arm to grab one of the rings clutched in the lion's mouth, but before I touched it, the head came to life and let out a deafening roar. A pulse of energy washed over me, causing me to take a step back. I rubbed my arms as an icy chill ran down my spine, enveloping me in a cool breeze. The sky overhead appeared lighter, and the lion's head was once again in a bronzed state.

The sudden environment change was weird. Had the sky really been darker a minute ago, or had I just not noticed the full moon?

I reached my hand toward the other lion, but pulled back as both doors slowly opened.

Fresh baked cookies wafted through the doors, flooding me with a sense of love and trust. Before I could decide what this meant, I registered new scents and feelings. The aroma switched to a bouquet of fresh flowers, and an overwhelming mood of home and safety. My eyes drifted closed as I recognized crisp apples sliced fresh for a pie, just as the feeling of hope and promise engulfed me.

I liked it.

My eyes shot open when I registered the scent of roses. I shook my head, trying to clear it, and took a tentative step back.

As if the savory odors somehow held power, an invisible force surrounded me. I had to stay alert, and sharp. I couldn't let the smells affect my other senses. Being tricked into one of Cinnamon's games wasn't my idea of fun. She'd sent me on more than one useless errand in the past just to piss off her father.

Inside the giant doors was a beautiful garden courtyard—in daylight; while outside it was night. The garden stretched impossibly far into the distance. The door was obviously a portal, but to where?

"Who are you, and what do you want?" a voice said from somewhere inside the courtyard.

I dropped my gaze to see an uncommonly short man dressed in a red and purple outfit. The style—if not the color—matched something the king's guard would have worn in King Arthur's time. The man didn't go with the outfit. He was exceedingly round with a pudgy red face that would have better suited the court jester. His short, meaty fingers clutched a clipboard—very twenty-first century—with a blank piece of parchment trapped under the clip. He held what appeared to be a feather quill pen, but it was really just a fancy ballpoint.

"I'm here to see Cinnamon," I informed him. "It's a family matter."

The sentry dropped his head to check the blank parchment. "You're not on the list."

I paused, realizing he had, in fact, just checked a blank list. "It doesn't appear anyone is on the list."

"That's right," he confirmed. "We aren't expecting any visitors today."

"I didn't say I was an expected visitor."

"Well..." The man glanced at the parchment then focused on me. "What kind of visitor are you?"

That was certainly a loaded question. I wasn't on official family business, so anything I said would technically be a lie. But time was running out. Quaid was already hunting for me, and I needed to see all four quads before he found me. So I didn't give a rat's ass I was about to lie.

"Cinnamon asked me to come."

"You're invited?" His eyes maintained steady contact.

"Yes," I said, hoping he had no truth sense.

"Well, why didn't you say so? This way, please." The sentry fluttered aside and motioned for me to enter.

All thresholds are different. As soon as I passed through the one into Cinnamon's fortress, I realized how stupid I'd been to leap before I looked. The cyclone of energy that hit me dropped me to my knees with a sharp crippling pain leaving me crouching on hands and knees, unable to move.

Waves of energy rushed through me. A force I couldn't break free from held me to the ground. My eyes burned, and my skin tingled. Locked immobile on my hands and knees as a cold stabbing pain and wave upon wave of energy, sensations, and chills ran through my body, all I could do was scream, but no sound came out.

The energy increased as it flowed into the ground through my hands and legs before looping back around and shooting into me through my eyes. Each cycle was more intense. Cold. So cold. I shuddered as my body slowly froze.

A hand clutched my shoulder. The touch was so hot it burned. I was lifted—ripped away from the ground—breaking the energy loop. The cycle stopped, and my normal senses started to return. My head pounded. With shaking hands, I wiped away the blood dripping from my nose.

I jumped when the doors slammed shut behind me, and everything popped into crystal clear clarity.

My chest tightened. The veil detector was on overdrive. And I didn't just sense the veil. Now it was as if I could read it, and I knew it hid a demon.

I searched for the demon. The doorman was gone, but seven similarly dressed men circled me. I sensed no veils. They were all human.

With their chiseled faces and, I'm guessing, washboard abs, these guys were men Cinnamon would have dated. Not even the ridiculous red and purple king's guard outfits could make them look bad. Regrettably they were each holding a long spear, the point about a foot from my body. I stood perfectly still. I didn't want to die over a misunderstanding.

"I demand you explain yourself," I said, trying to sound as if they were wasting my time and would be sorry once Cinnamon found out.

No one moved.

"You weren't invited," accused the demon I hadn't yet seen. "In Purgatory, that's punishable by death."

Purgatory! Oh, shit, that's where Cinnamon's portal led? Of all the places I could have walked into, this realm was the worst. What the hell was she doing here? She was half pagan, but she hated this place. This wasn't good. Purgatory had very specific rules about who was and wasn't allowed in.

I wasn't an expert on the realm, but I knew the rule about being invited. I'd actually learned that in elementary school—long before I had any idea pagans were real. I'd read about pagans and other magical tales in a book I was given as a gift from one of my social services caseworkers. I didn't get any gifts growing up, so the book was treasured—and I'd jokingly thought maybe a little possessed.

It was one of the few things that made it through my childhood. The book always got packed or saved or sent to the new place. My birth certificate was lost six times, but not that book. I'd read it again after I learned pagans were real, and if everything in it was true, then being killed was the least of my worries. If I'd known this was Purgatory, I wouldn't have dared cross the threshold.

"You're not a pagan so why do you care?" I asked.

I heard the snap of the demon's fingers. The sentries inched closer, bringing the tips of their spears near my throat.

Okay, so he cared, but why? "My apologies, sir," I said. "If you notify Cinnamon I'm here, she will vouch for me."

He chuckled. "Unfortunately," he said, walking into my field of vision, "ignorance of the rules will not save you from them."

At first glance, he certainly appeared to be Cinnamon's type with his short brown hair that was long enough to curl at the ends, with more of a sexy just-out-of-bed style than full-on ringlets. His eyes were dark, but his features were more rugged than harsh. If I didn't know otherwise I'd say he was human.

"You do know the rules, don't you?" he purred.

He chortled at the expression on my face, so I concentrated on presenting a neutral expression, which was harder than one might think.

"Cinnamon isn't available at the moment," he added. "You will have to deal with me."

"Who exactly are you?"

"You're certainly bold," he said, smiling.

I rolled my eyes. If there was one thing that annoyed me the most about magic users, it was the superstition about knowing their Name. I wasn't sure what I could do with it exactly, but asking was generally considered rude.

"You may call me Charles."

Charles, if that was his real Name—but probably wasn't—slinked closer. He stood in front of me between two sentries. The slightest glint of red winked in his eyes, and I caught the scent of something old and ugly. For a moment, a glimmer of his true self was visible. He was still handsome, but the harder lines of his face made him look angry, as if he had a permanent scowl. I marveled at the enhancement to my ability. It was incredible. Then in a flash, the illusion returned. I'd seen through the veil—I was sure of it, but why couldn't I hold onto it? Why did his human facade return?

Was Charles's power that strong?

I couldn't even sense Omar or The Boss's veil before, but I'd never know if Charles was like them. The old power was gone. Now I had to learn to use this one. Maybe if I narrowed my focus, I could crack the illusion. I'd done it a few seconds ago. I just needed practice.

Lifting my chin, I said, "I am here on family business. I insist you find Cinnamon."

His smug expression unnerved me. He was arrogant, but I didn't think he would be bold enough to disobey The Boss.

"What's going on here?" Cinnamon's voice broke into our showdown.

When she came into sight, the first thing I noticed was her height. She usually wore killer five-inch heels that made her the same height as her brothers. Today her feet were bare, which put her six-foot frame even with Charles. Her absent shoes weren't the only things different. Her usual little black dress had been replaced by a casual lemon-yellow sundress that flowed around her flawless body like silk. She wore it with all the poise and grace of a goddess, but it wasn't her usual style. The hair was wrong too. She usually wore her long blonde locks down—perfectly straight, not pulled back into a tidy ponytail.

I moved toward her. Matching me, the sentries marched forward. I froze, not wanting to be impaled.

"It's nothing, dear," Charles said to her, never taking his eyes off me.

Cinnamon glanced between us. "It looks like you're planning to kill my father's favorite."

I held back a disgusted huff. She only called me that to piss me off. If the Devil was even capable of having a favorite, it sure as hell wasn't me.

She smiled. "Not that I care, exactly, but I don't want to have to explain her death to him."

I was sure she was joking. Not about not caring—that part was true—but she'd never let Charles kill me. Her brothers would have, but not Cinnamon. Sage would have walked away as if he knew nothing about it. Sorrel would have watched. Mace would have killed me himself. Cinnamon, however, wouldn't want to disappoint her father. She might not have been so generous if she knew I was here on my own.

Charles's tight grin wavered. He turned his gaze on Cinnamon. She stood tall and regal. Despite her clothing, she was her confident self, exactly as I expected. He was handsome, but she was the one in control. Her boy toys did what she said.

She beamed when she caught his eyes. I smelled the sickly sweet aromas I'd caught before, but it wasn't as pleasing now. She slid into his embrace. Willingly. My mouth dropped open.

"She came in uninvited," he said. "I was thinking I might have her run the maze."

Cinnamon's eyes went glassy as she leaned into him. Her interest in me vanished. His voice was hypnotizing her— enchanting her!

"Cinnamon," I shouted, trying to get her attention. "I must speak with you in private. It's very urgent family business."

Charles's lip curled as he glanced back at me. Cinnamon was so wrapped in his spell she couldn't hear me. When my vision sharpened, his true form peeked out again then his human mask returned.

I started to speak again. He motioned for one of the sentries. I lifted my head to avoid the point as he inched the blade closer. If I remained still the blade wouldn't cut me.

In a sleepy voice, Cinnamon asked, "What were we talking about, dear?"

"Nothing," he crooned. "You should go lie down as you need your rest."

With a vacant nod, she slipped out of his arms and headed toward the main house. She stumbled through the courtyard until a demon woman hurried out to help her.

The demon woman's pale blue sundress matched Cinnamon's in style. The female's dark hair was gathered into a high ponytail with a wild streak of indigo blue running along the left side of her head. She stopped for a moment when she noticed me. She eyed Charles before bowing her head slightly. His attention remained fixed on me so he didn't see the demon woman's gesture. I was sure I'd never seen her before, at least not in her demon form, but she recognized me.

She tugged Cinnamon toward the house.

Demons in Purgatory enchanting hellspawn—that wasn't supposed to happen, right? Cinnamon was in trouble. There was no way she'd let anyone control her. Based on her reactions, she'd obviously forgotten that he'd spelled her once it wore off. Did The Boss know she was in Purgatory? Did he care? I'd always considered her his favorite, which really meant he didn't have a scowl on his face when she left his office. Would he leave her trapped under Charles's control if he knew? Was I supposed to help her?

Omar's instructions were vague. He'd only said to *visit* the quads. Could I walk away? The cold blade of the spear pressed against my skin, reminding me the first thing I had to do was figure out how to avoid getting killed in Purgatory.

"Now, back to you," Charles said, trying to charm me.

The magic power of his spell radiated off him in waves, but the enchantment didn't have the same effect on me as it had on Cinnamon. The smell was still overwhelming, but there was no sense of distraction. I wasn't being lulled by its charms any longer. "I know what you are, demon. The Boss will not be pleased."

Charles put his hands to his mouth in mock surprise, but the wicked glint in his eyes was cold and calculating. "If I were you," he threatened. "I would worry less about me and more about getting through the maze."

The sentries took hold of me and, led by the little man with the clipboard, marched me to the edge of a tall hedge. He said something I didn't quite catch, then shoved me through the foliage.

Charles called it the maze. So naturally, I expected to fall face down onto a grassy path between another equally large hedge. Instead, I stumbled into the middle of a road, where I was almost run over by an ice cream truck. I jumped out of the way just in time, as it barreled past, turning left onto a side street, blaring a tune any kid in America would recognize.

I leaned over resting my hands on my knees. My heart thumped from the adrenaline rush of nearly being hit. I forced myself to take long, slow breaths. Hyperventilating right now wasn't going to help.

After a minute I stood, taking in my surroundings. I was on a two-lane highway in the middle of nowhere. Behind me, a rusty barbed-wire fence stretched into the distance. Beyond that a field of grass so brown and lifeless rolled over small hills and into valleys. Its appearance made me wonder why it hadn't already returned to dirt.

Across the road in front of me sat an old weathered farmhouse. The deserted wraparound porch contained a single broken rocking chair—tilting from its missing rocker. The cracked and peeling white clapboard siding was dull and lifeless, leaving no question as to why the yard was little more than dirt and weeds.

Where the hell was I? I trudged forward. The crunch of gravel under my feet pierced the dead silence. I stopped moving and listened, which was when I understood why everything seemed off. There wasn't *any* sound. The trees weren't rustling, the wind wasn't whistling, and the birds weren't singing. To be more accurate, there were no birds to sing. Now, I couldn't even hear the ice cream truck. Nothing, except for me, seemed alive at all in this place. It couldn't be real.

I reached into my bag for my phone. If I was right, it would confirm I was still in Purgatory. Not some abandoned road in the middle of nowhere.

I groaned. "Not again."

The GPS readout was flipping between China, Purgatory, and nothing as if the phone couldn't decide where it was. My perfect phone was losing it, but that wasn't my real problem. The battery indicator was flashing yellow. Earlier in the day it was three-quarters full, now it was almost dead. It had a similar problem last Friday, which I'd ignored because a full charge later that night seemed to sort it out. It was obvious now there must be a bigger problem with the battery. I listened for a dial tone, but whatever caused the GPS to go bonkers affected my service.

I switched the phone off and threw it back into my bag. I wanted to scream. I was trapped with a busted phone in an abandoned world with no obvious way out. Frustrated, I kicked a pebble across the street. It skittered along the asphalt breaking the quiet. I took a deep breath and looked down the road both ways. To the left was an industrial building in the near distance; to the right at least a mile down the road was another farmhouse.

"Which way?" I muttered, shaking my head.

My wrist tingled. I checked my watch and barked out a laugh. Of all days. The hands of the watch were spinning around wildly in both directions.

Exhaling with a long breath, I dropped my hand. The damn thing was nearly perfect. For the past five years, it always had the right time and even morphed itself into a style appropriate for my wardrobe. Jeans and a t-shirt equaled rugged hiking watch; office suit equaled silver bracelet watch. The fact I couldn't remove it and I hated wearing a watch at all was apparently inconsequential.

Now the nearly perfect, completely annoying watch didn't tell time.

"Awesome," I screamed. Maybe an overreaction but I wanted to hear...something.

I headed to the left toward the industrial building. It was closer than the other farmhouse, and the ice cream truck had come from that direction. Maybe the building would lead to something, or someone.

Ten minutes later, I stood in front of the industrial building ready to scream again. It was an empty shell of brick and concrete.

Every other window was busted, and any unpaved areas were overrun with weeds. The lines of the parking lot were so faded they almost didn't exist.

The road I'd traveled along continued further into the distance where I saw more buildings clustered together. The steeple of a church loomed nearby. Unless the entire town was deserted, there had to be something there. I started walking.

When I reached the town, sadly it was no more alive than the farmhouse or the industrial building. I passed three churches, a large cemetery, another manufacturing plant of some sort, and an empty diner called the Liberty Bell. All were intermixed with single-family homes and the occasional oddly placed plantation-style home.

Everything appeared as if its heyday had come and gone fifty years ago—a snapshot in time of a small town in middle America. Except there weren't any people.

I was heading down the empty Main Street when a faint breeze passed over me. The threshold was light—no more than a whisper so it wouldn't have disturbed a feather, but when there's nothing else to feel, everything can be felt. I spun around. The road behind me was gone. Instead, I stared at a brick wall. I turned when a soft noise whistled in from the street.

I was at the dead end of an alley. At first I thought I might be in the middle of a movie set. The concrete and brick were meticulously clean—almost sterile. The street and sidewalks ahead were perfectly pristine. Nothing like the grungy decay of the dead town I'd just walked through.

I breathed a sigh of relief. Civilization—finally.

I checked my phone, but it was still on the fritz. A sharp clink drew my gaze up. Striding toward me was a man in a white ten-gallon hat and a tin star reminiscent of an Old West sheriff. His hair was white enough to be a pagan, but his bent nose and cold brown eyes looked more druid. He was neither; just an average human.

His shiny spurs clinked as he walked. Tipping his hat, he said, "Good day, miss. Have you seen the postman yet?"

This was not what I'd expected to hear, but at least he seemed friendly. "I'm sorry," I said. "I'm new to town. Can you tell me where I am?"

"You're in Hell." He paused then continued, "Montana."

I held back a snicker. I'd heard of Hell, Michigan before and often wondered if telling tourists they were in Hell was a running joke. Despite the amusement factor, I didn't have time for jokes. I needed to find my way out of this place, and so far, this guy wasn't helping. "Well...I'm fairly sure I'm not in Hell or Montana, so...is there someone around here I can talk to who might know what's going on?"

"It's better if you accept things now." His tone was sympathetic and condescending. "The longer you wait, the unhappier you'll make everyone else." Then his voice hardened, and he shifted his belt to make sure I noticed the six-shooter. "I'd hate to have to retire you so early." He smiled again. "It's not like we get new people every day."

Okay, not so friendly after all. My gaze darted from the gun to his face. "Right. So you said something about the postman?"

The sheriff motioned for me to follow him. He stopped when we reached the sidewalk and pointed to a sand-colored brick building at the end of the street.

I smiled. "Thanks."

I headed toward the building, glancing back a few times. The sheriff continued to watch me.

There were a few other people on the street, but they avoided eye contact as they hurried past me. My senses told me they were all human, but who were they and why were they here? Someone had to have answers.

I peered in through the large windows at the front of the post office. No one was at the counter. I glanced back toward the sheriff. He shifted his belt again—watching and waiting. I put my hand on the doorknob, took a deep breath, and opened the door.

The top edge of the door smacked a small bell dangling from above. The loud chime announced my arrival and dropped a blanket of energy on my head.

It didn't hurt, but a tingle of magic rippled across my skin. For a moment, the room became vibrant and warm. A yellow flyer, pinned to a nearby corkboard, rustled in the breeze from the door. The flyer announced a bake sale on Main Street tomorrow. I was happy and content. I wasn't in a rush to do anything. Nothing at all seemed important, except going to the bake sale.

Just as I was thinking about what I might bake, the magic reversed. The happy feelings backed away from me, as if the blanket of energy had been removed. The flyer was now curled and faded—barely readable. The dull reality returned, and my happy, contented state dissipated.

What happened?

The sound of shuffling came from the back. A second later, a gaunt, haggard-looking demon shambled out of the backroom. The craggy lines on his face weathered him beyond his years. Like most demons, his eyes were dark, with the slightest red shine. He appeared hungry, tired, and rundown. "Good afternoon, miss, how can I help you?"

He greeted me with a smile, as if he were simply another friendly inhabitant of the town. His veiled form was unknown to me, but I had to assume he'd project a more appealing countenance, than the scrawny, worn-down demon in front of me. I was just as sure he had no idea I was seeing through his veil. I played along. If he thought his disguise was fooling me, he might give me more information than he intended.

"Good afternoon, sir. I was wondering if you could tell me where I am."

He pointed to the wall behind him, where the words 'Hell, Montana' were painted in bold black letters.

"I see, and where can I get a bus out of town?"

"Sorry, miss, no buses in or out of town. Once you're in Hell, you're in Hell."

A small laugh escaped my lips, but I coughed to cover my reaction. The absurdity of this place being Hell was funny—Mayberry maybe, a trap definitely, but Hell—the realm owned and controlled by the Devil—no.

"Really? Because the one who sent me here called it the maze, which makes me think there could be a way out." He wasn't going to cooperate, so I took a different approach. "How long have you been stuck here? Are you keeping the illusion or are you just part of the audience, *demon*?"

Letting out a relieved sigh, he dropped his veil. Having already seen through it, I still saw the same rundown demon I had a minute ago. The constant work of displaying it was probably why he looked so haggard. He took a deep breath, as if filling his lungs with air had been impossible before. "If I knew how to get out of this place, don't you think I would? I've been here fifty-nine-and-a-half-years. I added the spells to make everyone think they lived here. Then I made one of them sheriff so he could send all the newbies here to get the whammy on them before they caused any problems."

"The whammy?" I eyed the bell above the door. *Is that what I felt walking in?* "For a minute everything seemed wonderful, then it disappeared."

He pursed his lips and studied me. "You should have walked through that door into Hell, Montana. Why didn't it work on you?"

Good question.

I shrugged. "I'm not completely sure about that myself, but I don't think you have enough power to make me see something that isn't real." I glanced back toward the bell. "Not in Purgatory, anyway."

The demon's eyes widened when I mentioned Purgatory.

"I have to get out of here," I said. "There must be a way."

"There isn't. Trust me, I've tried."

He spent the next twenty minutes telling me how he'd arrived here almost sixty years ago. Everything was the same, but the people, all thirty of them at that time, were confused and trying to kill each other. He'd cast the first spell when he arrived so they wouldn't mob him for being a demon. He finally got everyone to believe this was a place called Hell, Montana, and that they all lived here. Disturbingly, no one ever grew old or left, and now they had a population of one hundred and twenty residents, all playing their part in the illusion.

He sighed. "They do the same thing every day. They wake up and think it's the same day as yesterday. All waiting for that damn bake sale." He snorted. "So nothing ever changes, unless new people are added. They come to the post office, and I assign them a place to live, and they're off to become part of—the Maze, you called it."

"There has to be a way out." I pivoted to face the street through the large windows. "I'm going to find it," I muttered.

The demon was quiet.

"What about the ice cream truck—who drives it?"

His brows pinched together, and his gaze dropped as if he were thinking. "Ice cream truck?" He shook his head, then his eyes widened. "That's right. The ice cream truck. I'd forgotten. Do you mean it's still out there?"

"Yes, and it's outside the bubble."

"The bubble?"

"Outside, in the dead part of town. Do you know how to get back there?"

He shook his head. "You can't. Once you pass into town, you're here to stay. No one has ever left." He leaned forward and lowered his voice, as if someone might be listening. I was fairly sure absolutely no one monitored this depot of forgotten souls. "Do you have a power that might be able to help us get out of here? Find the ice cream truck perhaps?"

"A power?" I shook my head. "I'm human."

He gave me a steady look. "A human wouldn't have known I was a demon, and the whammy would have worked."

He was right.

Pinching my brows together, I considered what this meant. I didn't have an answer. "It's complicated," I said.

There was no reason to explain my life to this guy.

It was an unexpected bonus that my painful passage into Purgatory had amped up my veil detector, but that was it. It wasn't as if it transformed me into a pagan or gave me special powers. Did it? I didn't have an answer for what happened with *the whammy*. Maybe the spell over the town was sort of like a veil—a really big veil.

I thought about the other perks. The phone was a lost cause, and the watch couldn't even be trusted to tell time. Plus, those were both just things. The translator, which was implanted technology, was all that was left. If it was like the phone and the watch, then it too was probably broken—of course, I was hearing English from the demon.

"Are you speaking English?"

"Yes," he said hesitantly.

"Can you speak Demon?"

"What would you like for me to say?"

I heard English, but I knew it was Demon. *Cool.* Could I hear Ancient now too? "Can you speak Ancient?" I asked.

He shook his head.

Damn.

"What's this all about?" he asked.

"Nothing. I'm just thinking."

What else? I could try to listen to the street outside. Maybe I had more range now. I remembered the pain from the early days before I had control. When I'd catch a faint whisper and immediately my hearing would hone in on the conversation. Unfortunately, I didn't know how to ignore what was happening around me, so the amplified volume would make a normal voice near me sound like it was being shouted from an ear-splitting megaphone. But the quietness of this town could make it the safest place to try. The risk of pain was low.

"There's one thing I can try. It might help us locate the ice cream truck. Although I don't know what good that will do us."

"Maybe it will help us find the exit—to the dead part of town," he suggested, excited.

Who wouldn't be after sixty years in this prison?

Taking a deep breath, I closed my eyes. Picturing the town in my mind, I thought about the street outside the post office. I wanted to start slow. Before I attempted to increase the range, I had to control it. I focused on the sidewalk outside the door. An odd disconnected sensation covered me. It was as if my mind had stepped outside my body. At the same moment, the picture inside my head became real, things appeared as if my eyes were open, and I was physically on the sidewalk outside the post office.

My true eyes flew open, and my mind was slammed back into my body. I lost my balance and had to grab onto the wall for support. "Oh, boy," I said.

"Are you okay?" the demon asked. He'd stepped around in front of the counter.

"Did I disappear?"

He opened his mouth then closed it. "No," he said cautiously.

I looked outside at the sidewalk. I could have sworn I'd been out there, but I never left the building. Somehow I'd separated from my body. As if my mind—my presence—was free to roam around on its own. *Holy shit, that's cool.*

"Are you sure you're okay?" he asked.

I nodded. "I'm going to try that again."

I didn't know why or how—maybe I didn't care—but whatever this was, it had nothing to do with the translator. It was a new ability. I remembered the blanket of energy that fell over me as I entered. The room had been vibrant for a moment, then the illusion broke. Had I done that too? What else could I do?

I caught sight of the demon just before I closed my eyes. His gaze darted around as if he were looking for something. I ignored him.

I pictured the post office I stood in. It was easier this time to pull my presence away, and I found myself outside my body, watching myself and the demon. *Cool.*

I thought of the street in front of the post office. In a flash, my presence blinked to the sidewalk.

Amazing. Everything was as vivid as if I were physically standing outside. The view of the picture-perfect shops lining the street was exactly the same. The red and blue of the spinning barber's pole, and the smile on the face of the security guard who opened the bank door as customers approached. *Freaking amazing.*

The sheriff was across the street talking to someone. A faint sensation of someone brushing past me clipped my presence as people moved around me. They couldn't see me. Of course, they couldn't see me; I wasn't really here.

I walked toward the four-way stop and concentrated on listening for the ice cream truck. It had been outside the bubble. If I could hear it then maybe I could follow it. Find the edge between this fake reality and the dead town I'd walked through.

Tuning out everything else, I listened for that familiar sound. At first I heard nothing, but then, as if a mosquito had flown too close to my ear, the sound popped into focus. It was faint, but it was there.

I spun around quickly when another brushing sensation hit me, but there was no one there. I was alone on the street, and I'd lost the sound of the ice cream truck. *Damn.*

After another brush, I realized too late that it wasn't my presence that sensed the movement. It was my physical body.

Opening my eyes, I was jerked back to the post office, right before someone whacked me on the back of the head.

CHAPTER 7

I woke with a splitting headache and a large lump on my head.

The old springs of the cot creaked as I sat up. Yep, I was in Mayberry's jail. I closed my eyes and rested my head in my hands. There was a strong bleach smell wafting in from the other cell. Combined with my headache, the pungent scent made me want to hurl.

Other than today, I'd only been unconscious four times in my entire life. Three of those had been in the last five years—and two of those three had been courtesy of Mace. One more today and I'd be doubling my record. At least I was adding variety: tranquilizer dart, right hook, and now a whack on the back of the head.

I pushed back the nausea. I was alone, but I could hear noise from the front room through a partially opened door. There was a short hallway that led to the back, but there was no way I was getting past the thick bars.

Other than my watch and my clothes, they'd taken everything else—even my shoes. I shook my head. Did they think I'd hang myself with the laces?

"Well, well," the sheriff said, swinging the door to the front room open wide. "I thought I told you to fit in." He leaned against the doorframe.

"Where's the postman?" I asked.

"He'll be along directly." The sheriff had a smug grin. Did he know what was going on?

"Well, let me know when *your boss* gets here."

I had to hold in a snort when he straightened and puffed out his chest. Obviously, I'd hit a nerve.

"He's not my boss. There's always two. Equals."

As if I was skeptical about his declaration, I raised one of my eyebrows in an attempt to piss him off. No need to give him any respect. "Right. Equals. Looks more like a leader and a *follower* to me." I pointed at him as I said follower.

His lips formed a thin line. "It's about time, not rank. He's just got more at the moment."

I chuckled. "Time is constant. Won't he always have more?"

"He's out in six months," the sheriff snarled. "Then I'm the one with more time." With a cocky snort, he added, "Unless there's a screw up. Then I'm on top sooner. Either way, in six months I'll be number one."

Was this a prison sentence for them? The postman said he'd been here fifty-nine and a half years. Another six months would be a sixty-year stretch. He's out in six months unless there's a screw up—someone getting out would certainly be a screw up. *Great.* A man with nothing to lose but his freedom.

"So second fiddle," I chided, "low man on the totem pole—like I said, let me know when your boss gets here."

The sheriff's eyes narrowed. He put his hand on his revolver, but stopped when he heard a bell ring behind him. He glanced back then dropped his hand away from the gun.

"Where did you get this?" the postman asked, holding up my phone.

Dropping The Boss's name might be my only chance to survive long enough to escape. The sheriff had been a bit too eager to reach for his gun. "*He* gave it to me."

The sheriff's brows pulled together.

The postman considered the phone, pursed his lips, then said, "The phone doesn't work here. Which means *He* can't find you."

I held his gaze without giving anything away. I dealt with the Demon King five days a week. This guy was a joke. He couldn't intimidate me if he tried. "Whatever, man. The GPS in that thing has been busted for weeks. I just haven't had a chance to get it fixed. He will come searching for me."

I eyed the sheriff. "So I better be breathing when *He* finds me."

"Who the hell are you talking about?" the sheriff blurted.

I chuckled.

The postman sneered at the sheriff. "She means the Demon King. The Devil. This is a phone from Hell—the real one."

"Oh, shit."

Taunting the sheriff, I raised and lowered my right eyebrow. His eyes were wide. Good. Now he understood what he was dealing with.

"If she belongs to *Him*," he whined. "We're screwed. He'll kill us all when he comes for her."

"She's lying," the postman scoffed. "This phone doesn't work here. He didn't create this place—another did, one of his own. He won't come for her."

"If you say so," I said smugly. There was no reason to let him know he was right, and not just for the reasons he listed. "Do you really think the Demon King uses GPS to keep track of me? You can't take these." I held out my right arm. I expected the mark to show itself, as it had when Wylan James asked for proof. It didn't appear.

The postman snorted. "What? Did Daddy lose the end of your leash?"

"He's not my father," I snapped.

Still smiling, he said, "We don't need to eat or drink here to survive. This is the nothing of nowhere, and you can sit in that cell and rot for eternity for all I care, but you're not getting out of here." He threw the phone into my bag. His gaze dropped to my watch. "I told you to take everything," he snapped at the sheriff.

The sheriff bristled. "I couldn't get the watch off. I tried while she was unconscious. The damn thing shocked me twice."

"Take it off," the postman said to me.

"I'd love to. Tell me how and it's yours."

His eyebrows rose a fraction. Looking at the sheriff, he said, "Don't open this cell for any reason. You got me?"

The sheriff stared, slack-jawed. "Wasn't planning to."

The postman glared at him and walked out. I heard a thump like my bag hitting the top of a wooden desk, before the bell from the door clanged.

The sheriff put his hand back on his gun. "Just you and me now."

I shrugged and leaned back against the bars. "Your *boss* might be right. The Demon King may not be able to find me here, but how difficult do you think it will be once you've sent me to the real Hell with that revolver?"

The sheriff snorted as if my threat was empty then returned to the main room.

My head hurt. I reached back and touched the lump. I'd kill for some Tylenol. I wasn't sure how I'd get out of the cell, but I refused to sit and do nothing. I closed my eyes and stepped outside my body. The transition was getting easier. It didn't hurt as much this time.

I thought about the crossroads and blinked my presence to the four-way stop.

I listened for the music. After a few seconds, I caught the ice cream truck melody. I followed the song. It grew louder as I passed the small church at the corner of the town square. The music led me toward the railroad tracks. I continued until the notes dropped away and I stared at a brick wall.

What just happened?

I was back in the alley, the one I'd arrived at after walking through the threshold in the dead town.

Frustrated, I tried again, but again hit the wall.

The demon was right. There was no exit. I'd attempted every logical path that led out of town. They all dumped me into the alley. It didn't make sense. It wasn't even my body that was getting dropped at square one—it was my presence.

Was any of it real?

I opened my eyes, hauling my presence to my body. The dizziness wasn't as bad this time. I recovered quickly, but my head seemed to hurt more. Great, either it was a side effect of my new ability or my presence didn't feel the pain of the blow to my head when I was outside my body.

I guess it didn't really matter. I stretched out on the cot to rest.

~ # ~

I woke to the faint echo of a ringing bell jarring me from my nap. My headache was better, but the lump still throbbed. I sat up on the cot.

"Sheriff," I called, but there was no answer.

I closed my eyes and popped my presence into the other room. Empty. The sheriff was gone. I opened my eyes.

A bright line of sunlight was now three-quarters up the wall. The sun was setting. Had time really passed? The watch hands were still spinning. I sighed in disgust. I'd forgotten the one thing I could never lose was now useless.

I was about to look away when the hands slowed and stopped at twelve o'clock. Then the big hand pointed toward the back of the cells, away from the front room. I raised one of my eyebrows. *Unbelievable.*

"I need a way out of the cell, not a compass." I sighed, dropping my hand. I was talking to my watch.

The watch started vibrating. When I looked, the hands were back at midnight. My stomach twisted and turned as a burst of energy pulsed from the watch. Weird. The vibrations increased, and the watch emitted a high-pitched whine. The sickness rolling in my gut was followed by another short burst of energy. The vibrations increased, and the whine soared in volume.

Wincing, I gripped my side just before the third wave pulsed. Every time it happened, the pain, vibrations, and whine increased. By the fourth, I was bent double and the whine had escalated to the point it went silent.

The cell's bars rattled and shook.

I wailed as the fifth pulse slammed into the room with enough force to knock the door off its hinges—literally. The door clanged loudly as it hit the floor.

I didn't move, paralyzed by what just happened. The pain was fading, but not gone. The watch was spinning again, making me grimace from the pain it caused my red and raw wrist.

A noise from outside snapped me to attention.

It was time to move.

I stood, groaning from the dig at my side and rushed out to the front room. Grabbing up my bag, I slung it over my head. My shoes had been stuffed inside with the phone and my wallet. I dropped the shoes on the floor and jammed my feet into them. Reaching for the doorknob, I hissed when the sudden movement reminded me of my raw wrist. I checked the watch. The hands still spun. I concentrated on the face. Like before, a second later the spinning stopped, and the big hand pointed to seven.

"What? Are these directions?" I asked, then rolled my eyes at how crazy that sounded.

The big hand circled once and stopped on seven. Now I was sure I was crazy because I think the watch just answered me. I moved my wrist. Like a compass, the big hand continued to point behind me. It was a watch that could rattle metal hinges until they disintegrated.

I looked back at the cell. Before I could decide if I trusted it, the sheriff's voice outside propelled me into action. "Okay, you win," I said to the watch. "Get me out of here."

The watch continued to point to the back. I found a door at the end of the hall beside the cells. It led to an alley behind the jail. When I emerged, the sky was almost dark, but the moon was full and cast an eerie pale light over everything.

I glanced at the watch and followed the big hand, which pointed to the right. I kept an eye on the watch as I ran through back alleys and side streets, trying not to get spotted. All my careful dodging was almost ruined when I slammed into a man as I veered on to a blind alley. We both wound up sprawled on the ground.

Scrambling to my feet, I reached out to help the stranger. A shock of static energy passed between us as I took his hand. "Sorry," I said.

At the same time, his arm went limp, his eyes closed, and he crashed to the ground. A moment later he opened his eyes, his expression confused. When I reached a second time to help him, he cringed away. I guess he didn't want to be shocked again.

"Where the hell am I?" he wailed.

Okay, I wasn't expecting a newbie. Was he not spelled to believe he was part of this crazy town?

I heard voices. They were getting closer. I had taken a step to flee just as the stranger clasped my wrist.

"Where am I?" His eyes were wide with fear.

"I don't know either." I wrenched my arm away. "Follow me if you want out."

I took off. I had no idea if the guy was behind me or not. I could hear the sheriff barking orders nearby. I reached the end of a side street—right across from the alley I kept being dumped in. Why was it leading me there?

Before I had time to think, someone hollered, "Sheriff! There she is."

I didn't try to see who shouted. I ran, full speed, across the street to the alley. I glanced down one more time to make sure the watch was pointing straight ahead, then closed my eyes and headed for the wall. It was freedom or Hell, Montana forever.

I braced myself to hit the wall, but I passed through as if it wasn't there—as if the wall had been an illusion. I passed back through the threshold as easily as I had the first time.

The quiet of the dead town was back until a man's earsplitting wail went off beside me. I opened my eyes and found myself at the farmhouse where it all started. The man I'd run into was now lying on the ground beside me writhing in pain.

"Are you okay?" I asked, but clearly he wasn't.

His eyes were vacant.

I gasped in horror as he began to age. His skin sagged with lines, and his cheeks became hollowed and sunken. Rapidly, he was changing from a young man in his thirties to an old man—wrinkled by age. He panted then his hips bucked off the ground as his body convulsed and spasmed.

"Thank you," he whispered through contorted wails.

"For what?"

"Waking me." He cried out and clutched his chest. His body went rigid, then limp.

Cautiously, I touched the side of his neck. He was warm, but there was no pulse.

Dead.

I stood. What had he meant? What did I wake him from? The demon's spell? The Whammy? The demon said nothing ever changed, but clearly time had not stopped. It was just waiting for them to leave.

I jumped when the high-pitched sound of the ice cream truck barreled toward me. Was that the exit? The other direction hadn't worked.

I ran after the truck. It was moving faster than I could run, but I kept trying to keep it in sight. I rounded the corner, following the truck around the turn. I was losing ground. It was at least a half-mile ahead of me now.

"No," I screamed as it disappeared, but I didn't stop running.

I headed toward the spot where the truck disappeared. Maybe it was a portal—a way out. Something. As I drew closer, a force pulled me in.

Please don't drop me back in Hell, Montana.

CHAPTER 8

The trip back took only seconds. I was drawn through and propelled out the other side of the hedge.

"Yes!" I jumped into the air, then immediately slapped my hand over my mouth.

I waited a minute to make sure I wasn't heard. I breathed a sigh of relief when no one came bursting around the corner.

I brushed myself off and took out my phone. Mentally crossing my fingers, I hit the power button. A minute later the home screen appeared. The battery indicator flashed yellow, but at least it was working. Breathing a sigh of relief, I powered off the phone to save the battery and dropped it back into my bag.

Someone cackled, drawing my attention back to the hedge. The chortle had come from the other side. I took a few steps back, looking in both directions. Crap. The hedge appeared endless. Tilting my head up, I frowned. Climbing over the thirty-plus-foot hedge wasn't going to happen, and I sure as hell wasn't walking back through it. There had to be a way around.

Another burst of laughter pierced the silence. I had to find a way around that didn't involve going through the hedge, which might drop me back into Hell, Montana—no thank you. I would have said it was impossible to cross the thick, gnarled foliage if I hadn't just done it, but there was no way I'd risk another chance to be stuck in that trap. Using my new ability, I closed my eyes and stepped outside my body. I barely felt anything as I transitioned to my disembodied form.

I thought of the other side, the side I'd originally been pushed through the hedge from, and blinked there.

A harem of drunken maidens was dancing and lounging around as a band of minstrels played music for Charles's court. Expensive oriental carpets and huge fluffy pillows were strewn under a large awning. He sat high above the melee on an elaborate gilded throne. The scowl on his face was unbecoming. He lifted his chin, putting his nose high in the air. As a maiden dared touch him, he jerked his hand away, throwing her off.

She didn't seem to mind. The same way Cinnamon hadn't minded earlier. Were they all under his spell?

My eyes widened as I recognized the woman. Cinnamon. She twirled around as if she were high. Her blonde hair was pulled up into an almost comical style—a massive beehive of curls and flowers—and she was wearing a *toga*.

I focused on Cinnamon and blinked my presence closer to her location. She was making a fool of herself, but clearly didn't seem to mind. His spell was strong, but how did she let herself get trapped? And how was he keeping her under his spell?

I spotted the demon woman, who'd helped Cinnamon into the house earlier, heading toward Charles. I studied her. Her long dark hair was down, but the indigo streak was still prominent among the ebony waves. Her sundress was gone. She wore black pants and a casual cotton top.

"Is the girl still with us?" she asked.

Charles narrowed his eyes. "Why do you wish to know?"

Indigo lowered her head. "I was just curious if I should expect another at dinner tonight."

He snorted. "No, she's already left."

"Very well. I'll be in town for a few hours. I'll return before dinner."

"You may go." He waved his hand, shooing her away.

Indigo left the courtyard. Did she believe Charles? If not, would she call The Boss? *Probably not.* She had to know Charles was manipulating Cinnamon. She was clearly helping to keep Cinnamon here. The Boss wouldn't appreciate her role; therefore, she wouldn't draw attention to herself by telling him about me, but then why had she asked?

I tried again to place her. Given my role, she had to know who

I was from the office—unless she didn't know me at all. Could she be working for the double?

Were the quads next on my double's hit list?

Was this why Omar told me to visit them?

To save them?

Cinnamon's peal of laughter drew my attention. She needed my help either way.

I headed back toward the hedge. I scanned the foliage and found an opening about twenty meters down from where I'd been shoved through earlier.

I opened my eyes and drew back into my body. I reached out my hand to steady myself, but the sensation was barely noticeable this time.

I eyed the watch, but my handy compass wasn't moving. "Let's go," I said.

Staring at the unmoving hands, I considered what had made it work before. Nothing, it just started giving directions in the cell. *No.* It first went crazy on the road.

"Which way," I said, remembering the command I'd unknowingly given it before.

The watch hands spun. I focused my eyes, zeroing in on the hands, which stopped and pointed right. I walked until the hand moved left. The hedge in front of me appeared as thick and gnarled as the rest, but if the watch was directing me forward, there had to be something there. Maybe it was a hidden door, like the brick wall to Cinnamon's compound.

I stretched out my hand and walked forward. I expected to run into the hedge or pass through a threshold, but I didn't. There wasn't anything there except a small corridor between two identical hedge walls. The thickly gnarled hedge was only an optical illusion. No magic needed.

I followed the watch's directions until I reached the opening on the other side. I cautiously approached the exit, but wanted to scream when Cinnamon called my name.

She'd spotted me and wasted no time announcing my presence to the others. "Claire, darling," she squealed. "What are you doing here?"

When I looked at Charles, his eyes were wide. He stepped from his throne and stalked toward me. He barreled past Cinnamon, who was tripping over herself to reach me.

She recovered from being shoved. "Oh, Charles, this is my father's assistant, Claire."

I moved away from the hedge. I didn't want him to throw me back in.

"Yes, we met earlier today," he said dryly.

Earlier today. I must not have been in the Maze as long as I thought. I stiffened when Charles stopped in front of me given that he was close enough to touch me. I lurched back. He inched forward. I took another step and slammed into one of the sentries.

Charles was inches from my face. He smelled of sweet lilac and eucalyptus. The compulsion was stronger now. It was so thick around me I could barely breathe. I was afraid to willingly touch him. The power he had over Cinnamon appeared to intensify when she touched him.

He smiled at my reluctance to push him away. "I'm not sure how you made it out of the maze, but you can't resist me forever." He leaned in.

His power crashed against me, as if the spell were a physical force. "Back the fuck off jackass, I'm not going to touch you."

"Are you sure about that?" He licked his lips, parting them as if he might try to kiss me. He was arrogant and cocky and nothing like the kind of man Cinnamon dated.

I swallowed, pressing against the guard at my back. A second later Cinnamon not so gracefully snorted and clumsily toppled into Charles.

He stumbled, shoving me at the sentry. Furious, Charles snarled and pushed himself away. His touch sent a surge of power crashing over my entire body. It shot through me like a bolt of lightning, and I howled at the jolt of pain.

In the time it took to blink, the spell wrapped around me like a suffocating blanket. As it took hold, pain became love. I loved Charles. I'd die if I couldn't have him. I stretched out my hand to stroke down his long luscious body, but he spun toward Cinnamon—ignoring me.

My eyes widened with outrage. That bitch couldn't have him. He was mine. I lunged forward ready to attack. I stopped when a sharp pain bent me double as the spell unraveled, taking the agony as it fell away.

I straightened. Any good feelings I had for Charles were gone. *How?* The whammy. The reversal happened the same way in the

Maze, from bake sale to dull reality. With Charles, one minute I'm willing to kill for his love, the next I'm seeing his true form and hating him. Magic nulling? Another new ability?

My eyes focused on Charles. His veil was gone too; only the demon remained.

"You idiot," he spat, shoving Cinnamon away.

Oblivious to his anger, she scurried forward to the dancing maidens.

Charles rounded on me. He smelled of fire and brimstone, all sweetness gone.

"I can see you," I warned.

His expression changed into a smug scowl. He glanced back at Cinnamon, who was dancing and twirling near us. "You'll never convince her."

He was right. Cinnamon was still trapped by the illusion, and he wasn't going to let either of us walk out of here. She needed to wake up from la-la-land and take control of the situation.

Wake up. Yeah. That was exactly what she needed to do. The man in the Maze—he'd said I'd woken him. Could de-spelling her be that simple? Did I have that power? The man from the Maze seemed to think so.

Would it work every time? What if there were consequences? Did I care if there were consequences?

The weight of the sentry's hands pressed on my shoulders. Charles sneered. He didn't see me as a threat. The sentry's hands tightened. I looked up into his eyes; they were empty. Was he under the same spell? Purposefully I touched his hand. A tiny static shock went between us. The same had happened in Hell, Montana. I gasped when his eyes rolled back, and he dropped to the ground like a stone.

I stood there gaping for a moment, then remembered something similar happening to the man in the Maze.

"What the hell?" Charles blurted, eyeing the sentry's crumpled body.

Cinnamon was only a few feet away. I darted around Charles and ran for her.

"Come, Claire," she said. "Come dance with me."

I reached for her.

She stretched out her hand, then whipped it back and spun around laughing.

Ugh. Could she at least help me save her?

"Come, join me Claire."

I took another step forward. Charles spun on his heels and grabbed me before I could get to her. I struggled to wrench away, but he was stronger. He growled, yanking me closer. I twisted back toward Cinnamon.

"Cinnamon," I snapped, getting her attention. "Dance with me," I begged, stretching out my hand for her.

Her face lit up. She stopped spinning long enough to move near my outstretched hand. Charles's grip tightened, but before he could drag me back, I lunged. Our fingertips brushed lightly, and a small static charge passed between us.

Charles jerked me around to face him.

Cinnamon's body hit the ground behind me with a thud.

Charles's shocked gaze landed on me. "What are you?" he muttered.

Sadly, I didn't know anymore. "I'm the Devil's assistant," I said, as if that explained it—but it didn't. These abilities were new. I was different. How much different—I had no clue.

The vein on the side of his neck pulsed. His nails dug into my arm. I ignored him.

The sentry was standing, rubbing the back of his neck. His wide-eyed stare was confused and scared as it flitted around the courtyard.

Charles was oblivious to the man's distress. He shoved me at the confused sentry. "Take her to the dungeon," Charles barked.

The sentry's eyes were fearful. I don't think he knew what to do.

"Run," I commanded, nodding at the front gate.

He studied the gates for a second then took off. He didn't get far before Charles threw his will at the fleeing sentry. Several maidens screamed as the guard went flying through the air, crashing into the minstrels.

Another sentry hurried forward, but before Charles could give him an order, his body was thrown several feet away.

I spun around and saw Cinnamon. Her eyes, normally blue, were an impossible black. The power she wielded crackled around her.

"You certainly know how to make an entrance, Claire." She sneered, although I was fairly sure her anger was directed at

Charles, not me. "You've had your fun, but it's my turn now."

Fun. Was she serious? "You're welcome," I said sarcastically.

She ignored me. Her gaze was fixed on Charles, who was visibly trembling. He took a step back, then froze, his body going rigid. Raising her hand, she lifted him off the ground with her will.

She grimaced as she glanced down at herself. "A toga—you made me wear a *toga*?" Cinnamon threw him without remorse across the courtyard. He crashed into his gilded throne with a loud thunk, destroying it in the process. "Claire, you can go. Tell my father I'm going to be busy for a few days. His request will need to wait."

"But I need to speak with you. Ju—"

She silenced me with her will before I could tell her Junior was dead. "Go now before I change my mind."

Furious at her dismissive attitude, I marched to the exit, ready to get the hell out of Purgatory. She couldn't exactly help me, not that she would, and I still had to see the others.

The large doors to the garden slammed behind me, ending her hold over my voice. The sky was darker now, although the moon still shown bright.

I took out my phone and prayed it would power on and the battery wasn't completely dead. After a few tense seconds the screen flickered to life. Thankfully, I was back in China, but the yellow battery indicator still flashed.

I had no way to charge my phone. I had to hope it would hold on for a while longer.

I found Mike's card and dialed the otherworldly taxi service. As I expected, the dispatcher seemed uncertain about my request. I assured him Mike said he would return and reminded him I was a good tipper. Reluctantly, the dispatcher agreed to send Mike. I ended the call and immediately powered off the phone.

There were no texts or voicemails from Jack. I didn't try to call him. I refused to risk involving him. He would understand once I could explain. For now I had to trust he wouldn't think the worst.

I breathed a sigh of relief when Mike rolled up ten minutes later. "Hey, Mike. Good thing you didn't wait. I didn't think seeing Cinnamon would take that long."

"What was that?" Mike asked, raising his eyes from his logbook.

Not bothering to repeat myself, I said, "I need to see Sage and Sorrel."

"Sure thing."

Within minutes we were back in New York City. Mike stopped in front of a large apartment building on the upper east side of Manhattan. From the outside it appeared to be a normal multi-family complex. The redbrick and wrought iron was a common theme in this neighborhood, but that was where the similarities ended. Unlike the others, this structure had only two residents: Sage, who lived on the left side and Sorrel, who lived on the right.

Sage and Sorrel were identical twins. The middle two quads resembled their father. Their dark hair and arched eyebrows gave them an edgy look, but their pagan side made them irresistibly attractive. Sage hated almost everyone. I was no exception. Midge called Sorrel the nice one. Of course, since she appeared to be about sixty, he'd never hit on her, and she'd never had to reject his advances. The *nice one* hated me because I wouldn't sleep with him.

"I'll call when I'm ready to be picked up."

Mike smiled when he saw the tip. "Anytime."

I headed up the walkway. Once both of my feet were firmly on the first step of the stairs, the front entrance split in two. Very much like Cinnamon's hidden fortress, all the quads liked their privacy. What had once been a small alcove with one door from the road was now a wide porch with two different doors on either end.

I rang the bell on the left side, but no one answered. I rang it again, and this time a breathless voice answered over the intercom, "What?"

"It's Claire. I need to see you."

"Go away."

Sage was never the friendliest—none of the hellspawn were—but he was more likely to agree to see me and trick me into doing something I wouldn't want to do. Either way, I didn't have time for his bullshit. "Your father sent me. Now let me in."

"I—no. I—" After, I'm sure, he ran through all the excuses he could think of in his head, with a deep sigh, he finally said, "Fine, but make it quick. I don't have all day."

The door swung open, and I strolled in. I was surprised to see him running down the stairs from the second floor. He was moving so fast I half expected him to run right past me. Instead, he stopped short about a foot from me, breathing heavily and fidgeting from foot to foot.

His short black hair was unkempt, sticking up in all directions. He wore a bright green and orange shirt, the kind you might expect to see on an African tribesman, not a hellspawn from New York City. It wasn't a toga, but it sure as hell wasn't his style. My eyes dropped to his bare feet. There was a crescent-shaped bruise on the top of his right foot. Ragged sweatpants completed the style. For someone who usually dressed to impress, this version of him was ridiculous.

I took a step back. He definitely hadn't showered today—or yesterday from the smell of it. Of course, it could have just as easily been a week. "What are you wearing?" I asked.

He beamed at me with wide eyes and raised brows as if I'd complimented his tailor. He twirled around and said, "It's a dashiki. Do you like it?" He waited expectantly. When I didn't respond, he turned up his nose and said, "I think it's absolutely divine."

I opened my mouth, then closed it. I wasn't exactly sure who this crazy was, but Sage didn't use words like divine. He didn't twirl to be admired. And there was no way in hell he'd wear a pair of high-end sweatpants, much less this pathetically tattered pair he must have stolen from a homeless person.

"Are you alone?" I asked, peering around him.

He spun as if someone was trying to sneak up behind him. He craned his neck to look into the formal living room and jumped when he found me standing in his foyer. As if he hadn't remembered I was there.

"When was the last time you left the house?" I asked.

"Hmm, let me think." He tapped his index finger on his bottom lip and gazed up at the ceiling.

His eyes fixed on something. I followed his gaze, but there was nothing above except crown molding and track lighting. I cleared my throat and asked again.

"Oh, right. Um...I haven't left since the funeral."

My heart skipped a beat. He couldn't mean Junior. "What funeral?"

Sage dropped his head as if fondly remembering someone. I breathed a sigh of relief. He wasn't talking about Junior.

"Sage," I said, getting his attention. "What funeral?"

He gawked at me, as if seeing me for the first time—again. I was beginning to think he was schizophrenic. His eyes were wide, childlike, and teary. "Sorrel's, of course."

"Sorrel's dead?" Impossible.

"You were at the funeral too, you idiot."

That had to mean Sorrel wasn't dead. Oh god, unless my double was there? No. He wasn't dead. "I wasn't at any funeral. When did he die? How did he die? Are you sure he's dead?"

I studied Sage. He was confused and sad, but his eyes were also empty—like the sentry's had been in the courtyard. I took a deep breath and crossed my fingers this would work.

Sage narrowed his eyes when I reached forward to touch him. I lowered my hand. I'd have to try something else. "Are you sure he's dead?"

His brows dropped into a line. He tilted his head. It was obvious he didn't understand what I was asking. He broke the stare first, lowering his gaze to the floor.

It was time for some tough love. He needed to wake up. I took a step forward. He jumped back as if I was about to attack him. I smiled and opened my mouth to calm his fears. His eyes widened, and his mouth went slack as if I were a super villain about to pounce.

He threw his will toward me, pinning me against the wall. "T-Thanks for stopping by," he blurted, almost in a panic. "You can show yourself out."

I gaped at him as he sprinted up the stairs. Unbelievable.

My gaze tracked him until he reached the top. He paused for a moment, then took a step—vanishing out of sight. At the same time his will disappeared, and I fell to my hands and knees.

I jumped to my feet. "Sage," I shouted, rushing to the stairs.

He didn't answer. I called his name again, but the house was quiet.

I closed my eyes and stepped outside my body. I checked the house, blinking upstairs, then into the various rooms. I scanned every room. Sage wasn't in the apartment. He was gone.

I opened my eyes and almost tripped on the fifth stair. What the hell? My body wasn't in the foyer where I left it. Instead, it was halfway to the second floor. I gripped the banister, trying to stop myself from moving.

"Claire."

Something was calling me. Something wanted me on the second floor. I resisted the compulsion to continue up the stairs.

"Claire," it said, yet it wasn't a voice. It was a feeling.

I tried to resist, but the call beckoned to me, pulling me closer. "Stop," I commanded, coming to a halt just before the landing.

My right leg shook with the desire to move. I wouldn't be able to hold back forever. Whoever called to me wasn't letting me go, and for some reason I couldn't break free. Apparently, my magic nulling powers had no effect on something I couldn't see or touch.

The watch. *Okay, think. What can I ask it to do? What do I need it to do?*

I thought back to what happened to Sage. He'd disappeared after darting onto the landing. I didn't want the same thing to happen to me. I didn't want to be trapped in another Hell, Montana.

I concentrated on the watch. "If I'm not back in ten minutes," I said, but I had no clue what to ask for. *Oh, screw it.* "You know what to do."

And…the watch did nothing. No once-around-the-dial acknowledgement. Nada.

Giving up on the watch, I turned my energy to the problem at hand. But my right foot was on the next step before I could stop it. I crossed the threshold, passing through a wave of energy so cold it sent a chill down my spine.

"Claire."

This time the voice appeared to come from the large mirror that hung on the wall across from the stairs. I closed my eyes and stepped out of my body.

The mirror in front of me was illuminated with a halo of white energy. Power pulsed from it as my name was called. Not surprisingly, since I hadn't been able to stop it before, my body continued forward.

I opened my eyes. The thick mahogany frame was carved with vines that spiraled through a labyrinth of hypnotic geometric shapes. The vines snaked around the frame, twisting and turning through the wooden maze, growing thicker and denser as I watched. I cast no reflection in the glass, and whatever lived inside of it had the power to control me. Sage too, I suspected.

I gripped the frame with both hands to stop myself from falling into the mirror. Everything went quiet.

Dropping my hands, I looked behind me. I wasn't at the top of the stairs in Sage's apartment anymore. I was back at the company, standing in the doorway to The Boss's office suite.

"Are you just going to stand there," a voice in front of me said. "Or are you going to let me in?"

I spun around, coming face-to-face with myself. Not a reflection. My red hair was gathered back in a loose twist. I was dressed in my favorite gray suit, but the shoes were wrong. I'd never wear heels that high to the office.

After a moment of stunned silence, I asked, "Who are you?"

The other me ignored my question.

I asked again, "How did I get here?"

She smiled, but still didn't respond.

Was I really back at the company? *Is this my double?* Was The Boss in his office?

She cleared her throat.

My eyes lowered. She was carrying a large stack of red file folders. I'd never seen that many early retirements at one time. This couldn't be real. I let her pass. She dumped the folders on my desk, then turned slowly, leaning on the edge.

"Who are you?" I asked.

Her eyes widened. "You don't remember?"

"Remember what?"

"You'll see soon enough," she said. "I'm the Keeper."

The Keeper?

She winked and blew me a kiss. "The one and only."

Is she reading my thoughts?

"Yes," she purred.

Oh my god, she's reading my thoughts!

She threw her head back and roared with laughter.

A slow nagging pain crept up my neck. *I have to stop thinking.*

Her movements were a blur, and she was in my face, staring into my eyes. "You can certainly try."

I took a step back, running into the glass door behind me.

Her eyes bored into me—the most vibrant shade of gray—not blue or green. For a moment, the image flickered. Green tendrils of hair fanned out around her head. This wasn't my double. "You've changed," she cooed. "I see you have your power back. Good. You'll need it."

My power? Back? What did she mean?

She clutched my right arm and squeezed. The Boss's mark flashed. "He can't protect you here," she sneered.

Protect me? Here? I jerked my arm away. "He'd never protect

me." I rubbed my wrist where she held me. "My watch." It wasn't on my wrist. My hand went to my hip. "My bag." Where did they go?

She raised an eyebrow. Her lips curved up as if she knew a secret.

"Why am I here?"

She shrugged. "Lucky, I guess." Before I could speak she confessed, "Not for you, of course."

The slow pain inched up my head. "Get out of my head and answer my questions."

As if I'd hit her, she staggered back a step. The intrusive pain disappeared. My head was clear. *Can you hear me?* She didn't respond.

My shoulders sagged, and I breathed a little easier. "Why did you bring me here?"

She shrugged. "You came when I called."

"I want to leave."

"I'm not stopping you."

Ugh, was she kidding me?

She huffed as if she were bored. "You're still bound by Winter. No fun at all."

Bound by Winter? What the hell did that mean? Before I could ask, she continued, "Summer can't protect you now. Spring shouldn't have given him the job. I suppose no one wants it really, but someone has to have it." Her matter-of-fact tone told me she believed she was making complete sense.

Summer can't protect me? I glanced down at my arm. Was The Boss Summer? Nothing about this seemed true. "You're crazy. You know that, right?"

"Yes, of course, but you would be too if they'd starved you for nearly twelve years."

"Who?"

"The royals. Your precious master and his ilk. But now you're mine again, and he can't protect you here."

The royals. The Druid King, the Pagan Queen, and the Demon King—The Boss. That's whom she meant, but why was she calling them seasons, and which one was Spring? And why wasn't there a Fall?

This was stupid. Squaring my shoulders, I took a step forward. She wasn't going to bully me. "Who says I need his protection?"

She jumped up and down, bouncing on the balls of her feet. "Oh, goodie, Summer's pet is going to play." Her gaze studied me from top to bottom. "You don't have *all* your power yet, but it'll have to do."

Her singsong version of my voice was starting to get on my nerves. And why was she calling me a pet? A pet was a human that druids, demons, or pagans kept with them in their homes. Did she think I was The Boss's pet?

"At least you're not human now. It was no fun at all before," she prattled on as if we were planning a party.

"What? I'm human," I said. "Before?"

She giggled. "Silly pet, not anymore." Her voice lowered, whispering conspiratorially, "Technically you never were, but being bound can have such dire consequences."

What? I considered her face. She was grinning from ear to ear, but there was no hint of deception. She believed it without doubt. I'm not human? Never was? How was that even possible?

"If I'm not human, then what the hell am I?" A sudden fear ran through me.

"Poor baby—doesn't know who Daddy is," she chided.

I shook my head involuntarily. There was no father's name listed on my birth certificate. If I'm not human, did that mean I was, what, a druid, a pagan—a hellspawn? Could The Boss be my—? I wouldn't even consider it. I swallowed, trying to keep down the bile in my throat. The Devil was not my father, and I wasn't sure how the power thing worked, but I was human.

"The watch has the power." I feebly attempted to explain it away.

She chuckled. "Winter's blood will break the curse."

My eyes widened. "What curse?"

She sagged her shoulders and sighed. "It doesn't matter now—now we play. I do hope you remember our games. We used to have so much fun."

I crossed my arms. I wasn't going to play her stupid games. "I suppose Fall wants to screw me over too."

Her eyes flared white. Her jovial nature vanished. Before my eyes, her body morphed into a ghostly siren with radiating static energy covering her naked form. A wild mess of green hair stood out from her head as if the strands were being blown by an invisible wind. In a deep voice, she said, "Do not joke of things you do not understand. Fall is the reason you exist. Your heart belongs to her."

"But there's only three realms," I challenged.

A low rumble started, which must have been her laughing, before she said, "Now there are three. Then there were four."

There used to be a fourth realm?

"Choose," she spat.

Choose what?

Her form changed. Within seconds, she showed me seventeen different, yet familiar, people. Everyone from the grocer in my local supermarket to the homeless man I passed on my way to work. She paused on my second-grade teacher, Mrs. Gage, an older woman with graying hair and pointy horn-rimmed glasses that seemed to stare at you on their own.

Her voice was loud and shrill, sounding the same as I remembered Mrs. Gage sounding. "This was a popular choice once."

No. Not the nightmares.

"Summer's pet is starting to remember. Good."

I may have been twenty-one, but at that moment, I felt like nine-year-old Claire—the scared little girl plagued by nightmares. This couldn't be happening. Those had disappeared years ago.

Ignoring my distress, the other me continued, "Maybe someone more recent." Quickly, she shifted through images until she stopped on my beautiful dark-haired, blue-eyed boyfriend.

Jack.

He stood there in his low hung jeans, looking all bad-boy sexy. "Hey babe, what's up?" he said.

"No. Not him. Please."

He winked, and she started shifting through images again. She stopped on a big, blurry blob in the shape of a woman. I knew immediately it was my mother. I shook my head again. I didn't want to see this thing's version of her.

The blob shrugged, and the Keeper switched again. This time it landed on Mace.

I sucked in a breath. My body tensed.

"Shall I read you poetry or cut out your heart?" Mace said with a wicked laugh.

"Why are you doing this?"

Ignoring me, the Keeper waved his hand. The office

disappeared. We were now in Hell—at least what I expected Hell to be like—a desolate wasteland of destruction.

"I guess it's too late to pick poetry?" I said nervously.

He licked his lips, then winked before giving me a wide Cheshire cat grin. The Keeper's version of Mace was somehow more vicious and cold. His god-like good looks were hardened, as if he was wearing a mask. The wind picked up, and a chill ran through me.

"Please don't bring back the nightmares," I whispered, more to myself than any plea to the Keeper.

His smile faded as he calmly started removing his jacket. I was in the middle of a war-torn city. Gutted, bombed, and crumbling buildings were all around me. Debris was everywhere. I stumbled and almost fell backing up.

He was taking his time, rolling up each shirtsleeve. "You should start running now—a head start," he said. "I'll be very disappointed if you're too easy to catch," he warned.

I ran. An unseen force slammed me against a crumbling chunk of concrete. I guess I should have known the Keeper wasn't going to play fair. I winced as I heaved myself from the rubble. A pole protruding from the block of concrete jabbed painfully into my side. The skin wasn't broken, but it hurt like hell.

"Ten, nine, eight..." Mace started counting down.

I ran. There was no way to out run him, but I had to try.

"...seven, six, five..."

I ducked behind a building, still within earshot.

"...four, three, two, one."

My heart skipped a beat.

"Ready or not, here I come," he teased.

I crouched low, trying to quiet my breathing—trying not to panic. Waiting for him to pass by, I held my breath as he approached. I gave him a minute to put distance between us, then bolted to another building. Staying low, I hugged the wall. I jumped when an invisible blast struck near my head. Tiny chips of concrete debris flew out in every direction. I ducked as one of the larger chunks flew at my head. I nearly tripped, almost falling into a pile of steel and sharp glass.

I lost sight of him, but I was sure he was still chasing me. Without warning, I slammed into an abandoned car. Its alarm started blaring. I lunged away, stumbling this time, and ran. I reached the next building, stopping to catch my breath.

"Come out, come out, wherever you are," he taunted.

The crunch of his footsteps neared. I saw a broken piece of two-by-four lying on the ground. It had four rusty nails jutting from the underside of one end. I scooped it up and ducked behind a wall—waiting for him to get closer.

Wind howled through the buildings. I closed my eyes, trying to focus on his sound. "Just go away," I pleaded quietly into the night.

Everything stilled.

I cautiously opened my eyes, hoping I was back in Sage's apartment. I wasn't. I was in my childhood nightmare, the one from my past, a scary version of my old elementary school.

I froze and looked around. The classrooms on either side of the hallway were filled with children—at least they appeared to be children. They were really scary little monsters who were just waiting to break out of their skins and eat me.

An innocent giggle sounded behind me. I thought my heart might stop beating. I spun around. It was Beatrice—a little five-year-old with cute blonde curls that bounced in time with her steps. She giggled again and skipped toward me. Exactly as I remembered.

I gripped the plank tighter, holding it up like a baseball bat. "Stay the hell away from me, bitch."

The sound of her patent leather shoes hitting the floor sent chills down my spine. She scared me more than anything else ever had, before or since. When I was younger, I actually thought she was the Devil—that was before I met him, of course.

Get a hold of yourself. I backed up, but stopped when I hit something.

"Boo." I shivered as his breath brushed the back of my neck.

I spun around.

Mace ripped the board from my hands and tossed it away. "There you are." He caught me by the hair and jerked me close.

I slammed my elbow into his side, but he wouldn't budge. He tugged my head back and leaned in for a kiss. With my fingers shaped like claws, I grabbed at his face, pushing him away. He snarled and yanked my hair. I yelped, but still tried to claw him.

With his free hand, he held my arms away from him. I struggled, but it did no good. He was bigger and stronger. He angled my head, exposing my neck, but this time he wasn't going to kiss me. Opening his mouth, he bared his teeth. They were now disgustingly sharp and dripping with saliva.

My heart beat like a drum. Struggling free was impossible. I arched my face, screaming when his wet lips touched my neck— burning my skin. I felt a tug against my core, as if he was somehow sucking my life away.

"Stop," I panted.

The Keeper stilled.

I took a few deep breaths. I closed my eyes and shouted, "Wake-up!"

Everything stopped. My hands ached. The burn of his lips on my neck faded. I slowly opened my eyes. I was back in Sage's apartment, gawking at a very disappointed—pissed off—version of myself.

I sighed with relief just as an annoying beep-beep, beep-beep started. I checked my watch and let out a disbelieving snort. I released the mirror's frame, flexing my hands to relieve the stiffness. I switched off the alarm.

I was shaking, cold, and scared, but I was free of the Keeper's influence.

The reflection of me started to fade. "Until next time," she mouthed, before backing away and disappearing into the mist.

CHAPTER 9

I hurried down the stairs, pausing at the bottom to catch my breath. My hands were still shaking when I spotted a small bathroom off the foyer. I splashed water on my face, then dried it with a hand towel by the sink.

My reflection in the mirror was pale, but my color was returning. I took several deep breaths. My hands weren't shaking as much, but I was still wired. I inspected my neck, expecting to see where Mace had bitten me, but there was nothing there.

This whole time, I'd never left the apartment.

I took a long calming breath and attempted to forget the memory of the nightmares. I hadn't thought about them in years. I hadn't run from Mrs. Gage, or Beatrice, or the scary monster children since I was nine. I was still having difficulty wrapping my head around what had happened, now *and* then. To think that years ago my nightmares had been caused by this creature—the Keeper—deliberately trying to hurt me.

The nightmares had ended the summer before I turned ten. At the time, I'd given credit for chasing the nightmares away to my new caseworker, Mr. Harrison. He was the New York City social worker who had been assigned to me after my previous social worker mysteriously disappeared. I felt horrible for him the first time I met him. Getting assigned my case was like the lottery win of bad luck. Up until then, I'd had a different caseworker every six months—and they weren't all lucky enough to just disappear.

Mr. Harrison hadn't really taken away the nightmares. He was my caseworker, not my savior, but he'd removed me from more horrible foster families than I could count. I considered the nightmares part of that package. He was the only good thing that had ever happened to me.

Now I had a new hell to deal with. Could I trust anything the Keeper said?

I glanced at my right arm—The Boss's mark. The watch. *My power.*

Spring's pet. Bound by Winter. Protected by Summer. *Screwed by Fall.*

Not human.

I shook my head. I was tired and hungry. I wanted this day to end. I wanted to go home to Jack and make love to him. Fix the misunderstanding between us. Quit my job. Live a normal life. Win the lottery. I chuckled. What was one more impossible thing on the list?

I flexed my hands which were still sore from the tight hold I'd had on the frame. "Enough," I said, pounding my fist on the counter. "Suck it up, Red, and solve Junior's murder." I laughed at my own serious expression, but I couldn't just stand here and do nothing.

Sage was MIA. I took out my phone and considered calling Quaid. No, I couldn't give up yet. I shoved it back into my bag. I wasn't willing to risk involving him. I had to stick to the plan. Sorrel—as long as he wasn't actually dead—was next on the list.

I moved to leave then stopped when I spied an old-looking set of keys on the marble table by the door. I hadn't seen those before, but I'd been distracted by Sage's behavior. I picked them up and examined them.

There were two skeleton keys, one slightly larger than the other, and two ordinary house keys. They were each engraved with a hellspawn symbol. If I was right about the symbols, the house keys belonged to Sage and Sorrel, the larger skeleton key had Cinnamon's mark, and the smaller key, embossed with a silver snake, was for Mace.

Why would Sage have all of their keys?

I stuffed them into my bag. If they belonged to Sage, he wouldn't miss them right away, and if not, they could be a clue to what was going on.

I left the apartment and walked over to Sorrel's door. I considered using his key to enter his apartment, but decided it was safer to ring the bell. After the day I'd had so far, I didn't want to walk in uninvited.

I rang twice before he answered. Good, not dead. He partially opened the door, leaving the chain attached. More strange behavior. Most things coming after him wouldn't be stopped by a door chain.

He wore a white tank top and was just as unkempt as his brother. At least he wasn't wearing a dashiki.

"I need to speak to you," I said. "Your father sent me." I opted to start with a lie. I certainly didn't want him to think I'd come for any other reason.

Sorrel sniffed. "I told him I don't ever want to speak to him again."

Okay, like that was possible. "Since when?"

"Since the funeral," he said.

"Whose funeral? Yours?"

"No, idiot. I'm standing right here," he admonished, then muttered, "Why does no one ever see me? Why do they only ever think about him?"

Sorrel was definitely the neurotic one, but this wasn't like him. He'd never admit he thought everyone favored Sage, no matter how much he believed it. Not that I was surprised, but he clearly wasn't himself.

"Sorrel," I said, getting his attention. "Who died?" I asked, to confirm what I already suspected.

"What? Oh, Daddy's favorite is still here," he sneered, raising his chin.

"His favorite what? Slave?" I wasn't The Boss's favorite anything. "Who died?" I demanded.

"Sage. Sage is dead. Now go away."

Sorrel shifted and his right leg came into view. I recognized the sweat pants Sage had been wearing earlier. I looked closer. He had the same bruise on his right foot. *Oh, crap.* This was the same twin, but did that mean the other twin was really dead?

"Sorrel," I said, continuing to address his current personality. "I need for you to let me in. Your father sent me with a gift for you. I must come in to give it to you."

His eyebrows lifted. "A gift?" Then they fell into a frown. "He can't win my love so easily."

Oh, for heaven's sake. It was sad I wanted the uncaring, selfish assholes back, but the emotionally exaggerated drama queen personas were frustrating. "Open the damn door," I demanded. "Or I'll tell him you refused the gift, and he will come up here himself to give it to you. Now, you know what happened the last time he came up to see you, right?"

Sorrel was quiet, likely remembering his father's visit. At least he could still be threatened. "You can come in, but only for a minute." He closed the door, and the chain slid back before he opened it.

Cinnamon had been dancing around in a toga. Sage had been modeling garish tribal wear, but nothing prepared me for Sorrel's foyer full of secondhand furniture. I could barely squeeze through the entrance, and once in I was practically nose-to-nose with him— or Sage, whichever twin it actually was.

"Are you remodeling?" I asked.

"No," he said, sounding offended.

The only plus to being so close was that he couldn't get away quickly. Regrettably, it also put me in direct contact with his smell. Unwashed hellspawn wasn't pretty. I tried not to breathe. "Here's the gift." I touched him on the forehead.

A slight shock passed from me to him, but he didn't drop to the floor like the sentry or Cinnamon. I tapped him again—it couldn't hurt. This time he passed out and almost crushed me as he fell forward.

"Sage, Sorrel?" I said, shaking him by the shoulder. "Can you hear me?"

After a few seconds, a very startled, very pissed head popped up. He glared at me and growled. I would have skittered backward, but I was pinned between him and the oversized chest of drawers behind me. He pushed himself off, yanking me up with him as he got to his feet. "What have you done to me?"

I clutched his arms, trying to push him away. To prove his strength, he lifted me off the floor. It gave me the perfect opportunity to kick him in the groin.

He dropped me and doubled over. "You bitch," he shrieked. Straightening quickly, he launched at me. "I'll kill you for what you've done."

"Wait!" I cried, pushing my hands out to stop him.

He froze, but his eyes were still wild with fury.

"I didn't do it. I brought you out of the spell, but I don't know who cast it. We need to find Sorrel. He could be hurt."

By his temper, I was certain this was Sage, although to be honest I had never been able to tell them apart. They were identical in every way, and if I hadn't seen them at least once together in the same room, I would have suspected there was really only one of them. Sage was, of course, the bigger asshole, and if this were Sorrel, he would have already tried to kiss me.

"What do you mean?" he snarled, twisting his hand in my shirt and heaving me forward.

I tried not to panic. He was angry and strong—a hothead, but he wasn't stupid. He'd listen to reason—I hoped.

"Look, when I got here you were over in your apartment wearing a dashiki and acting like you were crazy, saying that Sorrel was dead. I decided to see what Sorrel had to say and came over here, where I find *you* again—now sans the dashiki, pretending to be Sorrel and saying that you, Sage, are dead." I left out the part about me snooping around his house and getting trapped by the life-sucking Keeper imprisoned in his upstairs mirror. It wasn't important right now.

"What the hell is a dashiki?" he asked, his nostrils flaring.

"Tribal shirt. Not your best look."

He tightened his fists, drawing me closer. "How did you break the spell?"

"I have no idea," I admitted without going into the details.

He frowned. "Where's Sorrel?"

"I don't know. That's what I was trying to tell you. He could be in trouble. You have clearly," I said, turning up my nose, "not bathed in days, and both times you thought your twin was dead. We need to find him. Now."

"Unless he did this to me," Sage said coldly.

"Why would Sorrel do this to you?"

The idea was ridiculous. Sorrel was the least likely of the quads to do anything against the others. He was a lover not a fighter, and he was the weakest. He couldn't have taken Sage, and no way in hell could he have taken Cinnamon. She would have broken him in half if he tried.

"Cinnamon was trapped too, there's no way he—ugh." I gasped as Sage shoved me against the door.

"Cinnamon." His voice was calm, quiet, and deadly serious. "What has she to do with this?"

"Nothing," I said quickly. "She's been some demon's plaything for the past few days. It isn't Cinnamon or Sorrel. We need to find Sorrel, bef—"

I was about to add, before he winds up dead like Junior, but Sage didn't give me a chance. He opened the door and shoved me outside. "You can go now. I'll handle it." He slammed the door in my face.

"You're welcome," I shouted at the closed door.

Selfish bastard. I reached for my phone, but stopped when I heard a noise coming from Sage's apartment. I inched to the door and heard a woman's voice. "Shit, where are they?" she snarled, followed by footsteps padding away.

I fingered the keys in my bag. Was she searching for these?

I used Sage's key and, making sure to be quiet, opened the door. The place was silent. I was about to close my eyes and let my presence find the intruder when the faintest puff of air came from my right. I spun just as a woman rushed me. She knocked me into the table by the door. My left arm was pinned as we crashed to the floor.

"These are mine," she said, snatching the keys.

I recognized her as the demon woman I'd called Indigo from the garden in Purgatory. She was dressed the same—dark pants and a casual top. She froze when she realized who I was.

"Forgive me, mistress," she said frantically. She held out her hand to help me up, but stopped suddenly. Her eyes focused on mine. "You're not the one I serve," she accused, shoving me away. She snatched the keys and disappeared.

I sat there—stunned. Indigo hadn't recognized me in the garden. She'd thought I was the double. But how did Charles fit into all this? He had no doubts I wasn't the double. Was he working for someone else? Great, another player—a mystery player.

A bump and thud came from upstairs. Sage must have heard the commotion. It was time to leave. I pushed to my feet, rubbing my scrapped arm, and headed for the door.

I took my phone out and powered it on. Thankfully, it still had some juice. No messages or texts from Jack—where was he? Why hadn't he attempted to contact me? Scrolling to find his name in the contact list, I stopped when the screen dimmed and reminded me how drained my battery was. Holding my breath, I dialed the otherworldly taxi service. I cursed when the phone died in the middle of my call. Removing the battery, tapping and holding down every button, nothing I did woke it up. Dead, damn it. I threw it back into my bag.

At least I was in New York City. There'd be a payphone within a block or two of Sage's apartment. I fished out Mike's card and searched for a payphone. I spotted one on the corner near a drug store, right beside another New York City staple: a hotdog vendor.

Mike's familiar brakes screeched to a halt just as I bought my dog.

"Where to this time?" he asked as I inhaled the lifesaving processed meat.

I couldn't believe I was about to willingly go to Mace. A chill ran through me as I remembered the Keeper's chase. I know it wasn't really him, but the effect was the same. Unfortunately, with Sorrel MIA and Sage refusing to cooperate, Mace was the next piece of Omar's puzzle. He was also the reason The Boss didn't send me on hellspawn errands anymore.

Mace was the youngest quad. He was gorgeous and, according to Midge, looked the most like their mother, but his wicked violet eyes kept him from passing as a full pagan.

He wasn't someone I trusted, but I had no choice. I trusted Omar. I had to believe Mace was trapped like the others. Enthralled to an unattractive demon that wanted him to rub her feet and feed her bonbons—would certainly be a just reward. None of the others had been themselves, and their alters hadn't really been the cutthroat variety. I would be okay. Tap and go. That was the plan. By the time he was Mace again, I'd be out of there.

"Hey, you still with me?" Mike asked.

"Yeah. Sorry, it's been a long day." I pasted a smile on my face. "I need to see Mace."

Mike raised both eyebrows. Clearly, Mace's reputation preceded him. "Are you sure?"

No. "Yes." *Please believe me.*

He took a long look at me. I wasn't in the best shape, but I had a black eye when he met me. I could tell he was a nice guy. I didn't like lying to him, but I wouldn't risk his life by roping him into my problems.

His brows drew together. "You don't seem sure."

He genuinely seemed to care—not something I was used to. Not since Mr. Harrison, my social services caseworker, anyway.

"Are you okay?" Mike asked.

I opened my mouth to say no and caught a glimpse of a picture taped to his dash. A towheaded little girl with pigtails was smiling at the camera. My voice caught in my throat. He had a family who cared about him—a daughter who loved and depended on him. I closed my mouth. I wouldn't drag him into this mess.

I smiled, this time more convincingly. "I'm okay. Just business for The Boss."

Obviously still not convinced, he hesitated.

I glanced at the photo again. "Your daughter is beautiful," I said. "I never knew my dad. She's lucky to have you—to keep *her* safe."

He studied the picture, his brows drawing together again.

"My job's not nearly as rewarding," I said, "but someone's got to do it. Right?"

His eyes were still fixed on her picture.

"Just another day at the office for me."

After a few seconds he nodded. I was sure he didn't believe me, but he understood. It was his job to keep her safe. He couldn't do that if he got hurt helping me. He couldn't save us both.

"Mace it is," he said, putting the car into drive.

I dreaded seeing Mace, but going to The Boss with a crazy story of look-a-likes and mystery players wasn't a better option. I had to find Junior's killer.

"Why me?" Mike asked, dragging my attention back to him. "Why not one of the company cars?"

I didn't have a good answer. He was challenging my 'just another day at the office' line. He really was a good guy, but I couldn't tell him the truth. "Because you were nice and gave me your card and promised you'd come back for me." I smiled, hoping that would be enough.

"My card?"

"Yeah, this afternoon when you picked me up."

"This afternoon. In the city?"

"Yeah," I said, realizing I wasn't the only one having a long day.

His brows furrowed, and he peered at his daughter's picture again. Then smiled. "Right, it was over on 52nd and..."

"No," I said, thinking back to exactly where he'd picked me up. "54th and…Park, I think." Was that the cross street? *Close enough.*

"That's right." He shook his head. "Too many long days in a row. Eventually it catches up with you."

"Tell me about it," I murmured.

Within minutes, the taxi stopped outside a villa in Grand Cayman. It wasn't Mace's style. He preferred five-star hotels to quiet bungalows by the sea. Of course, Cinnamon had been trapped in Purgatory, Sage had been prancing around in a dashiki, and a demon woman working for my double was carrying around keys for all four. I was sure this place wasn't his doing.

The tropical heat weighed on me as I exited the taxi. I glanced around. There was a payphone by a convenience store on the corner. I'd be able to call for a pick-up as soon as I de-spelled Mace. I tilted my head at Mike.

"I can wait a few minutes if—" His phone chirped, interrupting him. He scowled at the text.

"Don't worry," I said. I didn't want him to break the rules on my account. "I'll call when I'm done."

He raised his head. "You'll call when you're ready?"

"I promise." Part of me wanted him to wait, but I wouldn't put anyone in Mace's crosshairs. The only way he could keep his daughter safe was to stay out of my trouble. And he certainly didn't want to be on Mace's radar.

Mike looked at his phone one more time, then at the picture of his little girl. He smiled and gave me a parting wave.

I waited for Mike to drive off, then headed for the bungalow. My hands were sweaty, and my heart was beating faster than normal. Mace had messed with my head the last time I'd seen him. He put me in a dream state for three days, but I experienced weeks trapped in a past reality that never happened. When he finally let me out, I had difficulty knowing what was real and what had been the dream. I didn't trust my own memory from that time. It took weeks to fully recover, and that was only after The Boss had medical fix my memories.

Jack had been there for me too. He saved me from the darkness and gave me hope.

The Boss punished Mace. It was the only time he'd ever intervened on my behalf. Not that he told me any of this, or that I was supposed to know it happened. I'd overheard Quaid complaining. He was pissed that he now had to do my job, especially after Mace promised to never do *it* again. I was sure *it* was the mini trip into hell he'd sent me on.

I hadn't seen Mace since the incident. He was dangerous, but he wasn't stupid enough to defy his father. I just needed to take precautions. I couldn't lose my memory again. It had been so difficult to come back the last time. I was hoping to find Mace inside rubbing an ugly demon's feet, but I couldn't count on that being the only option. The others hadn't been violent—at least not until I de-spelled them—but Mace wasn't exactly the poster child for good behavior.

I didn't know what power I really had, or how to use it. For all I knew the Keeper lied and it was all the watch. Considering everything that happened, I didn't really believe that, but it wasn't like I had a user's guide, so it really didn't matter where it came from. Whether it was from me or the watch—same difference—it would work or it wouldn't.

Putting as much conviction as possible into my words, I said, "Don't let me forget anything."

A strange tingling sensation ran from my right wrist to the base of my neck and over my scalp. An odd glow rimmed my vision, blinding me for a moment. Everything popped into sharp focus when I could see clearly. I was alert—aware of my surroundings. As if the sky had been cloudy before and now everything was sunny and bright.

I immediately regretted casting the spell. I shook my head, but the overwhelming sense of total awareness didn't go away. *Crap.* This couldn't be good.

"Suck it up, what's done is done," I muttered.

Blowing out a breath. I raised my hand to knock, then hesitated. Could I really do this? I considered throwing up, but I resisted. It wouldn't help. He scared me, but losing my lifesaving hotdog wouldn't change that.

I can do this.

Quickly, before I chickened out, I rapped my knuckles on the door.

Within seconds shuffling footsteps approached. I released a breath I didn't realize I was holding when the door opened, and it wasn't Mace. It was a very old man dressed in an elaborate butler's uniform. He had close-cut gray hair combed back with so much gel it was wet. He was human. His outfit reminded me of the costumes the sentries had worn—too perfect to be real.

"Yes, miss, how may I help you?" he said, in a very formal British accent.

"I'm here to see Mace."

"May I inquire as to your business with the master?"

The master? "It's a family matter." No need to discuss this with the help.

"And you are?" he asked, looking down his nose at me.

"Claire, his father's assistant." There was no understanding of my position in his eyes. Either he didn't care or he didn't know. Could be both.

"Please follow me."

I followed him into the villa's main room, which was a large open room designed in a tropical style. The eclectic collection of couches and chairs seemed to be the kind of furnishings someone might choose if they could only buy what was already on the island.

My voice caught in my throat the moment I saw him. He was sitting, surrounded by several young pagans tightly huddled around him. The girls were dressed in barely-there string bikinis and wrap-around sarongs. The boys wore what I believe they called banana hammocks and nothing else.

I was anxious, but it wasn't my fear of Mace. Someone in the room was veiled, and not who they appeared to be.

Mace's eyes were glazed, but snapped to attention when he saw me. One of the pagan women had her head between his legs. I blushed and turned away when I realized what she was doing.

Pagans weren't exactly shy about sex—with anyone. I attempted to ignore him and concentrate on figuring out which pagan was veiled, but the men and women were all too close together. I couldn't pinpoint the source.

A couple of *long* minutes later she let out a wail of pleasure. Mace unceremoniously shoved her off and righted himself. Thank God, *he* wasn't a screamer. I couldn't say the same about her. She'd carried on as if she was auditioning for voice-over work in adult films. He hadn't made a sound. His piercing gaze was on me the entire time, which was uncomfortable enough.

"Did you enjoy the show?" he asked.

I rolled my eyes. Mace was too attractive to be human. His pale violet eyes were unusual and unnerving. They weren't quite blue enough for a full pagan, but they weren't red like a demon either. He ran his hand through his short-ish blond hair and flashed a wicked grin. He could have rocked California surfer or Norwegian god. He would have looked just as good bald, and he knew it.

I didn't respond. Instead, I scanned the pagans, who were now fanned out around him making it easier for me to see each of them.

"Would you like to go next?" he asked.

My eyes widened and snapped to his beautiful face. A woman to his right growled, but his gaze stayed on me. I didn't like the way he eyed me. Like all pagans, Mace wasn't timid about sex, but Sorrel had always been the amorous one toward me.

My heart beat fast, and my palms were sweaty. Not wanting to show fear, I purposefully kept my breathing slow and steady. The others had been nothing like themselves. Mace was maybe a hair more preoccupied with sex—especially with me—and I'd never seen him in jeans before—but those were the only differences. Of course, Cinnamon had seemed normal until Charles turned his attention on her. Maybe Mace just needed another jolt of— whatever—to be the fully oblivious sex god he was acting like now.

If he didn't need my help and this was just Mace then I should run. If he did need my help and I left him trapped, he'd get even. I really had no choice. At this point, I had to attempt to de-spell him.

Mace sat up straighter and cocked one of his perfect eyebrows as I sidestepped the butler and approached him. *Oh god, he probably thinks I want to be next.* I ignored that thought, but the woman to his right certainly didn't. Her body language told me she was ready to fight for her spot in line.

I swallowed my fear and continued with my plan—the absolutely stupid plan of tap and go. Especially now that he thought I wanted to go next.

He bit his lip as I approached. I leaned forward—ignoring the low snarls from the pagan on my left—and touched his right hand. I expected the same static energy to pass between us that I experienced with the others. My mouth fell open when nothing happened. He really wasn't spelled.

I jerked my hand away. His brows pinched together. I took a step back, planning to run, but before I could move the woman to my left grabbed me by the hair.

"He's mine next," she hissed.

"I don't want him," I blurted.

Mace's expression darkened. Was he actually surprised I didn't want him?

"Everyone wants him," she argued.

"Everyone else, maybe. Not me."

Mace's mouth pinched together. He had the ability to know when someone was lying. I wasn't lying, and for some reason that seemed to piss him off.

"Tell her, please," I urged, but he kept his mouth closed

She growled, "You know you want him too."

For the love of God, could she be more delusional? "Please, Mace."

His eyes never left mine. He was enjoying this. In a low silky voice, he said, "Leah, she's like family."

I was so *not* like family, but I wasn't about to argue that point.

"Leah," he barked when she didn't react.

With a petulant groan Leah shoved me forward. Off balance, I stumbled. In a blur of motion, Mace stood and caught me. He spun me around so I was facing away from him. Trapping my arm between our bodies, he held me close with his suffocating embrace. "Did you miss me, Claire?" he cooed in my ear.

I sucked in air to keep from snorting. One, because this was Mace, and although he was being a bit touchy-feely right now, he was an ass, and two, he could hurt me if he really wanted to.

With his nose in my hair, he inhaled deeply before putting a light kiss on my cheek. "Have you come to play?" he asked then kissed me again.

"No." I cringed when he drew my earlobe into his mouth. "I came to help you. That's all. I swear."

"I'd rather play."

Oh, god no. Lovey-dovey Mace was really starting to piss me off. With a firm tone, I said, "You're in danger."

He wasn't under the spell, but maybe he was next. I could warn him, and he wouldn't get trapped. If only he would listen. He swayed our bodies back and forth as if we were slow dancing. He either didn't care or he didn't believe me.

"Look at me and you'll know I'm telling the truth," I insisted.

He stopped and spun me around to face him. His lips were pressed into a firm line. He'd gone from playful to pissed in a heartbeat. "Speak."

Assuming he wouldn't placate me long, I blurted everything out quickly. "Cinnamon was trapped in Purgatory. Sage was at his apartment, but not himself. Sorrel is missing. I thought you might be trapped too."

I gasped when Mace yanked me forward. His hands tightened around my arms. His jaw was clenched, and his violet eyes were somehow lighter—more threatening.

"I—" My voice cracked. I swallowed, trying to ignore the lump in my throat. He wouldn't hurt me like before. He wouldn't go back on his word to the king. "Mace," I stammered, not sure what to say.

All eyes in the room were on us. The pagans glared at me. Leah—the woman who'd grabbed me—licked her lips. Were they just going to watch him hurt me? She smiled, then leaned over to whisper to the girl on her left. The woman behind her shifted to hide, but not before I saw her.

Indigo. She wore a tropical sarong over a colorful bikini, like the others, but it was her. She was the one veiled. The one I'd sensed when I walked in. The veil had no effect on me—not since my trip to Purgatory, but Mace and the others would see her as a pagan. I breathed a sigh of relief. Mace would have to believe me now. He couldn't ignore a veiled demon in his harem of pagans.

I moistened my dry lips and looked at Indigo. "Demon," I accused.

Mace followed the path of my gaze. He snarled at her before shoving me to the ground and stalking toward her. The other pagans scattered, disappearing one by one. Indigo turned to run, but he stopped her with his will.

I pushed to my feet, intent on getting to the door while he was busy with her. At this point, I didn't care if Mace was in danger. Hell, *I* was in danger.

Mace had other plans. He threw his will, tripping me. "Stay," he commanded.

Indigo yelped.

"Show yourself," he yelled.

I sensed her release her veil as I launched toward the door again. A loud thump sounded behind me just before I was yanked backward by his will. I braced myself for the impact. As I slammed into the wall, my breath was knocked out of me. Wheezing I peered down. Indigo was crumpled, unconscious, on the floor at my feet.

"You aren't getting away from me that easily," Mace said. "Not after what you've done."

After what I've done? He was acting as if I'd come here to kill him not save him. "I was just trying to help. I told you about the demon."

He barked out a short laugh. "Do you really think I didn't know about her?"

If he knew about her, then why didn't he get rid of her? Why did he keep her around? "I have important business for your father—"

Mace's violet eyes widened. "You're lying, Claire," he said through gritted teeth.

Oh, crap. "You promised him you wouldn't do this again."

His smile faded, and his eyes narrowed. "Did he send you here?"

"Ye—" I started to say yes, but my words were cut off as he wrapped his will around me and squeezed. He'd seen through the lie before it was off my tongue.

He leaned in, pushing my body against the wall. "You came to me willingly, not as my father's servant." His cocked eyebrow sent a shiver down my spine. Mace twined his hand in my hair. "All bets are off now, little girl."

I gasped as he pressed our bodies closer together. "No. Please. I won't tell your father. I promise. Just let me go."

"How do you know you won't like it?" he asked, rubbing against me. "Father has been keeping you away from me," he said, trailing light kisses down my neck. "You came to me willingly." He inhaled deeply, as if my scent were an elixir. "You're mine now."

"No—"

He cupped my face in his hands. Lifting my chin, he kissed me on the lips. I tried to pull away, but his firm grip prevented it. I gasped when his hand snaked under the hem of my shirt, which allowed him to push his tongue into my mouth. Turning my head, I slid away as he bent forward to deepen the kiss. Undeterred he returned his warm lips to my neck.

I wanted to scream in frustration. His touch was setting me on fire, but I shouldn't be feeling anything. I didn't love Mace. I hated him, but his hands roved over my body caressing and stroking as if we were lovers. I cried out as he bit on my neck then licked over the spot.

"Stop," I demanded, and he froze.

A guttural rumble came from his throat.

"Master," the butler called from behind him, breaking the tension

Mace pushed away from me. My legs like jelly, I slid down the wall, trying to catch my breath.

He glared at the butler. "What," he barked.

"Your message has been sent," the butler said, bowing his head.

"Shit," Mace said, glancing back at me. Through gritted teeth, he said, "Collins, you are nothing if not efficient."

"Thank you, sir," Collins said with a slight nod.

I started to lift myself off the floor.

Mace pushed me back down with his will. "Sit, stay," he chided, as if I were his pet.

Collins spoke again. "What shall I do with Miss Lily?"

Mace's attention swiveled back to the butler. "Take her below to the basement."

Collins nodded.

Mace turned back to me. "And prepare a circle of salt for Claire."

I opened my mouth, but Mace tightened his will, keeping me quiet.

Although Collins appeared quite old, he easily bent down and scooped up Indigo—Lily's—unconscious form. He threw her limp body over his shoulder and carried her toward a blank wall on the far side of the room. He tapped it three times, and a door appeared. A portal...of course. Beach houses didn't have basements.

Mace stared at me for a long minute, then sighed. "This is a royal fucking mess," he said, more at me than to me. He squeezed the back of his neck and paced the room.

My body was stiff from the tight hold of his will. I cleared my throat.

His head whipped around. Cocking an eyebrow and actually snapping his finger, he said, "I know just the thing for you. Don't go away."

As if I could go anywhere right now. I couldn't even move.

Five minutes later, Mace returned. His cocky expression, with his almost-smile, unnerved me. He was spinning two small metal bands around his finger. He clasped them in his hand, stopping their spin, then fanned them out as if showing me something cool. Crouching down he pulled one of my hands to his lips for a light kiss. I had to stop myself from rolling my eyes.

With quick efficiency, he clicked the thin delicate bands on my wrists. A tingle of sensation washed over me as the last bracelet closed. He chanted, a low murmuring unintelligible sound. I sucked in a quick breath as the metal resized to conform to each wrist, melding against my skin perfectly. A surge of energy enveloped my hands as the bands settled into place.

Mace pulled me to my feet. He tilted my head up to kiss me. I pushed him away.

"Ouch," I said as a powerful shock surged up my arm. I jerked my hand away. "What was that for?"

His mouth turned into a mischievous grin. "I can't have you going around touching people. Can I?"

I rung out my hand. The pain was dissipating to a dull throb, but I still had chills from the contact. I studied the bracelet. "Seriously? That will happen anytime I touch someone?"

He stifled a quiet chuckle.

"I'm sorry I touched you without permission, but don't you think this is a bit extreme?"

He tapped me on the nose like I was a spoiled child then pulled me toward the basement stairs.

The basement was nothing more than a concrete box. Probably no more than fifteen-foot square. Half of the room looked as though a graffiti artist had tagged it while on crack. It was painted with hundreds of black and gold markings that covered the floor, walls, and ceiling. The other half was just bare gray cinderblocks and concrete—a stark contrast from its gilded neighbor.

Some of the markings were in the same Ancient script as the Devil's brand on my arm. Others resembled Egyptian hieroglyphics. I had no clue what any of the symbols meant.

Collins was in the painted half of the room, creating a circle of salt. Lily's unconscious body was lying outside the circle but inside the painted half.

"Will there be anything else, sir?" Collins asked, once the circle was complete.

"No, you may go," Mace said.

As soon as we were alone, he started chanting. The melodious words could have been a song, but it was nothing the translator recognized. He was casting a spell in the Ancient language. I took an involuntary step back when a ripple of light pulsed through the markings causing them to flare and glow. Mace pulled me forward as the salt ring flashed red, and the glow from the room rippled around it. He spun me and pushed me through the threshold of the warded room. A pop sounded as his hands passed through the invisible wall. The glow faded when his chant ended.

I rubbed my arms. The room had become noticeably colder, dropping several degrees within seconds. "Why are you doing this?"

Ignoring my question, he said, "Stay inside the circle. It will protect you." With his hands in his pockets, he turned on his heels to leave.

"Wait, you can't just leave me down here."

He pivoted to face me. "Would you rather come upstairs to my bed?"

My mouth dropped open. It took me a moment, then I said, "No."

He grinned, as if he knew I was lying.

I shook away the memory of his hands on my body. Damn pagans and their sex on legs appeal.

"Don't try to leave," he warned. "The barrier won't let you pass. It will knock you unconscious if you try."

"The Boss—"

"You came here of your own free will, Claire. I won't be denied. You're mine now, and I intend to keep you."

I stood there gaping. Was he serious?

Before words could return to me, he said, "Now I'm off to fix the mess you've made. We'll settle up later, and finish the little game we started upstairs."

CHAPTER 10

The basement was completely dark. Mace had switched off the lights on his way out. I sat in the circle of salt, my legs crossed to be sure I was fully inside it.

Salt magic was old and powerful. I had no idea how it worked. But it would protect me as intended, which meant it would keep me safely out of Lily's reach for as long as Mace wanted it to, or until he broke the salt line.

I could hear the low moans and whimpers of Lily's fitful sleep. She would be awake soon. I closed my eyes and stepped outside my body. The symbols and markings glowed a bright green illuminating the darkened room.

The threshold that separated the painted half from the rest of the basement resembled a green wall of steel, with a transparent shimmer rippling over it like a wave in a pond. A faint blue halo circled one of the bricks on the far wall. I hurried forward to investigate, but my presence slammed into the barrier. I attempted to blink to the other side, but that didn't work either. The halo disappeared moments later.

Frustrated, I stomped back to my body, ready to open my eyes. I stopped when I realized my physical form was bathed in white light. The salt circle protected me from the sickly green cast surrounding everything else, including Lily. Every square inch of the enclosure was marked or covered by the green glow that connected all the symbols. My presence was trapped by the markings as surely as my body was trapped by the threshold.

Thinking back, I remembered how the pulse activated the enclosure, sealing it off completely. I peered at my body, thinking about the wave and how it wrapped around the circle. The salt protected it. I studied the floor closely. The markings under the circle weren't glowing. The salt prevented them from connecting to the other symbols.

Maybe it was my way out.

I jumped into the circle, basically standing on top of my body, which was weird. I thought of the main room upstairs. The one I'd been in with Mace. Instantly I blinked to that location.

The living room was empty. I stilled for a moment and listened. His voice drifted from one of the upstairs rooms. I followed the sound and found him in an office. The tropical theme had missed this room. It was an ultra-modern example of cold glass and steel. The only color in the marshmallow white room came from a large abstract painting. The vibrant red was splashed against the canvas as if it were a study in splatter patterns.

Mace was on the phone. Pacing. "Sin, we will figure out who did this. They will pay."

There was a pause. I moved closer, but I couldn't hear Cinnamon's voice through the phone.

"Quit screwing around and bring the demon here. I'll get him to talk, then you can kill him." Mace's neck corded as she spoke again. His tone was strained when he responded, "Yes, she's here. No, I don't know how she discovered you."

He ran his hand through his hair, scratching the back of his head. "Yes, the twins are on their way. Sorrel isn't well..." He paused.

Sorrel had been found. *Good.* I couldn't complete Omar's task without seeing them all. Of course getting away from Mace was going to be a challenge.

He sighed. "I agree. She can fix him— We'll figure this out *together.*"

The desperation in his voice caught my attention. Why was he so adamant she come?

The twins were already on their way. "Why did he need Cinnamon?" I muttered.

"Because we're stronger as one," he snapped, and for a minute I thought he was answering my question. Running his hand through his hair, he sighed. "Look, no, I mean yes, you must join us." He took another turn around the room, holding the back of his neck, waiting for her answer. After several tense seconds, he dropped his hand, and his rigid stance relaxed a fraction. His lips curved in his usual smirk. "Excellent. I'll see you then."

Cinnamon was coming, and she was bringing Charles.

I jumped when a pagan woman materialized in the office. She was beautiful—of course—her skin pale and flawless. She had blonde hair so light and translucent it was almost white. It appeared as fine as silk, and flowed down her back in long cascading waves. She was as tall as Mace's six-foot-five frame. I dropped my gaze to see if she was wearing heels, but her airy dress covered her feet. Mace's posture stiffened in her presence.

"Nephew, how are you?" she asked.

Nephew? Obviously from his mother's side of the family.

Mace bowed his head, but his shoulders remained tense. "Hello, Aunt. You look well." His greeting was formal. Was he afraid of her?

"I received your message." Her voice was delicate and melodic, but their tense postures made it clear the situation was painfully strained.

Mace's head remained lowered. The muscles in his neck flexed. "I apologize for sending it, but the situation has changed. The others will be here soon."

Her smile faded. Through gritted teeth, she asked, "What has caused this change?"

As if he were considering his words carefully, he paused then said, "Claire, Father's assistant. She's involved—I don't know how, but she woke them." He swallowed, then added in a pleading tone, "I'm afraid it hasn't been enough time. They won't cooperate willingly."

The aunt's arched eyebrow relaxed. A wicked grin crossed her face, which, for some reason, sent a chill down my spine. She ambled forward and lifted his chin. His eyes were still wide with fear, but softened a bit at her smile.

"She was in Purgatory?"

Mace opened his mouth to respond.

Without thinking I yelled, "Don't tell her anything!"

He closed his mouth. As if he'd heard me, his eyes darted around the room.

The aunt swiveled her head to look in my direction. I gasped when her eyes met mine. Her smile widened. *Oh, shit.* She could sense me.

"I'll take that as a yes," she said, more to me than Mace.

"Aunt?" He followed her stare. His eyes scanned the area, but when he didn't remark about my presence, I took that to mean he *saw* nothing. He couldn't sense me, but he'd somehow heard me.

"Don't worry, Nephew. All will be fine."

"But you said—"

She put a finger against his lips. "We will discuss that later. Does your father know she's here?"

"No."

"I must speak with her...alone."

Mace hesitated. "Alone?"

Her eyes became cold slits when he didn't immediately agree. "Yes, alone," she demanded.

Back-pedaling, he said, "Of course, Aunt. She is in the basement."

She smiled, caressing the side of his face. "We will speak when I return."

As she passed me, her cold essence rolled over my presence. "Are you coming?" she whispered.

My eyes flew open. I was back in the dark basement. Adrenalin pulsed through me. My heart rate increased with every second. She'd scared Mace—the scariest pagan I knew—and now she wanted to see me. Alone.

I swallowed, pushing down the knot in my throat as footsteps stopped at the basement door. Why was she happy I'd been in Purgatory? I flinched when the door clicked open. The lights flashed on overhead, causing me to squint.

An unveiled human with dark hair glided down the stairs, but I was sure it was the aunt. Her hair, which had been straight down her back before, was gathered up into a neat bun. Her flowing full-length dress was now a suit that reminded me of a modern-day Jackie-O—complete with a small strand of white pearls and earrings. She looked to be in her late thirties or early forties. Pretty, but not beautiful.

I was confused by the new style. She'd sensed me; didn't she know I'd seen her? The hidden veil worried me. Someone who could scare Mace would have to be strong—Omar strong.

Obviously, there were more people than I thought who could hide their veil.

She lowered her gaze to Lily, who was starting to stir. "Sleep," she commanded, and Lily's body went limp. Turning to face me, the woman said, "Do not worry, child. You're safe from me...for now."

My eyes widened.

She chortled. "The game will be so much more rewarding now."

"The game?"

She studied me. "You look different than I imagined."

I furrowed my brow. "How did you expect me to look?"

"Like a human, of course."

"I am human." Although I believed it less every time I said it.

Her grin broadened. "Your features are more pagan than human."

Oh, please. "You're the pagan here, not me."

She gasped, covering her mouth playfully with one hand. "Ah, clever girl. What else have you seen?"

Had she really not known I'd seen her true form upstairs?

I wanted to take a step back, but she'd wrapped her will around me so fast and effortlessly I didn't even see it coming. Our eyes locked.

There was an increased pressure on my head, similar to the way it felt when the Keeper read my mind. I wanted to turn away, but couldn't. The pain started almost immediately. I could smell the blood as it trickled down my upper lip. A ringing sounded in my ears. I couldn't breathe.

"Stop," I managed to force out.

I fell to my hands and knees when she released me. My lungs burned as I sucked in air as fast as I could. Still gasping, I raised my head.

She was in her true form now. Her simple long dress flowed effortlessly around her lithe body. The dress shimmered with an iridescent lushness I hadn't noticed upstairs. Her hair was once again white-blonde, loose and flowing down her back.

"I'm surprised you made it out of Purgatory alive," she said. "We will deal with that later. For now, I am more interested in your predicament."

"Which predicament?" I wheezed out between gasps. The pain

shooting through my head was relentless. My breathing was returning to normal, but every lungful still burned. I managed to push myself off the floor and stand.

She crowed a mirthless laugh. "Which one, indeed."

"Yes, which one?" I demanded.

Her wicked grin returned. "Traveling between the realms is very dangerous for humans—especially from Earth. Underworld portals are more predictable."

"So now I'm human," I said, bent over, hands on my knees, looking up at her.

She raised one of her perfect eyebrows. "That was a general statement, dear. However, you were more human before, which is why you're here—now."

Now? "What is that supposed to mean?"

"You arrived three days before you went in."

"What?" This really made no sense.

She sighed.

I straightened, finally able to catch my breath.

"I'll try to explain the situation more clearly. You think today is?" She looked at me, expectant.

After a few heartbeats, I said, "Monday?"

"When, in fact, today is Friday." She grinned. "Last Friday from your perspective."

I shook my head. Time travel? That was impossible. Time travel wasn't real. *Was it?* "I went back in *time?*"

"It would appear so," she said. "Those pesky Earth portals can be so unreliable. You should be thanking whatever you pray to that it didn't drop you in the eighteen hundreds. Three days is just a mere inconvenience. Don't you think?"

"*Back* in time? Time travel?" I said, shaking my head. How was that possible? I looked up, realizing what she'd said—the eighteen hundreds—three days were bad enough. Three days ago—not Monday. I gasped. "Junior's not dead!"

My body went rigid. Her will, holding me in place.

"That's exactly the kind of information I don't want you sharing."

"But I can save him." *And save myself.*

She waggled a finger. "That isn't quite how it works, dear. The decisions they make must be their own. No helping."

Decisions? "Are you saying the quads are going to kill him?"

Was Junior the one who trapped them? Was he the mystery player—the one who hired Charles?

The aunt's lips pressed into a line. "Enough," she said, waving her hand at me.

Her will tightened around me like a giant fist, making it impossible for me to move. I gaped as she stepped through the salt circle as if it weren't there. She towered over my five-foot-eight-inch frame. My back ached with increased pressure as she lifted me to eye level.

"You will not speak of these events." She raised her hand. A tiny shock zapped me as she touched my jaw. I opened my mouth to ask about Junior. A cold sensation rippled over my face, forcing me to clamp my mouth shut. Words were on my tongue to speak, but the spell kept me tight-lipped. A moment later the sensation receded. My jaw loosened. I was able to speak.

"Junior trapped them. That's why—" I cried out in pain as she tightened her hold.

"Indeed," she said, drawing me closer. "There is more than one way to get what I want. The first way would have been far less painful."

My eyes widened with fear. I couldn't look away.

"Snow of winter, rain of spring, leaves of fall and summer's green. Keep this child of mine I see from telling tales of future deeds."

Her eyelids dropped, and a white-hot stream of energy shot from her eyes into mine. My head exploded with fire. I opened my mouth to scream, but nothing came out.

I waited for the darkness to come—for the searing abyss of pain to abate—but it didn't. My entire body shook as the aunt's power drained me.

CHAPTER 11

My body tingled as if I'd been zapped with a Taser. The aftershocks rippled through me, making everything ache. I was curled in a ball on the floor. A drip of blood fell from my nose. I opened my eyes to see nothing but dark shadows over my vision.

Jumbled thoughts ran through my head. A dull thumping sound blocked out all others. Where was I? Did I black out again?

No, I heard a voice surface from the melee. *You're in the basement.*

The basement. As soon as the words crossed my mind, a flood of images popped into my head. One image of Mace's butler pouring a circle of salt. The markings on the wall as they activated and flashed. The eerie green glow of the wards trapping me. It was difficult to concentrate at first. My brain was scrambled, my thoughts scattered, but the images kept coming. The image of the pagan—the aunt—in the office with Mace. Everything connected to this basement was flooding my conscious thoughts.

My eyelids fluttered as I focused. The aunt's spell had been so bright—blinding. The dark shadows were fading.

The thumping turned to ringing in my ears, then stopped. A split second later the room snapped into clear view. I could hear everything. The hum of the air conditioner, the sound of water running through pipes, Lily's breathing as she lingered outside the circle. I was acutely aware of the smallest things. It was all so loud. I covered my ears with my hands.

Translator, the voice said.

I wasn't blocking the tech—the translator's ability to bring quiet sounds near. Everything—all the sounds—were coming in. The soft shuffle of feet from above sounded like sandpaper scraping against wood. I had to stop it. I had to turn down the volume before my ears bled.

I closed my eyes and attempted to block the sounds. I zeroed in on Lily. I heard her heart beat—steady and calm. Thump, thump. Thump, thump. One by one the other sounds quieted.

I breathed a sigh of relief and uncovered my ears. All I could hear now was Lily cursing under her breath. "Stupid girl," she muttered.

Now that I had control I could ignore her too. Tuning her out, I concentrated on the jumbled mess in my head. My mind worked to piece together the developments of the day. One thought led to another. Events, people, places, all settling back into place. Why did the aunt do this?

You canceled the first spell, the voice whispered.

The aunt hadn't wanted me to say anything. She cast a spell to keep me quiet, but my magic reversed it.

As it did in Purgatory.

Her words came rushing back. "Keep this child of mine I see from telling tales of future deeds."

She hadn't called me a pagan, not exactly. But a child of hers didn't make sense at all. Had going to Purgatory done more than give me powers? Did it make me a pagan? And why would I be hers if it did? I shook my head. I wasn't a pagan. That was impossible.

The voice was quiet. Did it disagree?

Great. I'm going crazy. Talking about my subconscious like it was a real person. I laughed.

Lily hissed.

"I know you're work—" working for my double, I tried to say, but my voice box seized, sending a sharp spike of pain down the back of my throat. "Ju—" I wanted to say: Junior's not dead! but my throat closed up again, and I groaned. "Time—" Time Travel. I couldn't say it.

What did she do to me?

The spell. Future deeds, you can't speak them, the voice said in a matter-of-fact tone.

Thank you, Captain Obvious. Why?

Lily muttered something, then cried out as she hit her hand against the wall protecting me.

The aunt had been able to cross the salt barrier. *Lily can't. I guess friendlies can get through.*

Perhaps.

You can't actually believe she's stronger than salt magic.

No comment.

Lily was getting harder to ignore, and my body was stiff from being curled up on the cold concrete floor.

The decisions they make must be their own, the voice repeated something the aunt said.

Returning my thoughts to the conversation I had with the aunt—*I remember, she didn't reply when I asked if the quads were going to kill Junior.* Nor had she confirmed that Junior trapped them.

How would she know?

I shrugged. Then I recalled I was talking to myself and shrugged again. *I have no idea, but if the quads suspect him—*

They'll want revenge.

I agreed. I had to get out of here. Junior could still be saved. He didn't have to die. I could save him and get out of this mess.

The double.

The video of Junior at his desk flashed before me. The memory of the blood running down the walls and the sick copper smell of his office caused saliva to well in my mouth. I swallowed it and pushed the memory back. I refused to throw up.

"Claire, baby," he'd said. She was there when he was shot.

Was she?

Why was I questioning that? *Oh, crap,* Omar said it was me. He'd seen me both times—me, not the double. I didn't believe him. How could I believe him? It hadn't occurred to me that going back in time was an option.

Because no one factors in time travel.

I let out an erratic giggle. *No one factors in time travel.*

My thoughts were starting to clear.

Lily was eyeing me. "Are you insane?"

Being sure to stay tucked safely inside the circle, I sat up. "It's certainly possible." I stretched out the muscles in my neck and wiped the blood off my nose with the hem of my t-shirt. There wasn't much of it now, but a small puddle had dried on the floor.

She glared at me. The red swollen mark under her eye and a

small cut over her left eyebrow looked painful. "What did you tell him about me?"

"Nothing."

"You lie," she whined. "My mistress hid me from his eyes. You told him."

"True, I pointed you out, but I didn't tell him anything else. He found out on his own."

"Impossible," she sneered.

"You don't know the half of it."

A car door slammed up above. I closed my eyes and blinked to the living room.

Sage strode into the main room. He was back to his normal style in a dark suit that settled against his lean frame perfectly. I certainly wasn't going to miss the dashiki. The butler carried in Sorrel. He was unconscious and in worse shape than Sage had been in earlier.

Mace and Sage exchanged awkward pleasantries. This was probably the first time the two had been together at a non-family event since they were kids, and that was over five hundred years ago.

Sage watched as the butler carried Sorrel toward the stairs. His brows were lowered. "What if she can't fix him?"

"She can," Mace said with confidence. "But we will wait until Sin arrives."

Sage gave Mace a sidelong look. "Why?"

"Because I say so."

Sage faced his brother, his lips pressed into a hard line. "You aren't in charge here. I want Claire to fix him now."

"I'm in the basement," I said, without thinking.

He scanned the room, his gaze stopping on the wall that hid the portal to the basement. He heard me, just as Mace had before in the office.

"We wait for Cinnamon," Mace said, not seeming to notice Sage wasn't listening.

"Don't wait," I encouraged. "Come get me now."

Sage glanced from the wall to Mace, then back. "I'll get her myself," Sage said, heading toward the portal.

In a flash, Mace threw his will, slamming Sage against the wall and holding him there. "I said we will wait."

Sage struggled, but Mace's hold was stronger. "I said I would stay."

A cruel grin curved Mace's lips. "I don't believe you, so we'll wait."

"Fine," Sage growled.

"The girl stays put."

"I've already agreed, now release me."

Mace waited for his brother's eyes to meet his.

Through clenched teeth, Sage snarled, "Please."

With a twisted smirk, Mace dropped his will. Sage barreled past him toward the bedrooms.

"You're giving up that easy?" I yelled after him.

"Fuck you," Sage muttered.

Mace raised both his eyebrows.

"He's not talking to you," I said, before slamming my hand over my mouth.

Mace spun around, scanning the room. After a minute, he gave up looking and returned to his office. He couldn't sense me, not like the aunt. However, he—both of them—could hear me somehow. But it was subconscious. I don't think either of them realized they heard me, yet both acted on my suggestions.

I decided to stay upstairs and explore the bungalow. Cinnamon would arrive soon. Mace would ignore me until then.

The place was huge. The upper floor had four bedrooms and Mace's office. Along with the main room, the downstairs consisted of an eat-in kitchen, dining room, media room, and master bedroom. The tropical eclectic ensemble of furniture continued throughout the house. I found an oil painting propped against the wall in one of the bedrooms. The image reminded me of the butler. Maybe this was his house?

I watched the sun set from the deck off the master suite. I thought of Jack and the vacation cruise we'd been promising ourselves we'd take as soon as he finished his degree. I wished he was here with me and this was our vacation, instead of this miserable nightmare I couldn't control.

I blinked back inside when Cinnamon's voice rolled in from the main room. Part of me was glad she'd arrived. The other part was scared at what she and the boys might do to me. I returned to the living room. She was in her signature black dress, blood-red lipstick, and killer high heels. Her hair was once again flowing down her back, perfectly straight. The toga princess she'd been in the garden was gone.

She didn't bother with pleasantries. She started barking orders the moment she arrived. "Put him below with the others," she ordered her manservant—one of the sentries from the garden. He was having difficulty controlling the thing that was tied up in the sack, which I assumed was Charles.

"You," she said to Collins, "be a dear and fix me a drink."

Mace entered the room, his face expressionless. Sage carried Sorrel. Cinnamon motioned for him to lay Sorrel on the sofa. She hovered over him, studying him.

"What's wrong with him?" Sage asked.

Cinnamon placed her hand above Sorrel's body. She left her hand there for a few minutes before dropping it. "It's some sort of spell—obviously—but I'm not getting any readings off him."

"We should try together," Mace suggested. "There must be something there."

"Agreed," Cinnamon said, placing her hand above Sorrel again.

Sage and Mace joined her, each holding their hands above his body. Tendrils of power swirled around them as purple streams merged and coalesced.

"Wait," Cinnamon said, glancing around the room. "Something else is here—listening. Do either of you feel..."

I opened my eyes and returned to the basement just as Cinnamon focused on me. Had she seen me like the aunt had? I assumed the aunt, being older and stronger than Mace, was the only one who could sense me. I had somehow influenced the boys with suggestion, but Cinnamon actually pin pointed my presence. Maybe it was the melded power of all three that let her sense me. I would have to be careful when she was near.

Charles was out of the bag. There was more than one bruise already forming on his swollen face. He'd have raccoon eyes by tomorrow. His lip was split open on one side, but that didn't stop him from snarling at Lily.

She cowered in the corner as if she were scared of him, but relaxed her posture as soon as he looked away, which gave me the impression she wasn't actually scared of him at all. He studied the circle, as if he could penetrate it. His cold stare shifted to me. I was careful to stay inside the salt ring.

"Hi, miss me?" I said to Charles.

"Get up!" he snapped at Lily.

"Yes, *master*."

Charles didn't seem to hear Lily's obviously condescending tone. She wasn't working with him, but, from what I could tell, he had no clue. He glowered at her until she was in place on the opposite side of the circle.

They started walking the circle in unison, chanting in Ancient, something the translator couldn't decipher. After a few minutes, they both walked forward, but were immediately thrown back, landing hard on the floor.

"It's salt," I said. "Even I know that's unbreakable."

"Shut up," he snarled at me, quickly getting back to his feet.

"I told you, master," Lily said in Demon. "I've tried everything. The youngest one wants her protected."

"We must summon our lord. He will know what to do."

That got my full attention. Charles was going to summon his master—the Mystery Player—would it be Junior as I suspected?

"Yes," Lily said. "But it won't work. I've tried."

I snorted. She glared at me. I covered by mumbling a woe-is-me remark and acting as if I had no clue what they were talking about. Lily was lying. She hadn't summoned anyone.

"We'll try together," he said. "Join me."

Charles sneered at me. I stared at him and mouthed 'salt,' as if he were trying to break the circle again. Not everyone knew about the translator. Now that I could tell when they weren't speaking English, I could fake my ignorance more convincingly.

Charles raised his head, tilting his nose up. His wicked grin exuded confidence as he and Lily started chanting. Their chants were in Ancient, although I doubted they actually knew the language. Like their chant to break the circle, they had probably memorized the spell to summon their master.

My head snapped up when I heard Maliki. It was one of Junior's given names.

He never told anyone his real name. For some, the superstition about names ran deep. Midge had let his given name slip once when we were talking. It was the last time I saw her. She went on a break and never came back. I'd forgotten about that until now. Hearing that name reminded me.

Although I suspected since the aunt's visit, the chant using Junior's name was proof. Charles was working for Junior. He *was* the Mystery Player. But did Charles actually know that? Or did he just know his master was Maliki?

If Junior never revealed his true identity, Charles might not actually know it was him. That was a big if. Either way, Mace would get the name Maliki out of him for sure. I hoped Junior was secretive enough about his name that the quads didn't know it. If they couldn't pin the traps on Junior, they might not go after him. They needed to know about the double, but just thinking about saying that out loud made my throat tighten.

As I expected, nothing happened when the chanting stopped. Charles hit the circle with both hands. Lily cowered back into the corner. I rolled my eyes at her. She stuck her tongue out at me when Charles wasn't looking.

My attention went to the stairs when the door above creaked. Charles backed away from the circle, flattening himself against the wall. I got to my feet, looping my fingers in my jeans, trying to appear more relaxed and confident than I felt.

The three siblings entered the basement. Mace was now dressed in his usual style, an expensive charcoal suit tailored to fit him perfectly. His arms were crossed over his chest. He winked at me, before schooling his expression into his usual wicked sneer. They all stood outside the enclosure observing me as if I were a lab rat in a cage.

Cinnamon was front and center with Mace and Sage on either side flanking her. Sage paled slightly when compared to Cinnamon and Mace, but even the twins were supermodels compared to normal humans.

I looked at Charles. He was visibly trembling. Cinnamon blew him a kiss. He shuddered.

Her gaze landed on me next. Her face was impassive. "Why are you here?"

"Your father sent me."

"She's lying," Mace interjected.

He was right.

"Why did father send you?" Cinnamon asked, ignoring Mace.

"He wants to see you. All of you."

Mace cocked his eyebrow. He knew I was lying.

"I can call him if you like," I offered.

"She fixes Sorrel before she calls anyone," Sage interrupted, taking a step forward.

Cinnamon held up her hand, stopping him. He growled,

running his hand through his hair, before reluctantly stepping back.

"Do you think you're safe from us?" Cinnamon asked.

She had no reason to doubt me. "Is anyone?"

Her upper lip curved into a dangerous grin. "Do you think we won't hurt you to get what we want," Cinnamon asked. "Maybe even kill you, if it comes to that?"

My eyes widened. "Seriously? I helped you."

She tilted her head to the side, inspecting me. Could she see the same truth that Mace saw? "What happened to us, Claire?" Cinnamon asked.

I opened my mouth to tell them about the double, but my throat closed, sending ripples of pain shooting over my jaw. I glanced between Lily and Charles. "You should ask your demon friends why they did it. They know more than I do."

Charles extended his hand as if he could reach me, but skittered back when Cinnamon glared at him. I didn't move. I couldn't risk leaning outside the salt's protection.

"Lily has been with all of you," I continued. "You should talk to her alone."

Lily's eyes widened in shock, but I needed the siblings focused on the real danger. Charles could only give up Maliki or Junior. Lily could give up the double.

Cinnamon turned to Mace who nodded. She eyed Sage. His hands curled into fists, then relaxed. His grim expression was clearly pained as if pleading.

"She's not telling us everything, brother," Mace said, as if answering his unspoken question. "It will be easier to make her talk."

"No," I said, but they ignored me.

Sage looked down, hands shoved in his pockets, and shoulders slumped. "Fine."

"I don't know anything," I argued. "All I did was try to help you. All of you."

"She's lying," Mace said.

Bullshit. "Cinnamon, why—"

"Yes, Claire, why are you lying?" she interrupted.

Oh, shit. My mouth went dry. She could tell I was lying about something. "Cinnamon, please. They're the ones who know what's going on. Not me."

Her eyes never left me. She wasn't convinced. Frustrated, Sage paced.

I opened my mouth, racking my brain to think of anything I could tell them. "Lily—" I got out before my throat constricted, cutting off my words.

"Let's make things more interesting, shall we?" Mace smirked. He took a deep breath and using his will directed a stream of air toward the salt. Granules skidded off in every direction, eating away at the edge of my protection.

"Are you mad?" I asked, stealing a quick look at the demons. Charles, whose eyes were on the salt, licked his lips, waiting. "They'll kill me."

"And that would be *so* tragic," Cinnamon said. "Maybe you should start telling us the truth."

The aunt's spell wouldn't let me tell them the whole truth. Giving up Junior would only seal my fate. My eyes locked on Sage. "I can't fix Sorrel if I'm dead."

Sage rushed forward. Cinnamon knocked him away. Jumping back to his feet, he tackled Mace from behind. Caught off guard Mace's will derailed, cutting a hard line through the salt.

"Oh, hell," I cursed.

CHAPTER 12

Charles reached into the broken circle and yanked me out.

I wanted to shout, but his fingers were wrapped around my throat. I could barely breathe. I kicked him, but he ignored it.

"You bitch, do you know what she did to me?" Charles yelled, slamming me against the wall, hitting my shoulder hard.

I howled in pain as he wrenched me forward. I scanned for Sage, but he was being held against the wall by Mace. I found Cinnamon. She was examining at her nails, ignoring the melee happening all around her.

As if she knew I was looking, she said, "I need a name."

What? She wasn't going to help me? Charles's hand tightened around my throat. He was going to kill me. Die now, or tell them about Junior and die later? Later worked better for me.

I reached up and raked my fingernails down Charles's face. My wrists burned as Mace's bracelets shocked me. Charles faltered enough to drop me, releasing my voice.

"Maliki," I wheezed out in a gasp of breath, before he was on me again.

Cinnamon's brow arched, but she didn't move. Crap, she didn't know who Maliki was.

I caught sight of Lily from the corner of my eye. This was probably a stupid plan, but she and Charles didn't have the same goals, and she needed them to know who Maliki was. As far as I could tell, she was the only one who knew except me, and I doubt she wanted Mace beating it out of her.

"Lily," I whispered, because that was all I could manage. "Help me."

She looked at me dismissively.

"They don't know who Mali—" Maliki is, I mouthed.

I clawed at the fingers wrapped around my throat. My hands fell, as my eyes started to close. Charles was killing me.

Just before I lost consciousness, the most wonderfully calming force washed over me. The peaceful warmth was beautiful. I wasn't scared or cold. I was free from the pain, and the quads, and my crazy life.

The peacefulness only lasted a few seconds. The bliss of what I imagined Heaven felt like was over, replaced by the bitter cold of the basement as Lily ripped me from Charles's grip.

I leaned against the concrete wall of the painted half of the basement, gasping for breath. Charles and Lily were fighting, yelling at each other in Demon.

My gaze found Sage. "Get me out of here."

He pushed away from Mace, causing his brother to stumble back into the painted enclosure, breaking the barrier as he did. The symbols on the walls flashed, blinding me for a second.

As my vision returned I felt hands on me, jerking me to my feet. At the same time, Charles threw Lily at the barrier. She flew through it, crashing into Mace as he got back to his feet.

My shoulder ached as Sage rushed me up the stairs.

Lily and Charles's wails followed us through the bungalow.

I glanced behind me when the noise stopped. Mace bolted up the stairs to the second floor. Cinnamon wasn't far behind. I winced from the pain when he yanked me out of Sage's hold.

He tossed me into the bedroom at the end of the hall. The lock clicked before I could get to my feet.

"She will fix him now," Sage demanded. "One touch to make him right. That's all."

There was a grunt, then a loud thump, before an all-out brawl started. Clearly, Mace wasn't finished teaching his brother a lesson.

"Enough," Cinnamon said, before sending them away.

I winced as I struggled to my feet, holding onto the twin bed for support. My shoulder throbbed. Exhausted, I fell on to the bed. Everything was finally catching up to me. I had no idea how long it had been since I woke up this morning. This morning, I scoffed. I was still three days away from *this morning*.

~ # ~

My eyes popped open when I heard them coming. The room was dark now. I'd only meant to rest for a minute, but I must have fallen asleep.

Sage's voice roared louder than the others. "She fixes him now, or I'll go to Father myself and tell him."

"You're such a softy," Cinnamon purred. "Don't worry, we'll let her fix him first."

"She may be too weak," Mace warned.

"She has rested long enough. She will try," Cinnamon said, ending the discussion.

She was the first to enter. I squinted when she flipped on the light. Mace bustled past her and marched over to me.

He put his hand above me. "Stay," he said, trapping me under his will.

"That's enough." Cinnamon pushed his will away. "You can play with her later. She fixes Sorrel first."

Cinnamon came around to stand across from Mace. Sage's eyes narrowed on me as if everything was somehow my fault.

The air was heavier with them in the room. The power that swirled around them was palpable. I could sense the purple energy I'd seen swirling around them before.

The butler and Cinnamon's manservant carried Sorrel in. She yanked my arm and unceremoniously placed my hand on Sorrel's head. I pulled away when the bracelet zapped me, wrenching my sore shoulder.

"Wake him up, now," Cinnamon said.

"Mace has to remove the bracelets before I can touch him."

She dropped her eyes to the metal band around my wrist. Raising one of her brows, she fixed her eyes on Mace.

"Hell shackles," she said. "Really?"

He shrugged. "They're mine. I can do what I want with them."

"Remove it," she said to Mace.

With a sigh, Mace clasped the bracelet on my right hand between his fingers. I heard a click, and the energy surrounding my right hand fell away. He removed the cuff, letting my hand drop back down to the bed. I reached forward, brushing my hand against Sorrel's head. A faint shock passed from me to him as my fingers made contact with his skin.

A minute passed. Sage glared at me, the vein beneath his eye pulsing. I willed Sorrel to move. Another minute passed. A low growl came from Sage's throat.

"It's going to work," I said to Sage. "Give it a minute."

Mace caught my wrist and clicked the bracelet back into place. He brushed the skin on the back of my hand, sending a jolt of pain through my arm. I scowled at him, but he just looked away.

"Why isn't it working?" Sage grumbled. His patience was running out.

"Are you refusing to help, Claire?" Cinnamon asked.

"No," I said, not liking the vulnerable position I was in, laying flat on the bed surrounded by them.

Sage ran his hands through his hair. "Make her fix him."

"I've already fixed him," I yelled, defiantly at Sage.

Mace brushed my hand again.

"What?" I said, but his gaze was on Sorrel. I glared at Mace for a moment, willing him to look at me. His face was turned away, but I could see the tiniest upturn at the corner of his mouth. He wanted me to look at him, not Sage. Was he jealous? Unbelievable.

"He's waking," Cinnamon said, and immediately some of the tension left the room.

Sorrel's eyes were open, but he was still dazed and confused. His brow furrowed when our eyes met.

Sage rushed to Sorrel's side, helping him to his feet. "It will pass, brother," Sage said, leading Sorrel from the room.

After the twins and servants left, Mace started in with his usual posturing. "Shall we throw her back to the demons?"

Cinnamon sighed, as if tired of this game already. "She'll tell us what she knows after they've loosened her tongue."

I glared at him. "You're the one who knows something. Why don't we let them loosen your tongue?"

A glint of fury flashed in his eyes, but his demeanor didn't change. He quickly silenced me with his will.

Cinnamon's gaze hardened. She'd caught the look. "What does she mean, brother?"

"She's trying to trick us."

I shook my head.

Cinnamon pushed his will away. "Let her speak."

Mace scared me, but she was not one to ignore. She could easily take control if she had a reason, and giving up the aunt's connection to Mace might take her attention away from me. *And keep him away from me.* "Ask him about your aunt," I said. "Ask him why she was here. Why he sent for her—"

Mace silenced me again, but it was too late. Cinnamon went from normal to scary as hell in about half a second. I was sure she'd care about the aunt, but I had no idea how she would react.

"Aunt Mab," she screamed, actually sending tiny sparks out of her fingers. "You called Aunt Mab!"

Mab! Pagan Queen Mab? *Oh, shit.* Child of mine! *Oh, shit.* Had she claimed me in the basement? She couldn't just make me a pagan? *Right?* The dark hair, I remembered. I can't believe I didn't guess before. Human history gets a lot of things wrong about the big three, but apparently Mab really does appear to them with dark hair. My thoughts returned to the room when I heard Mace cry out.

As if swatting a fly, Cinnamon captured him with her will and hurled him across the room. He was tossed like a ragdoll, and she wasn't breaking a sweat.

Ignoring the throbbing soreness in my shoulder, I rolled off the bed out of their way. I was on the wrong side to leave the room, and there was no way past them. I pressed against the wall, hoping to avoid being hit.

Mace threw his will back at Cinnamon with enough force to shake the walls. She countered and deflected his attempt with no effort. It was obvious now why he needed her cooperation. An uncooperative Cinnamon would be impossible to control.

She deflected another of Mace's attacks before suspending him by the throat with her will. She smashed him into the wall, cracking the plaster. He attempted to say something, but she was too mad to listen. She flung him across the room again, nearly throwing him through the wall. He staggered as he stood, catching the edge of the dresser for support. He held his hands up, putting his will between them. With a wave of her hand, she batted his protection away. He was going to lose. His eyes found mine.

"She owns you," I mouthed.

His violet eyes flared with cold fire just before he dropped to one knee. He bowed his head toward Cinnamon. "I can explain," he said.

She raised her hand to strike. Glaring, she closed her fist. "You know I don't trust her, so tell me quickly before I kill you for involving her."

"She contacted me," he said. "I swear it on our mother's name."

Cinnamon's demeanor changed. Her shoulders relaxed. Dropping her hand to her side, she released him.

"What?" I said, glancing between them.

She was still furious, but something was different.

Mace stood, glaring at me.

Cinnamon smoothed out her dress. She was cool and collected again, as if she hadn't just wiped the floor with him. In her normal voice, she asked, "Why did she contact you?"

He ran his hand through his hair and tugged the sleeves of his jacket down. He didn't appear as un-fazed as Cinnamon, but his cool hardened visage was back. In a quiet, deadly tone, he said, "Why do you think?"

Cinnamon cocked one of her perfect eyebrows.

"She knows everything that happens in Purgatory. Did you think your presence there went unnoticed?"

Her lips pinched into a hard line. "Then why didn't she contact me?"

"I have no idea."

He was lying. The aunt—Mab—may have contacted him first, but he was willingly helping her now.

A line appeared between Cinnamon's brows. "I was the one in Purgatory."

He answered with a small nod. "True, but maybe she wanted to make sure you weren't just there to piss off Daddy."

"As if I would ever willingly stay in Purgatory," Cinnamon scoffed.

I didn't understand why she hated Purgatory. She was half pagan. Of course, I didn't want to go back either, and I'd only been there a few hours.

I pressed into the wall when Mace walked toward me.

"Mab found me in a very bad state." He shrugged. "I thought I was the butler, as if Collins was my master. She saved me," he said, glancing back at Cinnamon. "Before we could save you," his brows lifted at me, "Claire found you."

I opened my mouth to speak, but there was nothing to say. Everything about why I found Cinnamon was from the future. My throat tightened just at the thought.

"Claire knows something we don't. She knows who did this to

us, and she will tell us, or I'll kill her," Mace said, although I doubted he would do it quickly. He'd want to play first.

"Ask the demons—Lily, ask Lily. Please," I begged.

Mace leaned in, crowding me against the wall. I reached up to shove him away, but dropped my hands when the shock of touching him increased.

Cinnamon stepped up, putting her hand on his shoulder. She tugged. Mace resisted at first, continuing to pin me with his stare. She tugged again. He dropped his shoulder, pulling out of her hold and paced toward the door.

She pushed the hair back from my face. Running her hand down my arm, she stopped just before passing the metal band. "You have one chance to tell me the truth, Claire," Cinnamon said. "Who is Maliki?"

She was deadly serious. I couldn't hide the truth, and she was done wasting time. She'd throw me back to the demons if I lied, or let Mace finish me off. She didn't care.

I couldn't give her the answer I wanted to give her. My throat tightened. The double was off limits. I'd have to give them Junior. Not as if that would save me from Mace. I would save myself another way. Blinking back the sting of tears, I said, "Junior."

You could have heard a pin drop it was so quiet.

Before she could comment, Mace was behind her, a hand on one arm. He muttered a few words in Ancient. Through my connection with her, a strong surge of power washed over me, just as it had when Charles touched me in Purgatory.

For a moment, I trusted Mace completely.

Cinnamon's hand dropped from my arm, as a very sweet scent wafted in the air. Moments later the spell rolled back over me— away from me. I no longer trusted him anymore than I had before. The sweet smell was gone.

Unfortunately, Cinnamon was still caught by the spell. I could see it in her eyes. I reached out to touch her hand, but winced when the bracelets shocked me. My hands fell away. I couldn't help her. Mace's eyes narrowed on me. He'd witnessed my attempt to de-spell her.

"Cinnamon," he said, drawing her attention. Just as Charles had done in the garden.

"What?" she said, but her voice had lost its edge.

"You need to convince the twins that we must strike now,

before Junior realizes his efforts to trap us have failed."

Cinnamon's face was pensive, as if she were considering his request. His hold wasn't as strong. She had followed Charles without question.

In the garden, I'd felt love for Charles; this time it was trust for Mace. The spells were different, but oddly similar. Unfortunately, trust would probably be enough to make Cinnamon comply. She'd want revenge.

"We can end this now, before the situation becomes an issue," Mace continued.

"What about Claire?" she asked.

My eyes locked on Mace.

"Would you like to keep her as a pet?" he asked, his eyebrow arched at me.

"I'm no one's pet," I said.

Cinnamon smiled. After a long moment, she sighed. "She wouldn't be worth the trouble."

"Let me go. You don't need me. I don't care what you do to Junior," I lied.

Ignoring me, she turned to Mace. "I will speak with the twins."

He locked the door behind her when she left. "You really shouldn't have told Cinnamon about Mab." He still faced the door. "I was just going to have some fun. Even after you messed up my plans."

"Yeah, right."

In a flash, he was in my face, flattening my body against the wall and twining his fingers in my hair. "Now I'm going to take everything from you. Your protection, your love, your freedom. Everything."

I stifled a yelp when he put pressure on my shoulder. As he chanted in Ancient, his hand warmed. I whimpered from the heat that concentrated on the damage in my shoulder. I cried out as the soft tissue was mended and fused together.

He wiped away a tear. I resisted when he pulled me in for a kiss. Tightening his hold on my hair, he growled, "You're mine now. Get used to it."

CHAPTER 13

I was sitting on the floor, when Mace returned two hours later. I'd been all over the room, but there was no way out. The windows were too high and small for me to reach, and the door was locked and warded.

My back straightened. I didn't want him picking up where he'd left off. His hot kiss lingered on my lips, and pagans weren't exactly picky about who they slept with. Sex was as precious to them as day old bread. I didn't want him taking liberties with me. Just because he put no emotional attachment to it, didn't mean I felt the same way.

He'd never shown any interest in me before—not that I'd spent that much time with him. Sorrel, on the other hand, had come on to me from the first moment I met him. He'd been clear from the get-go that he planned to have me in his bed. It never happened, but that was because he could be scared by the threat of his father's wrath. Mace had no such fear.

Mace sat down on the floor beside me. He still wore his suit pants, but the jacket was gone. His white button down was open at the collar, and his sleeves were rolled up. He placed a small silver tray on the floor next to him. I couldn't see what was on it, but I caught the smell of something sweet.

He placed my arm on his lap, running a finger along the line of the bracelet at my wrist. "How are you feeling, Claire?"

Jerking my hand away, I said, "How the hell do you think I'm feeling? I want to leave."

His lip turned up into that annoyingly handsome smirk of his. He pulled my arm back to his lap, this time keeping it trapped. "Would you like something to eat?"

As if on cue my stomach rumbled. I thought of the sweet aroma. I was hungry, but my stomach roiled at the thought of eating anything from him. I pressed my lips together.

He touched my hand, giving me a little shock.

I winced then growled, "No, thank you."

His twisted smile faltered a bit. When he stroked the side of my face, I flinched. "I knew there was something special about you the moment I laid eyes on you."

"Yeah, I think you mean cursed."

His hand was back on my wrist.

I hated the way he touched me. I wanted him to go away and leave me alone.

"It was the mark," he said. "Father doesn't mark just anyone, but he marked you."

I frowned, drawing my brows together. The mark was a very painful reminder of The Boss's power. I never gave much thought to whom else he might have marked.

"Do you know what it says?"

"Property of?" I offered.

"No," he sneered, twisting my wrist to bare the mark. He sent a pulse of energy through my arm. Like it had at the deli, the mark illuminated. He ran his finger along the mark, sending a shiver down my spine. "The first two symbols here," he gestured at the two closest to my wrist, "mean protected by. The last two," he indicated the others, "are the symbols for my father."

Protected by. The Keeper said the same thing. I didn't buy it then, and I don't buy it now. The Boss had proven too often how willing he was to leave me unprotected, but why would Mace lie?

"Protected by—or property of, I don't see the difference," I countered. "And if I'm so damn special and so damn protected then why am I here with you?"

I studied the mark. It had caused me nothing but pain—protected by the Demon King—what a joke. I remember the first day I saw the mark five years ago. The day everything changed.

Today was going to be another day like that one. Tears stung my eyes. Mace wasn't going to let me go. The Boss wouldn't save me once Junior died. I was screwed.

"Special is just another word for damned." I blinked back the tears. I wouldn't let Mace see me cry.

"You have no idea how wrong you are." His voice was different. Distant—frustrated—hostile. He had some serious daddy issues. And I was somehow in the middle of his twisted game. "When I saw your mark, I did some research. Do you want to know what I found?"

"No, but you want to tell me, so go ahead."

I don't know what he expected me to say, but I tensed when he slid my arm back into his lap, running his finger along my wrist.

"Your mother, Melinda, made a deal with my father."

I looked away. I didn't want to hear his version of those events.

His hand cupped my face, forcing me to look at him. "Years later she died giving birth to you."

"I know the story." The Boss had explained it to me. When he told me I belonged to him.

Mace smiled, clutching my chin. "You think you know the story, but you don't." His grip tightened. "Now be quiet and pay attention while I finish."

I resisted when he drew me in. Ignoring my pathetic attempts to avoid him, he gave me a quick chaste, kiss on the lips. Pagans were so damn confusing. I hated him, and I was sure the feeling was mutual, but he had no issues giving me a playful peck.

"Because of a loophole," he continued. "She was allowed to go to Paradise instead of Hell."

I didn't have all the specifics, but he wasn't telling me anything I hadn't already heard. I stayed quiet to avoid another kiss.

"Did you know he had the chance to close the loophole a few years ago?" Mace paused as if he expected an answer.

"How would I know that?" I asked quickly before he decided to encourage my participation.

He shrugged, picking up a strand of my hair. "It has been my experience that you know a lot of things you shouldn't."

He was right. I was the Devil's assistant, obviously I'd know some things, but why he thought I'd know the inner workings of Paradise and Hell politics was beyond me.

Mace frowned. "Daddy didn't take the deal. Do you know why?"

"No clue."

He twined the loose strand he'd been playing with behind my ear. "Because if he had, the rule would have reversed completely."

I waited for him to explain, but when he didn't I asked, "That's important because?"

He rubbed my wrist along the edge of the bracelet. "He didn't change the law so your mother could stay in Paradise with her family."

"Why would The Boss give a rat's ass about one random soul?"

Mace's grip hardened. The finger rubbing along the line of the bracelet slid over to the other side, shocking me. "Why do you think?"

I attempted to wrench my arm away. His grip tightened. An unnerving thought occurred. "Because of me?" *Please don't say it's because of me.*

Mace's face steeled. "No, not because of you."

"Then why?" I asked, jerking my arm from his grasp.

"It was because of his love for your mother."

My mouth hung open. *Love?* I shook my head. *He loved her?* The Devil loved my mother? *No, no, no.* Panic suddenly hit me. "Are you saying he's my—"

Mace scowled. "I never said *she* loved him. You're not one of us."

"Thank God, I'm not one of you psycho crazies," I shouted.

He hated me—for something I couldn't control. He hated me because his father loved my mother. Fuck.

"He protects you because of *his* feelings for *her.*"

"You're wrong. He doesn't protect me."

Mace's hatred was clouding his perception of how things really were. I'd never seen The Boss show the least bit of compassion for anyone, much less me. I couldn't believe he loved my mother, or that she was the reason he did anything. But Mace certainly did, and that was a problem.

"*She* is his weakness," he added. He caressed my face, his gaze fixed on me. "You've benefitted from that—not anymore."

I laughed. "Benefitted, right. What world are you living in?"

His eyebrows rose when I denied his claim.

"I said I was going to take everything from you, Claire. That includes my father's protection." Mace smiled as he caressed the side of my cheek. "To do that, you'll need to bind yourself to me."

"What? Are you insane? I already belong to him. Property of or protected by—you can't change that fact."

Mace chuckled, shaking his head as if I were a simpleton that understood nothing. I pulled back when he moved in to kiss me. He fisted his hand in my hair, holding me still. "That's where you're wrong. He marked you because he doesn't own you."

"Hu—"

Mace tugged me forward crushing our lips together. His tongue possessively slipped into my mouth to take what he wanted. His kiss was long and deep and demanding. I didn't want to be kissed. Not by him and not like this, but the bastard knew how to kiss. I was panting for breath when he released me.

"You're lying," I accused between jagged breaths. "The Boss owns me."

Mace smiled and cocked one of his perfect eyebrows. "Did you like the kiss?"

Speechless, I gaped at him. His smug smile pissed me off. "No, I didn't like the kiss, you bastard."

"You're lying."

Heat rose to my cheeks. I shook my head. "I don't want you."

He shrugged. "What you want is irrelevant."

"I know," I said. "It's been irrelevant for the last five years—because he owns me."

Nothing I'd ever wanted mattered. I'd gone from one totally screwed up foster family to the next, until I turned sixteen—the age of maturity in Hell. Thanks to my mom, The Boss put his claim on me and that was it. What I wanted would never matter again. Mace couldn't change that.

He smiled. "You know nothing. He can't take an innocent's soul, Claire. You have to willingly give yourself to him." He stroked my face again. "I'm sure that's something you'd never do."

Impossible. The Boss owned me. He had to. Why else would he have taken me?

What if Mace is right? the voice whispered.

"He really doesn't own me?" I asked, trying to confirm.

Mace's grin didn't waiver. It's not true. Why wouldn't Omar have told me? We were friends, sort of. I sagged back against the wall. Was nothing real?

Unless he couldn't tell you.

I remembered how Omar acted at the office. He'd stopped in the middle of saying something, as if there were things about me that couldn't be said.

I was pulled back to the present when the silver tray brushed my hand and sent a tiny shock up my arm. The tray was filled with five petit fours, decadent looking mini cake squares. It was a pastel smorgasbord of pink, purple, green, yellow, and blue. Their sugary smell filled my nostrils.

He clutched my face and peered into my eyes. "You'll pledge yourself to me."

He tightened his grip, stopping me before I could lean away.

"If you refuse," he said, pecking me on the lips. "I'll have my way with you, then throw you back in the basement with the demons. I don't think Lily will save you this time."

I was sure Lily wouldn't help me again. I jerked my head away. "I don't believe you. I belong to your father."

Mace cupped my chin, drawing my face back to his. "How many people do you think carry his mark?"

"Hundreds?"

"I only know of one."

"You're lying." I couldn't be the only one he'd marked.

Mace kissed me again. Another long demanding kiss.

I pulled away. "You hate me for something I have no control over."

"I hate my father for that. I hate you because you told Cinnamon about Aunt Mab. She will be harder to control now, and Aunt Mab will not be happy when she finds out." He twisted a strand of my hair around his finger.

"Please don't touch me—not like that. I don't want that."

He chuckled. "You'd enjoy it."

"I wouldn't."

"I've never had any complaints," he scoffed, offended.

"Please. Not that." *Anything but that.*

"You have two options, Claire," he said, caressing my hair. "I recommend you pledge yourself to me—willingly."

There weren't two options—there were never two options. He does whatever he wants to me then throws me to the demons, or I willingly pledge myself to him, binding me to him forever, then he does whatever he wants to me. Neither *option* was desirable and seeing as there was no option to leave and return to The Boss, there was only one I could choose.

I took a deep breath. "I agree to pledge myself to you."

"I want it sealed with a kiss."

"No."

He smiled and tucked my hair behind my ear. "Pretty soon you won't be able to say no."

"What!" That couldn't be how it worked—could it? "You promised."

"I never promised not to kiss you, Claire. I quite enjoy it. Now, let's start with this." He picked up the small pink square from the tray. "Once you eat this, you'll belong to me—forever."

I eyed the cake suspiciously.

"A kiss would be more fun, Claire, but the cake seals the bond. By accepting what I offer, you will be bound to me forever. I'll own you, like my father never has."

The smell of the pink square was cloying. "What is it?"

He held the cake to my lips. "Pagan cake."

"From Purgatory?" I rasped, my mouth dry.

His wide grin was unnerving. I hesitated a moment, swallowing hard, before I opened my mouth. He placed the moist square on my tongue. It was dense like pound cake, and the icing tasted a bit like almonds and licorice. Not really a good combination.

As the cake slid down my throat, a warm sensation spread through my body. I didn't like the fuzziness the cake created in my head.

The initial wave of warmth was immediately followed by a swell of cold. Goosebumps rose all over my skin. My head tingled. My sight went in and out of focus. My thoughts started running together. I couldn't think straight.

Mace held up another piece of cake. It smelled sickeningly sweet so close to my nose. I didn't want it. I shook my head and pushed at his hand, not even wincing at the shock. Cradling my jaw, he tugged down, and forced my mouth open.

"Only the first must be willing," he said.

Each piece of cake was the same—first a wave of warmth, then cold.

Once I'd eaten the last piece, he put the empty tray off to the side. Snaking his hand around my neck, he pulled me in close. I studied his lips, fascinated by what they could do. I thought he was going to kiss me, but he didn't. For some reason, that disappointed me.

"What aren't you telling me?" he asked.

I didn't understand what he meant. I was too busy thinking about—longing for—his almost kiss. The cake made me foggy, disoriented, and giddy. I laughed. "What?" I asked, my gaze fixated on the pout of his beautiful lips.

"What aren't you telling me?" he shouted.

I touched his pillow soft lips. "Ouch." I giggled. What did he want to know? I couldn't remember.

He asked me again, this time keeping my attention on his eyes with his will. I was compelled to tell him the truth—my throat closed up immediately.

Was I drugged? Or was this longing a result of my pledge to him? Not that it mattered. Mab's magic was stronger. I giggled again. He'd never get what he wanted. I still couldn't speak about the future.

I touched his face. The bracelet shocked me; I didn't care. The pain was dulled. I could ignore it, but I couldn't ignore him. I wanted him. Fisting my hands in his hair, I yanked him forward for a kiss. If he wouldn't give it to me, I would take it. A long passionate, breathless kiss. He was mine now. His lips were so soft and his breath was so warm and inviting. I wanted him—all of him.

I pushed him back to the floor, rolling him over and straddling him.

No! I heard a faint scream in my head. I ignored it.

A new wave of warmth washed over me. His hand tightened in my hair, wrenching my head back. "What aren't you telling me?"

I leaned in. My body was responding to his touch. "I want you inside me. Now. Then I want to curl up in your arms and sleep." I just wanted him to hold me—*Stop it! No, you don't.*

Was that the voice? I snorted. It was trying to remind me. I was in love with Jack.

I smiled at Mace. I couldn't stop myself. "You're beautiful. Make love to me."

I touched his face—those beautiful lips.

Fight it, the voice demanded.

"I don't want to fight."

The voice was angry with me—I giggled. The voice—who did she think she was? This was my life. My sucky crap-ass life. "I want to go home now."

"You are home," Mace said.

"Could he read my mind?"

"No, you're thinking out loud."

"Of course I am." My head was swimming. I couldn't concentrate. I couldn't stop thinking about Mace. I couldn't stop wanting him to touch me. This wasn't what I wanted, but at the same time, it was what I wanted.

"Tell me, Claire. What are you hiding?"

"I love you," I said with the conviction of a high school crush.

His lips turned down. "Tell me your secrets, and I'll let you have me."

"I love Jack—and he—" *Loves me*. My throat closed before I could say it out loud. I hated Mab's spell.

Mace's lips curled into a snarl. He flipped me over. Now he was on top.

"Yes, take me. I'm yours."

"Fuck. Too much cake," he muttered.

Was he angry with me because I loved someone else? "I love you too."

Mace kissed me, but it was too short. He rested his forehead against mine. I studied his lips. I wanted them on me. "Tell me, baby," he said, in that beautiful voice of his.

"I love—"

"Tell me what I want to know." He ran his hands down my shirt, cupping my breasts. "I'll give you everything you want if you do." He was back in my face, but his lips were too far away.

Licking my lips, I willed him closer. I groaned when he wouldn't. The tingling burn at my wrist started to hurt. I didn't care.

"Tell me," Mace demanded.

I smiled up at him, incapable of keeping any thoughts in my head. "I love you."

He pushed me away, getting to his feet in one fluid movement.

"No, stay with me," I whispered as the warmth of his body left me.

He muttered a curse before slamming the door as he left.

CHAPTER 14

The room was bright from the sun outside when I woke. I was on the bed, twisted in the sheets. The room had been put back together and someone had tucked me in.

Cringing at how I'd practically thrown myself at Mace, I thought of the night before and wanted to scream. I moved my head and almost hurled. Nausea was not my friend. I nearly tripped detangling myself from the sheets.

I ran to the bathroom and made it just before I threw up.

After flushing away the cotton candy sludge—the remains of Pagan cake—I sank to the floor. My conversation with Mace ran through my head.

I'd kissed *him*. I'd begged him to stay with me. God, make love to me.

I wanted to go home, curl up on the couch with *Jack*—not Mace—and have him hold me. I'd go crazy if I didn't have something that was normal soon, something that didn't have anything to do with my insane reality.

My stomach gurgled. I leaned over the toilet and threw up again. Crying wouldn't help. I had to get out of here. Screw Mace and my pledge to him. I could leave—go to The Boss—he'd fix everything. He might kill me too, but that would be better than pining for Mace.

I stood and washed out my mouth. After drinking several handfuls of water, I splashed more on my face then glanced at the shower, then at my clothes. I'd been in the same shirt and pants for what seemed like days. I needed the clothes off, and to wash away the memory of Mace's hands and lips.

I peeled off my clothes and started the shower. It was hot and steamy within seconds. Inside, the water washed over me, soothing my nerves and sore muscles. I washed, but no amount of scrubbing made me feel clean. My skin tingled as if his hands were still on me. His touch, his kiss, his smell—it was all around me. Resting my head against the tile, I closed my eyes and thought about home—about Jack. What if I never saw him again? I started to cry. *What would he think if I never came home?*

I stayed in the shower until the water ran cold. When I stood in front of the vanity, I didn't recognize the girl who stared back at me. Her color was sickly pale, red hair dull and lifeless. She had bruises everywhere and scars. Twisting around to see my back, I gaped at my gaunt reflection and Mace's mark!

She's still you, the voice whispered.

I know. I didn't need to be reminded of everything. Taking a deep breath, I wiped my eyes. I couldn't lie down and accept this hell. I had to fight.

I leaned in closer to the mirror to more clearly see the mark. It was a red tattoo, a cord of vines and jagged edges circling the emblem of a serpent. It rested in the center of my back, between my shoulder blades. I loathed it and what it represented.

The click of a door shutting brought my attention back to the room. I shrugged into the robe hanging by the door. When I returned to the bedroom, it was still empty, but a tray of food had been left on the bed. The savory smells of a warm breakfast reminded me how hungry I was. Yesterday's lifesaving hotdog was barely a memory. And the god-awful Pagan cake was gone too.

Ravenously I devoured the food before I considered what I was eating. From the few remaining crumbs I decided my breakfast had been bacon, eggs, and toast with orange juice. Not that it mattered—considering it was almost gone—but the food tasted normal. No licorice and almond aftertaste. I hoped that meant I wouldn't be a lovesick puppy for Mace today.

After breakfast, I found clothes in the chest of drawers. The choices were limited, but I was glad to have something clean to wear. I put on the capri pants and tank top, then blow-dried my hair.

I slipped my shoes on and headed for the door. Remembering the door was locked and warded when I tried to twist the unmoving knob. Still, I needed to know what was going on. I wouldn't be able to physically leave until they let me out of this room, but anything I could learn about them would only help me escape.

I laid down on the bed and closed my eyes, pushing my presence outside my body. Now that I was rested, it was easy. The warding on the door had a yellow glow to it, but unlike the basement prison downstairs, which had wards up and down every wall, floor, and ceiling tile, this one just covered the door. I blinked to the hall and headed toward the main room on the first floor.

The doors to the other bedrooms were open, and I could see what each of the quads was doing. Cinnamon sat at a dressing table preening in front of the mirror. She'd gathered her hair into a messy twist similar to the style she'd worn in the garden. Sage was ironing a bright green tie. I chuckled. The tie reminded me of the dashiki—I guess he'd forgotten to pack it. Sorrel was asleep.

I stopped, pivoting around to peer at the open doors. Sorrel had been unconscious before and now he was just sleeping. Sage was ironing a green tie, which wasn't really one of his normal colors, and except for the garden, I'd never seen Cinnamon with anything but straight hair.

Why did Mace's spell appear to affect them the same as Junior's?

Voices from the living room pulled my attention away from the quads. As I got closer I heard Mace and Aunt Mab speaking Pagan. "I agree, that is very bad news about Cinnamon, but it is not entirely your fault. I should not have made myself known to the girl so soon. But the spell is working?" Mab asked.

It was Mab's spell?

"Yes, but I thought you said it would make them cooperative."

"Claire's abilities had an unintended side-effect. I couldn't use the same spell," Mab said.

The same spell? Was there just one book of them? How would she know the spell Junior used?

"Her abilities?" Mace's tone was clipped telling me he was annoyed.

"Nothing for you to worry about, dear, and no need to worry about the others."

"They must willingly cooperate. You said that was imperative."

"Yes, but that was before."

"Before?"

"Yes, before Claire got involved. She changes everything."

Me? How do I change everything?

"Everything," Mace scoffed. "How?"

"Do not worry, dear Nephew. It is nothing you need to be concerned about."

"But she belongs to me now," he said, almost whining.

I hated the way that sounded, and wished it wasn't true.

As if to stifle her chuckle, Mab put her hand to her lips. "I wouldn't get too attached, my boy."

I really didn't like the way that sounded.

Mace was disappointed, but he didn't challenge her.

"Ask her why," I prompted and immediately wanted to kick myself. For a moment I thought the corner of Mab's lip curved up. *Oh, yeah, she heard me.*

Mace hesitated. The suggestion in my voice was clearly enough to nudge him, even though he couldn't sense me in the same way Mab could.

"My father can't claim her," Mace said. "So why can't she be mine?"

Can't claim me? Why couldn't The Boss claim me?

Mab waved her hand in the air as if shooing away his question. "Something else is on your mind, Nephew. What is it?"

No, no, no. Go back to the other question.

Before I could suggest this to Mace, he sighed and continued.

"I've been contacted by an unexpected ally," he began cautiously. "But his timing is too coincidental for my liking."

She raised her eyebrows. "A traitor? In your father's organization?"

"It would seem so," Mace confirmed. "He claims to know things about the future."

"That's highly suspect." She paused. "But we must not rule out his usefulness."

"What do you mean?"

"Let me worry about that. You have other matters to attend. Have you contacted the blacksmith as I suggested?"

He rubbed the back of his neck. "I have, but she is reluctant to trade with me."

"What is her concern?"

"Retribution, perhaps. I'm not sure." He lifted a shoulder. "If you—"

"That's not possible, but I'm sure we can find something she wants."

Mab glanced in my direction. I ducked behind the wall. I sensed her smile at my attempt to hide. Realizing it was stupid, I moved back into the room. She clearly had no intention of telling Mace I was here.

"What of the girl?" she asked. "Is she well?"

"She will live."

Mab's eyes narrowed. "Be sure she does. Especially now that we have a traitor."

His brow furrowed, but he said nothing.

Ugh, I'd never get any information with him asking the questions.

"You must go to the blacksmith," Mab said. "Take the girl with you, and she will trade with you."

He needed another nudge. "Why? Ask her why."

"Why?" he blurted out, then snapped his mouth shut. His gaze searched the empty space near my presence. He was getting better at sensing me. "I don't trust Claire. She's not being completely honest with me. My methods of persuasion have not been as effective as I would have liked."

I rolled my eyes. "He means threatening and drugging me didn't work."

Mab's lip curled. "I have looked into her mind, Nephew. She doesn't know more than she's telling you."

"Bullshit," I said.

This time Mab had to cough to cover her laugh, but she regained her composure when Mace spoke.

"Bullshit. I agree. She's not telling me everything," Mace countered, then realized who he was talking to. "Forgive my outburst Aunt. It's just—I could tell she was holding something back."

Mab smiled. She strolled forward and took hold of his hands. "Don't worry. Move forward with the plan. Everyone will play their part."

He nodded.

Unbelievable. He was going to take her word for it.

She's the Pagan Queen, the voice reminded me.

Whatever.

"I must go now. I have business to attend to. Take the girl to see the blacksmith. She will trade with you, but don't let her kill the girl." Mab winked at me before disappearing.

~ # ~

I was beyond sick of being in the room when Mace finally opened the door. He'd called for a car about an hour ago, and it just arrived. He was dressed in jeans and a black t-shirt. Not a style he wore often. He, of course, rocked it, but that was because he was perfect. I was sure his body had been the inspiration for countless marble statues over time. At least I didn't have the urge to throw myself at him today. That was a plus.

He leered at me with possessive eyes. A warm tingle ran over my body as his fingers stroked my arm. I turned away. He cupped my face, tugging it back around. He kissed me, holding me in place. I eventually gave up trying to resist and opened my mouth to let him in. Guilt crowded my mind every time he touched me. I forced back tears. I wasn't going to cry. Not about this.

He finished and leaned his forehead against mine. "You belong to me," he said. "No matter what she says."

I didn't want to belong to him or The Boss or Mab. I wanted to belong to Jack.

Mace's mood darkened. "It's time for your next punishment."

My eyes widened. "What was the first one?"

The Boss's protection, the voice reminded me.

Right. I couldn't even think of that without adding air quotes in my mind. Protection. Indeed.

"You must let go of your silly human notions. I've removed your protection. Now I'm going to take your love."

"What the hell is that supposed to mean?" Jack, no, he couldn't mean Jack. "Don't hurt him. Please."

Mace smiled at the fear in my eyes. He caressed the side of my face, then quickly kissed me on the lips. "We must hurry. There's a lot to do." Taking my hand in his, he led me along behind him.

The car was waiting outside the bungalow. The driver held the door as Mace shoved me into the backseat.

Clutching my chin, he fixed me with his eyes. "You belong to me."

I didn't look away. His claim wasn't my biggest concern right now. What he might do to Jack was what scared me.

"We have an errand to run, but first I have something to show you."

Show me? Did he mean the blacksmith, or was she the errand?

Deep lines formed on his forehead as his eyebrows drew together. "You know," he accused.

"I don't—"

"Don't lie to me, Claire. I can see the truth in your eyes. You know where we're going…how?" He pushed forward, bringing us nose to nose.

"I—I overheard you and Mab talking."

The cords of his neck stood out. "Cinnamon was right. You were in the room earlier when you were supposed to be in the basement. What *ability* is this?"

"It's complicated, and I don't know how it works."

He glared at me.

"It's some sort of astral projection—I guess. I don't know. I can go places, outside my body. Mab can sense me, she knew I was there."

"Why didn't she prevent it?" he asked in Pagan.

"How the hell should I know," I answered without thinking. *Shit.*

"I see Father gave you all the company perks. I'm sorry, but you won't be allowed to keep those." He turned my head to the right. I could barely make out what he spoke, as he whispered something in my left ear. I hadn't understood the words, but I think they were in Pagan. After glancing at my face, he rotated my head to the left. This time I clearly heard the English translation of, "Can you hear me now?" that he whispered into my right ear in Pagan.

His eyes narrowed on me. I saw the light flash in the violet depths as he realized I'd understood. "The right ear, then." As he held my head steady, he chanted a swirl of words in Ancient.

I tried to pull away, but his firm grip kept me in place. I jumped as he slammed his cupped hand over my right ear. A shock wave reverberated through my ear canal, creating a high-pitched sound that burned as it bounced off my eardrum. I screamed and cursed at the top of my lungs. I clawed at Mace's arms, digging my nails into his biceps. It wasn't until the noise in my head died down that the searing pain of the electric shocks from the bracelets forced me to drop my hands.

Mace shoved me away. "You will have nothing of my father's," he muttered.

"Fuck you." I leaned against the door, numb with shock from the throbbing pain in my ear. I couldn't hear anything out of my right ear. The translator was gone. I closed my eyes and stepped out of my body. Mace was staring at me.

He reached over, running his finger down my arm. My body tensed. "It's time," he said.

Time? I opened my eyes, returning to my body. "Time for what?"

"It's time to take your love away."

"Please don't hurt Jack. He doesn't deserve it. He knows nothing about this world."

Mace laughed so hard his body shook. "You may not want him after I'm done."

I drew my eyebrows together.

"You must suffer the loss. It wouldn't be a very good lesson otherwise. Although, once the facts are known, you may thank me for saving you."

"Don't do this. You have me. Leave him alone. Please. I'm begging you."

"I'm actually surprised you like him so much, then again most of Father's servants do their jobs well."

"What?" Jack was the only normal thing in my life. He didn't work for The Boss. "You're lying."

Coldly Mace said, "Do you actually think Father would let you pick your own boyfriend? Some random guy he couldn't control?" He gripped my wrist and painlessly ignited The Boss's mark. "Protected by, remember?"

I yanked my arm away. "The Boss wouldn't do that." Even as I said it, I doubted my own words. "You're lying," I said weakly.

His grin widened. "You really didn't know," he said in mock wonder. "You never even suspected."

Lips pressed flat, I refused to play his twisted game. I'd never believe him. I knew what Jack and I had. It wasn't fake. The Boss wouldn't—

"He's been scripting your life since the day you were born. Do you think it was chance that you were never adopted, that you were always in foster care? He couldn't risk you actually getting a family who might love you."

Mace was trying to twist it all around. He wanted me to think everything that had ever happened to me was because of the Devil. Mace was lying. This hell started five years ago, and Jack wasn't part of it.

"I can see you aren't convinced, but you will be soon," Mace said.

The driver said something I could no longer interpret.

"Good, we're almost there."

I looked around, but we were just on some random street in Underworld.

Mace was lying. He had to be. Jack was real, not some demon from Hell hired by The Boss to be my boyfriend.

I stared out at the changing landscape. We were zipping through a part of town I'd never been to before. Mace shifted forward and said something to the driver. A few minutes later, the driver parked outside a pub. The Fire Pit. He went inside and yanked out a young demon.

I gasped. My mouth dropped open. "No," I said. I turned away, tears stinging my eyes. I didn't want to see Mace's proof.

Mace clasped my head between his hands and forced me to stare at Jack. "I said I would take everything away," he said. "How am I doing so far?"

A tingling sensation began in my chest. My breathing became labored, and my stomach hardened into a tight knot. Hot spikes of pain shot through the right side of my head as my damaged ear strained to work. "That's not him. This is a trick."

Mace chuckled. "Trust me, that's him."

The bracelet on my right arm tingled, but I wasn't touching anyone. I glanced down. Tiny hair thin wisps of white energy were sparking off the metal.

"What the hell," Mace said, releasing me and looking down at my wrist. "Stop it."

Hot pressure pushed against my eyes. The wisps of current crackled around the band like burning flames.

"Stop." Mace commanded. "Turn it off." He grabbed my hand, then dropped it just as quickly.

I hadn't felt the shock that time, but it looked like he had. Narrowing my eyes, I raised my hand to use as a weapon.

He held his hands up as if blocking me, but also afraid to touch me. I lunged for him. I slammed my hand against his chest. He clamped his mouth shut, refusing to scream. The bracelets were doing to him what they'd been doing to me, and it had to hurt.

"How does that feel you bastard," I yelled as I kept my hand against his chest. Catching a flash of something green, I stared into his eyes. I looked closer, only to realize it was a reflection of the shine on my eyes. My hand slipped as my power drained. The green shine on my eyes flickered, then went out.

My body went cold. I shivered and shook as Mace threw me off him.

"You bitch," he spat, rubbing his chest. "He's dead now."

"No," I pleaded through chattering teeth. "I'm sorry." I wasn't sorry, but I didn't want him to hurt Jack. "I won't do that again." I had no idea how I'd done it this time, so that really wouldn't be a hard promise to keep.

I turned back to look out the window. I was numb, shaking with cold like a junky needing a fix. Jack was—everything. He still appeared to be my Jack, but with my new ability, I could sense he was a demon. I closed my eyes and stepped outside my body.

I was on the sidewalk now. Standing beside him. I wanted him to wrap me in his arms and tell me everything would be okay. Jack and the driver were arguing. I couldn't understand anything they were saying. I glanced back. The car windows were tinted; he couldn't see me.

"I love you," I said.

Jack looked back toward me. The driver roughly nudged his shoulder to get his attention. They argued a minute more before Jack was thrown back inside the pub.

I opened my eyes, wiping away a few tears. I still felt shaky and drained, but I wasn't as cold. Mace was pissed, but he didn't send the driver back to the bar for Jack.

I sank down in the seat as the car pulled away from the curb.

"I want a thank you," Mace said, breaking the silence.

"Thank you," I said, without hesitation.

He chuckled. "Oh, no sweetheart. It'll take more than that for his life."

"What?"

"I want *you* to fuck *me*."

I swallowed past the lump in my throat. *Fuck him, here?* I eyed the driver. "I can't—"

"Calm yourself, Claire, not here. I want more room to move

147

when you finally take your turn."

I wanted to throw up.

"For now, I'll just take a kiss, and make sure you mean it. I can tell."

I hesitated. I wouldn't want Jack kissing another girl. I guess I was splitting hairs. I'd already kissed him once, and I would have done more if he'd let me. But that was while I was drugged.

Yeah, I'm not sure that matters.

"Does the driver need to turn around, Claire?"

"No." I took a deep breath, licked my dry lips, and slid over to Mace.

He stayed still.

Right, I was supposed to kiss him. Channeling the lovesick, nothing to lose, drug-crazed Claire from last night, I snaked my hands through his hair and roughly pulled his lips down to mine. I shoved my tongue in his mouth, and yanked his hair harder than necessary.

He groaned, moving to hold me in place.

I pushed him away and scooted back to my side. Fire burned in his eyes at being shortchanged.

"You said you wanted me to mean it. Well, that was all your kiss meant to me."

Snarling, he said, "You'll do better when we're alone, or I'll hunt down that worthless demon you think you love and make you watch as I rip out his heart, and trust me when I say I mean it."

I looked away. I could see the conviction in his eyes.

Thankfully, Mace took out his smart phone and ignored me for the rest of the trip.

I leaned my head against the window, trying to ignore the throbbing pain in my right ear.

The car stopped outside a large brick building. I glanced around, but there wasn't much to see. The shop across the street sold Harleys, and the one beside the warehouse sold surf and ski equipment. A demon was coming out of the Harley store. He flipped the sign to closed and locked the door. It was still early, but the fight was tonight. Every business downtown would be closed within a few hours.

Mace dragged me out of the car, keeping a firm hold on my elbow. He guided me toward the entrance of the blacksmith's shop.

A very large, very wide druid, between seven and eight feet tall, was pounding out a length of metal. After a few more strikes of the hammer, he dropped the formed metal into a vat of oil. He drew another sword from the forge. It appeared child sized in his large hand. It was clear he had no intention of helping us.

The narrow room was made of stone. Large extended hooks hung from the wooden beams running along the ceiling. Sturdy tables and benches lined the walls. Two large anvils bordered the enormous forge, which took up more than six square feet of floor space. Piles of wood were stacked along the back wall, and everything had a metallic burnt smell.

Weapons of every type hung on the walls. Raw materials and half-finished pieces were haphazardly stacked around the room. At least it was an organized mess.

"I said no." The woman's voice came from the office to our right.

Mace turned us to face her. She was not at all what I had expected. She was smaller than me by at least half a foot. Her slender petite frame appeared dainty—almost fragile. She had long silvery hair with ribbons of black, gold, red, and brown running through it. The streaks weren't manmade, they were natural. Surprisingly they weren't the oddest thing about her appearance. She had two different colored eyes, which might not have been obvious if one were brown and the other hazel, but one was red and one was bright blue.

I lowered my gaze when she fixed both her eyes on me.

"Are you sure we can't come to some sort of an arrangement?" Mace asked. They were both speaking English, but I'm sure it wasn't for my benefit. She wasn't a demon or a pagan or a druid for that matter. I didn't know what she was, but clearly they had no common language.

She was staring at Mace again, but I could tell she wasn't impressed. Her upturned nose said she wasn't scared of him either. He was no concern to her, and she had no interest in trading with him.

A drop of something wet hit my shoulder. I looked over. Blood. The entire left side of my head was numb, and I hadn't realized my ear was bleeding.

I flinched as she wiped off the drop of blood, bringing her fingertip to her nose to smell. She then licked it off her finger as if it were frosting.

Her eyes widened, and she circled me. "What is she?" the woman asked. "A gift?"

I sidled closer to Mace. He chuckled. I ignored him. I didn't want this blood-loving whatever sinking her claws into me.

"She's human and not for sale."

"Human, hardly," she scoffed.

"She bears the Demon King's mark," Mace said, as if that explained it.

He had no clue—neither did I, but the blacksmith seemed to know something.

"Why have you brought her here if I can't have her?"

"She belongs to me," he said. "I'm here to see if you have reconsidered my offer."

"Interesting," she said, studying me. "You have a new offer, but it's not the girl." She smirked, turning her cold eyes back to him. "I'll give you what you want for two quarts of her blood."

"No," I said, finding my voice. There were only five quarts in the human body. Two quarts—four times the amount normally taken during blood donation—would be too much.

Mace touched my face, running his finger along the outside of my right eye. He watched me. "Interesting," he said as if he saw something unexpected. He glanced back at the blacksmith, then back to me. "Interesting, indeed," he murmured.

"Do we have a deal?"

"No," I said again, this time more firm.

Mace wrapped his will around me. "Yes."

"It must be given willingly," the blacksmith said.

I shook my head. Hell no.

"What a pity."

Mace leaned close. "This for Jack's life."

I held his gaze for a moment. He was offering me an opportunity to change our deal. I suppose if the excessive blood loss didn't kill me than at least I didn't have to willingly sleep with Mace. Not so sure this was a win, win, but it was a better bargain. I nodded once.

The blacksmith clapped her hands. "Goodie. Follow me."

I stopped short when she led me toward a macabre-looking dentist's chair, circa 1920's insane asylum. The chair had more straps attached to it than padding. Mace nudged me forward. Reluctantly I laid down on the chair and tried not to freak out as she buckled me in.

Mace was standing near enough to touch, but he was busy texting and not paying attention to me. I could hear the woman off to the side, but I couldn't see what she was doing until she wheeled a hospital-style tray over to my trapped body. I eyed the needles as she hung the collection bags at the base of the chair.

She examined both my arms before deciding to use the left one. After tying a rubber hose around my bicep, she tapped the soft flesh on the inside of my elbow, then picked up a needle. She smiled at me as she slid the needle into the largest vein on my arm.

She grabbed and held my left eyelid open. My eyes widened when she lifted the second needle into view. She was seconds away from contact when Mace caught her wrist.

"No," he said. "You said blood, and I don't want her blind. Pick another spot."

A tear leaked from my eye when she released me.

"Oh, well," she said, winking at me. "He's so protective."

I really hoped that was sarcasm, because I didn't want anyone completely bat-shit crazy having any of my blood. Her bedside manner sucked. All four needles hurt as they drained my life away. I had never liked donating blood, but after this experience I was sure I'd never willingly donate blood again.

Mace appeared unconcerned about the amount of blood flowing out of my body. He left at one point to take a call, leaving me alone with the crazy lady.

The blacksmith bent and peered into my face. She studied me, as if I were a scientific oddity. "He has no idea what you are," she whispered, a wicked grin crossing her face. "But I do."

"Tell me," I pleaded.

"Sorry." She smiled. "It's forbidden."

Forbidden?

The slightest hint of green glint flashed in her eyes. A color I'd never seen before, until today when my own green shine was reflected in Mace's eyes.

"Your eyes," I said, but my voice was weak.

"A relic of time," she said, cryptic and vague. "Have you seen it before?"

I started to tell her what had happened in the car, but I couldn't concentrate long enough to put my words in order. Unable to keep my eyes open, darkness came quickly.

CHAPTER 15

When I opened my eyes, I was lying on a wooden bench in the middle of a vast garden wearing a white nightgown that was soft against my skin. I was calm and relaxed and peaceful. The sun was shining overhead, but it wasn't hot. The air brushing against my face was temperate, comfortably cool. I sat up on the bench. There were flowers everywhere. They were beautiful with their vibrant reds, yellows, and blues dotting the picture-perfect landscape, but I couldn't smell them.

Was any of this real? Something brushed by me.

The beat of my heart thumped louder, and panic flooded my system. Almost immediately, a tranquil hush enveloped me. It was like before when I'd been in the basement of the bungalow. When I thought I was dying. I stood and turned a slow circle. Was I dead? I didn't feel dead.

"Where am I?" I called into the emptiness.

Again, the strange essence passed near me, something pleasant, soothing, and warm. I spun, trying to determine what the presence could be, but I saw nothing. For a third time, it brushed past me, this time touching my shoulder, and the serenity I'd felt before was magnified tenfold. My soul was weightless and free, without a care in the world. I took a step back. I didn't want the other presence touching me.

This place scared me, and I wanted to feel scared. I wanted my heart to beat faster, and my palms to be sweaty. I didn't want this feeling of tranquility masking the truth.

"Please stop," I called to the nothingness.

But the presence continued toward me. I backed away. My knees hit the bench behind me, and I fell over.

"Don't be afraid, Claire," a harmonious voice said as the most handsome man I'd ever seen appeared before me.

His golden-brown hair and golden eyes that sparked like fire were striking. His body, lean and muscled, was a good foot taller than me. The strong line of his jaw and chiseled chin had a rough character that made his handsome masculinity mouthwatering. But it lacked emotion.

His movements were so precise, his manner so deliberate, but not cold or uncaring. He just didn't feel real to me. It was as if I could tell he veiled his true self from me, although I couldn't actually sense a veil.

"I will not hurt you," he said, holding out his hand.

I hesitated. "What are you?"

"I can't hurt you. I promise."

Even though he didn't answer my question, something about his voice made me want to trust him. I took his hand, and again, the peaceful warmth I'd felt before washed over me. It lingered when he released me.

"Where am I?"

"A safe place."

"How did I get here? Where's Mace?"

His brows drew together, and his features turned sad. "You're still with him."

I whirled around. How could I still be with Mace? *Oh, no.* "Is this a dream?" I didn't want to be trapped in Mace's version of my nightmares. Not again.

The man reached forward and steadied me. His touch sent a new wave of peacefulness over me. "No. This isn't a dream."

I shrugged from his hold.

Reluctantly, he let me go.

"Am I dying—dead?"

"No," he said, but his gaze skittered away as if I might see some other truth in his soul.

A rush of dread overwhelmed me. "Who are you?"

He tried to touch me again. I backed away. He wasn't safe. Why did I think he was? He was excessively nonthreatening, and it was starting to make me nervous—no, afraid. "Don't touch me."

"It will help."

"I don't care. Just don't."

He must have read something in my expression because before I could run, he caught my arm and a small shock traveled through me. His calming influence was gone. I no longer felt safe. Frantically, I twisted, trying face him.

"Stop," he said, holding me in place. "You must let me back in." His voice was rushed.

I couldn't see him, but the flowers before me were dead. Their petals and stems were dried up and baking in the sun. I shivered as the heat left my body.

When I looked down, I gasped at the hand holding me in place. The skin was weathered and cracked as if the hand was decaying—very, very slowly.

"What are you? Why am I here?"

"Let me back in," he pleaded. "You don't have to see me this way."

"What way? As you really are?"

"No one sees me as I am. I'm a reflection of their past."

"What does that mean?"

"I'm not allowed to explain. However, you may see the handsome me if you choose."

"Why? What makes me so lucky?" The words caught in my throat.

"You have seen me before."

My heart rate increased. "When?"

He didn't answer my question. "You must let me in before you see me as I am now."

I was scared, and I was cold. This place was now barren, everything in it dead or dying. Just as I imagined he was. I didn't want to see that version of him, but I didn't know how to let him back in.

"Why do you care how I see you? Why should I be different?"

"Give me permission to be near you. To touch your skin," he said, again without answering my question. "It will reverse the effect your power had on my spell."

"What spell?"

"The one that lets you see me as I was the first time we met. Please, it's the best I can offer."

I looked at the hand holding my arm again. It was dying. I didn't want to see him that way. "I don't know how to let you in."

"Simply think it. As long as you mean it, you will see me as you did before."

I closed my eyes and thought of the way he was before. A sensation, which was almost the same as when the other spells reversed, enveloped me as if I were casting a spell on myself. Immediately, the calming sensation of his touch returned.

I was back in the beautiful garden, but the chill remained. He was a handsome man again. I caught a glimpse of his hand as he attempted to hide it. The part I'd seen before was still old and cracked.

"Thank you," he said.

"Why?"

"You're unique." He paused. "I would prefer you always see me in this form."

I rubbed my arms as a chill ran through me. "Why am I cold?"

"Do not be frightened. You will return soon. It's not your time yet."

My time for what? Before I could ask, fatigue caused my legs to give out. He caught me as I fell and held me in his warm embrace. "You're so beautiful," he murmured as I drifted off to sleep.

~ # ~

With a gasp, I opened my eyes. I couldn't move, but not because anything was holding me down. I was weak, only able to shift my head. An IV was hooked to my right arm. The bag contained a transparent green fluid. The medicine pulsed through me, as if it were somehow keeping me alive. There was a bandage on my left arm from where the blacksmith had taken the blood. A bruise ran along the vein, and I felt the pull from the tape securing the gauze to the other three spots.

A rush of adrenaline pulsed through me as another wave of medicine dripped from the IV. My right ear, which was not bandaged, seemed half stuffed with cotton. Some sounds were getting through, with a twinge of pain when I wiggled my jaw.

My attention sharpened when I recognized their voices. The door to the room was open, but I was too weak to try and escape. I closed my eyes, trying to step outside my body. On the second attempt, I pushed my presence into the room. It hurt, but I'd done it.

155

I found the quads in the main room. They were arguing in English. It never occurred to me they might prefer English to Pagan or Demon. Of course, if they knew I was listening, they wouldn't hesitate to switch. I hung back hoping Cinnamon wouldn't sense me.

"It can be done," Mace insisted.

"Is it worth father's wrath?" she asked.

Sage and Sorrel glanced at each other. Sage tilted his head toward Cinnamon, and Sorrel nodded. They were clearly backing their sister.

"Enough," Mace said. "We have the weapon. We have the opportunity. I have assurances the plan will succeed. We will get our revenge."

"Assurances from whom?" Cinnamon asked.

"Someone who has seen Junior's dead body."

"A seer?"

Mace smiled, but he didn't give up the source.

The others were quiet for a moment, then Sorrel spoke. "We didn't start this. If you're sure Father will not take revenge, I'm in."

Sage seemed surprised by his brother's change in attitude. I considered Mace. His eyes were locked on Sorrel. Mace's hand flexed toward the twin. Was he manipulating him?

I was about to say something to Sage, hoping he'd hear me as he had before, when Mace spoke.

"He has no right to interfere," Mace argued. "We are doing nothing more than Junior has done a hundred times over. It is our right to get justice."

Cinnamon eyed the others. She'd want revenge as much as Mace, but she was more cautious. She didn't want to anger her father.

Mace touched her arm. "It is our right to get justice," he repeated, but this time he made sure Cinnamon heard him.

She leaned back. He was relentlessly pushing his suggestion. Maybe she was starting to fight his hold. She moved her arm away, then rubbed her head as if it hurt. Noticing their stares, she tossed her hair back as if she'd been primping.

He focused his attention on Sage.

Was his hold waning? "We'll settle the score," she announced, dashing my hopes she'd refuse to help. "He'll die at the fight."

Mace's smug grin annoyed me.

She pushed to her feet, then stopped. Her gaze met mine. "Well, well, someone's awake."

I opened my eyes, returning to the bedroom. My arms and legs felt like lead. Exhausted pain slammed into me. I wasn't going anywhere. I had no choice but to wait as their footsteps stomped toward me.

Cinnamon entered the room and ripped the IV out of my arm. "You don't deserve this," she snarled.

I cried out from the shock and the pain. Half-dead, I lay there and laughed at her. "Then let me die," I challenged.

"She's no threat," Sage said. "Look at her. She can't even move."

He was right, and they all knew it.

"We can play with her later," Sorrel said. He tapped Mace with his elbow and said something in Pagan.

Mace's jaw tightened. "She's mine."

"Fine, little brother, she's yours, but I get first dibs when you're through."

"Leave us," Mace barked.

Cinnamon said something in Pagan; the twins laughed, then followed her out of the room.

Mace's nostrils flared. He sniffed the air. "You smell of Death. You should be glad we saved you in time. I've heard he is quite hideous."

Death? I turned away, but not fast enough.

Mace caught my chin and jerked my gaze back to his. "Impossible," he said. His expression was a mix of confusion and anger. "How are you doing this?"

"I don't know what you mean," I confessed.

"Your eyes have seen Death."

"No," I shook my head. "I haven't."

Mace brushed the hair away from my eyes to take a closer look. Obviously not satisfied with what he saw, he drew back and scowled.

"When I return," he said, kissing me on the forehead, "we'll figure out what makes you tick. Either your eyes are lying or you are." He stood. "The eyes never lie, but neither do the fates. No one sees Death and lives."

~ # ~

Startled, I woke with the pain of someone plunging a needle

into my arm. I was momentarily disoriented, until the voice in my head reminded me why I was here.

I was shocked to see Lily standing over me, taping a new IV in place.

"What are you doing?"

"Saving your life. Again," she said, clear disdain in her voice.

"Why?"

"My mistress has instructed me to," she said. "That is all you need to know."

Her mistress—the double.

"How did you know I wasn't your mistress?" It had to be the eyes, but I wanted her to confirm. She said nothing. Fine, I'd give her a hint. "The eyes aren't the same."

Lily remained silent. She didn't want to tell me anything, but the way her lips pursed together made me think she wanted to say something. I just needed to push harder.

"You can't change the windows to the soul, especially if you don't have one," I goaded. That worked.

"You will be sorry once she has you. She has changed her plans to include you."

Changed her plans? How would Lily know that? "When did you speak to her?" It couldn't have been since she got to the bungalow. Could it?

As if considering her words, she paused for a moment, then said, "After seeing you in the garden."

She was lying and not very well. "You thought I was her in the garden. You didn't know I wasn't her until you saw me at Sage's apartment."

Her eyes slid away. She adjusted the IV, causing a new twinge of pain. "You know nothing."

"I know you didn't speak to her after seeing me in the garden," I pressed. "You had to come straight from Sage's or you wouldn't have been here when I arrived. You had to see her here. In this house."

Lily opened her mouth to say something, but closed it immediately.

"Was it Mab?" I asked. She schooled her features, but she did it too well. "She didn't want you to wake up while she was talking to me," I said, watching Lily closely, "but she could have awakened you while I was blinded."

My mind had been a jumbled mess. It had taken me several minutes to bring it all back together. Mab could have easily spoken to her during that time. Or after, when Mab returned to speak to Mace.

"You know nothing," she spat. "She has tied your tongue."

I smiled as some pieces fell into place. Only one person had spelled me to keep me quiet. Mab was the double. She'd manipulated Junior and convinced him to trap the quads. That would explain how she knew exactly what spell was used on them. She must have given the spell to Junior. Just as she gave the second spell to Mace.

She'd refused to help Mace convince the blacksmith. She couldn't risk having proof she was involved. Mace had no idea she'd used Junior to set them up. She'd manipulated everything.

"Only one person has tied my tongue," I said.

Lily scowled, her eyes cold and calculating. "You're a particular favorite of hers or I would kill you," she finally admitted. Smiling, she pressed a fingernail into the crease of my bandaged arm, hurting me. "She will have you before it's over."

"I'll die before I let that happen."

Lily laughed. "You'll certainly wish you had before she's through." She took a key from her pocket, which she put on the bedside table. "That key will take you to Underworld. You're on your own after that."

"Why are you helping me?"

"Who says I am?" she said, then disappeared.

My mind was racing as I waited for the green liquid to flow into me. Mab was the double, the one who set me up. The one who wanted Junior dead and for the quads to kill him. But why did she involve me? Was it just convenient? Or did she somehow know I'd get pulled into this mess? As Lily said, I'm a particular favorite. *Yay, me.*

Ten minutes later, after the bag was empty, I ripped off the tape and winced as I slid the needle out. I closed my elbow and studied the key. Could I trust her, or should I try to call for a taxi?

No money, the voice helpfully reminded me.

I palmed the key, hoping it wasn't some sort of trap. I concentrated on the watch. "Get me the hell out of here."

The watch guided me to the basement where I spotted Charles in the enclosure. He was sleeping—scratch that, he was dead. Lily had tied up the loose ends nicely.

The watch led me to the back wall. When the key got closer, the brick that had glowed blue before started glowing again. The key emitted a faint hiss as I touched the marked brick and disappeared.

CHAPTER 16

The portal took me to a street, where everyone looked as if they'd just walked off the runway. It had to be Little Purgatory. I was startled as the door to the proudly proclaimed Wild Hare Bar and Grill slammed open, and a demon came flying past me.

The bouncer, a tattooed pagan the size of a linebacker, followed him out. With no effort, he picked up the demon and tossed him into the wall behind me. The uninvited rule wasn't as strictly enforced outside Purgatory, but obviously the Wild Hare had its own set of rules, and this guy clearly hadn't been invited.

I didn't stick around to watch more.

I was sure Mace had no clue I'd just escaped the bungalow. Since it was still two days before Johnny and his crew would harass me for being in Underworld, I could assume—at least for the moment—no one was looking for me.

I considered my options. I could go to The Boss or Quaid and tell them what was happening—well, not tell them because Mab's spell wouldn't allow that, but I could point them in the right direction. Getting out of downtown and back to the company would be the difficult part since I had no money. There was also the matter of the traitor, someone who had seen Junior's dead body. And that someone was working with Mace.

Omar was certainly a powerful enough seer to have seen the body, but would he really betray The Boss? I couldn't picture him as the traitor, but he'd sent me on this fool's errand. He had to know what would happen, but he'd seemed genuinely surprised by Junior's death.

That could have been his plan, the voice suggested.

I shook my head. I didn't want to believe Omar had betrayed me. Either way I needed to get out of Little Purgatory.

I had two options: try to save Junior by warning him or try to get to The Boss or Quaid and hope they believed me. The quads had a head start, and Junior was downtown. Finding him—

"Ow." I cried out as someone brushed past me, clipping my hand and activating the bracelets. Okay, new goal, lose the bracelets. Then find Junior.

I headed out of Little Purgatory toward the arena. I wasn't exactly sure where I was. Based on all the red and purple armbands it was obvious everyone on foot, in groups of two or more, was going to the fight. I followed three pagans, keeping a decent distance, so I didn't get noticed. They were wearing red armbands—demon colors. They didn't have their own fighter this year. It was a druid and demon match-up, and there was no way the pagans were rooting for the druids.

I loped onto a side street as soon as I crossed out of Little Purgatory. Downtown was gridded out in blocks, but it wasn't as if I knew the place well. The few times I'd been down here, I had a driver and my phone. I needed to get my bearings, make a plan, and remove the bracelets.

I tried the obvious approach first and concentrated on the watch. "Remove the bracelets."

Nothing happened.

I surveyed the area. There were a few shops along the street, but most of them were closed. The watch or my power was good with directions, but I had no idea what to ask for. And would it lead me to a closed business? I really didn't know enough about how it all worked, but I didn't have another option.

"Take me to…" I paused. *Where can I have them removed?* "Take me—"

"To your leader," some guy quipped as he ambled past.

I was attracting attention. I glanced around, but he was the only guy who seemed to notice me, and he wasn't exactly stopping to chat. No, he was heading for the pawnshop across the street.

When he opened the door, the glass reflected a red sign hanging under the awning. I hadn't noticed it before, but it was exactly what

I was looking for: Jewelry Repair—perfect.

I crossed the street. Catching sight of myself in the glass storefront, I noticed that the bandages were giving me a hospital escapee vibe. It also appeared most of my bruises were gone. The skin around my wrists was still raw but improving. I removed the bandages and tossed them into the trashcan outside the store. I'd be less suspicious this way. At least I hoped I would.

I peered through the glass door, scanning the inside of the shop. There was a scruffy middle-aged demon standing at the counter. His arms were folded over his chest as he watched the guy who'd walked past me. The demon answered a question, then shook his head, never changing his unapproachable stance. A minute later the customer left without buying anything, and I slid through the door before it closed.

The shop was grimy but well lit. There wasn't much security in place—a couple of round mirrors and a camera perched behind the register. The shop was empty except for me, so there was no surprise that the demon behind the counter was staring. He had the same unapproachable stance he had with the last guy, which normally might bother me, but not today.

I sauntered up to the end of the counter, the one farthest away from the video surveillance. The demon sighed before reluctantly walking over to me. I kept my head down and my face pointed away from the all-seeing eye of the camera.

"Can I help you?" he asked, returning to his arms crossed over his chest stance. He wore a red armband so he probably wanted to close up early and head to the fight.

"What are these worth?" I asked, holding out my arms and ignoring his attitude.

Cinnamon had called them Hell shackles. I assumed that meant something. I was hoping it meant they were *worth* something.

"Well, that depends," the demon said dryly. "Why are you wearing them?"

I cocked one of my eyebrows. "Do you want them or not?"

"Well," he said, eyeing my watch. "I'd rather have the watch."

"Not a chance." I couldn't remove the watch, but even if I could, I wouldn't trade it for anything in this hellhole.

He shrugged, then pursed his lips. "I guess I'll just have to settle for the bracelets, but I'm not sure I know how to get them off." He called toward the back. "Luke, get in here."

I tensed when I sensed a druid coming from the back. A minute later, a thin fragile druid shuffled through the curtain. He was very old with a bad left leg that caused him to limp. He couldn't have been more than five feet tall, if that, and his head appeared to be too big for his body. Although he wore a really cheap brown suit, the odds were good he wasn't one of Johnny's boys.

"Yes, sir," Luke said.

"Can you remove these?" the demon asked.

Luke slid a wooden box over to the counter and stepped up on it. I moved my hands away as he reached for them.

I caught the barest hint of a brown shine to his eyes when he said, "Don't worry, miss. I won't touch your hands."

His smile put me at ease. I held my hands out for him to inspect. He clutched my right wrist, bringing the band closer to his face. He slipped down one of the jeweler loupes on his glasses.

The curtain to the back room swooshed, drawing my attention away from Luke. The demon owner was no longer in the shop. I was about to close my eyes and follow him, when he returned a moment later. He reached under the counter for something, then glanced out the window.

Before he could catch me spying, I moved my eyes to his reflection in one of the round mirrors. I didn't like the way his gaze darted to the window, or the shifty way he held whatever he pulled from under the counter, which I suspected was a gun.

It was taking too long to remove the bracelets. I wanted to tug my hand away, but Luke had a good grip for someone his age. A car drove by outside. The owner shifted, bringing up the butt of the gun he was trying to hide into view.

He must have called someone when he ducked into the back. His fake casual demeanor was inconsistent with his twitchy behavior. He was waiting for someone. I was sure of it. I wanted out of here, but getting out of Luke's grasp wouldn't be easy or quiet.

"It doesn't look like—" I started, but the words died in my throat when an audible click sounded, and the first bracelet fell off into Luke's hand. The other one weakened, as if it might be unlocked. I concentrated on the watch, to focus my power. "Open the other bracelet," I said.

"Humm," Luke said, still scrutinizing the bracelet in his hand.

With the same click as before, the second fell off, clanking loudly on the glass counter. I examined the open band and realized what Luke was studying. Several Ancient characters and Mace's serpent mark were etched into the inside of the band.

I really hoped he didn't recognize Mace's mark. I eyed the demon. He was ready to pounce.

Luke clasped my wrist before I had a chance to escape. "We got a problem," he said to the demon.

Just as a car screeched to a stop outside the shop, I snatched my arm away. I glanced back to see two of Johnny's goons getting out of a lime-green convertible. *Great. I don't have time for this.*

The demon was now pointing his gun at me.

"She's marked," Luke said, pointing a crooked finger in my direction.

"He wants to kill me himself," I told the owner. "I'm worth nothing dead."

Before he could react, I rushed him, jumping over the counter. The stunned demon jerked to avoid me and tripped. The gun went off as he hit the ground. I didn't look back. I ran through the curtain and into the rear room just as the buzzer on the front door sounded.

"She's back there," Luke shouted.

I spotted a side door. A gunshot dinged off the doorframe as I hit the alley. Without slowing, I hauled ass through the alley, down a few cross streets, before finally ducking behind a dumpster to catch my breath. My heart raced. I closed my eyes, took a few deep breaths, and stepped outside my body.

I could have blinked to the pawnshop, but I wanted to see if the goons were following me.

I reentered the shop, breathing a little easier since I hadn't passed Johnny's boys on my walk here. The demon was now inspecting the bracelets.

"Should we call?" Luke asked.

"I already called Johnny's people. It's better if we let them handle it."

"What are we going to do with the bracelets?"

The demon visibly tensed. "Destroy them. I don't need any of Mace's kind of trouble here."

"But they're worth a fortune. Real Hell shackles."

"Yeah, and they're only good for finding her, or for him to find you if you keep them. I said destroy them, unless you want to explain why you removed them?" The demon lifted his brows as he threatened Luke.

I should have taken the bracelets and destroyed them myself, but it was too late now.

Gruff voices came from the back. The demon handed the bracelets to Luke. "Get rid of these."

Luke shoved the bracelets into his pocket, then grabbed his coat and hat and headed out the front door. The buzzer sounded as the tough guys walked through the curtain.

"Why was she here?" the taller man asked without preamble.

"She was interested in this lovely item," the demon said, holding up a brooch that had been in the glass case.

The tall thug gave him a level stare. The shorter man scanned the shop. "Where's the old man?"

"He's already left for the day," the demon said cautiously. I didn't blame him. Nobody wanted to get on Johnny's bad side. "Look, I called you boys first. I could have called The Boss's people."

"This is a waste of time," the shorter man said. The taller man nodded.

I relaxed as the two men got into their car and drove away. The bracelets were off, and Johnny's boys had lost my scent. I was about to open my eyes when the demon picked up the phone. I waited a minute to see if he changed his mind about calling Mace. I doubted he'd call The Boss at this point.

"Yeah, you don't know me, but I got some information you might be interested in," the demon said. He was silent for a moment, then said, "The girl was down here. I let Johnny's boys know, but that was before I knew she was marked by Mace." Another pause. "I just thought you might like to know."

He hung up the phone.

"Who did you call?" I asked. Would it have been The Boss? I gasped—or Mab?

He opened his mouth as if to say something, then closed it. For a second, I thought he saw me, but then the buzzer from the door sounded behind me. He crossed his arms over his chest, eyeing the new customer.

Opening my eyes, I returned to the alley and concentrated on the watch. "I need to find Junior."

~ # ~

I rubbed my arms. The capri pants and tank top were fine for the Grand Caymans, but the sun would be down soon in Underworld, and the temperature was dropping fast.

The crowds were heavy on both sides of the street, which made the guy walking against traffic stick out like a sore thumb. I was shocked to recognize Omar as the wake of pedestrians drew closer.

I wanted answers. He had to know the truth. Why wouldn't he have told me The Boss didn't own my soul? I was about to yell his name when I stopped myself. What if he was Mace's traitor? I couldn't risk it, not when there was another way.

I glanced around, then ducked into the nearest alley. It was a dead end, but there wasn't anything to hide behind. I sidled up to the wall a few feet from the main street and closed my eyes.

I blinked to the other side of the road, right behind Omar. His brisk walk against the flow was annoying a few in the crowd. His frustrated attitude wasn't helping. "Move," he bellowed at one fight fan.

The fan was at least a foot taller than Omar. He wore a red armband over his sexy as hell leather jacket. His eyes flashed red as he focused them on Omar who was dressed in his usual high school chemistry teacher style, which couldn't have been less threatening. The fan puffed up his chest until Omar stopped, cocked his head, and glared at him.

The fan's face went white. "Sorry, man," he said, before bounding off the sidewalk toward the other street. A car horn blared, but the guy didn't look. He kept moving, his hand clutching a woman who kept glancing back as if they were being followed.

After that, everyone gave Omar a wide berth. I kept my distance too. I didn't want to take the chance that he could sense me.

Omar picked up his pace. He headed down another side street, cut across another main thoroughfare, before winding up on an avenue I recognized. He was headed straight for the blacksmith's shop.

He didn't knock; he just walked in. I jumped inside after him. The blacksmith was alone, pacing. The giant wasn't around, and the sidewalk outside had been deserted. She jerked when Omar spoke. He was speaking Ancient. I didn't understand it, but from her non-verbal cues, I could tell something was wrong.

She rubbed the back of her neck, nodding toward the office.

The only words I could pick out were Mace's name and mine. The conversation sounded so foreign. This was the first time I'd ever heard a full conversation in Ancient by speakers so fluent as to make it seem natural.

She jerked again when someone knocked on the door. She motioned for Omar to wait in the back room. I moved with him. So far he hadn't sensed me.

"Enter," the blacksmith said in English.

I peeked out from the back room. Wylan James bowed to the blacksmith and said something I didn't understand.

"English, please," she said to him. "You may understand Ancient, but you cannot speak it worth a damn, old man. I refuse to hear you butcher it."

The blacksmith was no longer nervous. She was as strong and confident as she had been when Mace and I were here earlier.

"As you wish, my lady," he said in English.

"Why are you here?"

"The blood," he said. "The seer has seen it. He wishes for you to confirm its authenticity."

"You're not the first to arrive, but I will tell you what I have told all the others. There is no blood."

James crossed his arms. "I have been contacted by more than a dozen. How can they all be wrong?"

"I wasn't aware you were so influential among them," the blacksmith said bluntly.

"They called once they saw I planned to come here. They wanted to make sure I knew how many had seen the truth."

"This is not the first time they have been wrong," she said, moving her hands casually behind her back and smiling in an innocent way.

"But this would be the first time so many have been wrong about the blood. You will not be able to hide the truth forever."

Her smile faded. Obviously, her innocent demeanor wasn't working on him. "You may go now." Her voice was clipped and cold. "Do not return. You're no longer welcome."

James's brow furrowed, but he bowed his head politely before leaving.

"He won't be the last to come about the blood," Omar said, returning from the back room.

The blacksmith replied in Ancient.

"Are you okay?" asked a voice that was so close I could smell the beer on his breath.

I opened my eyes when someone touched my shoulder.

Two druids were standing in front of me. The one touching me repeated, "Are you okay?" His buddy scanned the street, wiping his hand down his mouth.

I shrugged out of his hold. "I'm fine," I said, then moved past the druids and headed for the arena. I glanced back a moment later, but they weren't following me.

I made it a few more blocks before I slowed. I was too far away from the blacksmith's shop to turn back. Omar was clearly more aware of my situation than I'd ever thought, but I no longer considered him Mace's traitor. He didn't know about Mace. He'd gone to the blacksmith because of the blood—*my blood*. Wylan James had gone there too.

You're the one? You will save us? the voice reminded me of what James said.

The deli flashed in my mind. I remembered. He couldn't believe I was the one, but what did it mean? I was too close to the arena to give up on my plan to stop the quads from killing Junior. My blood was another issue. One I'd have to figure out later.

I was making good time, until the crowds grew so thick there was barely enough room to stand. I was still six blocks from the arena.

The setting sun made the day darker and colder. I kept checking the watch, hoping it would take me down a less crowded side street, but no luck. I was headed right toward The Grand—where anyone who was anyone would be staying—and where I would find Junior.

The streets were blocked off. There were people everywhere. I was close enough to start worrying about how I was going to get in. Junior would have guards at the elevator, and I wasn't dressed for the event. I wouldn't be able to talk my way in only wearing capri pants and a tank top. I hoped the watch knew another less direct way in.

I stepped off the curb, about to cross the street, when a mob of Densmore supporters rushed into the crowd. "Densmore! Densmore!" shouted the purple armband druid fans.

Within a few seconds, the crowd swelled into an impromptu pep rally, and I was driven to the side by the mob. Resting, I waited for the group to pass. I caught sight of myself in a shop window. My bruises had healed, and my wrists were almost completely unmarked. Only the faintest red line remained. My black eye had finally faded. My physical pain was gone too. All things considered, I felt pretty good—better than I had in days.

The Densmore pack was thinning. I shifted to move into the flow of people when a familiar voice caught my focus. I slunk into the shadows. My heartbeat increased as I searched for the owner of the voice. My eyes watered, but I refused to cry. The voice was getting louder. I couldn't understand what he was saying, but it was him. Jack. I would have known his voice anywhere.

Searching the crowd, I finally spotted him. A group of young demons walked my way. My beautiful, well-muscled, dark-haired human with ice-blue eyes ambled along with his friends. I say human because that was how he still appeared to me. He wore his most sinful blue jeans, the ones that hung so well on his hips I wanted to jump his bones when he was in them. His All-American bad-boy style was topped off with a white t-shirt and well-used leather jacket—the one with white racing stripes down the arms and a been-there-done-that amount of wear that made my mouth water. Okay, so maybe I'd ripped those jeans off him a time or two and had my wicked way with his sexy body while he still wore that jacket. I was the girlfriend. I had rights.

Past tense.

I forced back tears, refusing to cry. He didn't fit in with the other demons, but I was the only one who thought that. Everyone else would see the real him. I wondered which demon traits he possessed. Would he resemble my Jack, or would his features appear too angular and intense? His veil was unnaturally strong, which was probably courtesy of The Boss. One of the girls moved back to walk beside him, draping her arm over his shoulders and whispering something into his ear.

"That bitch," I grumbled under my breath. I took a step forward, then stopped when he smiled. It was his awkward smile. The one he had when someone said something that embarrassed him.

His veil flickered. Changing my mind, I dropped my gaze. I didn't want to see the real Jack. I wanted my Jack.

I wanted to confront him. Ask him why he did it. I wanted to know if he cared at all, but I already knew the answer. I just didn't want to admit it.

I waited for their voices to fade away, then I searched for him again. The same girl was standing beside him. He shrugged and her arm fell from around him. She moved over to another demon and draped her arm around him. Jack was walking alone now, with the group, but not close to anyone.

He came home early, the voice whispered.

Yeah, because the fight was canceled.

He came home before the fight started.

I recalled Saturday night. He'd come home with a movie we planned to rent and a tub of my favorite ice cream. That was the night he'd been different. He said he loved me, which he'd done before, but this time it felt different. I couldn't explain it, but I knew he meant it. More tears ran down my cheek.

Thinking of that night brought back a flood of emotion. This wasn't just a job for him. Maybe in the beginning, but not now. He wanted to be with me. I wasn't wrong about that, and nothing Mace said would convince me otherwise.

I wanted to run to Jack, to go home with him, to be with him, but I couldn't.

The me of that perfect night was already at home. I couldn't change that without changing everything. I had to save Junior if I wanted any part of that life back. If I didn't save him, that life was over.

I glanced at the watch, which was still pointing toward the hotel. The path was now clear. In the distance, I could still hear the druids chanting, "Densmore! Densmore!"

I lost sight of Jack as he headed away from the arena. He was going home. My heart wanted to follow him, but my head was going to win this round.

I had to save Junior—and myself—first.

CHAPTER 17

The crowded lobby of the hotel did nothing to conceal me. In my plain-Jane clothing, I stuck out in a room full of designer clothes and elaborate up-dos. I moved behind a large potted plant when I spotted Jenny from the office.

She was one of those spreading rumors about Junior and me.

They're not rumors if they're true, the voice said.

I ignored the voice, my subconscious or whatever this thing was in my head. It was starting to get on my nerves.

Only because you know I'm right.

Why all of a sudden are you Chatty Kathy? I knew I would regret casting that spell.

I rolled my eyes when the voice didn't respond. Shouldn't my subconscious be on my side?

I needed a way up to the top floor and wasn't sure how I would get there without being seen. There was only one elevator, and two of Junior's bodyguards guarded it.

Jenny moved away from a group of people I didn't recognize and walked up to Junior's guards. She flipped her hair and smiled. They ignored her. Chewing on her bottom lip, she nervously glanced at the waiting group.

She pursed her lips and balled her hands into fists. Turning back to the guards, she reached forward with one hand, but jerked it back quickly when the guard on the right snarled at her.

The train wreck that was the finance admin's attempt to get

access to Junior's floor might be fun to watch if I had nothing better to do, but I needed to find Junior.

I checked the watch. It was pointing toward the restaurant, not the elevators. Considering my clothes, I didn't think I'd have much luck making it to the kitchen to find a service elevator.

His guards might believe I was on official business. Then again, Junior hated his father. I'm sure the guards had a standing order to deny me just to piss off The Boss. Plus Jenny was still trying to get access. If I went to them now, she'd see me.

The kitchen was my only option. Maybe the hotel staff would be too busy to care. I waited a minute for Jenny to skulk back to her friends then I leaped out from behind the potted plant as a large figure blocked my path. I gasped as he clutched my elbow and yanked me forward for a kiss.

Unlike Mace's kiss, Junior's technique was more akin to complete suffocation. I was smothered as he eagerly plundered my mouth with his tongue.

I gasped again from lack of breath when he let go.

Junior said something I couldn't understand. He snaked his hand through my hair and planted another kiss on my lips. I pushed against his chest. He was holding on so tight I couldn't move. He started to say something else.

"English," I said, breathless from the kiss and the bear hug.

"I didn't think you were coming. You said you couldn't come." He playfully tugged on my hair with his free hand.

"I need to talk to you," I said.

"We can talk when we get upstairs." He stared down at my outfit. "You need something better to wear." He said something in Demon to one of his boys.

Junior spun me around and draped his arm over my shoulders—trapping me at his side. Jenny's mouth hung open as we walked past her. I could already see the glee in her eyes at the story she would get to tell on Monday—only now I knew it was true. She was probably tweeting what she'd seen right now.

By the time the elevator doors finally popped open, the walls had closed in on me, and I couldn't wait to get out. Junior hurried us into his suite. The others headed toward another.

Junior wore his tux—all except the tie. The top button of his white shirt was undone, giving him a dangerously sexy vibe. The fabric was so lush and rich it hugged his body perfectly. Clearly not a rental.

I didn't want to be alone with him. I drifted away once we were inside the posh suite. As if he didn't want to let go, he kept his hands lightly touching me.

I quickly scurried over to the bar. "Do you want a drink?"

"Sure," he said, smiling.

"What would you like?"

"The usual."

Great, I had no idea what his usual was. I scanned the selection. The bar was completely stocked. I was about to ask when I discovered that only one bottle had been opened. I lifted the Macallan 1926 scotch and poured him a drink.

He took the drink with one hand and clasped my wrist with the other. He lowered us to the sofa, discarding his drink on the table. His icy vermillion eyes bored into mine. When I shifted to rise, he stopped me. His hands were all over me. He leaned in for another kiss.

I put my hand on his chest. "I need to talk to you," I said, holding him at arm's length. "The quads are trying to kill you."

He straightened his elbows, levering off me. He pinched my chin between his index finger and thumb. Giving my head a playful shake. "I know. I'm taking care of it." His thumb stroked my bottom lip as he licked his.

"No, you don't understand," I said, drawing his eyes back to mine. "They're out of your trap. They're here tonight to kill you."

His lip quirked, then he smiled. "That's impossible."

"No, it's the—"

His lips were pressed against mine before I could argue. I turned my head away. Undeterred, he began kissing across my jaw and down my neck. My body relaxed, letting his weight settle against me. I gasped when his hand found the hem of my shirt, and his fingers slid under to touch bare skin.

Clearly "boyfriend Junior" was in the mood. I tried not to tense. I needed him to hear me.

"I'm serious, you need to listen. Trapping them was maybe not your best plan."

"You were fine with it last week," he said, continuing his sensual exploration of my neck.

Yeah, last week I was probably leading you around by your—

"Oh, no, not yet," I said, pushing his hands away from my pants.

"I promise you, they're out and coming after you."

Chuckling he brushed my hand away. Panicking I pushed against his big chest. The strong, powerful demon on top of me wasn't going to move. My vision faded as he loomed over me.

~ # ~

I woke up naked on the bathroom floor.

What happened?

The voice was silent. I picked myself off the floor, wincing as pain shot through my hip. The floor was covered in water. The capri pants and tank top were lying crumpled and soaked on the floor.

Junior, the voice whispered.

I remembered being in the sitting room with him. His hands were all over me. I rubbed my stomach where he'd touched me. In the blink of an eye, two images flashed in my mind. The first was of Junior and me on the couch in the living room, which I sort of remembered. In the picture, he was on top of me, kissing me. Not exactly the way I remembered it. The second was Death. His golden eyes were haunted, his face pale.

Dizziness swarmed me. I closed my eyes and clutched the sink so I didn't fall.

The voice was quiet again. Why couldn't I remember?

I gently pressed the knot on the back of my head. My feet were wet. I touched my hip, which was sore. There was a red mark. Had I slipped?

I remembered coming up in the elevator. I told Junior about the quads, but he didn't believe me. That was it. I woke up in the bathroom with a pounding head and, checking my watch, at least thirty minutes of missing time. Did I pass out after slipping on the water? I touched the back of my head again. I didn't feel any blood.

What happened, damnit?

I jumped from a knock at the door. "What's taking so long?" Junior asked.

"Shower," I said, breathless.

"Hurry."

I took a shower, hoping it would help clear my head. It didn't. The images were my only memory of the last half hour, and I didn't like what they were showing me. I'd kissed Junior—had I done more? Why had Death looked so sad?

There was a dress waiting for me on the bed. It was beautiful, although royal blue wasn't my best color. I was so tired. I wanted to crawl into the bed, not into the dress. My soaked clothing was another mystery from the missing half hour, which made the dress my only option.

I was halfway into the dress when the hotel phone startled me. I lifted the corner of the comforter and found the phone flashing. Junior picked it up from the other room. I waited for him to hang up, then picked up the receiver.

I dialed the office first, but no one answered. Then I punched in The Boss's mobile. I wasn't supposed to call it, but this was definitely an emergency. He didn't answer that one either. I was about to leave a voicemail when a demon girl from Junior's entourage came in—without knocking. I hung up the phone without leaving a message.

I yanked the dress up, covering my nakedness. She didn't seem to care.

She was tiny, almost a foot shorter than me in her four-inch platform heels, which meant she probably topped out at four foot five in bare feet. Her white-blonde hair was unusual for a demon. She sneered, giving me a once over and obviously finding me lacking. "Good, you're able to dress yourself." She dropped a shoebox on the bed, then turned on her heel to leave.

"Hey," I said quickly.

She sighed, turning to face me.

"Have you seen any of the quads tonight?"

She narrowed her eyes skeptically. "Why?"

"I have a message for Cinnamon. Have you seen them? Or The Boss?"

"You know as well as anyone that he never comes to Fight Night."

"Can you get a message to him?"

She glared at me for a second, mouth closed. Then regaining her voice, and her indignant attitude, she snapped, "You're his assistant." As if I actually wanted the job.

"Right." She wasn't going to be any help, but I didn't want her to leave me alone with Junior. "Who do you think will win?"

"Wagner, of course."

I snorted. *Obviously*.

Her eyebrows rose. "Wagner's undefeated."

I started to say, he won't win tonight, when my throat

tightened, cutting off my words.

Her eyes widened. Taking my false start as something more than it was, she whispered in a conspiratorial tone, "Is it fixed?"

I wanted to say no, but I couldn't. The fight was fixed. I knew it from the future. Shit. I couldn't even move my head. She decided that meant the fight was fixed. She rushed out of the room before I could stop her.

Great. Johnny was right. I had just started the biggest betting debacle in Underworld history. Everything I thought I had nothing to do with: Jenny's rumor, the bets, had actually been caused by me. All those events were happening again.

I thought about Junior. He hadn't died at the fight. Maybe I could save him now, but maybe that was because I was supposed to—only to have him die later at the company. I considered the phone again. I could call Quaid. He would have to pick up.

I reached for the receiver just as Junior opened the door.

"It's time to go," he said, leaning against the doorjamb.

I took my hand off the phone. Raising the lid off the shoebox, I found the highest most absurd platform high heels imaginable. They put Blondie's four-inch skyscrapers to shame.

I wasn't going to be able to walk in these, much less run if I needed to. I glanced down. My sneakers were lying on the floor by the bed. Thankfully, not wet in the bathroom.

"I'll be right out," I said.

Junior's eyes dimmed. His mouth fell into a flat line.

"I need to put on my shoes. I'll be right there."

He sighed, returning to the sitting room. "It's taking you long enough. I'd like to get there tonight," he called back over his shoulder.

I tossed the heels aside and slipped on my completely inappropriate running shoes. I concentrated on the watch and whispered, "Don't let Junior notice the shoes."

Junior wrapped his strong arms around me when I joined him. Again, I was smothered and trapped by his large embrace. "You're beautiful," he breathed into my ear, placing soft kisses on my neck.

I was shaking.

"Are you cold?" he asked.

"No." *I'm nervous and don't want to be alone with you.* "You need to watch out for the quads," I said, trying again to get him to acknowledge the danger.

Hugging me close, he softly patted the back of my head, unintentionally sending a twinge of pain through it. "Stop worrying about the quads. They're in no condition to hurt me."

"You're wrong," I whispered. "They're free."

He tensed, but not out of fear. He twined his hand in my hair and tugged my head back. "I said not to worry about it."

I pressed my lips together in a tight smile. "Okay, I'm sorry," I said, coaxing his hand down, away from my hair and the sore knot on my head. "Let's go."

The arena was packed and loud with the drone of excited voices. We walked in on the middle tier and headed toward the main floor. There were two other decks above us full of fight fans.

I was anxious about where the quads were and from sensing so many veils in one place. Underworld was usually a veil-free zone, but it had become common practice on Fight Night, the one night demons, pagans, and druids would bring their human pets downtown. Most of the humans appeared dazed. They wouldn't remember much of what they saw, but in recent years, bringing a human had become quite popular, so almost everyone did it.

The butterflies in my stomach were even more noticeable tonight. The number of veils was staggering, but sensing the veils had become more automatic since my visit to Purgatory, which had actually diminished the antsy feeling from sensing them one at a time.

The fight usually drew a crowd, but this year it was the hottest ticket. There hadn't been a druid-demon match in over a hundred years. The elite were all dressed to the nines. At least that meant I didn't stick out in my royal blue party dress. I spotted a few wandering gazes checking out my shoes. Luckily, Junior wasn't one of them.

I kept my eyes open for the quads. Unfortunately, more than one of the bookies taking bets noticed me. I overheard several betters put money on Wagner not to win. Junior's groupie had certainly been busy.

Security was everywhere. They had a "take no prisoners" attitude. Action was swift and immediate when anyone got out of line. More than one drunken fan was pulled aside. It seemed impossible that any type of disturbance would get out of hand with these guys around, but something was going to happen. I just didn't know what it was, or when it would. I continued scanning the crowd and spotted a few people from the office, but they didn't see me.

Junior was keeping me close, but I felt more like a hostage than a girlfriend. Our seats were dead center on the front row of what I assumed was the best side, AKA sitting ducks. I continued to scan the crowds. I started to step away when I caught a glimpse of Quaid.

Junior dragged me down into the seat beside him. He gripped the back of my neck and gave me a light squeeze. "Eyes on me— not other guys."

"It's just Quaid," I said quickly.

"I don't fucking care. You're here with me," he growled.

Jealous much? I smiled and gave him a quick peck on the cheek. "I'm here with you."

He smiled and kissed me for real. I wanted away from him, especially now that he was being alpha-male asshole in possessive, controlling mode, but he didn't know the danger he was in. I couldn't just leave him here to be picked off by Mace.

I got a break from his attention when the demon behind me spilled half of his drink down my back. Junior's eyes flashed red. He shoved the guy back into his seat. "Sit down," he ordered.

With Junior distracted, I scanned the crowd again. He hadn't died here, but I still didn't know if that was the future I needed to avoid, or if being here already changed things. Maybe he would be shot in this place—that's right; he was shot. The weapon Mace got from the blacksmith must have been a gun. It would take a special gun to kill a hellspawn—wouldn't it? At least now I had an idea of what to look for. The bullet hole was too small to be from a rifle. They would need to get close.

The crowd behind us thrummed with rowdy shouts and cheers. Words bounced around us like chants. Most of them were drunk. The mass of fans was mixed; there were as many purple armbands as red ones.

I swept my gaze over the immediate crowd. Someone who resembled Sage was coming our way, but I could tell it wasn't him as he drew closer. I kept sweeping my focus back and forth, but jumped out of my seat when the guy behind me soaked my back with the rest of his rum and coke. At least it wasn't beer.

"Hey, jackass," Junior shouted. "I'm not going to tell you again. Watch what you're doing."

The guy behind us snorted as if he was actually offended Junior had called him a jackass. "Oh, yeah?" he slurred, so drunk he didn't seem to have a clue who he was talking to. "What are you going to do about it, twinkle toes?"

Oh, hell. This was going from bad to worse. I searched for one of the security guards. Junior was about to rip this guy's head off. A minute ago, the place had been crawling with them, now this idiot was going to get killed because they were all on break.

I put my hand on Junior's arm, trying to get his attention. As if Mace was near, the mark on my back tingled. My breath caught as I spotted him coming down the far aisle. His eyes flashed with violet rage when they locked on mine. With lips pressed into a straight line, he searched the crowd for a second. Sage was coming down the aisle closer to us. Mace, teeth clenched, face dark with fury, tilted his head in my direction. The others wouldn't be far behind.

Glancing around, I spotted another drunken fan stupidly about to join the Junior discussion. "Hey," I said, getting the drunk's attention. "That guy—" I pointed at Sage— "said you look like a druid."

The guy's eyes flashed red, and his lip curled into a snarl. He barreled toward Sage, knocking him to the ground. He was throwing punches before Sage knew what hit him. A minute later, the guy was flying through the air as Sage threw him off as if he weighed nothing. The other crazy fans in our section took notice as the demon's body careened into the ring.

"That guy said Wagner sucks," I called into the crowd, drawing their attention to Sage.

Not everyone attacked. Some might have known who he was, and the druids agreed with his supposed view of Wagner. But enough had no clue how dangerous he was, and threw themselves into the fracas. He was back on the floor before he could get to his feet. Cinnamon had joined Mace, and they were both trying to stay out of the fray, which was quickly turning into a free-for-all.

Mace's eyes were locked on mine. His eyes had lightened. He raised his hand, I assumed, to throw his will at me, but lost focus when Cinnamon yanked him from the crowd. He glared at me once more before letting her lead him away.

I tugged at Junior's arm. He didn't budge. He was still arguing with the first drunk fan, who I honestly couldn't believe wasn't already dead.

Sorrel rushed into the melee, shoving people out of the way, trying to get to Sage. Junior didn't see either twin. The fight was spreading. The whole arena would be at it before long.

Sorrel helped Sage to his feet. They didn't look back as he and Sage escaped. Junior wouldn't die tonight.

He didn't the first time either, the voice reminded.

I know that.

I just didn't know what that really meant. I couldn't stay with Junior until Monday. With the immediate threat neutralized, I had to move on to Plan B. I had to get to either Quaid or The Boss. They would be able to sort this out before it became an issue.

I slunk away from Junior. I kept my gaze on him, expecting him to latch onto my arm and yank me back to his side. Fortunately, he was too busy watching the chaos to realize I was leaving.

I darted through the crowd, trying not to run into anyone. I was glad I wasn't wearing the high heels. Security rushed past me as I reached the stairs.

"Where's Marco's team?" a guard's walkie-talkie squawked.

"Attention everyone," the announcer boomed over the loud speaker. "Please take your seats."

"It'll be a bloodbath if they cancel," someone nearby observed.

The red exit sign above the door shined against the darkened arena. There were only a few more steps to climb. I swerved to miss a woman getting out of her seat and ran into a man wearing a fedora. *Oh, no.* He was one of the bookies I'd seen taking bets earlier. I didn't wait for him to figure out who I was. I shoved off and kept moving.

I glanced back when a really loud whistle pierced the noise. The man in the fedora was pointing at me. Crap, Johnny's bookie realized who I was, and knew there was a standing order to take me in if I was ever downtown alone.

The sound of the crowd was deepening, getting angrier. The rumor had already spread that the fight would be canceled. The announcer bellowed, "Unfortunately," but that was all I heard.

The crowd was on its feet screaming, "Fight, fight, fight."

I kicked something with my foot. It was a ball cap. I picked it up and put it on.

I burst through the exit doors into the main lobby. The doors closed behind me, blocking out most of the noise. I concentrated on my watch. "Which way?"

The hands pointed me down a dead-end corridor. I hesitated for a minute, until another loud whistle sounded from behind the closed door.

I turned all the knobs as I went down the hall. The fourth one was unlocked. I ducked inside as the door to the arena flew open. I closed my eyes and sent my presence back out into the corridor.

The man in the fedora just cleared the door. Another heavyset guy was with him. He let the doors slam, shutting out the noise. "Where did she go?"

Fedora shook his head. "She just disappeared."

The other man looked right at my presence but couldn't see me.

"She didn't go down there," Fedora said. "It's a dead end."

"Well, she didn't disappear," the other man argued.

Fedora took out his cell phone. "Vinnie just texted me. They're not going to cancel the fight."

"Good, because we took way too many 'Wagner's not going to win' bets for the fight to be canceled."

"You got that right."

"I'll text dispatch," he said, as if these guys were really cops. "Let them know she's been spotted."

"Yeah, she can be someone else's problem tonight. Let's go."

With one more glance down the empty corridor, they both went back into the arena.

I waited for the doors to close, then opened my eyes. The quads could try again tonight if they didn't cancel the fight. I glanced around. I was in a room full of computers, similar to the server room at the office. This one was not as high-tech and definitely lacking in security.

All the servers had labels. Some were half curled up on the end. One read "Scoreboard", another read "Tickets." Only one was re-taped half a dozen times. I grinned when I read the label: "Do not turn off or you will get fired."

I reached around to the back of the computer and pulled the power plug. The computer immediately powered down, which caused a chain reaction with every computer in the room. One by one, they all started shutting off.

I left the server room and headed back to the lobby. A clamor of footsteps rushed down a set of stairs to the right just before two men burst through a door a few feet ahead of me. The sign above the door read Control Booth with an arrow pointing up.

The men ran past me, not even looking my way. "Oh, shit," the first guy cursed.

"Time to go," I said to the watch. The hands spun around, then pointed toward the nearest exit.

Two seconds later, the building shut down—every light went dark and every sound went quiet. The main doors to the arena flew open. A few gasps sounded, and a brief murmur of panic until the emergency lights clicked on. Then all hell broke loose. I didn't wait around to see the chaos. I needed to get out of there and get back to the company. It was time to see The Boss.

I made it to the street before anyone else was out of the arena. It wasn't long, however, before throngs of people were pushing their way out the glass doors. Loud cracks and crashes happened as more than one pane shattered. The paper hadn't mentioned anything about a high body count. I hoped everyone made it out safely. I hurried across the street and headed for a taxi. Once I got back to the office, the motor pool manager would pay the cab fare.

The Boss isn't at the office, the voice said.

"What?" I said, then remembered I was talking to myself. I stopped for a minute. I checked my watch. It was a little after six on Saturday night, but he was always there late.

If he's not at the office, smarty pants, where is he?

There was a pause, then the voice said, *the Lux Hotel.*

I remembered. He had a standing meeting on the first Saturday of every month at the Lux. It was on his calendar. I could see the image in my head, clear as day.

I eyed my watch. "Take me to the Lux."

CHAPTER 18

I was ahead of the foot traffic of fans from the fight, walking alone on mostly deserted streets. Almost every business was closed. No one could compete with Fight Night. A few bars had signs on the doors that read 'Open after the fight', but like everything else, they were still closed.

I was shivering. The cocktail dress did nothing to keep me warm. I was hungry too, and tired. At least my feet weren't hurting. I trudged on for another twenty minutes before finally seeing some signs of life. The Lux was busy with activity. There were several cars waiting for a valet, with more than a few vehicles honking their horns. With the unexpected cancellation, the hotel was short staffed. Everyone was scrambling, and no one was happy.

I kept an eye on the watch. I expected the hands to lead me into the lobby, but instead I was directed to a dark alley down the side of the hotel. I hesitated for a moment, but the watch hadn't steered me wrong yet. The face lit up as I left the sidewalk, and several doors had lights overhead that gave off enough illumination I didn't trip over debris.

I followed the watch's directions toward an alcove. As I got closer, I could clearly see the three or four steps that led to a weathered door. I took the stairs down and tried the door. The knob wouldn't turn, but based on the shadow cast by the light, it was obvious the connection wasn't flush.

I yanked on the knob. The door budged an inch so I stepped

back to access. The top part of the door was protruding more than the bottom. I took hold of the knob with my left hand and pushed the top with my right. With a firm back and forth motion, I wiggled the door loose. I walked through a few cobwebs into a cluttered room that had been long forgotten. The only light came from under the door on the far side.

I banged my knee twice as I made my way across. I closed my eyes and stepped outside my body. I blinked to the hall. A dozen cleaning carts lined one side of the corridor. They were parked between small closets that ran the length. I opened my eyes when I didn't see anything or anyone.

I rested my ear against the door, one last check before I slipped out. The watch pointed right. I'd only taken a few steps when I heard approaching footsteps.

I ducked into one of the closets and shut the door. A door near me creaked, followed by someone wheeling out a squeaky mop bucket. I peered around the closet, hoping they didn't need anything. The room was dark, but light coming from under the door illuminated stacks of fabric. I ran my hand over a few. They were too uneven to be sheets. Uniforms, I guessed. I listened as the squeaky bucket passed by, then waited until the sound was so faint I could barely hear it.

I had my hand on the doorknob when it occurred to me that I would be a lot less conspicuous in one of the uniforms. The blue party dress was cold and would standout below stairs. I needed to blend in. I paused for a second to make sure all was still quiet, then I switched on the lights. Quickly, I scanned the garments and selected a set of maintenance coveralls, mainly because they would be warmer than a maid's uniform, and I didn't think a guest would stop a maintenance worker for help.

I slipped out of the dress and hid it back behind the folded uniforms, then shimmied into the coveralls and stuffed my hair beneath the ball cap I'd found at the arena. I needed to keep a low profile, and I hoped this would do it.

I flipped off the light and closed my eyes. The hallway was still clear. I left the closet, but froze when I realized one of the carts up ahead was moving. I didn't see anyone at first, but then I spotted the top of a head. A maid was crouched down, refilling her cart with tiny bottles of shampoo and conditioner. I spotted her key card lying on top. Quietly, I shut the door to the uniform closet and headed down the hall. Without pausing or making a sound, I snatched her key card.

I checked the watch and followed it to a service elevator. When I pressed the call button, the doors immediately popped open. The Lux was a big hotel. With forty-three floors to choose from, I had no idea where to begin. Checking every floor wasn't an option. I concentrated on the watch, but it didn't do anything.

"Which one?" I finally said, but still nothing.

I spotted the door to the stairwell. I really hoped the watch wasn't expecting me to take the stairs. I focused again, and this time the hand pointed toward the buttons. I moved closer, and the hands started spinning then slowed as I passed each button. The big hand pointed away until I reached thirteen. Ignoring the irony, I swiped the key card and stabbed the circle.

It only took a few seconds for the elevator to reach the thirteenth floor. I followed the watch's directions, which stopped me in front of room 1313. Had I not been so tired, I would have laughed.

My journey was about to end. The Boss would handle the situation. He'd call Quaid. They'd sort everything out. Junior wouldn't die. I wouldn't belong to Mace. I'd get to go back to my crappy life.

One that would be even crappier without Jack.

I dismissed those thoughts. I was still conflicted about his true identity, but I knew he loved me. This wasn't just a job for him. But would The Boss even let me keep him? If he never wanted me happy—which I believed—he'd use this as an excuse to take Jack away.

I squared my shoulders. I couldn't show The Boss any weakness. He wasn't known for his patience, and I was sure he was going to be royally pissed that I was interrupting his meeting.

I started to swipe the key card but quickly decided it was better to knock.

"Yes," a *woman's* voice answered.

"Maintenance," I said, keeping my head down so she wouldn't see my face through the peephole.

"Just a minute, please."

A few seconds later, a tall woman dressed in white opened the door. She wore a large hat swathed in a veil that made her resemble a beekeeper. Her perfume had a light, sweet smell to it. The scent reminded me of someone, but I couldn't remember who, and oddly, the voice hadn't helped. She wasn't who I was expecting to find in The Boss's room. For a minute I was speechless.

"Yes?" she finally prompted.

"Um," I said, finding my voice. "I'm looking for...Conrad...Bosh." I assumed she knew him by his human name, but why I decided that I wasn't sure.

She chuckled. "Sorry, you just missed him."

I dropped my shoulders. I was so tired. I wanted—needed—to find him. I wasn't going to make it much longer at this pace.

"Are you okay?" she asked. "You look ill."

I raised my head. "I'm fine," I lied. "I just haven't eaten much today." Her perfume seemed so familiar. She must have been in the office before. Although I think I would have remembered a veiled woman in white. "I really need to find him."

"Wait here," she said.

She dashed back into the room and returned with two dinner rolls and a bottle of orange juice. I shook my head, but I would have given almost anything for those rolls.

She held out the rolls. "They're cold now, but you look like you need them."

I was starving. I took them. "Thank you, miss..."

"You'll find *The Boss* downstairs in the theater, but he's not alone—you'll need to wait for him to finish," she said.

My mouth was still gaping when she closed the door. She called him The Boss—not Conrad. Who was she? Not now. It didn't matter. I headed for the elevator.

As I went, I shoved the first roll into my mouth and ate it in two bites. I was halfway through the second one when I opened the juice and chugged it down. I finished off the second roll by the time the elevator dinged at my floor.

The car wasn't empty when it arrived. An old woman in a maid's uniform, with raven hair so dark it must be dyed, was already inside. Her expression seemed warm and friendly, but there was something cold about her eyes. I decided it was best not to stare. I didn't need anyone asking to see my ID.

"Are you coming, dear?" she asked.

I cautiously entered the elevator, and the door closed behind me. I studied the buttons, unsure how I'd figure out which one to press to get to the theater. I couldn't use the watch without making the maid suspicious.

"Do you need help, dear?"

I smiled. "Which floor is the theater on?"

"Three, but you can enter quietly through the balcony from four."

Her voice was light and airy, nothing like what I would expect from an old woman. Something was eerily familiar about her, but I decided it was best to stop thinking about her and get on with the task at hand. Three was already selected. I swiped my card and pressed four, then slid against the back wall.

Another employee got on and off before we reached the fourth floor. I looked back at the old woman. She winked and pointed toward the right as the doors closed. A chill ran down my spine. I wasn't sure what it was about her, but I hoped I wouldn't run into her again.

I followed the corridor to a small door tucked into a corner. Ignoring the sign that said 'Employees Only', I quietly opened the door and found myself in a narrow hallway behind the theater's balcony boxes. The guests would use this passage to enter their box; however, they would have to come up the stairs from the main entrance on three, not sneak in through the back.

I could hear voices, but not clearly. I crouched down and crept into the box closest to me. Peeking over the railing, I was shocked to see the two men who had most impacted my life. The Boss was standing there with his hands in his pockets. His suit was as impeccable as always if not a bit rumpled—his hair still wet from a shower. The other man was someone I didn't think I'd ever see again—Mr. Harrison, my old foster care caseworker. He was as I remembered, dull and average, but not as underpaid. His suit was clearly several steps up from his days as my caseworker.

Before I could fully absorb the sight of the two men before me, the doors at the back of the theater opened. I ducked down again to make sure no one saw me.

"Good evening, Sister," The Boss said.

Sister!

"Yes, Sister, it is good to see you looking so well," Mr. Harrison said.

I peered over the railing again. Who were they both calling sister?

My heart skipped a beat. Mab. She floated down the aisle

toward them, her delicate dress draped over her statuesque body as if she were an ethereal angel. A cold shiver passed through me as I observed her. I couldn't believe how wrong I'd been about her connection to the quads. She wasn't their pagan mother's sister. She was related to their father, The Boss.

The Demon King and the Pagan Queen were siblings? And Mr. Harrison, how did he fit? *Oh my god, no.* He couldn't be the Druid King. How was that even possible? I'd trusted so few people in my life I could count them on one hand. Three fingers: Jack, Omar, and Mr. Harrison.

I guess I shouldn't have been that surprised I was fooled on all counts. My boyfriend was really a servant of the Demon King, my caseworker was most likely the Druid King himself, and Omar knew more about me and my blood than I did.

I ducked as Mab glanced at the box where I hid. She'd sensed my presence easily enough. I'm sure she knew I was here in the flesh. I considered sneaking out the way I'd come in, but I needed to see The Boss. I'd deal with the fallout if she decided to rat me out. I was running out of options, and clearly, there was more going on here than I knew.

"Brothers," Mab said. "It's good to see you both again so soon."

Okay, so she wasn't going to rat me out. I took a chance and spied over the railing.

Mab stared at The Boss. "How are your children doing?"

"You're the one who called the meeting, Sister," The Boss said, his lips tight and teeth ground together. He was clearly pissed to be here. And from the looks of it, with the woman upstairs in his room, I could guess what this meeting had interrupted. "I assumed you would be the one to tell me," he finished.

"I did not call the meeting to discuss any of your children," she replied. "I was merely being polite. I have come to discuss the girl."

Mab's lips turned up in a cruel smile. *Oh, shit. She was talking about me.*

The Boss pulled his hands from his pockets and clasped them in front of his body. He narrowed his eyes at her. Then he glanced over at Mr. Harrison.

"What is your claim this time?" Mr. Harrison asked.

This time?

"She has entered my realm uninvited."

Mr. Harrison and The Boss stared at each other but didn't say anything. Mab's confident grin didn't waver.

The Boss straightened, standing more erect. "When?"

"Time is not always as it seems," she said smugly.

I rolled my eyes. The *me* from this time hadn't yet been to Purgatory. Maybe The Boss would know.

"Why?" he asked.

Or maybe not.

"Something to do with your four, I suspect. It is so hard to keep track."

"Did she intend to enter your realm?"

Mab waved a slender hand, dismissing his question. "We both know that isn't relevant. The rules are clear. I can claim her for breaking the rule and entering my realm, if I choose."

What rule? The uninvited rule? But that would just let her kill me, right? Was there another rule I didn't know about? A rule that gave her the right to claim me?

The Boss's face hardened. He didn't seem pleased with her answers. Although it didn't seem to me he was putting up much of a fight.

"Harry," she said, then paused.

Harry... Mr. Harrison was Harry—the Godfather. I'd forgotten. The Druid King was the Godfather.

"What a droll name you're using these days, Brother," Mab continued. "You'll confirm my right to the girl."

Mr. Harrison eyed The Boss and shrugged. "She has a claim—if she wants her." He lifted a brow at Mab. "You're one to talk. You haven't changed your name since Shakespeare used it in one of his plays. And dark hair on you has never been very becoming."

She laughed. "Classic is still better than *Harry*, Harry. I'm a pagan no matter my hair color, I am always becoming."

Oh my god, these were the people screwing with my life— bickering like children.

Addressing Mab, The Boss interrupted, "Why do you want her? She's no different from the rest."

There was the protector I'd always known. I was glad to know at least one person didn't think I was special.

Mab smiled at The Boss. "She is your weakness, Brother."

The Boss's face darkened with rage. "Hardly," he growled.

Mab's lips curved up in a wicked grin. "And we *all* know she is different from the rest."

Who were the rest?

"You can't control fate by controlling her," Mr. Harrison added.

Mab ignored him, focusing on The Boss. "There is one who will be unhappy if you lose her. Do tell, Brother, is she still in the hotel or have you already sent her away?"

His eyes flashed red, and he glared at her, teeth bared. "That deal has already been made," he said. "We will speak of it no longer."

"It may have been a mistake," Mr. Harrison intervened, stepping between them, "but Melinda is off-limits. What do you really want?"

I stopped listening at the word "Melinda." They were talking about her—my mother. I sank down to the floor with my back against the box.

The perfume, the voice said.

Images flashed in my head. Images of a blurry figure surrounded by a light beautiful fragrance. How could I have forgotten?

The angelic beekeeper—the woman in 1313—was my mother. The only person who'd ever loved me.

Not caring if they heard me, I scurried out of the box. I bolted down the hall toward the service elevator. It seemed to take forever to get to the thirteenth floor. I almost ran into a maid as I rushed out. Dodging her, I headed toward the room. I rounded the corner, then stopped dead in my tracks.

Mace was standing outside the door of 1313, tapping on the screen of his phone.

"No," I whispered.

His head raised. Smiling, he returned his phone to his pocket. His lip curled up on one side. "Everything," he said, raising one eyebrow in smug satisfaction, nodding toward the hotel room.

No, no, no. I shook my head. He couldn't have her. Not her. The rage in me grew. A fire at the pit of my stomach churned. I wanted to kill him.

A tingling sensation started at my wrist. My chest constricted, and my breathing became labored. Hard knots tightened in my stomach, and a hot pressure pushed against my eyes. It was happening again. It was similar to the pain I'd felt when he showed me that Jack was a demon.

Tiny crackles of current sparked off my watch. White wisps of electricity were swirling around the band, the action identical to what it had done with the bracelet.

Mace's eyes widened as the pressure increased against my eyes. I assumed they were flashing green again, but I had no way to know.

The cart is new, the voice said.

What? I looked behind him. There was a maid's cart outside my mother's room. She'd been dressed and ready to leave before. The maid was cleaning—my mother was gone. Thank God. Mace didn't have her.

The pressure eased, and the sparks dissipated.

His gaze followed mine to the cart. He shrugged. "Next time."

He would never take her. The Boss wouldn't let that happen.

"I need a way out," I said to the watch, not that I believed it held the power. I was now sure the power came from within, but I had no clue how to use it. The Keeper said I was bound by Winter, but the watch somehow let me channel my power—as crazy as that seemed.

I caught sight of the billowing drapes before I sensed the cool air against my face.

You'll die, the voice warned.

That doesn't sound like a memory. What are you really?

The voice stayed quiet.

I hadn't noticed the window until I'd asked for a way out. Maybe I had too much faith in my power. Maybe I wanted another visit with Death.

I glanced at the window again, but turned back when Mace spoke.

"Have you learned to fly, Claire," he asked, his lip curled in that gorgeous sneer.

I cocked one of my eyebrows. "We're about to find out."

I spun on my heel and ran. I wasn't returning to his care. I'd die before I let that happen. He'd already taken everything—Jack. There was nothing left if I couldn't have my freedom. Thirteenth floor or not, I had nothing to lose.

"Don't let me die," I said to the watch as the cool air hit my face.

CHAPTER 19

I dove through the window as if I were jumping through a ring of fire. I spread my arms out wide after I cleared the windowsill. For a second, I was suspended in a perfect swan dive over one of the busiest streets in Underworld. I was free.

At that moment, I didn't actually care what happened—but magic doesn't always work the way you expect it to—and I guess fate really did have bigger plans for me.

I hadn't been very specific in my instructions. Don't let me die and give me a soft landing was what I should have said. Instead, in the blink of an eye, I was skidding, arms first, onto the roof of the building across the street. I was glad I had chosen the maintenance coveralls, or I would have had cuts and bruises all over. Instead, I wound up with a bruised elbow and two scraped knees—it could have been worse.

I stood on wobbly legs. I went to the edge and looked over. I couldn't really believe the jump had worked. For a second, I thought Mr. Harrison was standing on the street in front of the hotel, but whoever it was disappeared before I could be sure. I lifted my gaze to the window across the way and saw Mace.

Shock and fury turned his face red. "You can't hide from me," he mouthed, retrieving one of the Hell shackles from his pocket.

"Oh yeah?" I challenged. "Watch me." I snapped my fingers, then whispered, "Hide me," to the watch.

My head was swimming so I shut my eyes to shake the lightheadedness. My presence pulled from my body. I ignored the fatigue and prayed my power would hide me.

I stood there watching my body. *Please work.*

I breathed a sigh of relief when I began to fade. One minute I was there, the next I was gone.

"No," Mace mouthed, astonished.

As if the heat were draining out of my body, I was cold and began to shiver. My breathing became labored, and I watched in horror as my shield started failing. I started flickering back into visibility, and there was nothing I could do to stop it.

I opened my eyes just as I fell to my knees, then passed out.

~ # ~

I ached. I hurt. I could barely move. Not dead. I was too miserable to be dead. Exhausted, mentally and physically drained, but not dead. Death would have been easier.

My mother. I'd seen her—sort of. She'd called him The Boss, not Conrad. Did that mean anything? Did I mean anything?

She fed you, the voice said.

I remembered the rolls and the orange juice. The voice was being helpful again. My stomach grumbled. She didn't tell me who she was. She hid her identity. Were all first-Saturday-of-every-month meetings with her at the hotel?

Don't, I thought before the voice could argue. *There's nothing else to remember.*

I opened my eyes. The room was dark, but not pitch black. I failed to sit up on the first two attempts. On the third, I took a few deep breaths then swung my legs off the brick they called a cot. I closed my eyes again so I wouldn't pass out or throw up from the spinning room. I was so tired and exhausted my muscles shook from the exertion. After a few minutes, my breathing slowed. I opened my eyes again.

I was propped against the bars of the cell. I guess my days of getting my own room were over. As my eyes adjusted, I realized I was no longer wearing the maintenance coveralls. Someone had cleaned me up and changed my clothes. I was dressed in a green loose fitting shirt and pants, hospital scrubs or prison uniform, take your pick. I took stock of everything else. No shoes or socks—no watch!

I studied my bare wrist. I had been wishing I could get the watch off for over five years. Now that it was gone I wanted it back. How the hell did they remove it? I was sure no one, except maybe The Boss, could remove it. And who were they? Mace? He'd seen me on the rooftop. This must be another of his prisons. It was so quiet. I was isolated and alone, as if he'd left me here to die. If this was Mace's doing, I'm sure I wouldn't be that lucky.

Unlike the basement at the bungalow, this room resembled an actual prison. The concrete room was filled with four identical cells, with no separation from one to the next. The bars I was leaning against were the bars separating the cell next door. The walls beyond the cells were bare unpainted concrete, which made the room feel cold. A flight of stairs rose out of sight, but that was it—no door or windows.

The other cells were empty. There was a blanket rumpled on the floor, and the cot was slightly askew in the cell on the far end. The room also had a faint musky-sweaty scent as if someone had recently spent some time down here. Good to know this was an active prison.

I closed my eyes, to step outside my body, but nothing happened. There was no spark of power. Nothing that made me even think it was possible. I wasn't sure I'd ever felt more human than I did right now. Funny how I didn't like it.

I heaved myself to a sitting position away from the bars. I wanted to stand—make sure the door was locked, but with the way I felt, I was lucky to sit-up on my own. Standing wasn't going to happen.

There was a small crate beside the cot. A note leaned against a carton of something. I'd seen that type of tetra-pak packaging before on fancy protein energy drinks, but this one, with its bold red and blue design, didn't look familiar. With effort, I picked up the note: "Drink this, you need your strength."

Yeah, right. With my luck, this would shrink me like Alice in Wonderland. *No thanks.*

You could walk through the bars if it does, the voice said.

Cute. I rolled my eyes. *Stop talking to me.*

The note slipped out of my hand and landed upside down on the cot. This side said: "You won't fully recover without it." I tried to laugh, but it was a pathetic attempt seeing as how I could barely keep my eyes open.

After another five minutes, when sitting was becoming an issue, I picked up the carton and read the label: Berry Blast. It didn't sound very appetizing to me, and the big blue and red graphics, which were maybe supposed to be a blueberry and a strawberry, just looked weird. Food shouldn't look like expressionist art. I pried open the lid and took a sniff then I couldn't close it fast enough. It smelled awful. Just as I stretched to put it back on the crate, my stomach grumbled loudly. I was starving, but I wasn't sure Berry Blast was the answer. Of course, it was the only option. I reopened the carton, held my nose, and drank.

Just for the record, *Berry Blast sucks*.

I twisted the top back onto the carton and returned it to the crate.

There was nothing instant about Berry Blast, and sitting up wasn't accomplishing much. I laid back down on the cot and closed my eyes.

My stomach roiled, but I didn't throw up. However, I did have a really sudden need to stand, which I thought was impossible considering how tired and drained I was. I braced myself for the effort of swinging my legs over the side of the cot. I was surprised when the motion practically propelled me to a standing position. I grabbed the bars to steady myself. My head was dizzy from the sudden movement, but I could stand on my own.

Holy shit, *Berry Blast rocks*!

I paced around the cell with a gnawing restlessness in my gut. My heart was pounding, my hands shaking. Lying in the bed wasn't an option. I had to keep moving around. It was like a caffeine rush times ten. I wanted to climb the walls—literally. Clearly, I had underestimated the power of Berry Blast.

I checked the cell door for the twentieth time. It was still locked. I tried to step outside my body now that my energy returned and I didn't feel like death, but I was too wired to keep my eyes closed. I stopped trying after noticing that every square inch of the cement walls were covered by invisible glyphs. I couldn't see them now, but the green glow was crystal clear to my presence. Like the basement in Mace's bungalow, this place was warded to keep people in. The bars were for show.

After thirty minutes of pacing, the door at the top of the stairs opened. I squinted when the lights flipped on, but my eyes adjusted quickly.

The wooden steps creaked under his weight. My heart thudded. I was sure Mace was ready to punish me for leaving without permission and screwing up his attempt to kill Junior. I expected to feel the tingle of his mark, but nothing was there. He slowly descended the stairs into view.

Only it wasn't Mace.

It was Mr. Harrison—Harry—the Godfather—the Druid King.

He'd been my protector as a child. There was an amber glint that ran across his eyes now, but that was the only difference. He had the same amount of gray hair as before, although I'd never thought it suited him. He was exactly as I remembered: taller than average, a nondescript face, and light brown hair. A druid.

The Druid, I supposed.

Of course, I'd never really met the man in front of me. There was no Mr. Harrison.

He gave me a steady look but didn't immediately speak. I suspected he didn't know what to say. He didn't know I already knew who he was—who he really was.

We both stood there staring at the other. I had trusted this man. He was the one person I considered trying to contact when The Boss took me, but I couldn't do that to him. The Boss made the rules very clear. No one could know whom I really worked for. What sucked now was that I was sure Mr. Harrison had always known what happened. Hell, he probably had his boys pick me up and deliver me to The Boss.

At least, I had my answer as to why he wasn't there five years ago. Why he hadn't ridden in on a white horse and saved the day? I blinked back the tears that threatened.

Mr. Harrison grew solemn. "Claire... There is a lot you don't understand."

"Harry." I tilted my head. "You don't mind if I call you Harry, right? Or should I remain formal? Mr. Harrison? The Druid King seems a bit arrogant, but hey, whatever you want."

He smiled. "Harry will do."

"So, did someone call the police? Did you come to save me again?" I asked sarcastically.

"Claire—"

I held up my hand. "Don't." I didn't want to hear his excuses. "I need to speak to the Demon King. Can you take me to him?"

His gaze slid to the side. Frowning, he said, "You don't belong to him anymore."

"Anymore? Did I ever? What claim did he make when you

handed me over at sixteen? Did you get any proof? Did you get any proof from her? Am I just some prize you people collect and pass around? Is it her turn?"

He opened his mouth—closed it. Opened it again. "Claire, you're—" He paused.

"Different from the rest?"

His eyebrows rose, then dropped as if he were considering something. After a few seconds, he said, "You were there? At the meeting?"

"Yes."

"How? We should have sensed you," he said. "And how did you understand us?"

I had no reason to hide the truth. I suspected Mab made it all possible, but I had no proof. I shrugged. "I have no idea, and I heard English."

His eyes narrowed as if he didn't believe me. After a moment, he looked away. "Interesting," he finally said. "She wanted you to hear us—but why?"

"Who the hell knows? She's your sister. Why don't you ask her?"

His lip curled into an amused grin.

"How can you do this to me?" I asked. "Give me to her? Or him? Or even keep me here at all? What is so different about me that I need to be owned by one of you?"

"Mab is using you to get what she wants from our brother. She will throw you back once she has it."

Harry was lying. He couldn't know what Mab would do. She'd have no reason to give me back. According to her, this wasn't her first claim. Obviously, she wanted me, but why? "You don't know that, and I don't even think you believe it." I called his bluff. "Of course, who am I kidding? Why would the Druid King—the most feared of the royals—care?"

Harry's mouth twitched. "He will save you if he can."

"Right," I drawled. "Don't hold it against me if I don't consider that money in the bank."

"Claire—"

"So that's it. You're going to hand me over to Mab and hope she loses interest, or The Boss saves me?"

"It's the law."

"The law. Unbelievable."

"Claire—"

"Okay, fine, the law," I said, making the quote mark gesture. "I don't understand why *you* have to do it. Why not just let me walk out of here? Let her find me herself?"

"Because he didn't bring you here." Mace's voice came from the top of the stairs as I felt the tingle of proximity affecting his mark.

I backed away from the cell door, almost tripping over the crate.

"Hello, Uncle," Mace said, entering the basement. "Is she well enough to travel now?"

Harry's lips pressed together briefly before he answered. "She is."

Mace appeared calm, which was its own joke. I prevented him from killing Junior. He failed because of me, and Mab didn't strike me as a person who liked failure.

"Thank you, Uncle," Mace said, nodding at Harry.

Harry inclined his head.

"Wait," I said before he could leave. "You can't just leave me with him."

Harry eyed me but spoke to Mace. "I have no claim, as you know, Nephew, but I should remind you that my sister expects her property returned undamaged."

Mace pasted a tight smile on his face. "Yes, Uncle. You have no claim. Thank you, again for the hospitality of allowing me to use your residence."

"Of course, Nephew." Harry's nostrils flared. His cold dark eyes glowed with power.

Mace bowed his head and kept it lowered. "Thank you, sir," he said, this time sincerely. "I acknowledge your advice. I will not damage Aunt Mab's property. I swear it."

Without another word, Harry turned away. The creak of the stairs echoed as he left the basement, leaving me alone with Mace.

Mace was livid when he faced me. Not that it would do me any good, but I stayed pressed against the back wall of the cell, as far away from the door and any open bars as possible.

He caught me with his will and moved me to the cell door. A frozen expression hardened his face, and the fake smile didn't reach his eyes. Extending his hand through the bars, he touched my cheek. "You shouldn't have interfered."

He caught my face when I tried to look away and studied me. After a moment, his face changed. Maybe he saw something in my gaze—something that made a smile touch his eyes.

Sliding his hand around to the back of my neck, he pressed me flush with the bars then laid his other hand on my stomach. "I'm going to enjoy taking this away from you," he said with a wicked grin.

I glanced down at his hand, at how he cupped my belly. "No. You're lying."

He chanted a few words of Demon, I think, and a white-hot pain shot through my middle. As the energy flowed, it danced around inside me until it coalesced on something deep within my abdomen. I cried out when it cradled the tiny ball within.

I fell to the floor when he released me and curled into a ball. My stomach thrummed as if he'd sucker-punched me, but it was worse than that. I wrapped my arms around my waist and willed myself to stop shaking.

"You'll have nothing of his. Not unless I allow it."

I couldn't be pregnant, but if I was, had he just taken it? "You bastard. I don't believe you. And forget about killing Junior. I saw Quaid at the fight. You'll never get to him now."

Mace's smirk fell. Technically, everything I'd said was true. I had seen Quaid at the fight; I just never got the chance to talk to him.

After a few seconds, Mace roared with laughter. "That's good, Claire," he said chortling. "Some of it's even true, but unlike the baby, which you'll have to wait a few weeks to confirm, I can prove you wrong now about Quaid."

Still amused, he took out his phone and typed a few words, then dropped it back in his pocket.

Ignoring him, I inspected my stomach. He said it would take a few weeks to confirm, which meant he hadn't removed it…if it was real. I pushed myself off the floor. The pain had subsided, but I could still feel the knot in my stomach.

I heard movement from the top of the stairs. Heavy clomps came down at a quick clip. My mouth fell open.

"It was a good lie, Claire," Mace said, turning to face our guest. "Do tell me which part was really true."

I stood there gaping at the last man I ever thought would betray The Boss. Quaid—The Boss's right-hand man, sauntered in, as if he owned the place.

"Why?" I snarled at him.

"You look like hell, Claire," Quaid said, his grin more sneer than smile. He'd looked like one of the security team at the fight. Now he was dressed in a black on black suit, his short dark hair in a perfect military cut—his usual office look.

"Why?"

His lips dropped on one side, leaving a lopsided smirk. "I've got my reasons. Let's just say he's got it coming."

"Apparently," Mace interjected, "Junior killed his beloved. A thousand years ago, I believe you said."

Quaid scowled at Mace. All humor was gone from his face.

"I have my doubts, of course, but others were convinced. Not that you—"

"I cleared security out of the way," Quaid said. "This is what we agreed I'd do. You had your chance and blew it. The seer who came to me didn't tell me where he saw the body—just that he saw Junior dead."

Oh? "What seer?"

"Not Omar."

"He's not—" I cleared my throat when the spell wouldn't let me say he's not the only one I know.

"What's wrong with you?" Quaid asked.

"She does that a lot," Mace answered for me.

Quaid snorted.

"What's so funny?"

"Nothing. Is that all you need? I have things to do."

"You are in this until the end. You will accompany us to see Aunt Mab."

Already shaking his head, Quaid started to speak.

"It's not a request. The queen has commanded it."

Quaid glared at me as if I had something to do with his problems.

"This is all you, big guy," I said. He was the one going against The Boss.

"Leave," Quaid spat at Mace. "I wish to speak to Claire alone."

"No."

"Why? Are you afraid she'll beg me...to save her?"

"She's mine," Mace shouted. "My influence here is limited, but I'll have complete control in Purgatory."

Complete control. What the hell did that mean?

Quaid's jaw tightened.

"She has sworn her allegiance to me. A bond with a pagan over Pagan cake is almost impossible to break."

Quaid eyed me. "I was under the impression she belongs to Mab now."

The cords in Mace's neck tightened. "She will give her to me as a gift," he said confidently.

Quaid didn't hide his amusement.

Mace was a fool. I had no idea why exactly, but Mab would never give me up.

He scowled at Quaid. "You're walking a fine line," he growled. "If my father knew—"

"If your father knew you were trying to kill Junior," Quaid interrupted, "he would not be pleased."

"You should not be too quick to presume you're in Mab's favor," Mace warned.

"I would suggest you take your own advice." Quaid's tone was smug.

Mace was silent for a moment, but the anger in his eyes was clear. I don't think Quaid would have been so smug if he were an ordinary demon. His size was impressive, but hellspawn were more powerful than demons. Quaid, however, was protected from hellspawn vengeance by very strong spells given to him by The Boss. He would not have been very effective otherwise.

Mace had no choice but to back down. "Talk all you want, she will be mine." He sneered at me before leaving the basement.

Quaid stayed behind although I had no idea what he'd want to discuss.

"Why are you here? I don't believe that bullshit story about your beloved anymore than Mace."

Quaid shrugged. "I have my reasons."

"Good for you. Now if you aren't going to get me out of here, leave. I'm not in the mood."

I dropped back onto the cot, lying flat and closing my eyes. I studied him with my presence. He glanced back toward the stairs and lifted his hand as if he were going to open the door. He lowered it, shaking his head.

"Which devil are you really working for?" I asked him, hoping it would prompt him as it had with Mace. He didn't seem to notice.

He turned to leave the basement, pausing before he reached the stairs. "What has happened must happen," he muttered then climbed and left.

What the hell was that?

CHAPTER 20

"Claire," a woman's voice said, but it didn't sound like it came from a person. It sounded ethereal, if ethereal had a tone. "Claire," it called again, and this time I opened my eyes.

I wasn't in the cell in the basement anymore. Weightless, I was floating. Other than the voice, there was no noise in this place, only waves of glittery light cutting through the darkness.

"Who's there?" I asked.

The pressure of the light weighed on me as if I walked out of an air-conditioned room into a hot, humid summer day. But the temperature wasn't hot. It wasn't anything but an empty, insubstantial nothingness to float in.

"A friend," the woman said.

"Where are we? Who are you?"

I heard a small laugh, then she said, "Somewhere in your head, I suppose."

What? "Who are you?"

"You won't let me talk anymore. I'm lonely."

Was this the voice? I took a calming breath. "Okay, just so I'm clear. You're the voice?"

"I have a name."

"No, you don't. You're my subconscious that was spelled to not let me forget. You don't have a name." I paused for a beat, then added, "Only crazy people give the voices in their head names."

"It's Jayne."

"I'm not calling you Jayne…I can't believe my inner voice thinks it has a name."

"I'm not a result of the spell, but the spell did unlock me. You're not crazy."

"Right, the voice in my head assures me I'm not crazy." I rubbed my eyes. "This is a nightmare, and I need to wake up."

"I needed to tell you something, but you weren't listening," the voice admonished. "This was the only thing I could think of to get your attention."

If I stop listening, will it go away?

"No."

Ugh. The voice can read my mind. "Fine, what?"

"You must not eat or drink anything while you're in Purgatory."

"Why not?"

"It will give her too much control."

"Who, Mab?" But instead of getting an answer, I was sinking away from the darkness. I fought to stay in the void, but nothing worked. "Wait," I shouted.

"For what?" Harry asked.

My eyes shot open. He was standing outside the cell, studying me.

I sat up on the cot, dropping my legs over the side. I must have fallen asleep after Quaid left. "Nothing, just a bad dream," I said. Either that or I'm crazy and there really was a voice in my head named Jayne.

There was a new power shake sitting on the crate. I would have rather had real food, but another healing boost wouldn't hurt. The effects were more immediate this time. I was feeling them before I'd finished half the carton.

"Mace—the quads—are trying to kill Junior," I said before anyone could interrupt us again. I couldn't give him any of the specifics, but I could tell him what they planned.

Harry's expression didn't change.

"I guess that's not your problem," I said. Again, no reaction. I shook my head.

"Don't try that jump again," he warned. "I might not be there to save you next time."

I glared at him. It had been him outside the hotel, and now he wanted gratitude. "Don't pretend to care. I didn't ask you to save me this time."

His body stiffened, and his eyes flashed a wicked amber glow.

I still thought of him as Mr. Harrison, which was stupid. He was the Druid King, and I'd do well to remember that.

He took a deep breath. "I thought you might want this back before you leave." He held up my watch.

My watch! I pushed myself off the cot and crossed to the door.

He pulled it back. "Don't use this in Mab's presence. She'll sense it and take it from you." He extended it again.

"Okay." I took the watch and put it back on. It morphed into a black military-issue, ladies' watch. Very utilitarian—practical—something to go perfectly with my standard-issue prison scrubs. I'd wanted this thing off for years, now I was relieved to have it back. "How did you get it off?"

"It's one of mine," he said. "I created it for you."

Created it for me? "But I got this at the company."

He arched an eyebrow. "Are you sure about that?"

I thought back to the day I'd been kidnapped off the street. If it had been the mob—Harry's boys—they could have put it on me before delivering me to The Boss. I could have been wearing it when I arrived. I was unconscious—who knows when I actually got the watch.

"Okay, fine. I don't know where I got it, but why did you take it off?"

"The watch lets you access your power. When you jumped, you used too much of it and almost died," he said. "I had to remove it so you could heal."

"The Keeper said it was my power—"

"The Keeper?" Harry's expression hardened. "You've spoken to the Keeper? When?"

"Why do you care?"

My conversation with the Keeper ran through my head. She'd talked of the seasons. I'd decided The Boss was Summer. Harry's his opposite, right? Would that mean Harry was Winter? She hadn't declared Winter's sex, but Fall—the mysterious fourth realm—was a her, and Spring was a he. Mab wasn't hidden, so she couldn't be Fall and not Spring. She had to be Winter—which meant Harry had to be Spring.

Harry's pet? I let out a dry laugh. Better than Mab's, I suppose.

"Are you Spring?"

His brow wrinkled. Shoulders that had been relaxed before

were rigid.

"That makes total sense," I muttered, more to myself than him. "You really do pass me around. First you, then him, now her."

"You don't have all the facts," he said.

"Did you trap her—it—in the mirror?"

He became unnaturally still.

I took that to mean yes. "She called me your pet."

"It means nothing."

I snorted and sat back down on the cot. "Right."

After a long pause, he sighed and rubbed his forehead. His eyes were closed.

Regret or pity—did I care?

When he opened his eyes, Mr. Harrison's softer gaze met mine. "The power is yours, Claire, but—"

"I'm bound by Winter—yeah, I've seen the memo. Life sucks." Winter's blood will break the curse. Did he know that?

"Don't speak of things you don't understand," he warned.

I was sick of this cryptic bullshit. "Then explain. Make me understand."

Harry pursed his lips. "You're special—"

"Special," I shrieked, glaring at him. "I ask you to explain and you tell me I'm special! What am I really?"

"You're unique."

"Un-fucking-believable." I shook my head. "He switches out special for unique. Hallelujah, I'm getting answers now."

He rubbed the back of his neck.

I wasn't letting him off that easy. I wanted real answers. "Something's different about my blood," I prompted.

He stilled, but remained silent.

"The seers know about it," I continued, but he still said nothing. "What am I? What do they know?"

He stood there, impassive. This wasn't the man I knew. The man I'd known as a child would have answered me. He'd have explained—like always when I had questions.

I exhaled, thinking of the Keeper. She'd made it seem like they all had a hand in what I was or what I had become—not human. "Spring's pet. Bound by Winter. Protected by Summer. Screwed by Fall," I muttered.

Harry sucked in a sharp breath. His nostrils were flared—all passivity gone. I'd never seen him this angry. "You speak of fairytales and myths," he snarled.

"Fall is a fairytale?" I asked. "I must have missed that part in your book."

Harry's eyes flashed amber. "Speak of it no more."

"Then explain what makes me special. Why the Keeper's trapped and seers are so interested in my blood they seek proof of its existence."

Harry turned away from me, lips pressed together, as if he stopped himself from saying something.

"I'm not even human. Am I?"

He closed his eyes, pinching the bridge of his nose. After a minute, he started toward the door.

"Mr. Harrison, please tell me. Help me understand." I stood, rushing to the bars. "I trusted you once. At least explain to me why Mab wants me. What does it mean that I belong to her? How is this the second claim? It can't all be so bloody sacred."

His brows were drawn together when he faced me. He took a deep breath. "You were born with magic, which gave Mab the right to claim you at birth."

My eyebrows shot up. Born with magic? Claimed at birth? "How can she do that?"

Harry sighed. "It is our law. It is to maintain balance and prevent magic from being in the hands of humans."

"What kind of—"

"We will not debate its merit," he said, cutting me off.

"Okay—so why didn't she take me then? Did she want something else instead?" She must have gotten something to leave me alone. Although if the rule was to maintain balance, it seemed odd she had a choice at all.

"Hardly," he murmured, pushing his hand through his hair. "Nothing that simple, I'm afraid."

"What happened?"

"Bargains were struck. Sacrifices were made. You were spared your fate."

"Sacrifices?" I asked, thinking of what humans knew of druids, but Mab wasn't a druid, and I was fairly sure the sacrificing tendency of druids was urban legend. I pushed those thoughts out of my head. "Why now?"

"You broke the rules," he said, but offered no details.

"What rules?"

"You returned to Purgatory...uninvited."

"What? That's it. Just like that she can claim me?"

"Yes."

"How was I supposed to know this rule?"

Harry stared at me as if I were missing the obvious. "You were given the book."

"The fairytale book—the one that never got lost," I quipped. "That was my warning."

He nodded.

Unbelievable. My life hinged on a book I didn't know I needed to heed. I laughed and shook my head. *Un-freaking-believable.* "Next time, maybe a list. You know, something like, 'Things to Avoid. Number one is stay out of Purgatory, so the psycho sister of your ex-social worker doesn't drag your ass off to her realm to torture and maim you'. Something simple like that."

As if he'd seriously made note of my request, he inclined his head.

I gawked, slack-jawed, although I'm not sure why his attitude surprised me. "So that was the deal—not to break the rule. What was the sacrifice?"

"Your mother," he said.

Huh? "She died giving birth to me. Is that what you mean by sacrifice?"

"No."

"What happened to her?"

Harry seemed reluctant to tell me.

"You can't throw out that grenade, then refuse to tell me."

He dropped his gaze.

"Tell me. Please!"

Harry blew out an exacerbated sigh. "You were born with your power, and like all others, Mab took you to live in her realm. To be a pagan."

"Took me? How exactly?"

"You died."

"Er?" I choked for a minute, unable to draw air into my lungs. "If I died—how—" I didn't know how to ask the right question.

"My brother," Harry said. "He stole you from Death and returned you to Melinda."

Death—that's when I saw him the first time. When I was innocent.

Harry continued, "Mab retaliated by killing your mother, but it didn't end there."

Tears welled in my eyes. My mother was the sacrifice.

"Things had gotten out of hand," he said. "I was forced to intervene and resolve the issue to prevent war. I forced my siblings to compromise and stop their childish squabbles over one tiny human."

Ignoring his obvious jab at my insignificance, I asked, "The Boss was fighting because he loved my mother?"

"It would appear so."

"He would have gone to war for her?"

"Yes."

"Did she love him?" Part of me wanted Mace to be wrong.

"Very much. She still does."

I thought of the angelic beekeeper. "Is he my father?" I whispered, afraid the answer was going to be yes.

"Mab couldn't have claimed you if you'd been his," Harry answered.

His words caused some relief, but I would have rather heard him simply say no.

"What did Mab get?" She'd never walk away empty-handed.

"She would have gotten you had she not killed your mother. Instead, she was given the right to claim you in the future if you broke the rules by returning to Purgatory uninvited."

"Why did my mother hide herself from me in the hotel? I wouldn't have recognized her. And if she's able to visit the hotel—"

Harry held up his hand, stopping me. "She shields herself from everyone. Mab took her beauty before killing her, and she is not allowed to contact you."

"Part of the truce?"

He nodded.

"So, I've died. Good to know," I said, trying to push my thoughts from my mother. "But that doesn't explain my blood."

"Your power is in your blood. Your blood is unique. That is all I can say."

"Is that why Mab bound my powers?"

"She bound your powers to make you human. It was her concession for losing you."

"I changed things when I entered Purgatory? My powers started coming back. That's why it was forbidden?"

"One of the reasons."

"But the binding's not broken?"

"No, just weakened. The watch let you access some of the power, but the trip to Purgatory widened the gap. It may continue to expand over time, but it will never be broken. Part of you will always be human."

I thought of the Keeper's words. She'd said, "*Winter's blood would break the curse.*"

If the binding was the curse, which according to Harry couldn't be broken. How would Mab's blood change that? And why wouldn't Harry know her blood would have that effect? Of course, I had no clue how I'd get any of her blood or what I'd do with it once I had it.

"The seers know about my blood," I reminded him. "The blacksmith took a lot of it."

Harry's forehead wrinkled. "She shouldn't have been allowed to take any."

I shrugged. What did he expect me to do about it?

"Did you give it willingly?"

"Um—It's complicated."

He breathed out a frustrated sigh. I didn't care if he was angry. I wasn't willing to let Jack die.

Harry spun to leave.

"Wait," I said. "Why is it so important?"

He stopped. Glancing back, he said, "It's forbidden to discuss. Speak of it no more."

Forbidden? Harry's shoulders shifted. He was leaving.

"Was watching me your job while I was little?"

He ran his hand through his hair.

"Was it your job to save me from the Keeper? I seem to remember you saved me a lot." I studied my hands, not wanting to look at him. "But you never actually helped me." He'd always brought the police, rescued me from the latest bad foster situation, but he never made my life better. "Was helping me forbidden too?" I looked up.

He rubbed his forehead and opened his mouth as if he were going to say something. Pain flashed briefly before he turned and headed toward the stairs.

"I guess you really are the Druid King—the monster, not the

saint. Did you think this form would be easier for me? It's not. I would have rather died believing my Mr. Harrison was real."

Abruptly, as if my words had struck him, he stopped but didn't turn around. After a few seconds, he continued up the stairs and out the door.

Damnit. More questions; no answers. I started pacing. The energy from the power shake was making me restless. I wanted out of this hole. I backed against the wall when the basement door opened.

It was Quaid. He was alone.

"Why are you here?" I asked.

"Because Harry is in a mood," he said.

"No, jackass, I mean, why are you here helping them?"

He glanced back toward the stairs. "Why do you care?"

"Wow." My eyebrows raised. "For one, let's consider who's on which side of the bars. And if you were going to betray The Boss and help them, what reason would you have to lie to Mace?"

Quaid's smile faded. "I didn't lie."

"If he didn't believe your beloved story then it was a lie."

"He can't read me. It pisses him off, so he makes a point to insist I must be lying."

"Whatever."

Quaid checked his watch.

"What, are you late for a meeting?"

Ignoring me, he pulled out his phone and typed several messages, something I'd seen him do more than once at the office.

I peered at my own watch. "What day is it?"

"Monday," Quaid said, without looking up from his phone.

"Monday!" I'd lost a whole day. Had I been that drained?

Quaid stopped what he was doing and shoved his phone back into his pocket when the door at the top of the stairs opened. I felt the tingle of his proximity from his mark before I saw him.

Mace didn't appear happy Quaid was with me. His gaze darted back and forth between us. "I thought I told you to wait for me upstairs," he said, glaring at Quaid.

Quaid snorted. It was obvious he had no respect for Mace.

"Go!" Mace ordered.

Quaid gave him a tight smile, then flashed a glance at me before leaving.

"What were you and he doing?" Mace asked, his stare pinning

me in place.

"Doing...nothing. We were talking about what a dick you are."

His nostrils flared. Using his will, he forced me to stand and walk toward him. He focused on my belly as I approached. His fingers curled into claws. "I'll take this now. Maybe that will help you understand your place."

I fought to resist his pull. "Back off, asshole. Don't touch it."

"*It*...doesn't sound like you're all that attached to it."

Mace grinned, his will overpowering my struggle. I clutched my belly. He sent a pulse of energy through me. Like before, it felt as though the energy bounced around, until it found the knot in my stomach.

I took in a sharp breath. "Please don't." Now I was pleading.

"You still want it? Knowing what you know about Jack? He's a demon, Claire. He lied to you. He was just doing his job."

Every word struck me like a blow. I tore my eyes away. I didn't want him to see the truth. The truth about Jack and how I felt— *still feel*, about him.

Mace's will wrapped around me forcing me to look at him. "You still want him. And you would have his demon child too." He chanted in Ancient.

The energy coalesced into a sharp stab of pain in my gut. I wailed an ear-splitting cry. "No. Please stop. I'll do anything you want."

He dropped the pain to a dull throb. "Anything?"

"Yes," I whispered.

His eyes brightened, lips curving into a wicked smile. "Will you kill Junior for me?"

I gasped. *Oh, god...did I kill Junior?* My mouth went dry. I struggled to free myself, but his will tightened. Nausea rose to my throat. *No, I couldn't have done it. I wouldn't have.*

Mace clutched my chin, staring into my eyes. "You look guilty," he growled. "But Junior isn't dead yet."

I wanted to turn away from him.

A sneer twisted his lips. "Clearly, you're willing to do it."

His smug confidence scared me. He didn't understand why I was guilty—not that I'd killed Junior yet, but I'd seen the video. He'd called out my name just before he was shot. It could have been me. Tears welled as I cried for the family I wouldn't have. Even if Mace let me keep the baby, he wouldn't let me go. I'd never have a normal life. He'd make sure of that.

He studied me. His brow furrowed in confusion, but he held the power, and he knew it. "Are you ready to obey me now?"

I flinched as he moved his hand back toward my belly. He didn't try to hurt me, but the implied threat was there.

"Maybe if you're very good," he said, brushing the hair back from my face. "I'll let you raise the little bastard."

"Fuck you," I said, trying to blink back the tears.

He opened the door to my cell. Continuing as if I'd said nothing, he added, "I must deliver you to Mab, but I expect her to let me keep you."

I tried to school my emotions. I didn't want him to know what I thought of his plan. He was a fool to think she'd just let him have what he wanted.

He squeezed my arm as he pulled me from the basement. "Do you understand?"

"Yes."

"Good."

Once upstairs, he shoved me toward Quaid. I didn't see Harry again as we left the house. A car was waiting for us outside. Quaid hustled me into the back of the car. Cinnamon and the twins were already there. None of them acknowledged me, which was fine. Part of me wanted to warn them, but the other part knew it was useless, so I decided to keep quiet. Cinnamon's hair was still up, and Sage wore the green tie I had seen him ironing at the bungalow. He and Sorrel looked a little banged up, but neither of them seemed to care—or remember?—that I had caused the crazy fans to attack them.

"Why do we all have to go?" Cinnamon asked, scowling.

"Aunt Mab requested it," Sage said.

"Requested—commanded is more like it," she scoffed.

"She can't command you. You should have refused," I said, as Mace slid onto the seat.

Cinnamon's lips pursed together, and her eyebrows dropped into a line. Had she not even considered refusing?

I started to say as much, when Mace said, "Enough," and looked at my belly.

I turned my gaze away. Challenging him right now wasn't an option.

He leaned back against the seat and placed a hand on

Cinnamon's arm. "It's just a request for a visit."

Her face relaxed as she nodded. "Of course, you're right." She was still trapped by his spell and trusted him.

I knew when we crossed over into Purgatory. We'd driven down what appeared to be a dead-end alley in Underworld, only to end up in an ice-covered forest in the middle of nowhere. I had no negative reaction to the threshold this time, but I wondered how dangerous the portal really was. Mab said it wasn't safe to travel between Earth and the realms directly, but travel between Underworld and the realms was more stable. Actually, she'd said it wasn't safe for humans, so maybe I didn't have to worry as much about that now. That was if I ever got to leave, of course.

The tires of the town car crunched on the ice and snow as we drove to the castle. My stomach was full of ants—not butterflies; those would have been too tame for what was going on in the pit of my tummy. I just hoped I wouldn't get hungry anytime soon.

An arctic cold ran through me as we stepped out of the car. My clean change of clothes at Harry's hadn't included a pair of shoes. I was freezing.

Quaid ushered me toward the large doors of a huge castle. The stone structure was so tall and sprawling it made the forest around it seem small. I shivered when I registered where we were, and it wasn't from the permafrost beneath my bare feet. Mab's castle. Her claim had been granted. I was in Purgatory—maybe for good this time. The fear of what she could do to me—what she'd already done to my mother—came rushing back.

Trembling, I followed Quaid inside the great hall. The temperature inside wasn't much different from the frosty outside, but at least we'd left behind the biting wind. I was frozen to the bone, and the scrubs weren't providing any heat. It may have been my imagination, or the fact I'd just walked on ice outside, but the stone floor had warmth I wasn't expecting—not that it helped much, but at least I wasn't worried about losing any toes to frostbite.

Mab sat on a high throne, watching as we approached. The quads and Quaid bowed as they greeted her. Quaid yanked me down. She walked over to where I knelt. The temperature around me dropped further as she neared.

As if this was the first time we'd met, she tipped my head back and studied me. "Oh, look," she said gleefully. "You brought me a new toy."

I swallowed a sour taste in my mouth. She raised me to my feet.

The others stood, but she ignored them. Her eyes were so blue they were almost black. "You must be freezing, dear. Let me fetch you a warm drink."

Mace tensed beside me, but he didn't say anything.

I had no intention of eating or drinking anything. I remembered Jayne's warning—I couldn't believe I was actually giving the voice a name. "No, thank you," I said before Mab had a chance to summon a servant.

"I can see you're cold. Would you not like something to warm you?"

"No, thank you. I'm fine."

Her angelic face hid her true evil, but her shell was starting to crack. Fine lines appeared around her mouth as her lips formed a twisted smile. She hadn't expected me to refuse her.

Without so much as a twitch, she wrapped her will around me so tightly I could barely breathe. She lifted me a few inches off the ground to her eye level. "I must insist."

Mace hadn't been able to force me to eat the Pagan cake in the bungalow; I had to eat it willingly. I assumed the same rules applied to her. "I doubt it will have the desired effect if you force me." My voice was strained. I barely had enough air to get out the words.

Her hold tightened, suffocating me. She crowded closer, practically nose-to-nose. My lungs burned with the lack of oxygen.

In a lowered voice, she said, "You're in no position to refuse."

My eyelids drooped. She was very clearly proving her point. She smiled, then dropped me to the floor. I gasped, sucking in air as fast as possible. I was still trying to steady my breathing when Quaid put me on my feet.

"I'm sure some time to yourself will improve your attitude." She had a wicked gleam in her eyes. Waving her hand in a dismissive gesture, she said, "Take her to the Deeps."

Two of her guards, men I hadn't noticed before, came from behind her throne.

"Stop," Mace commanded before I could back away.

As if glued to the floor, with no real desire to move, I was stuck. Mace had commanded me to stop—a simple voice command—and now I was unable to move. *Oh, god. Complete control. This was what it meant?*

He bowed his head and went down to one knee. "May we speak first, Aunt, before you send her away?"

He looked up; his eyes were wide—hopeful—but I knew there was no way she was going to give him what he wanted. She had a smug look of indifference, but all I saw was death in her eyes. She wanted me agreeable. Apparently, whatever awaited me in the Deeps would make that happen.

She smiled. "She will go to the Deeps while we talk."

No longer arrogant, his dejected gaze met mine. Quietly, he said, "Go with them."

Without any conscious effort, I walked over to the guards. I wanted to run, but my body wouldn't obey. Not when Mace gave the order in Purgatory. Complete control sucked.

"You have your orders," Mab shouted at the guards. "To the Deeps with her."

The men led me from the great hall, taking me along a series of corridors to the back of the castle, then winding through another long corridor and into a spiraling stairwell that appeared to have no end. We went further and further down until finally it ended so deep in the ground it felt like a grave. My pulse quickened as we reached the bottom. A single dark door lay ahead.

CHAPTER 21

In China, the Taklamakan desert was said to mean, "go in, and you will never come out." The Deeps, as Mab called it, was nothing like the dreams Mace trapped me in or the nightmares controlled by the Keeper. The Deeps, as it turned out, was its own world, an endless Taklamakan, designed by Mab to make anyone go mad.

There was no mean foster father or sociopathic hellspawn here to torment me. There was nothing. Nothing but me and the wind or the rain or the snow or the searing hot summer sun on a vast, endless desert. So hot one's mouth was dry from the lack of water, and one's lips cracked and bled. This was the Deeps, the endless hell of nothingness that went on for days, then weeks, then years.

Aimlessly, I walked around. There was nothing to find or do or see. At first, I thought the desolate isolation would cause me to forget and drive me mad, but the spell I'd done made that impossible. I hadn't heard from the voice again, but images, the movie of my life, were relentlessly played over and over in my head. I couldn't forget—anything. This might drive me mad faster than if I was losing them.

The time of this place was different. The days ticked past like marks on a ruler. I watched them turn into weeks, then months. Forward and back, ending and beginning, as if I could somehow control time itself. Maybe in this hellhole I could.

I stumbled over a rock and fell to the ground but got back up quickly. Resting wasn't an option. Nor sleeping, sitting, or stopping. The elements would attack if I did. I would wind up in the middle of a raging storm or a freezing wind.

I groaned as the wind picked up. I hadn't gotten back to my feet fast enough. The dirt started to swirl. A sand storm was coming. I ran, trying to get ahead of the gale. Trying to get out of its way, but I was too late. Raging wind slammed into me, knocking me to the ground.

After too many times of this happening, in frustration, I cried, "Stop!"

Instantly, everything stilled. I pushed myself to my feet and looked around. I was in the middle of the storm, but it wasn't moving. Millions of tiny specs of sand were suspended in the air. Amazing. I spun around in all directions, gawking at the contained chaos. Raw power, suspended in time. It was beautiful.

A moment later, something struck my cheek with a sharp sting. Then another. The sand. As I studied the suspended particles, they moved, vibrating slightly before flying off on their former trajectory.

I had some control but not enough. I reeled around, searching for the best way out. A small patch of blue sky beckoned. I ran for the clearing as the storm roared again, the sand swirling faster and faster. It was getting harder to see. I kept going, running for the bright beacon of blue.

"Faster," I screamed at my legs.

Without warning, time jumped ahead, and I wasn't in the desert anymore. Instead, I stood in the frozen tundra, the storm long gone. Winter again.

"Four months," I said, knowing that was the time that had passed. It was strange how I could sense the time here. I could see it as if it were laid out before me in a timeline.

Of course, I didn't actually believe it was real time—dream time perhaps. I wasn't completely sure.

I walked for another two days, making comments about the weather—talking to myself—actually wishing the voice would talk back.

"Jayne," I said hesitantly. I was so starved for interaction, I would gladly welcome her conversation. She remained quiet. "Please talk to me."

"Finally," she said in an exacerbated tone. "So, did it just occur to you that you had to give me permission to speak?"

"Um—" I wasn't sure what to say. I hadn't realized that at all.

"Fine, you're forgiven."

I'm losing it.

"You're not going crazy," she said.

"I've been here for seven years or two months or two seconds, depending on how you want to look at it. I'm tired. I can't sleep or rest. I've been watching a continuous loop of my life in movie form, and I don't know how the hell to get out of here, or when it will end on its own. So, yeah, I'm fairly sure I'm going crazy."

"You could shut it off."

The movie already felt like someone else's life, but I couldn't switch it off. "I have no idea how long I'll be here. If I switch it off, I could wind up forgetting my own name. Which is not a better option."

"Just a suggestion."

"You're talking to me now. Maybe I've already tipped the crazy scale."

The voice was silent.

"Fine, let's say I'm not crazy. What are you? Who are you?" I asked, realizing I had no idea how to phrase the right question.

"I'm Jayne," she said as if that explained it.

I wanted to beat my head against a wall. "Well, Jayne, what the hell does that mean exactly?"

She didn't say anything.

I sighed. "Where are you?"

"Trapped in you, somehow, I don't know," she admitted.

"Have you always been there, just silent? Which is creepy, by the way, if you have."

"No, I only regained awareness after you entered Purgatory the first time. I decided to use the spell you cast as a way to talk to you."

"So why did you shut up?"

"You commanded me, and for some reason, I couldn't talk to you after that."

I thought about that for a minute. Did my words have that much power? Was it like the suggestions I'd made to Mace and Sage?

"Yes, I think so," Jayne said.

"Right, you can hear everything I'm thinking."

She was quiet.

"I think we need to get past these secrets. Especially if I have none from you."

"I don't exactly understand it myself, but it's like I am you, but I have no control of the body."

A split personality?

"No, that's not it," she said quickly.

"How do you know?" That would explain a few things—wouldn't it? I'd seen a special on TV.

"No, look, I know I have memories that aren't from your life. I can't access all of them, but I know they're there. And I don't have the ability to take control of your body. If I were an alternate personality I'd be able to do that, and we couldn't have a conversation."

My head hurt thinking about it.

"Look out," she said, before I almost tripped over another rock.

I was so tired, I just wanted to sit down for a minute and do nothing.

"Maybe we should try to get out?"

"I'd love to. Do *you* have any ideas?"

"We could let the storms kill us?"

"That's an interesting thought, but what happens if it doesn't work? She may be planning to keep us down here forever."

"I doubt it. What fun would that be?"

"I assume you mean for her since she wouldn't have the gratification of screwing with us on a daily basis."

"Yes, of course."

I had no response to that. Sadly, I was sure she was right.

"You could try stopping things again."

"What good will that do? It didn't last very long the first time."

"Maybe try fast forwarding."

"Yeah, and sometimes time reverses. Plus we don't know if that will help us get out."

"Okay, this is getting us nowhere. Are we going to talk about the real problem then?"

I snorted. "Which one?"

"The baby. Jack and Junior. Don't act like I don't know what you're thinking."

"I don't want to think about it. If it's real and Mace takes it—"

"If the baby is real and it's Junior's, will you want it?"

I'd been ignoring my concerns of what really happened with

"boyfriend Junior" in his hotel room, and whether or not the baby could be his. Mace hadn't sensed it until after I'd come back from Fight Night, but that might not mean anything.

"Do you know what really happened?" I asked.

"No, I only know what you know."

So not helpful. "Yeah, and I was in that hotel room—alone with him—pretending to be his girlfriend. I have no memory of what really happened."

"Death was there."

"The bathroom floor was wet," I added.

"You could have slipped, fell, and hit your head."

Was that before or after I let Junior fuck me?

"I think Jack would understand if you did."

I brushed away a tear.

"Junior's a big guy," she said. "He could have hurt you if you'd resisted."

"Then why don't I remember?"

She was silent.

I started to run. From what I wasn't sure. I studied the vast desert before me, considering time as I ran. I imagined the seasons passing in front of my eyes. And they did.

Without knowing how I'd done it, Winter bled into Spring, which bled into Summer, then into Fall. The seasons rolled around in a continuous loop as I ran through the desert, thinking of the next season to come.

~ # ~

"Seven years," Jayne said, as if I couldn't sense the passage of time.

I'd figured out how to speed up time. Four or five times faster than normal, but there was still no end in sight. I'd been in the Deeps for almost a hundred years. Because of my ability to manipulate the time, it felt like a mere seven years, but even that was an eternity. My body moved on autopilot now, my mind a constant stream of Lifetime movies and talks with Jayne.

Dropping my gaze to my hands, I stopped. "We're getting older," I said, seeing the signs of age in front of me.

"No. Keep moving," she said. "Time's not moving on the outside."

"We don't know that."

"Yes, we do. There's no way this is real. And quit thinking

forever, we'll get out."

"Something will get out, but I don't know any more if it will be me."

She was quiet.

"I'm hungry," I mumbled.

"I know. I wish you'd stop thinking about it," she admonished.

"It's not like before. I'm actually hungry. I have been for months."

"We can't eat anything."

"I know."

"I know what you're thinking. Stop it. We can't let her have that power over us. Mace is bad enough. You know what he did to us. Complete control. We will die of hunger before we give that to her."

"I know," I snapped.

Time started moving faster. The seasons were whipping by us at a rate so fast it was dizzying.

"Enough," Jayne snapped.

"I'm not doing this."

"Stop it."

"I don't know if I can…the storm is coming."

"Start running."

"It won't help."

I sat, then laid down on the ground. My hands had withered as the years passed. Now they were old and craggy. The clock was nearing a hundred. I wanted it all to end.

"Don't give up," Jayne said.

I was ready to die. The wind started to howl. The dust and sand began to swirl. Beetles crawled up out of the ground beside me. I hadn't seen another living thing for a century, and now there were scary flesh eating bugs about to attack me. At least, I hoped this meant the hell was ending.

Within seconds, the beetles swarmed me and engulfed my entire body. They chewed at my flesh relentlessly. Mab would be disappointed I wasn't screaming, but I'd learned to ignore the perceived pain of this place long ago.

My body was a shell by the time the storm struck. It ripped the bugs off me before the sand finished the job of removing my flesh. In minutes, my bones were exposed to the elements, and bit-by-bit they were pulverized by the debris. I was conscious through the entire process, until the last part of my body was ground to dust and blew away on the wind.

That was the Deeps.

~ # ~

I bolted upright with a loud intake of breath. Rolling off the slab of rock, I rushed over to the tray in the center of the room. It overflowed with fruit so luscious they seemed unreal.

I salivated, eager to eat everything before me. Ripe bananas, tender strawberries, succulent peaches, and juicy apples called my name. I could smell their heady aroma. I picked up an apple. The skin glistened with beads of moisture. I could already taste the crisp sweetness as I brought the fruit to my lips.

Stop, Jayne cried.

"What?" I said, lowering the apple just as a droplet of water fell and splashed onto my chin.

Are you insane? put that down, right now!

As if it burned, I dropped the apple and wiped the water off my hands. "I wasn't thinking. I'm sorry."

Quit talking to me out loud. Do you want the guards outside to hear us?

"Sorry," I said, then, *Sorry*.

The smell of the food made my stomach roil.

Get away from it. Go check the door.

There was a large wooden door at the front of the room. I ran to it.

We should check with our presence.

I know. This isn't my first rodeo. And before you say anything, yes I'm okay.

I wasn't sure how true that really was, but I wasn't going to try to eat anything else. The movie had stopped, but the life it showed no longer felt like my own.

I closed my eyes and thought about the great hall. I was there instantly.

Cinnamon, Sage, and Sorrel were sitting by themselves gazing blankly into the room. Cinnamon slowly pivoted her head toward me, and although her lips didn't move, she said, *Wait*. Her face became strained. She closed her eyes and more clearly said, *I will not let Mab sense you, but I will not be able to hide you for long.*

Why?

You'll owe me.

I snorted. *Technically, you already owe me.*

Quit arguing, Jayne admonished. *She can't hide you forever.*

Fine, I'll owe her a favor.

I cautiously moved into the room. Mab and Mace were talking on the other side, but I couldn't understand what they were saying.

I looked at Cinnamon. *I can't understand them.* When she didn't offer any suggestions to solve my problem, I added, *Mace destroyed the translator.*

She sighed. *He can't destroy something one of the three created. He shut it off. Turn it back on.*

Could it be that easy? "Fix the translator," I whispered.

How am I supposed to do that, Jayne asked.

I'm not talking to you. I'm talking to the watch.

You are the watch.

I know, but since I don't know another way to access my power, I'm asking the watch.

Who are you talking to? Cinnamon asked.

None of your business, Jayne said.

A pop sounded in my ear, and I could hear Mace and Mab talking. *Be quiet, both of you.*

Mace was begging her, practically whining. "I'll bring her back as soon as I have completed the task. You must let me finish it."

He wants us to kill Junior, Jayne said.

I shushed her.

"And if you fail again?" Mab asked.

"I won't. We'll return before sundown."

Her eyes brightened. "Do you promise?"

He hesitated. Lowering his gaze, he clenched his fists, obviously not wanting to make that oath. The others were still sitting quietly by the wall. Cinnamon's brow was furrowed, and her lips were pressed together tightly, but he didn't appear to notice.

Returning his focus to Mab, he nodded. "I promise we'll return her before sundown. You have my word."

Mab's lips curved upward, apparently as happy with these terms as Mace was unhappy. They didn't discuss the consequences if he failed to return, but considering how overjoyed she appeared at the thought of his failure, I was sure he wouldn't miss the deadline.

"What about Quaid," Mace asked. "What are your plans for him?"

Mab straightened, sitting up taller. "Did he play his part at the fight?"

"Yes, he diverted the security team assigned to Junior's section to another location. We would have succeeded if Claire hadn't been with Junior."

"Good," Mab said, seemingly pleased Quaid had cooperated. "He will be my guest here at the castle. You will return without him."

Mace rubbed the back of his neck. "But I may need his help to enter the company."

As if dismissing the concern, Mab waved her hand in the air. "Use the girl."

Mace's eyebrows drew together. Quietly, he said, "She may not remember how to do it."

A wicked grin crossed Mab's face.

That heartless bitch, Jayne said. *She believes the Deeps broke us.*

I didn't agree or disagree. In my opinion, the jury was still out on whether I was broken.

"Her blood will get you in," Mab offered.

My blood. She's going to talk about my blood. I moved closer.

It's forbidden to talk about. Remember?

I shushed her again.

"Her blood?" Mace repeated. "Why is it so special? Why did the blacksmith want it?"

Mab's eyes became unfocused. She touched the pendant on her necklace, and a slight smile crossed her face.

That's a pretty pendant isn't it, Jayne said absently.

The pendant was antique silver with a red ruby in the center and etched black lines radiating all around. As with all the things I'd seen Mab wear, this was an exquisite piece of jewelry, but hardly anything to gush over. *Yeah, it's cute. Stay focused and ignore the shiny objects.*

"Aunt?" Mace said. "Is everything all right?"

I focused on him. "Ask her to tell you about her sister."

What are you doing? Jayne asked.

I want to hear her say it's a myth.

As if to clear it, Mace shook his head, then said, "Um...tell me about her. About your sister."

Mab's eyes narrowed. Sweeping her hand in a large arc toward the others, she said, "Quiet."

She moved so fast it was as if she'd disappeared, then reappeared in front of him. Lifting him off his feet by the neck, she snarled, "You speak of things you should not know." Mab searched the room as if someone might be listening.

Crap, she's hunting for us. Cinnamon, can she sense us?

Cinnamon remained quiet.

Mace placed his hand on the one around his neck. "I'm sorry. I didn't mean to upset you," he wheezed in a voice barely above a whisper.

She dropped him to the floor. Smiling, she cupped his cheek and lightly stroked it with her thumb. "You didn't upset me, my boy. It is so rare I get to speak of such things. And I don't want the others to hear."

"Of course," he said, voice trembling.

Mab returned to her throne. He got to his feet, nervously running his hand through his hair as if that might steady his nerves.

"First," she said. "How much blood did the blacksmith take?"

"A lot," he admitted. "Claire almost died."

"Almost?"

"Obviously she didn't," he added quickly.

"I will take care of the blacksmith," she said. His brows drew together. "Don't worry, it won't be traced back to you."

"As you wish," he said.

She touched her pendant again. "Have you heard of the fourth realm, Nephew?"

Mace smiled. "Yes, of course, in make-believe stories."

That's what Harry said, Jayne reminded me.

"What if I told you it was real?"

Mace smiled, shaking his head slightly. "It's impossible. I wouldn't believe you."

Mab's lips formed a tight line. "Why?"

He moved his right foot back, as if he might turn and run. She glanced at the movement. He stilled, then dropped to one knee. "Forgive me for doubting you, Aunt, but to believe the fourth realm was real, I would have to believe in its fate."

"You find it impossible to believe this?"

"For a realm to be destroyed? I would hope so," Mace said, his brows drawing closer together. "Am I wrong?"

"You're wrong."

He closed his mouth. I saw his Adam's apple bob up and down from swallowing.

It was destroyed.

No! Jayne said.

What did you think? They just abandoned it?

I don't know. Nothing. I'm being silly. You're right. It would have been destroyed.

I ignored Jayne's craziness and focused on Mace.

"The books speak of a great war," Mace said. "Of how time was torn apart, and the realms were divided. Is all of this true?"

"Yes," Mab said.

I zeroed in on him again. "The sister ruled the realm."

He parroted, "Your sister ruled the realm?"

She rubbed the pendant between her fingers. "She was my twin. How did you know to ask about her?"

"I don't know." His face was confused.

She searched the room again, but didn't appear to sense anything. "The fourth realm was real. It was ruled by my sister and destroyed ten millennia ago by your father, Harry, and myself."

Jayne gasped.

Mab touched a finger to the corner of her eye.

What is up with you? No answer. *Jayne, what is it?*

Sorry, Jayne said. *Is she wiping away a tear?*

Looks that way, I said to her. *What is up with you?*

It's nothing, but there's something about that pendant. It's stirring up memories.

Memories?

We'll talk about it later.

"How do we not know?" Mace asked, pulling my attention back to them. "Why is it believed to be a myth?"

Mab held out her hands and motioned for him to come closer. He stood, hesitating only briefly before walking to her.

Clutching his hands, then lightly touching his face to bring his eyes up to hers. "It is forbidden to discuss, but seeing Claire again has reminded me of her."

Any ideas on that one?

No, Jayne said.

"Claire?" Mace frowned. "How does she remind you of your sister?"

"Her blood is the same."

My blood. That's why it's special? That would explain why it was forbidden to discuss. If it was forbidden to discuss the fourth realm, it was forbidden to discuss my blood.

But why is it forbidden? Jayne asked.

I shrugged.

"Claire has fourth realm blood?" Mace asked. "How did the blacksmith know?"

"The blacksmith can sense the blood in others," Mab offered.

That's why we both have eyes that shine green. Did that make us mystically related? Were there others who had a green shine? I suppose it didn't matter. It wasn't as if all demons were related.

"How?" Mace asked.

"There aren't many left with the blood. She is a child of all realms, which makes her unpredictable and difficult to control. But that is not your concern."

"Claire's mother was human. If there aren't many left, who is her father?"

I took a step closer.

Don't, she might sense you. And you know she isn't going to tell him, Jayne said.

You don't know. She might.

Mab patted his cheek. "Claire has fourth realm blood, but she is not one of the Fallen."

"The Fallen?"

"It is what we call the fourth realm," she said. "Because of this, Claire's origin is unknown."

What? Jayne and I said in unison.

Mace's eyebrows shot up. "How can you not know?"

"It's complicated," Mab said, releasing his face.

He took a step back, running his hand through his hair. "Does my father know?"

She glanced at the others. They were still in their silent state. "Claire is very special."

I don't think I can handle another Claire is special discussion, Jayne said.

You and me both.

Mace wrinkled his nose. "You all favor her. Why?"

Her lips twisted into a crooked smile. "It is not favor, my boy. It is fate."

He raised an eyebrow. "Fate?"

"There is an ancient augury."

"You mean an omen? A prophecy?" he asked, eyes still wide.

Oh, this should be good, Jayne said.

I ignored her. Mab wouldn't be chatty for long, and she'd

certainly never tell me any of this.

He retreated a step when she stood. She took a turn around him, stopping with her back to Cinnamon and the twins. Mab's head tilted slightly, looking off to the side for a moment then at him again. As if finally making her decision, she fixed her eyes on his.

"A great mystic of the fourth realm foretold of a harbinger—a girl—who would set right what was lost by the Ancients. She would be of human birth, otherworldly lineage, and possess the blood of the Fallen. She would have the power to see the truth and would restore time within all the realms."

Holy shit. Did The Boss and Harry believe this too?

And which one of them is your father? Jayne asked.

One incredibly fucked-up problem at a time, please.

"Otherworldly lineage?" Mace asked. "Is my father her father?" He grimaced. "Is she one of us?"

"I don't want to be one of you," I shouted at him. He glanced in my direction, but thankfully, Mab hadn't noticed. Whatever Cinnamon was doing to keep her from sensing me must also prevent her from hearing me.

Chill out, Jayne said. *The guards might hear you.*

"No one knows for sure, but his actions have not always made his feelings clear. He did not publicly declare her as his."

This is what the seers think. They think I'm the harbinger.

It would seem so, Jayne agreed. *James called you the harbinger.*

I remembered now. He'd tried to tell me about the augury, but I wouldn't listen. I thought he was crazy.

Mace crossed his arms. "You all believe Claire is this girl?"

"She is the best fit, although it cannot be confirmed."

Because they don't know who my father is? How can they not know?

"So my father could be her father?"

Mab smiled. "You're forgetting. There are three contenders for otherworldly parent—if she is the girl, of course. But I seriously doubt Melinda was somehow impregnated with one of my ovum. Of course with magic I suppose anything is possible."

Mace's mouth hung open.

Don't even go there, I said

But she might be—Jayne started to say.

No.

"So you truly don't know?" Mace asked, running his hand

through his hair. "But you all believe she's the girl."

"Yes."

"Is that why you want her?"

"It is one of the reasons, but I have several."

Harry said she couldn't control fate by controlling us, Jayne reminded me.

One incredibly fucked-up problem at a time.

Mab looked at her nails then up at Mace as he paced back and forth, mumbling to himself. Rolling her eyes, she raised her hand as if she were about to end their discussion.

"How does she see the truth?" he asked. "You said the girl—the harbinger—could see the truth."

Mab lowered her hand. "I'm not sure which gift she has received. Seeing through veils perhaps?"

"Yes," Mace said, snapping his finger and pointing at Mab. He lowered his hand when she scowled at him. "She could see the blacksmith's true form...but then how did she see Death as beautiful?"

Mab's mouth fell open. She cleared her throat, absentmindedly touching her pendant. "When?"

"I told you, the blacksmith took too much blood. She almost died."

Her mouth pinched into a hard line. She released the pendant and balled her hands into fists. "Death cannot have her yet. He knows that. He shouldn't have interfered."

"He didn't keep her. She didn't die."

"He should not have made himself known to her. She should not have seen him."

Why does she care?

I don't know, Jayne said in a quiet voice as if I were asking her.

"He was not hideous to her. I'm sure of it. I could see the truth in her eyes," Mace said. "But how is that possible?"

"He was not always as he is now. He was once very dashing—beautiful. My sister loved him." Mab spoke without emotion. "They were soul mates, for lack of a better term."

Soul mates?

"What happened to him?"

"He betrayed us and was punished. He is hideous because his beauty is now tied to the eye of the beholder. You should hope, Nephew, you never have the honor of meeting him. I'm sure your past deeds would not paint him in a good light."

Mace remained silent.

"He is also incapable of loving anyone but my sister, and he was forced to kill her. In the end, she only saw his hideousness. She died without knowing his fate."

Jayne gasped.

What is up with you?

"That doesn't explain how Claire sees him as beautiful," Mace countered. "She's not perfect—no human is. Wouldn't her past deeds also paint an ugly picture?"

Mab grinned, baring her teeth. "Claire is not completely human, but you're right. She isn't perfect. She saw him when she was a baby. When she was innocent."

Mace's eyebrows pinched together. "But…"

She raised her hand and approached him. He body became unnaturally stiff and erect, but it wasn't from shock. She had him wrapped in her will. "That's enough about the past for now. I wouldn't worry yourself with these tedious affairs." She locked gazes with him, caressing his cheek with her hand "You have always been my favorite."

He smiled.

She continued, "Not because you're loyal, but because you're trusting."

His grin fell. The crease between his brows deepened. Moments later his face contorted in pain. Struggling, he tried to get away from her. She tightened her grip, stilling him.

Her lips curled into a vicious sneer. "Getting rid of Junior and weakening your father's powerbase is poetic, don't you think? The irony is that not even you realize how much power the four of you control."

Mace's eyes widened in shock.

"I can't let you remember this conversation," she said with mock sadness, "but I enjoyed having it. I don't often get to reminisce about my sister. If only she'd trusted me. We could have ruled the world together." Mab tapped his nose. "Forget."

She released him and returned to her throne.

He shook his head and opened his mouth, then closed it and opened it again. "I'm sorry, Aunt. What were we talking about?"

She didn't immediately answer. She glanced around, and her expression hardened.

She's searching for us, Jayne said.

I know. The strain was evident on Cinnamon's face. She couldn't hide us much longer.

"Her blood is not your concern. That is all I will say." Mab dismissed the matter.

I chuckled. Mab stood. She'd heard me.

Time to go, Jayne said.

CHAPTER 22

I stepped back when the door flew open. The taller man took me by the arm and led me up the stairs. The shorter man disappeared into the room before following behind us.

I was taken back through the corridors to the great hall. The twins and Cinnamon were still there, as they had been a minute ago, sitting off to one side. Mab was back on her throne, talking to Mace privately.

Her eyes fixed on the guards.

"We heard something," the taller man holding me said. "She was awake."

"Did she eat the food?"

The second guard spoke, "No, Your Highness, she did not."

She waved her hand shooing them away. Mab stood, looking down her nose at me as she approached. Her smile didn't quite reach her eyes. "How did you like the Deeps?"

"It was a bit windy for me," I said.

A small line formed between her eyebrows.

Mace stepped between us. "I promise she'll eat the food when she returns."

A chill ran down my spine, and the hairs on my neck stood. He'd be able to make me eat the food. Given he'd offered it, it must not be the same as Mab forcing me. I was sure my face was pale with fear as her eyes landed on me.

"You know," she accused.

That's too vague, I wouldn't give anything up, Jayne said.

Really, not the first rodeo, remember?

Stepping back Mace locked eyes with me. I didn't bother trying to look away. He'd see the truth in my eyes. He'd know I hadn't forgotten a thing.

"You're right, Aunt, she's the same," he said. "It's probably Father's doing."

Mab's brow cocked. "Explain."

"A few months ago he was angry with me for making her forget something. He may have made it so she can't."

I raised one of my eyebrows at Mace. His version of what he'd done to me was laughable.

Mab lifted my chin. "That can be a very dangerous thing to do to someone."

Why is it dangerous? Jayne asked. *It saved us, didn't it?*

Yes, that might be the problem. It saved us.

"You will be mine soon enough," Mab said. "I will have plenty of time to figure you out." She turned back to Mace, as if dismissing me.

I checked my watch. Mab would eventually figure out how it worked and take it from me. I needed some of her blood. That was the only way to break the curse permanently. Without my power, I'd have no protections against her. I couldn't be cut off from it by losing the watch.

When I looked up, she was casually laughing at something Mace said.

What are you going to do? Jayne asked.

I need her blood. I'm going to make her give it to me.

That sounds painful.

"Mab," I called out, ignoring Jayne's warning. "You'll never own me like The Boss does."

Pushing up my sleeve, I willed the mark to glow a fiery orange. I didn't take my eyes from her, but I could feel it dancing along my arm. I left it there long enough for her to get a glimpse. Mace said I was the only one marked by The Boss. Based on Mab's surprised look, I had to assume she hadn't known.

Mace is pissed, Jayne said.

His arms were crossed over his chest, and his eyes were narrowed on me.

I laughed at him.

"He's made his own claim. Did you know?" I asked her. "Maybe you should all get in line."

Mace started toward me, but Mab shoved him back and pinned him to the wall with her will.

A snicker escaped me before I could hold it back. "I can only have one master. So far, he and The Boss have a better hand."

What the hell are you doing? Trying to get us killed?

The Keeper said we need Winter's blood to break the curse. I don't have another way to get it, and you heard Mab. We're too important to them. We're the harbinger. She isn't going to kill us.

This isn't a good plan.

I ignored Jayne. If it was what I needed to do to unbind all of my powers, I had to do it. I wouldn't survive Mab without them. Harry said there was no way to break the curse, so I assume she doesn't know that either.

If this works at all, Jayne argued.

Mab's wicked grin widened. "You're mine, little one. Shall I prove it?"

"If you think you can."

Her lips thinned while her hands balled into fists as she glowered at me.

This isn't going to end well.

No, it's not. I shrugged, sending Mab over the edge.

She moved so fast it was a blur. She clutched my right arm, passing her hand over it. The Boss's mark glowed for a moment.

Holy, shit, do you see that? Jayne asked.

The Boss's mark still showed the symbols, but now the English translation was visible too. *Protected by.* At least now I knew Mace hadn't been lying.

Mab seized my left wrist and held my arm out straight. With an evil sneer, she held her right hand over my arm and started chanting; only this time I understood what she was saying.

We can read Ancient and hear it. Cool, Jayne said.

The translator understands Ancient, which makes sense, I guessed, *but why now? Why not before?*

Maybe Mom and Dad had the parental controls set to 'No Ancient,' Jayne said, sarcastically.

Maybe.

Even with the new ability to understand Ancient, Mab's chant had lots of nonsensical sounds that must have been used for rhyming. I stopped listening when blood dripped from her hand.

I howled in pain as molten lava seared into my skin. The fiery red blood pooled on my arm before etching its excruciating way into my flesh.

My torso bowed as if a surge of electrical current ran through it. The mark radiated energy as it formed, sending pinprick pulses all over me. I closed my eyes, and my presence was practically thrown out of my body.

My body flexed under the pain of her mark, but my presence could no longer feel it. White wisps of electricity swirled around the wrist Mab held. She didn't notice, but I was sure the power was building, just as it had before.

Tendrils of energy rode up my arm. The ghostly glow was visible to my presence, but it didn't appear Mab could see it. The white glimmer ran over my entire body, enveloping Mace's mark, but not The Boss's mark, as if the magic couldn't touch it. My body slumped to the floor when she released me. I watched as the mark faded.

Property of. No shock there.

I unsuccessfully attempted to open my eyes. My limp, seemingly lifeless, body lay there, helpless.

"You may go now," Mab said, dropping Mace from the wall.

He rushed over to me, lowering his ear to my mouth, as if checking to see I was still breathing.

I jumped when another version of my presence wandered up to him. "Mace looks concerned doesn't he?"

"Jayne?" I asked. "How?"

She shrugged, then faced me. That was when I noticed she held something small and glowing.

"What's that?"

She put her hand behind her back. "Nothing to worry about."

I crossed my arms over my chest. "I'm six degrees of crazy right now, so how about we don't play any of these silly keeping-information-from-me-to-protect-me-games. It's too late for that. Don't you think?"

She smiled, then held her palm open. It was a white radiant ball of light.

"What the hell is that?"

"It's how your mind sees the baby."

"What? Why do you have it? Why is it here?"

"I'm keeping it safe."

"I want to hold it," I said, reaching out my hand to take it.

"It's better if you don't."

"Why? It's mine!"

She raised one of her eyebrows at me and in a stern motherly tone, said, "It's safer with me."

I shook my head.

"They're moving the body. We have to go."

Mace was bowing one final time to Mab as the twins carried out my body. I stared right at Mab, but she didn't sense me.

I turned. "I want to hold—"

I was alone.

"Jayne!"

~ # ~

We returned to Harry's house in the Underworld, and they put my body in the basement. I didn't follow it down. I was afraid the markings would trap me, and I didn't want to be left alone with my thoughts. Jayne decided to hide and wasn't speaking to me.

Sage and Sorrel plopped down on the couch in the living room and pulled out the Xbox controllers, about to play Grand Theft Auto. They were obviously not preparing for the big showdown.

Cinnamon paced, walking between several of the posh rooms. Her brow was furrowed. She looked worried. I didn't blame her. She had no idea what Mab really wanted. But she wasn't going to sit around and watch the boys play video games. She left the living room and headed toward the back of the house. I followed her.

Cinnamon knocked on a door at the end of the hall.

"Enter," Harry's gruff voice said from within the room. He was standing in front of the window, gazing down on the street below. He faced her when she entered.

"Good afternoon, Uncle."

He inclined his head for her to continue.

Cinnamon clasped her hands behind her, almost as if she were at parade rest. "I'm concerned about Mab's interest in our affairs."

I noticed she didn't come right out and tell Harry their plans. Apparently, she couldn't be sure he would be sympathetic to their cause. I was sure he didn't give a rat's ass.

"She will keep her word. Why are you concerned?" His smile was weak and his voice flat.

Cinnamon attempted to smile back, but his uncaring gaze

forced her to lower her eyes. "Mace has been talking with her privately," she said quietly. "I don't know if he has all our best interests in mind when he deals with her."

Harry straightened. "He can't make a bargain with her on your behalf. You have to agree to the terms before you can be held accountable. She's not your master."

"I fear she has too great a hold on my brother." Cinnamon's voice warbled a bit.

Harry snorted, shaking his head. "He is old enough to make his own choices. He, alone, will have to live with them."

She tightened her left hand into a fist, released it. Her head hung, but I couldn't decide if it was from respect or fear? "I'm not so sure about that anymore."

Harry strode forward and put his hands on her arms, rubbing them in a comforting manner. "He can't make deals for you, my dear." He gave her a tight smile then returned to the window.

I assumed Cinnamon would leave, but she raised her head, pressed her lips together, and took a step forward. "This business with Claire is very peculiar."

His eyes closed. "Does he still have her?"

"Yes."

He sighed, opening his eyes. "I see."

"I don't believe as my brother. I don't believe she's favored, but she does seem to be of some interest to the three of you."

"She is of some interest, but not your concern," Harry admonished.

"Of course, Uncle." Cinnamon bowed her head. "Thank you for speaking with me."

I stayed behind as Cinnamon left. He hadn't appeared to sense me. He studied the street below, the cords in his neck protruding. He rolled his shoulders, as if trying to relieve some tension then rubbed his forehead, frowning.

I examined his features.

You look nothing like him, Jayne said.

I spun around, but she wasn't there. *You're speaking to me again?*

It's impossible not to.

I bobbed my head up and down. *Yeah, being crazy's a bitch.*

The phone on Harry's desk rang. He scowled, hitting the speakerphone. "What?"

"Hey, boss, this is Moe. I work for Johnny."

Harry grimaced. "Yes."

"Well, you see, we picked up that kid this morning, and I thought you might want to know Johnny's thinking about making an example of her. You know, because of the fight. To maybe enlighten the others."

His eyebrows knitted together. "What kid?"

"The girl, Claire."

Harry's nostrils flared. "You have Claire now?"

"Yeah, boss."

His face reddened and a vein in his neck pulsed. "When did you pick her up?"

"We had one of our boys on the inside drive her down here this morning."

Harry leaned over the phone. "I want you to listen to me very carefully." His voice was low and menacing. "I want her released. I don't want her harmed. No lesson is to be taught. No example is to be set. She isn't to be touched. Have I made myself clear?"

"Um...yeah, boss. Sorry, we didn't know she was off-limits." I could hear the worry in Moe's voice as it quavered.

"I don't want her touched ever again. Let her go. Now."

"Yeah, yeah, sure boss." Moe's voice was strained and scared. "I'll tell Johnny now. I'll take care of it."

Harry hung up the phone and disappeared.

"Claire."

Crap. He was in the basement with my body.

"Wake," he ordered.

My eyes shot open, and I was yanked back into my body. My arm throbbed where Mab marked me.

"Claire," he barked.

I sat up. "Yes."

"Why did Mab send you back with Mace?"

I just stared at him.

Harry narrowed his eyes. His face was still red. His pulse was still trying to beat its way out of his neck.

I smiled. "He asked her to."

"Why?"

"I told you why earlier. You don't care, remember?"

His voice lowered. "Why would Mab change her mind?"

I sighed. "I'd love to tell you."

He raised one of his eyebrows. "Don't assume I won't make

you." He was serious.

I'm not sure we'll survive him trying to make us talk, Jayne said.

He won't kill us.

I opened my mouth to say, Junior is being manipulated by Mab, and as expected, my throat closed up painfully.

Can't you get rid of the spell?

I don't know.

The curse is broken now. Try.

I held up my index finger. "Give me a minute."

I thought about all the other times I'd reversed a spell, and the one time I'd let Death's spell back in. I remembered how I'd inverted the power of the hell shackles and zapped Mace, and how the same energy formed again on the watchband when I thought he'd hurt my mother. Emotion had been a trigger.

Digging deep, I felt for the power within me and focused on the marks on each arm and the tattoo Mace left on me. I could sense the power of the blood used to mark me, as well as the potential within my own blood. Pulling those sensations together, and mingling their auras with the essence connected to my inner strength, I began to see the web of potency I held within me. Following the tendrils of power that coursed through me, I could visualize the places in my body where they connected. It was as if the foreign power was wrapped in a layer of my own.

I counted seven disturbances in the flow of my power. Some I recognized, like the one that was open for Death. And the ones closed from Purgatory—the whammy and Charles's love spell. They were still within me, which must have been how I could affect others.

As I searched for the right one, another came into view. I'd have to figure out what they all meant later. For now, I just needed to find Mab's spell and close it.

I ignored the spells that were already closed. More continued to surface as I looked for her spell. A lot of those were open. I'd have to worry about that later.

I heard Harry's weight shift, but I maintained focus on my hunt. He would just have to wait.

I visualized my search as if I were picking up rocks on the ground to see which ones were geodes. After finding three others that weren't her spell—or spells I recognized—I finally found the one I wanted. To my mind's eye, her spell's geode had an aquamarine and amethyst hue, and about a six-inch diameter. At first, I wasn't sure how to close it, until my mind's eye caught sight of a glowing geode with the same colors. I scooped it up and mentally slammed the two halves together.

My throat loosened and a heavy weight I hadn't even realized was there, lifted from my shoulders.

Harry cleared his throat.

"Your sister's a bitch," I said. "She spelled me not to speak of the future."

His expression didn't change. Clearly, he wasn't surprised.

"Mab wants Junior dead."

"Do you have proof?"

"Do I need it? She sent me back to help Mace do it, but I think he needs Cinnamon's help too, and she doesn't really want to do it. He has them all spelled."

Harry nodded, then steepled his fingers as if he was considering something. "Will they succeed in killing him?"

"I hope not. You can make sure they don't."

"I cannot interfere. It's the law."

"You can help fix things. He doesn't have to die."

His lips pressed into a flat line. "There may be nothing to fix."

I opened my mouth to argue, but stopped short. He'd listen, but he wouldn't help. I'd already mentioned Junior—he did nothing. "Is Junior's death so insignificant?"

Harry shrugged. "As I said, I'm not permitted to interfere. They must make their own decisions."

I jumped off the cot. "Even though your sister is manipulating everyone?"

He stared blankly at me.

"She put a love spell on Junior—pretending to be me! She had him trap the quads, so they would be angry enough to work together and kill him. Does none of this count as interfering?"

"It's complicated."

Complicated! The hairs on the back of my neck lifted. "In case you haven't figured it out yet, by everyone, I also mean *you*—the all-powerful Druid King—and The Boss. She counts on you both to follow your damn rules, while she's out running amok." I took a deep breath. Harry had to know the truth. He had to know I might be the one to pull the trigger. "Junior is going to die."

Don't tell him. You can't trust him as you once did, Jayne warned.

242

"Fine," I yelled at Jayne and threw myself back down on the cot. I crossed my arms and faced him. Waiting for him to speak.

Harry's brow creased, and I realized I'd just spoken to Jayne in front of him. "It's more complicated than you think," he said. "She can only be formally charged during an official meeting of the royal powers. I would have to convene a special session just to discuss it with them."

I threw up my hands. "Oh my god, no wonder you people winded up destroying yourselves. It's a miracle any of the realms survived."

Harry's eyes widened. He used his will to slide the cot to the bars, trapping my legs.

You shouldn't have said that, Jayne said.

No shit.

He leaned down and white-knuckled the bars near my head. "What do you know, Claire?" His voice was calm, but he wasn't.

I swallowed. "I overheard Mab telling Mace about the fourth realm," I confessed. "She said the blacksmith was a child of all realms, and I had fourth realm blood."

He arched a disbelieving eyebrow. "She discussed the fourth realm with Mace?"

"Yes, but she made him forget. She didn't know I was listening."

"She would have sensed you."

I shook my head. "I don't know how, but Cinnamon hid me from her."

His head cocked to one side. He didn't believe me.

"She also spoke of her twin."

"She mentioned Jayne?" Harry blurted out and stopped.

Jayne! Is he talking about you?

Jayne was silent.

Talk to me.

I don't know. No, it can't be, she muttered.

Harry cleared his throat again. I looked up. He was studying me.

"She said I reminded her of Jayne. Is it because of my blood? My fourth realm blood, or does she see a resemblance to her sister in my face?"

He frowned.

"You're not going to let me remember anyway. I've heard the omen. I know you think I'm the harbinger. Just tell me the truth."

His face went pale, and his expression went blank. He jerked from the bars. "It's forbidden to discuss."

"By who?"

"Royal decree."

"But you all are the royals—decree something else."

"It isn't that simple," he yelled, losing some of his composure.

I rolled my eyes, which didn't make him happy. I was trapped here. He could be pissed all he wanted. I wanted answers.

"Are you my father?" I asked him point blank.

He closed his eyes and rubbed his forehead. "I don't know. None of us do." His voice was quiet.

How is that possible? How can they not know?

"Did you ever sleep with my mother?"

Harry's eyes shot open. "Mab certainly didn't. You heard the omen. She is as likely as I am to be your parent."

"Right, but as she so eloquently put it—" In a horrible rendition of Mab's voice I said, "I seriously doubt Melinda was somehow impregnated with one of my ovum." Then I remembered her next line. *Of course, with magic, I suppose anything is possible.* "Fine. How did I get fourth realm blood? Was I born with it?"

"No, your original blood was replaced."

"Replaced? When?"

"We don't know."

"There's so much you don't know. How is that possible to be in charge and not know? You said she couldn't have taken a child of his. I assume that goes for you too, so wouldn't my blood have been checked when I was born? My mother was dating the Devil."

"At the time you were taken, there was no indication you were his child."

"You ran tests?"

"No." Harry shrugged. "He wasn't claiming you."

"That's it? You just took his word for it? Unbelievable. When was the fact that my blood was replaced discovered?"

"After you were found."

"Found?"

He paused and rubbed his forehead again. "After he took you back, before the deal was struck, he hid you and your mother. Your location was unknown for four years."

Four years, Jayne said. *We don't remember.*

"I was with my mother for four years?"

We should have remembered.

"Yeah, I know. I mean, I've been doing a lot of reminiscing lately, and we—I don't have any recollection of that time."

He'd started pacing.

"Please," I begged.

He stopped. "It was one of Mab's conditions."

Furious, I attempted to push away from the bars. I wanted to stand and throw the cot against the wall. "You let her take the memories of my mother," I screamed at him. "I have a million crappy memories of every other goddamn thing that has ever happened to me in my entire miserable life, but the one thing that might have made me happy was taken away. You intervened so there wouldn't be a war. You made the deal. You let her take them."

Without hesitation, he nodded.

"I hate you." I had total fucking recall of everything but my mother.

"Claire," he said. His voice was soft, the way he'd spoken to me as a child.

I blinked back tears. He wouldn't make me cry. "How exactly was my blood switched?" I asked. "Wouldn't it eventually go back to what I originally had? My body is making blood like everyone else's, right? And what about DNA—can't you do a paternity test?"

"Switched may have been the wrong word. It was more complete than that. Total replacement—everything was changed. Magically changed."

"Everything has DNA? It's in my hair, my skin, not just my blood. It was all changed?"

Harry sighed, the wrinkles around his eyes showing his age. "There is no DNA. Not with us."

"So without my original blood, we're just SOL."

"You could say that."

"You think I'm the harbinger because of the blood."

"Yes." He raised his hand, ready to cast the spell

"You're going to make me forget about all of this?"

"I must."

"How exactly am I going to fix time if I don't know I should be trying? The prophecy said I'd fix it, but how can I do that if I don't know about it?"

"If you're the girl, you will find a way."

OMG, was he kidding?

"Wait," I said, before he had a chance to wipe my memory. "Cinnamon doesn't want to go forward with the plan, but she believes Junior is the one who trapped them. She can be convinced not to participate. Please tell her the truth. She'll believe you."

He lowered his hand. "Have you seen Junior dead?"

"Yes."

"Cinnamon has already made her choice. I will not interfere with what is a certainty."

"But Mab is using them. She wants their power for her realm."

Harry's expression didn't change as he lifted his hand again. "I can't get involved."

"Can't or won't?"

Silence.

"Mab knows the blacksmith has my blood. Wylan James is going to figure out the blood is mine. I hope that's something you would prefer to keep quiet."

Harry slid the cot back against the wall.

"You're a bastard. No better than they are."

He waved his hand and said, "Forget."

CHAPTER 23

I lifted my head to see Harry studying me. How did I get back here, in the basement prison of his safe house?

I closed my eyes and pressed my hand to my forehead. A sharp pain was followed by images flooding back into my mind. Images of the conversation Mab and Mace had in Purgatory. Followed by the conversation Harry and I'd just had. My memories of figuring out how to reverse spells were all intertwined with the ones of my mother and Jayne. I held back a sob when I remembered what Mab had done to my mother—four years of missing memories.

In the blink of an eye, it was all returned to me by the spell I'd cast so Mace couldn't trap me in a nightmare and make me forget. In my mind's eye that spell's geode glowed a bright red, as it fixed the missing memories Harry had tried to remove.

His brows were lowered, his expression serious.

"What were we talking about?" I asked, as if I were trying to remember. I squinted and peered down just as Mace had done when Mab cast her forget spell on him.

When I lifted my gaze, Harry's face was now relaxed. A slow smile curved his lips, but there was no joy. His eyes were dark with sadness. "Nothing important," he said. "I'll leave you to rest."

He left as if we'd never discussed the fourth realm or my blood or my mother or the fact that none of them knew who my father was.

Nothing important. Do you agree, Jayne?

She was quiet.

Are you there?

Nothing.

I released a heavy breath. *Don't do this to me, not again.*

Jayne was silent—too silent. I closed my eyes and stepped outside my body.

"Where are you? Show yourself," I demanded, but she said nothing. "Please."

Nothing.

I opened my eyes and returned to my body. Jayne was gone. I looked inward at the other spells still within. Nothing was different. How could she be gone? Where could she have gone?

"You have permission to speak," I said, but nothing happened.

I closed my eyes and leaned back against the bars. The forgotten conversation with Harry swirled in my head. He hadn't cared about Junior's death. He'd refused to tell Cinnamon the truth.

What has happened must happen. Quaid's words.

Was that why Harry wouldn't help? He'd said Cinnamon already made her choice. Was there no way to save Junior? Were all my attempts destined to fail?

I put my hand to my stomach. "Do I kill Junior to save you, little one?"

I curled into a ball on the cot. I wanted to sleep, but my mind was too focused to rest. I was trying to reconcile the gaps in my memory. The four years I'd spent with my mother were gone. My first memories were from a hospital. I'd overlooked them before, as I assumed I'd been a baby, newly born.

Now I went deeper. I remembered the pretty smile of a young nurse named Sarah. She'd wanted custody, but because she was unmarried, they denied her. Single women weren't eligible to foster. This was the first in a long line of disappointments.

I didn't speak until I was six, when I had to call 9-1-1 because my foster mother OD'd on sleeping pills.

The more I recalled, the more the girl in my head was like someone else. I knew her hopes and dreams and disappointments. I knew the name and face of the first guy she ever slept with, but couldn't really remember the touch of his skin.

The door at the top of the stairs opened. Mace. The dull tingle of his mark was somehow dampened now by Mab's mark. I searched within and found the geode, a pale violet like his eyes. I picked up the two halves and slammed them together. I felt his mark on my back disappear.

"Get up," he commanded.

We weren't in Purgatory, but I obeyed. I had no choice. Not while he had the power to destroy the baby.

He steadied his gaze on me. "Come," he said, motioning me forward.

I walked over to the bars but didn't look into his eyes. I flinched when he reached through the bars to touch me. He held me in place with his will.

"Mace, please don't hurt the baby."

He placed his hand against my belly. I cried out as a sharp pain ran through me, but it wasn't focused, as before. It was different. The energy just bounced around, hitting nothing.

Stilling, he drew his hand back, fisting it at his side. "What did you do?"

I clutched my stomach. "Nothing."

He wrenched open the door, pushing his way into the cell. I backed against the wall.

"I thought I was clear," he said, pressing my body into the wall. "You belong to me now." He placed his hands on either side of me, caging me in. He leaned in close to my face. "I get to decide what you can and can't have."

"I don't know what you mean."

"You can't change the rules, Claire. Not in the middle of the game."

My heart raced. He was standing too close. I couldn't breathe. He pinned my wrists when I attempted to push him away. He wrapped his free hand around the nape of my neck. I struggled, but stopped fighting when he tightened his grip and crushed my body against the wall.

Power surged in me before I heard the tiny wisps of energy sparking off my left hand.

He was in my face, but I wasn't afraid he'd kiss me, this time. He was too angry for that. "Where is it?"

"What?" I gasped, barely able to breathe.

"Where's the tiny piece of Jack I need to collect?"

"What?" Again, I touched my belly. "No. Not the baby." Tears welled. "I didn't do anything. I swear it. It can't be gone."

"Yet, it is." His nails dug into my wrist.

The beat of my heart pounded loudly in my head. The baby was gone. I'd never see its heartbeat on the ultrasound or feel its kick. The crackle of power streamed to the surface. Wisps of energy covered my hand.

Mace was too close. He was suffocating me. I wanted him off. I needed him away. If he saw the truth in my eyes that I didn't know what happened to the baby, he'd be more reasonable.

I put my left hand to his face, hoping to push him back with the building power. On contact with his skin, a pulse of energy surged into the room as his eyes fixed on mine. Everything went quiet.

I took in a ragged breath. A tiny vein under his eye twitched. It beat a fast staccato, increasing when he realized he couldn't move. His eyes were angry, confused, and scared. He wasn't in control, and he knew it.

"Let me go," I whispered.

His hands loosened then fell away. With my hand still on his face, he stepped back giving me room to breathe. Our gazes stayed locked. He was trapped, but the power he was using to fight my hold hadn't let up.

"Stop fighting me."

His body relaxed, but his mind continued to struggle.

My grip trembled, but I didn't let go or break eye contact. The power felt like the suggestions I'd made before, only stronger. It was like all the magic I could do had a taste, and the more power that was needed, the stronger the taste. I could recognize it now by taste, or by mentally picturing the geodes.

"Was there ever a baby?" I had no doubts before, and Mace's actions had given me no reason to, but I wanted to hear him say it.

A vein at his eye continued to twitch. "Yes."

His resistance was making me weak, but I focused on his eyes ignoring how the power of the spell was draining my body. "What happened to it?"

"Stolen. Lost. Destroyed."

Destroyed? Did Mace think I'd killed the baby? Stolen? Who could have taken it? "Did you tell anyone about it?"

"No."

My concentration waned, and I almost lost eye contact. I had to hurry. "Could you tell it was Jack's?"

"No."

Not that it mattered, but I'd hoped he'd been sure.

I was losing focus; my hold was crumbling. The power to trap him was too draining. It would slip through my fingers soon. "You're going to forget about the baby," I said. "I was never pregnant."

"You were never pregnant," he repeated as my energy dropped, and I fell to the floor at his feet.

I could hear the whirl of the air conditioner and the hum of the florescent lights. The dead quiet of the spell was gone.

Mace backed away. He bent and pressed his right palm against his temple then touched the side of his face where my hand had been. "What did you do?" he wheezed.

I rubbed my palm. It was warm to the touch.

Mace yanked me off the floor, the sudden movement making me dizzy. "Answer me," he shouted. He threw me onto the cot when my legs gave out. He leaned over me, pulling me to a sitting position, then pushing my back against the bars as he squeezed my neck.

"I-I don't know what happened."

Without meaning to, I rubbed my palm again. Mace clasped my wrist, but dropped it quickly as if it burned him. His hand tightened around my throat. "We spoke. What was said?"

"I swear I have no idea."

His eyes narrowed and he jerked me forward—so close our heads were touching. His nostrils flared. He was angry. "You're lying."

I could feel the anger rolling off him like waves, but I sensed no conviction in his voice when he called me a liar. It was like he couldn't see the lie, but was sure I had lied. I was sure it was the spell. We'd spoken about the baby, but he was told to forget about the baby, which must be confusing his truth sense. I doubted I'd broken his ability completely where I was concerned, but about this one thing—the baby—he couldn't see the truth.

"You'd know if I was lying. You can see the truth, you just don't want to believe it." Trying to focus his attention on something else, I said, "You came down here for something. What was it?"

Looking down, as if trying to find the answer in his mind. He closed his eyes. A moment later he pushed himself off me and stood.

Glancing at the stairs, he pointed as if remembering then moved his finger over to the bars on the cell door, as if retracing his steps in his mind. Scratching the back of his head, he looked toward the stairs again then back at me, brows furrowed. He couldn't remember. He eyed my left arm and fisted the hand he'd burned.

"Maybe it's a don't touch what's hers reminder," I suggested, as if Mab's mark had somehow caused his pain.

He cocked an eyebrow. He could pretend I belonged to him all he wanted, but we both knew Mab called the shots. He flexed his hand. "You should hope she gives you to me or," he glanced around the cell, "this could be your new reality for years."

As if life as his slave would be any better.

He opened the cell door to leave. Glancing back, he said, "The Deeps may not be as forgiving next time. No one's ever the same when they return."

That record was still safe. He wouldn't understand, but I would never be the same. I dropped my gaze from his smug expression.

"I suggest you cooperate when you return," Mace said. "She can be cruel if you don't."

Was he serious? Did he actually think what she'd done so far was tame? I peered at him. "She dropped me into a hole for a hundred years. I had a conscious mind until I turned to dust and blew away on the wind. I'm more sure of what she's capable of than you can possibly imagine." The absurdity of his warning was laughable. *He* had no clue what she was capable of.

"We leave in an hour."

After he left, I slumped back. Mace's visit had, again, left more questions than answers. I put my hand on my belly and brushed away a tear. First Jayne, now the baby.

A calm peacefulness washed over me—Death. I sat up straighter. My eyes darted around the room. "Show yourself...please."

He materialized. His face was passive, but his look was intense.

"Why are you here?" I asked.

"Selfishness, I suppose," Death replied.

Selfishness? "What do you mean?"

He slid the wooden crate over and sat facing me. I had a feeling he was trying to see my soul. He stretched out a hand, but withdrew when I shied away from it.

"I know you know," he said.

I shook my head. "I—"

"Don't worry," he interrupted. "I should make you forget, but I won't. I can't."

I studied him. His expression hadn't changed. His gaze was on fire, but his body language was calm. He claimed he wouldn't, no couldn't, take my memories, but why? "Why can't you take them?"

"Selfish, remember."

Did he see something of her in me? "I don't understand what you mean? Do I look like her?"

"No," he said. "It's your blood."

"I know it's from the fourth realm, but—"

"No. It's not *from* the fourth realm." The longing in his eyes was clear. He touched my face gently. His calming influence intensified. "You have *her* blood."

I gasped. "What?"

He leaned forward as I pulled back. I had the blood of Jayne, not just fourth realm blood, but *her blood*. Was that where my Jayne had come from?

"You're all that remains of her," he said, sending another wave of his influence.

I shook my head. "Stop," I said. "Don't do this." I couldn't let the calm, relaxed, peacefulness that felt like Heaven make me lose focus.

"Don't be afraid," he said, backing away putting space between us. "I won't hurt you. I can't hurt you."

Death sat with his hands resting in his lap. I stayed against the bars. It felt good to have him touching me, but the emotions weren't real. He wanted to be near me because of Jayne. The only reason he wouldn't hurt me was because I was all that was left of her.

He'd been forced to kill the woman he loved, then cursed to love only her. I thought of Jack and the baby. Death's true feelings weren't for me, but I shouldn't be so harsh. I wasn't cursed, but my love was just as lost. I would never see Jack again if Mace had his way, and if I somehow managed to survive this and was saved by The Boss, he'd remove Jack for failing at his job—and the baby was gone. Death was only trying to be close to the thing he loved the most. It just happened to be a part of me.

I flinched when his hands lifted, although it was more of a

reaction to everything that had been happening to me, not necessarily because he was Death.

He stilled. "You're sad," he said. "Let me help you."

"There isn't anything you can do."

"I can comfort you."

His eyes were bright—hopeful—but the peacefulness he caused was an illusion. Not something I should let myself get lost in.

"Or I can go," he said, staring at his hands again resting in his lap, dejected.

I couldn't send him away. "You can stay."

He moved from the crate to sit beside me. My initial thought was to push him away, but the happiness and longing in his eyes stopped me. He'd been without his love for so long. It was an illusion, but I was the only one who could give it to him. He wanted to hold me—part of me wanted to be held.

Giving in to that desire, I rested my head on his chest, sinking into his embrace. I fell asleep cradled in his arms.

~ # ~

I woke as the door to the basement opened. I was cold, as if the warm body I'd been with had suddenly disappeared. Death didn't have a smell, but the buzz from his touch lingered a moment longer. I was surprised to see my visitor was Cinnamon.

I stretched my arms and neck. "What do you want?"

"Mace is ready for you."

"Since when are you his puppet?"

Her eyebrows rose. "Get up now, or you'll regret it."

I didn't jump to my feet. I wasn't afraid of her. There were bigger monsters in my life. Cinnamon was barely a guppy in that pond.

"Now," she said.

I slowly got to my feet.

She smiled. "Have we broken you, Claire?"

"Claire turned to dust earlier today. I'm who's left. You could say I've had enough."

She raised an eyebrow, probably thinking I was kidding. "If you—"

"Please." I held up my hand. Her threats would be wasted on me, and I really didn't want to hear them. "Dust, remember. Are you really going to be able to top that?"

Her smile dropped.

Harry didn't seem to think telling Cinnamon would change anything. I was hoping he was wrong. "You shouldn't do this. You don't need revenge. Mace is going to get you both screwed by Mab. Junior will die if you don't refuse to help."

I didn't go into all the specifics with her, but I'd given her enough reasons to back out. Mentally I found the geode for Mace's spell. Holding the power of it in my mind, I tapped Cinnamon's hand as I left the cell. A tiny static charge went from me to her.

"Even you deserve the truth," I said as her eyes rolled back in her head, and she dropped to the floor.

I stepped over her body and continued up the stairs. The boys were waiting, but didn't immediately realize Cinnamon wasn't behind me. She'd follow soon enough.

Mace barked orders. "You'll get us in through the portal in Junior's office, without setting off any alarms."

If he thought I was an expert on how to use the company portals he was about to be disappointed.

"She seems so willing to help, brother." Cinnamon's voice came from behind me. "Whatever did you do to convince her?"

He ignored her.

She was plucking the last pin out of her hair. She tilted her head toward me, but not enough for the others to notice.

That was the only acknowledgement I was getting, but I was hoping she'd go all I'm-in-charge-now-Cinnamon and put a stop to Mace's plan. Unfortunately, she didn't do anything, and I quickly decided Harry was right. She was going to let things play out.

She'd already made her choice.

"It's time," Mace said, opening a portal to his father's building.

I had almost no experience with this type of travel, but I had the basics. Not tripping alarms wasn't one of them. I thought of Junior's office, put my hand on the surface then closed my eyes.

At least I wasn't the one holding the gun.

CHAPTER 24

I slid through the portal into Junior's office. I wanted this nightmare to end, but I hadn't really considered what that meant. I was shocked to see his wide eyes staring back at me. At that moment, as he dropped his guard—just before Mace sidestepped me and pulled the trigger—I saw happiness.

"Claire," Junior said before the bullet struck him between the eyes and killed him instantly.

The ringing in my ears from the gunshot pulled all my attention to the bloody wall behind him.

Junior was dead. I hadn't shot him, but I was responsible for my actions. I'd let them in through the portal. I'd told them about Junior. There was no hope of returning to my old life now. My ears were still ringing when I heard the sound of voices arguing around me.

Sage and Sorrel were both pissed. They were awake now—the spell must be broken.

The hands of my watch were spinning around as they had many times before. They stopped when I concentrated on them and pointed back toward the portal. Was my watch trying to tell me to snap out of it and run? It didn't matter. I took the advice and ran. I didn't get very far, taking only one step toward the portal before I was thrown against the wall.

"Where do you think you're going, Claire?" Mace asked. He was in my face shoving the gun into my ribs.

"Mace," Cinnamon insisted. "We must go. *Now.*"

Mace was still eyeing me. Still pressing the gun against my ribs. He should have taken Cinnamon's advice.

Tsking came from behind us, then The Boss's unmistakable voice. "This is going to be a mess to clean up," he said. "I'm sure I'll hear about it from maintenance."

Mace sneered. "This isn't over," he whispered to me, then faced The Boss. "Father," he said, with a wave of his hand, a slight bow, and a jovial tone as if they were meeting over drinks.

The Boss had been examining Junior's body, but turned when Mace greeted him. He was never emotional. Today was no exception. He studied the others. Sage and Sorrel cowered off to one side. Cinnamon's fists were tightened, but she stood her ground, refusing to show any weakness.

"I think a new location is needed," The Boss said.

In a flash, we were all exactly as we had been, but now we were in Purgatory, in the great hall in Mab's castle. Mab sat on her throne, and Quaid hung by his arms from a wooden beam to the right of her chair. He was half-naked, his back a mass of angry red welts and blood. He'd clearly been whipped.

The Boss glanced at him but didn't comment.

"Brother, it is so good to see you again. I see you've brought back my property," Mab said, rising and walking over to me.

I scurried back.

She smiled and ignited her mark. She didn't make it too painful, just enough to get my attention.

I stopped and let her approach.

"You're trainable," she said. "Good." Turning back to The Boss, she lifted a brow. "I didn't expect you to deliver her personally, Brother."

"You're not really interested in the girl," he said. "What would you rather have?"

Mab left me where I stood and moved closer to him. "I see," she said, smiling. "You have come to trade." Her eyes briefly fell on the quads, but she didn't say anything. None of them reacted.

I gasped. The quads were all frozen like statues.

"Done," he said.

Done? Had he traded the quads for me? Harry said The Boss would save me if he could, but I didn't believe he actually would.

"And," The Boss continued. "I want my servant returned as

well."

Quaid lifted his head, and my shoulders slumped. She wanted Quaid to stay with her. Now she'd somehow trapped him, knowing The Boss would want him returned.

The wicked grin on her face was clear. He couldn't have both of us.

"I have a claim on both," she said. "You have only bartered for one. I'm willing to let you have either for your trade."

She knew as well as I did he would choose Quaid.

"It's against the rules to claim my property. He is not part of the bargain."

"He betrayed you, Brother. According to our rules, that makes him a free agent." Mab paused, smiling at Quaid as if they were lovers. "I discussed it with him at great length when he dined with me earlier."

She faced The Boss; her mouth formed a smug line. Jayne warned me about eating the food, but Quaid must not have known that rule, or why else would he have broken it?

"That will not work on him," The Boss said.

Huh? He's immune? Not fair.

"It's true I did not get the full benefit of his deed, but I do have a claim nonetheless. I have rights to one," she said, pointing at me. "And a hold on the other." She glanced back toward Quaid. "You may choose either for the bargain."

The Boss's mouth tightened, and his eyebrows dropped into a straight line. Mab smiled, her expression triumphant. She'd bartered for what she really wanted, the quads, and now she was going to get to keep the bonus prize as well—me. Seriously, why the hell did she want me so bad?

"I'll give you a minute to think about your choice." Mab walked over to where Quaid dangled. Tracing her hand along his side, she left four tiny lines of blood as her fingernails dug into his flesh. She stopped to check her reflection in the large mirror on the wall behind him.

My heart skipped a beat; the Keeper's mirror. The Keeper winked at me just before Mab walked away.

"You should take your servant," she said, glancing up at Quaid as she passed. "Then we will both have something to play with."

The Boss was apparently bored enough to check the time. He raised his head, but turned away quickly when he saw I was staring.

He'd pick Quaid, and that would be it. I'd be stuck in Purgatory forever. He wouldn't tell my mother the truth. He'd say his hands were tied and be done with it.

I flinched when Mab stopped beside me. I made a conscious effort not to back away from her.

"I'm quite interested in learning what makes her tick," she said, brushing hair back off my shoulder. "She was in the Deeps earlier, did they tell you?"

"No," he said, eyeing Mace.

"Do tell me how she managed to survive, Brother."

I clenched my fist, when she amped up the heat of her mark.

"The watch. It's one of Harry's."

I glared at him, but he wasn't looking at me. How dare he tell her anything?

Mab clutched my arm and twisted my wrists to see the watch.

I tried to pull my arm away.

She tightened her hold.

"Please stop her," I said to The Boss.

She laughed. "He hasn't yet decided, but we both know he's leaning toward his servant." Her wicked smile was confident he'd pick Quaid. "You and I will have plenty of time to talk about the Deeps after they have left."

I gazed down at the watch. I didn't want her to have it. In my mental landscape of geodes, I picked up the two halves that glowed a bright iridescent purple and slammed them together. The watch's clasp released.

"Go home," I commanded, and it disappeared from my wrist.

I was hoping it would find Harry, but with my luck it was probably sitting on the dresser in my apartment. Not that I had a clue what he would do if the watch went to him. It was probably against the rules to interfere, but the watch belonged to him, and I wanted him to have it back.

Mab growled and intensified the heat. Doing my best to ignore the pain, I searched around my mental garden of geodes. As I'd discovered, a geode in use would glow. Unfortunately, Mab's geode was black, and my power continued to uncover more geodes. Distracted by the pain of her mark, I couldn't find the other half. I couldn't turn her mark off, but at least I no longer needed the watch to use my power.

"Take your servant and leave us. I have decided you may not

choose the girl."

"That's not how the rules work, Sister," Harry said as he materialized in the great hall. He tucked my watch into his pocket.

Mab hissed and turned away from me, the pain of her mark returning to something more reasonable. "Why are you here, Brother? This matter does not concern you. You were not invited."

His mouth puckered and his eyebrows rose as he gave her an indignant look—it was clear he didn't need an invitation. "Where the girl is involved," he said. "It concerns me. I'm her guardian in these matters."

My guardian.

He strode over to where I was standing and placed his hand on my arm—turning off Mab's mark completely.

She pointed her finger at me and declared, "I have a legitimate claim to her. We agreed she belongs to me."

"Yes, but you offered her in trade. You cannot rescind that offer until he has decided which he will choose."

"Decide then," she spat and glared at The Boss.

He studied me, but I could tell he'd already chosen, and it wasn't me. I lowered my gaze. I didn't want him to see my disappointment at being left with her.

"Quaid," he said.

"Guards," Mab bellowed. "Remove the demon, and take the girl to the Deeps."

My mind was yelling at me to run, but I was frozen to the spot. There was no escape from her. Not in Purgatory. Even if I escaped the castle, I had no way out. I belonged to her now. My power, however, didn't like feeling trapped. I heard the faint crackle of energy as wisps of power formed around my left hand.

Quaid was lowered to the floor.

He was weak and unable to stand at first. But he was not easily broken. Mab had certainly given it her best shot. He stood with great effort, his jaw tight with determination. Without hesitation, he walked over and took his place behind The Boss. Quaid wasn't scared at the prospect of leaving with him. I wasn't sure how, but I was sure he hadn't betrayed anyone. He'd done his job, and now he was being rewarded by getting to go home.

The guards were on me, seizing me by the arms. The power building in my hand was starting to show. I tamped it down, hiding it until I was ready to use it.

"Wait," The Boss said. "I wish to challenge your claim to the girl."

"What?" Mab exclaimed. "That has already been decided. She belongs to me."

"Has she eaten anything while in Purgatory?" Harry asked.

Mab hesitated. "No, but..."

"What proof do you have to your claim, Brother?" Harry asked.

"She is under signed contract with me. She cannot be claimed by Mab."

"Signed contract?" Mab said in Ancient. "We agreed she could never be bound to you."

I was sure she thought she was speaking a language I couldn't possibly understand, but the parental controls were off on my translator. I could hear her perfectly.

"We also agreed you would have no direct contact," Harry said in Ancient. "If you swear an oath that you have not manipulated any of these events, then I will disallow his claim. If not, then you have both broken the agreement, therefore, neither of you will be at fault. Those are the rules, Sister."

Mab's eyes narrowed. I could tell she was trying to figure out her best strategy. If she tried to claim she wasn't involved, I was sure Harry would do everything in his power to prove she was. And if that happened she might lose the quads, which had been her original goal. There were probably other consequences too, but with these three who could keep track? I certainly didn't want to be trapped here with her while a court date was set.

She smiled and, in English, said, "She was not under contract when she entered my realm. If she had been, you would have stated it before."

The Boss snapped his fingers, and a signed piece of paper appeared in his hand.

I recognized it immediately. It was the receipt Mike asked me to sign. That seemed so long ago. He'd said I was signing my soul away. A requirement to seal the deal, but I'd thought he was joking. I thought The Boss already owned my soul.

Mab snatched the paper from his hand. "The blood is still wet," she pointed out as she inspected the document. "How, then, did she sign it before she entered Purgatory?"

"Time is not always as it seems," The Boss reminded her.

The same words she'd said to him earlier in the meeting at the

Lux. Harry smiled. I was sure he understood how it happened. He knew Johnny's boys had me until a few hours ago, and now the other me had just entered Purgatory. The Boss had been stalling. He had to wait for me to sign the receipt. Even though I had just signed it, I had, in fact, signed it before ever putting a foot in Purgatory.

"He has a claim, Sister," Harry said. "The girl signed it before entering your realm. Your claim is invalid."

Mab threw her will and shoved me up against the castle wall. I grunted, losing the air in my lungs. She kept up the pressure, pushing the air out of me until I could barely breathe. The Boss didn't flinch. He'd worked it so I belonged to him, but I don't think he actually cared about me.

"Stop!" Harry knocked Mab's will away.

I fell to the ground.

"You have what you really wanted." He motioned at the quads. "Now accept the bargain and leave her alone. Unless you have reconsidered and would like to claim no knowledge of events."

"You have no proof," she snapped.

"Then claim innocence," The Boss growled. "And we shall see."

I had no idea what making that claim meant, but her face made it clear. She wouldn't try that tactic if her life depended on it, which maybe it did.

Harry helped me up. I stayed close to him. He was the only one I trusted to play by the rules.

"Do not enter my realm again, child...unless you wish to die a thousand deaths." She turned away from us and returned to her throne. Before I'd become tangled in this mess, she'd been after the quads. So she'd gotten what she really wanted. She was just pissed I'd slipped through her fingers again.

The Boss waved his hand toward the quads. "Awake."

They peered around, all disoriented for a moment. The scowl on their faces said to me that none of them was happy to be standing in Mab's castle. The twins looked at each other, shrugging and shaking their heads. They had been under the spell the entire time. They appeared not to know what had happened. Considering her hatred for Mab, I was sure Cinnamon would have rather been anywhere else. She had no one to blame but herself. I opened her eyes before they killed Junior. She could have backed out but hadn't. The twins weren't innocent, but in this case they were victims of Mace's desire and Mab's plan.

Mace narrowed his eyes on Harry, then me. Quaid stood with The Boss, and I stood with Harry. Mace glanced around, seeing that he and his siblings were on Mab's side of the house.

Quaid and I would be leaving. If Mace hadn't already, he'd figure out soon enough that he and his siblings were staying with Mab. I don't think this was an option he considered when he decided to take this path. Maybe he'd never contemplated his father handing control of him over to Mab.

"You will remain in Purgatory," The Boss said. "All of you. Mab has control of you now."

Cinnamon's mouth opened as if she wanted to say something, but she was too smart to show her hand to Mab. She pressed her lips together, as if she knew it would do no good to beg her father to reconsider. She would have to stay like the others.

She looked away before The Boss did. Did that show compassion? I doubted she would see it that way if it were true, since his tough love basically sacrificed them for a glorified bodyguard. He had other plans all along for getting me back, but I guess he hadn't counted on Quaid's being trapped by Mab.

The Boss opened a portal, then motioned for us to leave.

I started forward, but stopped when Mace said, "Stay."

I lost the ability to move forward. My eyes widened as I realized Mace's control of me in Purgatory hadn't been removed when Mab's blood broke the curse and freed my powers. I couldn't walk toward the portal; his command wouldn't allow me to leave. Quaid had already passed through, when Harry realized I wasn't moving. He glared at Mab.

She sidled up to Mace and whispered something in his ear. He blanched. "Go," he whispered.

My legs could move again. Harry led me to the portal and waited for me to pass through. He and The Boss followed. I didn't look back again, hoping it would be the last time I was ever in Purgatory. Mace screamed while the portal closed. I guess he wasn't as favored by Mab as he'd thought.

The Boss called medical who immediately sent someone up for Quaid. He was taken away to be treated. He would be back to normal by tomorrow. I wasn't sure I would ever be normal again.

Harry handed me the watch. I put it back on. Technically, I

didn't need it anymore, but I didn't want them to know. Plus it was a very easy way to reach Harry. Having the Druid King on speed dial wasn't a bad thing.

"Thank you," I said.

He turned to The Boss. "We have many things to discuss," he said in Ancient. "I'll see you later tonight?"

"Yes," The Boss replied in Ancient.

Harry disappeared without another word.

Part of me wanted to know what they were going to talk about, but the other part wanted nothing more to do with these people. I was over the game they were playing with my life. I wanted to be that girl at the bus stop five years ago. The one who didn't know anything about this world or its people. I wanted to be her, not this screwed-up version of me who barely escaped Purgatory.

The Boss went back to his desk and sat down as if nothing had happened. "Do you need something, Claire?"

Did he really think things were just going to return to normal? "Did you love my mother?"

"Obviously," he said.

Obviously? I didn't think there was anything obvious about any of this. He loved her, but didn't bother claiming me. Not that I was necessarily his, but he didn't even check.

"Are you my father?"

"No." His answer was quick. No hesitation.

"Who is my father?"

He leaned back in his chair. "I have no idea. Your mother never told me."

Was he serious? "So she was pregnant before you met?"

I stiffened when he pushed back from his desk and stood, but didn't drop eye contact. I wasn't willing to let this go. He wouldn't tell me about the omen, or about the time I'd spent with her before we were discovered, but he had to know something.

He paced over to the window and gazed out over the city. It was another gray and gloomy day. Just like the first time I was in his office. His posture rigid, hands clasped behind his back. I expected him to turn on his mark, but he didn't.

"Do you want me to be your father, Claire?"

My mouth dropped open. "No. I just want the truth."

He turned. I saw the slightest hint of a raised eyebrow, before he schooled his features. "I can't tell you what I don't know. That's the truth. I don't consider you to be mine, if that's what you're asking."

I shook my head. "I'm well aware of your opinion of me."

He drew his eyebrows together a fraction. It wasn't much of a movement, but I got the impression I'd offended him.

"What about the prophecy?" I continued, knowing he'd think I meant the one from Wylan James.

"The prophecy is complete," he lied.

I crossed my arms over my chest. "So, I unleashed the great destroyer, created a divide among the realms, and brought about tyranny like no one has experienced in thousands of years?"

He shrugged in a dismissive way. "Prophecies are always a bit vague."

I gawked at him. He was going to let everything go as if it all meant nothing.

He started back toward his desk.

"I can't do this anymore."

"You don't have a choice," he said. This time he didn't even look at me.

I spun to leave. He stopped me with his will. He'd never done that before. Perhaps it was against the rules for someone not under his control. I guess now that he owned me he didn't have to hold back. The contract I'd signed meant he had complete control of me. Unless he wanted me to, I couldn't even move to face him.

"You tricked me into signing," I said, not that it mattered.

He swaggered over to me, holding the receipt up so I could see it. He pinched the contract at the top and slowly ripped it down the middle. The two halves burst into flames as they separated.

I could move again.

"I had to do that for your own safety. Mab would have kept you otherwise. She is not one to give up."

I moved to step past him.

He held out his hand to block my path. "You aren't safe if Mab thinks you're unprotected. If you leave, she will know I have released you."

"So I have to stay, or she'll try again?"

The confidence on his face was palpable.

"Bring it," I said, pushing his arm out of the way.

He switched on the only real power he had over me—his mark. He didn't make it hurt too badly, just enough to remind me who

265

was boss.

I spun back around to face him. "You're a heartless bastard. I have no idea what my mother sees in you, but maybe that's because I don't know her. I never will. Your sister has seen to that."

By the time I was finished speaking, I was shouting. I was mad, and I wanted him to know it. "You let her take everything from me. Everything!"

He didn't reply. Just stared at me.

I wanted to hit him. I felt the power in my hand building that tiny crackle of electricity as the wisps of energy gathered. I pivoted on my heel to leave before I did something stupid.

He extinguished the mark. "I didn't let her take you."

I closed my eyes for a second and took a deep breath. I was so tired. Everything had changed. I couldn't go home and be with Jack—but I wanted to. Instead, I was stuck living in this new hell. My mind was so overloaded with everything that had happened to me—ever. I wanted what I had that morning when I'd woken up in Jack's arms. Something real that felt right.

Without turning, I asked, "Where's Jack?" I assumed he'd know. "He and I need to talk."

"Claire," The Boss said, walking up behind me.

I went rigid when he rested his hands on my shoulders.

He'd never actually touched me before. "There's something we must discuss."

I turned to face him. "I know about Jack. It's not your business. It never should have been, and it never will be again. Do you understand? Never."

"I accept your terms."

My terms? "What's that supposed to mean?"

"I'll take care of the current problem. You're free to find a new acquaintance. I won't interfere," he said, as if that was the answer I was expecting.

"Jack is my problem. I'll take care of it." I didn't want him anywhere near Jack.

"Unfortunately he has already been transferred. At his own request."

No. He was lying. Jack was supposed to meet me for lunch. Today. We were happy—are happy. Jack wouldn't have requested a transfer. "What the hell is that supposed to mean?"

"It means you don't have to deal with it." The Boss returned to his desk as if the conversation was over.

"I don't accept your terms. Where is he?"

"It's over. Move on."

That was bullshit. There was no way Jack wanted out. The empty red ring box wasn't for nothing. He loved me. The Boss was hiding something.

A knock sounded at the door.

"Enter."

Quaid entered, but it wasn't the Quaid who'd come back with us. That Quaid was being treated in medical. This was the one from earlier in the day. The one The Boss was about to send back in time, I realized, to be the traitor.

Quaid was surprised to see me. He cupped his hands together, twisting a ring around on his pinky finger. He didn't wear jewelry, and he certainly wasn't going to start with an ill-fitting platinum pinky ring. "You needed to see me, Boss?" His hands were still cupped in front of him. He seemed uneasy.

"Claire. Go."

I studied Quaid's hands more carefully. The finger with the ring protruded more than the others, and the ring barely fit, riding high above his knuckle. I gasped, glaring up at his face. He didn't look at me. He kept his gaze forward.

It dawned on me. Quaid hadn't been searching for me at the apartment. He'd been hunting Jack, and now he wore a ring that clearly didn't fit on his pinky finger of all places. Was that my ring? The ring that belonged in the empty red ring box hidden in Jack's sock drawer? Jack would have had it with him for when he met me at lunch.

Tears welled in my eyes. Transferred. Was that like retired?

"Claire," The Boss said, but I ignored him.

I lunged at Quaid. He was a big man, but he wasn't expecting me to throw myself at him. I placed my left hand on the side of his face, the wisps of power flowing through me. His eyes locked on mine. "Where's Jack?"

"Retired."

Tears stung my eyes. "Is he already dead?"

Quaid nodded.

"Is that my ring?"

"Yes."

"Give it to me." I held out my hand.

He took it off. He'd twisted the diamond around to the back to hide it. He must have been bringing it back to The Boss as proof Jack was dead. I was never supposed to see it. I was never supposed to know Jack really loved me.

Quaid put the ring in my outstretched hand. I dropped my hand from his face. He immediately turned to The Boss.

"Claire," The Boss said.

I put the ring on my finger and wiped the tears from my face. Surprise number two. The ring was beautiful.

Meeting Quaid's eyes, I said, "What has happened must happen."

I spun to leave, then glanced back. "Give my regards to the queen."

The Boss turned on his mark, but that wasn't going to stop me from leaving this time. "You can't have me anymore."

"You won't be safe," he said, his tone somber as if he really cared.

"Then I die."

He didn't stop me from leaving.

I went back to my desk. The message light was on, but I ignored it. I opened the bottom drawer, the one where I kept my bag, but the bag wasn't there. It was still at Mace's bungalow in Grand Cayman. The drawer was empty except for an envelope with my name on it. The script was delicate and light, like a woman's handwriting, but I didn't recognize it.

I opened it. The note simply said *I'm sorry.*

It wasn't signed, but the paper smelled like the angelic beekeeper. Sliding it back into the envelope, I put the note in my pocket. Closing the drawer, I grabbed my spare key and picked up Jack's paper crane.

I was about to leave when I noticed the red file folder sitting in my out box. Picking it up, I opened the file to the last page. I never viewed this page, because I didn't want to know what they'd done to get retired. Something about this one made me curious.

I scanned the document. The reason was short and sweet and not what I expected. David Janis was retired because of: An inappropriate or fraudulent use of company assets: corporate credit card.

Slowly, I closed his file. He wasn't guilty. I'd taken his card and used it. Because of my unexpected time travel situation, it was also while he still had the card. I took the folder and fed it through the shredder. HR would eventually find the mistake, in fifty years or so—long after David Janus died of natural causes.

I stared back at my desk one last time from the glass doors. I hoped I would never see the place again. I pressed the button for the elevator and waited. Calmness washed over me as the doors popped open. The elevator appeared empty, but I could sense his presence.

"Can you give me a ride home?"

ABOUT THE AUTHOR

HD Smith has been writing as a hobby for over ten years. DARK HOPE is her first full length novel. She has previously published two middle grade novellas in ebook format. She is a software developer by day, working for an awesome cruise line in Celebration, FL.

HD grew up in South Carolina, but has called the Sunshine State home since 1997. She has Computer Science degrees from Clemson University (BS) and Florida Institute of Technology (MS). Her other hobbies include painting and screen printing. She enjoys creating t-shirts inspired by the places in her books. For more information, visit HD's website at http://www.hdsmithauthor.com/.

Photo by Stacie Lee